2

NO LONGER PROPERTY OF
SEATTLE PUBLIC LIBRARY

PRAISE FOR *ACTIVATED*

∞

"Jo Rivers is back and better than ever in ACTIVATED, the third installment of the Calculated series. With its stunning, cinematic descriptions, high-stakes action, intricately-woven plot, and a heart-racing, soul-penetrating love story for the ages, this book exceeds every expectation of the thriller genre. This is the best series in YA right now. Don't miss out."

— Chelsea Bobulski Author of THE WOOD, REMEMBER ME, and the ALL I WANT FOR CHRISTMAS series

"It is the rare story that has me gripping the edge of my seat while contemplating the meaning of life. Brilliantly inventive, Activated, the third book in the Calculated series, will break your heart and put it back together; captivate your imagination and set it free as Jo Rivers faces her greatest challenges yet. An epic continuation to this genre-defying series!"

— Lorie Langdon, Author of Olivia Twist and the Disney Villain Happily Never After Series

"Just when you think this series can't get any better, Activated soars to new heights in the snowy landscape of Finland's Arctic, where the setting is as dangerous as the stakes. McBee artfully elevates action, adventure, and romance while delivering all the elements we loved from Calculated and Simulated—readers will be enthralled."

— Tamara Girardi, Author of Gridiron Girl

"From the stars to the snow, Activated is an electrifying follow-up in the Calculated series that will stay with you for years. Raw and suspenseful, Jo River's story reaches a crescendo that will delight readers. With a witty cast, impossible odds, and heart-wrenching decisions at every turn, Activated will have you laughing, crying and racing through the pages only to wish for more at the end. Absolutely thrilling!"

— Candace Kade, forthcoming Author of Enhanced (coming 2023)

"A perfect storm of adrenaline, mystery, and romance! McBee does it again and delivers a novel of epic proportions. Activated, like it's

siblings in the Calculated series, is a classic in the making! Masterful, immensely enjoyable, and undeniably a ray of light."

— *Ellen McGinty, Author of The Water Child*

"Jo Rivers returns for another thrilling ride. Activated is full of edge-of-your-seat action, heart-stirring romance, and an intricately plotted story that will keep you glued to the pages. This series just keeps getting better."

— *Becky Dean, author of*
Love & Other Great Expectations

PRAISE FOR *SIMULATED*

∞

"*Calculated* was so incredible that I didn't think it was possible for the sequel to one-up it, and yet here we are. *Simulated* has all the mission impossible action you could hope for, paired with a love triangle that rivals the intensity of Twilight's. Be prepared to choose sides and hold on tight. You're in for one wild ride."

— Chelsea Bobulski, author of
THE WOOD and *REMEMBER ME*

"Full of global intrigue and the thrilling adventure of an action movie, Simulated transported me to the lush setting of North Africa as I cheered for an utterly unique heroine fighting for good and finding her place in the world. Action-packed and captivating - I couldn't put it down."

—Becky Dean, forthcoming author of
LOVE AND OTHER GREAT EXPECTATIONS,
2022, Delacorte/Penguin Random House

"Brilliantly crafted, this technological thriller delivers punch after punch of heart-pounding action. The fearless heroine and two equally intriguing love interests had me flying through the pages. I'm in love with this series!"

—Lorie Langdon, author of
the *Disney Villains Happily Never After* Series

"With thrilling adventure and cunning suspense, *Simulated* is the most riveting sequel I've ever read—a masterpiece destined for the stars!"

—Ellen McGinty, author of *THE WATER CHILD*

PRAISE FOR *CALCULATED*

∞

"A high-stakes YA tale of betrayal, revenge, and numbers... An enjoyable thriller with an intriguing, relatable protagonist."

— Kirkus Reviews

"A cunning story of strategy destined to keep readers chasing resolution from Seattle to Shanghai."

– Jennifer Jenkins, author of the *NAMELESS* series

"Calculated is an intelligent thrill ride! In Jo Rivers, author Nova McBee has given readers a heroine who is mathematically gifted beyond what most can imagine, and somehow immensely relatable, even as her greatest skills are exploited by international criminals. Sleek and sophisticated, with dark secrets at every turn, Calculated is impossible to put down."

– Shannon Dittemore, author of
WINTER, WHITE AND WICKED

"An intense and wonderfully complex thriller that kept me on the edge of my seat and turning pages!"

– Jessica Day George, NYT bestselling author of
SILVER IN THE BLOOD

"Calculated is smart with plenty of page-turning action, and a brave heroine who is deeply relatable. Twisty and original, this story will keep readers guessing and hoping to its pulse-pounding end!"

– Lorie Langdon, bestselling author of
DOON and *OLIVIA TWIST*

"[*Calculated*] is a thrill ride from start to finish, with so many twists and turns, you wonder how it could ever be wrapped up, only to have your mind blown at the end and your heart aching for the next chapter. Don't let another minute go by without reading this book."

— Chelsea Bobulski, author of
THE WOOD and *REMEMBER ME*

"Fast-paced and suspenseful. A thrilling debut!"

– Stephanie Morrill, author of *WITHIN THESE LINES*

"Calculated is a fast-paced and thrilling story that will keep you reading long into the night. Its twists and turns will take you from Shanghai's glittering high rises to underground prisons and the plights faced by the characters who feel achingly real. An action-packed adventure with heart."

– Judy Lin, author of the forthcoming
A MAGIC STEEPED IN POISON

"In this gripping thriller, McBee balances high-stakes, page-turning action with a powerful exploration of revenge, justice, forgiveness, and love, as well as an inspiring heroine readers won't soon forget."

– Kimberly Gabriel, award-winning author of
EVERY STOLEN BREATH

A CALCULATED NOVEL

ACTIVATED

NOVA MCBEE

WISE WOLF BOOKS LAS VEGAS

This is a work of fiction. All of the characters, organizations, publications, and events portrayed in this novel are either products of the author's imagination or are used fictitiously.

For information, address Wolfpack Publishing,
5130 S. Fort Apache Road 215-380 Las Vegas, NV 89148

wisewolfbooks.com

Cover design by Cherie Chapman

Hardcover ISBN 978-1-953944-61-0
Paperback ISBN 978-1-953944-60-3
eBook ISBN 978-1-953944-59-7

DEDICATION

∞

For my parents, Richard and Hellen
Your faithful love and support is one of my greatest treasures.

"We are slowed down sound and light waves,
a walking bundle of frequencies tuned into the cosmos..."

Albert Einstein

"Light is a dangerous thing to follow.
Before you know it,
it will drive you to the darkest corners of the earth."

-Red

PROLOGUE

∞

GENEVA, SWITZERLAND
EUROPEAN UNION ENERGY SUMMIT

Eighteen days after Tunisia...

The blackouts feel like a sign.

It's the first PSS assignment since my numbers returned. Maybe I'm foolish for jumping back into work so quickly after Tunisia, but an assignment to prevent darkness felt like a good place to start.

Since Tunisia, most of my time is spent in the midnight hours, searching for him—the one who turned my day into night. My sun into the moon. My sea into the stars. *For Noble.* Nothing is normal since I left him. Nothing will be until I find him. But even with the potent return of my mathematical gift, I still can't crack his code in the stars.

It's 6:32 pm in Geneva on the last night of the European Union Energy Summit. We're in an auditorium built like a coliseum, seated with 211 people. Experts from thirty nations are gathered here in Switzerland, home to the largest power grid in Europe, to discuss the sporadic blackouts that have been hitting Europe and other parts of the world, leaving hundreds of millions without electricity.

Prodigy Stealth Solutions was invited too, *discreetly* of course. Agent Ramos, Ms. Taylor's former boss at the Defense Intelligence Agency and PSS's government overseer, invited us to be extra ears and eyes at the Summit. Ramos said he wanted a different perspective on the blackouts. So here we are. But if I'm right, this will also lead me to Noble. There is no way he doesn't know what's going on with these blackouts.

On paper, we're just student observers. Ms. T and the PSS team sit beside me. We're seated near the back row, where journalists take notes and camera crews record the Summit.

Experts aren't sure what is causing the blackouts. Most scientists believe they're a result of the recent geomagnetic storms caused by solar flares, which are eruptions from the sun. They aren't normal power outages where electricity is simply cut off, but these intense surges of energy from the sun could severely damage power grids and mess with other electrical systems, which would explain why certain satellites are experiencing malfunctions and total failure. I came here with the intention of finding answers, maybe even solutions, but so far the trip is not what I had expected.

Ever since my gift returned in Tunisia, I've had to work double-time to pay attention. A new dimension of numbers has emerged, and now my numbers buzz with so many layers of information, it's hard to think straight.

I always assumed if my numbers returned they'd be the same as before. I was way off. Noble wasn't kidding when he said I'd need time to understand my new abilities. I've been upgraded to a new operating system without instructions. What he didn't tell me was that my gift would crescendo like water coming to a boil on the stove. Which leads me to a question—what happens when it boils over? I'm afraid to find out.

The ability to measure sounds and frequencies started when

I met Noble in the Bardo Museum in Tunis and now it increases daily. Not only do I pick up frequencies from humans, animals, electronics, vibrations—both manmade and natural—but I measure things unseen by human eyes, anything pulsing with energy around me. It takes time to identify the source of each frequency—if I can identify it all.

These unseen frequencies are hyper-visceral. They feel skin close, a whisper in my ear. I'm no stranger to paranoia—a product of the Pratt, no doubt—but everything feels like a threat. It's a maddening tickertape running at speeds too fast to comprehend. I'm starting to feel like Double-Eight again, checking over my shoulder and raising false alarms.

Where I once had a handle on my gift, this is a whole new level of non-stop input. I'm a toddler lost in a seven-story mall and can't find my way out—because the mall just keeps getting bigger. Which makes sitting in this room listening to experts discuss their theories about the blackouts incredibly challenging.

I shift in my seat, my mind galloping as I download 211 different people's heights, weights, movements, mannerisms, and intentions. Next, I study the dimensions and structure of the auditorium. Finally, I process every frequency that buzzes in the room—voices, heat signatures, cell phone signals. Apart from all this input, my mind is also still trying to solve the problem at hand.

Scientists and power engineers sit at a panel on the stage. I latch onto clips of what they say. "Our major satellites and power grids must be protected if we want to avoid a global crisis that could thrust us back to the Stone Age," an expert from the United States exaggerates.

"If the blackouts become longer or more widespread, it could be catastrophic," agrees a female expert with a French accent. "Apart from casualties, the economic loss alone would devastate most nations. The blackouts have already cost France billions of dollars in lost wages, spoiled inventory, delayed production, and damage to our electrical grid. Not to mention the GPS failures that caused accidents all over Europe. What if GPS systems for planes fail next time? What if the power outages last for weeks? Or months? Winter is coming. What then? People will freeze in their homes." Anxiety trembles in her voice.

I'm stumbling for answers in the dark like the rest of the world, only instead of focusing on the blackouts I'm still wrestling with what happened to my life after Tunisia.

I pinch my leg and try to focus. My mind traces the diagrams of international power grids that Agent Ramos shared with PSS, exploring different solutions—but none of it actually registers because something in this room is throwing me off.

My numbers, like algorithms, run analytics across the auditorium connecting faces and vibrations until I locate fourteen frequencies pulsing with negative numbers.

I pause. Identifying why my gift picks up on this activity is harder now. It could be any number of reasons, and without the right variables, finding a conclusion is like pulling one string out of a knotted ball of yarn. After sixteen equations and twenty-eight possibilities, I can't pinpoint anything immediately wrong at the Summit or in the crowd, or tell whether the problem is connected to the blackouts. Could be another false alarm.

Suddenly, a different frequency steals my attention altogether. This one is unlike anything I've ever felt. Once again, I can't identify what it is or where it's coming from. It's humming softly and boomeranging between me and an unknown source. Whatever it is, it's making me tipsy.

Ms. Taylor, the PSS Director, is sitting beside me. She listens to the various speakers intently, but numerically, her attention is on me, like she feels my unrest.

Pens, whose red hair is not in a bun on top of her head for

once but flows straight down her back, is taking notes with one hand, while searching something on her phone with the other. Harrison is multi-tasking too. He's researching every speaker invited to the Summit while he sorts every headline across the world related to the blackout. For the first time since I met Harrison, he isn't wearing a hoodie or jeans, but dark blue slacks and a button up. His shaggy blond hair is parted and styled. It's a version of him I've never seen before. Earlier I had joked that he actually looks like a prodigy now, whatever that looks like.

Felicia, who sits extra close to Harrison these days, looks so innocent in her white skirt and pink blouse, her shiny black hair dangling in a beautiful braid off her shoulder, but she's likely hacking into the power grid database and several world leaders' phones as we speak. Eddie, our inventor, uses a PSS program called *Expose* to scan everyone in the room for any ill-tech at work. Since he's also a language expert, he's been eavesdropping on foreign conversations since we arrived.

I shift uneasily in my seat.

Harrison moves a loose strand of his blond hair, and whispers, "You okay? You look pale."

"Not sure yet," I say. On one hand, I'm overjoyed my gift is back. I'm myself again and sizing up a situation is much easier. But on the other hand, if I can't figure out what all these new frequencies and equations mean, this upgrade might break me. Tapping into people's frequencies adds an extra layer of depth that isn't always clear. Sometimes a person's frequency fluctuates like a soft melody, other times it's a clanging cymbal. With so many frequencies happening simultaneously, it's critical to know exactly what you're tapping into.

An expert from Finland, Dr. Juho Salonen, a 6'2" man with sandy brown hair, joins the panel on stage. Numbers flicker around him like fireflies. My gift is highlighting him, so I pay attention. Leaning over to Harrison, I whisper, "Who is he?"

"Seriously, Jo. You don't know him?" Harrison asks, a horrified look on his face. I shake my head. "He's the most famous Finnish aerospace engineer. He is a satellite tech guru and the chief scientist and CEO of Scale Tech, the company that funds the International Space Collaboration. You do know what that is, right?"

"Of course," I respond. The International Space Collaboration is all over the news. It's like a global NASA on steroids. The ISC is making history with their upcoming launch of a multi-functional 'Super Satellite' that's been in the works for ten years. "But what is Scale Tech?"

"A private space tech company in Finland," he says. "It's small and their headquarters are in the remote Arctic region. They have some killer tech and the company is worth billions."

I nod at this information, then turn my attention to what Dr. Salonen is saying.

"The International Space Collaboration is planning to send up our first Super-Satellite in three months. We need to ensure it is successful or the geomagnetic storms could destroy ten years of work..." His voice fades because those fourteen negative frequencies draw my attention again.

My eyes dart across the room as numbers highlight a face, then two, then three, and finally all fourteen frequencies connect to one man like a leash to a master. A black-haired man dressed in a gray suit sits close to the stage listening intently to Dr. Juho Salonen.

I can't see his face but my analysis of his movements makes me shiver—he weighs the information thoughtfully, clearly knowledgeable about the discussion, but if I didn't know better, I'd say he was amused at the panic in the room. An uneasy feeling curls in my gut. I'm about to have Eddie get closer to run a facial scan on him when I stop myself. If I get on that bus I don't know where it will lead—and the last thing I need right now is more trouble.

In the last eighteen days, I've raised three false alarms. My numbers have made me paranoid again. The endless layers of frequencies in the conference room are messing with my head. I'm starting to sweat. Logically I know that every human reacts to a problem differently, and with frequencies, it's even harder to discern why people do the things they do. I make a mental note to investigate the man later, but right now I need to get some air.

I lean over to Ms. T. "I need to leave. I'll meet you at the hotel if that's okay?"

"Of course." She nods and leans over to one of our three bodyguards, Hank Wilson. He's very muscular, and tall like Qadar, winning the nickname, Tank. "Tank, please take her back."

Tank stands, and I follow. My teammates watch me with concern. They understand that my new gift is an adjustment. But it's not just that holding me back.

Outside, the city comes alive with numbers. In the span of twelve seconds, my numbers draw up five ways to walk to Lake Geneva. They count every window on five townhouses and cute European shops. They record the length of the street, the 21 steps it takes to cross the road, 9 cars speeding by and 13 pedestrians, speaking three different languages. The night is all lit up, like walking inside a computer hologram of dimensions and graphs. Part of me wants to roam the streets, but that nagging paranoia drives me toward the hotel. If I keep up with Tank's pace, we'll be there in six minutes.

We walk on cobblestone streets, the lovely European setting like a painting. The scent in the air is the frequency of blue. Ultraviolet. Whatever it is triggers me. It feels like the Pratt, like dangerous men are prowling. I can't tell if the threats are real or imagined. I could say something to the bodyguard, but I don't. A week ago, I scared my dad when we were walking on the beach. I was convinced we were being followed, so I forced him to run off Alki Beach and into a coffee shop while K2, my military grade smart watch, ran a surveillance grid. But I was wrong. I'm seeing too many ghosts behind the waves of oscillations crashing through me. What I need to do is focus on refining my new abilities and finding Noble.

The hotel doors are ten feet in front of us. A sudden dread comes over me. The sensation of being watched, followed, pours down on me like rain. I concentrate but there's nothing but cars pulling up, people getting out. I'm okay. I'm safe.

But inside, I'm a fist balling up—I could track whoever is closing in on me. I could hunt them down. *Get a grip, Jo.* I rein myself in. *What happened in Tunisia is messing with your mind again. Kai nearly died right in front of you.* An event I've not forgotten. Chaos is not what I need right now.

We reach the hotel. It's well lit, well-guarded. Surveillance is everywhere; so is the buzz of cameras and guards. Tank is right next to me. I rub a thumb over K2's screen. All tasers are operational. My tranq-earrings, too. Nothing is wrong.

Tank, like the other bodyguards, isn't obligated to stand watch over my room anymore. When we reach our rooms on the third floor he says, "I'm right next door." I nod my thanks, then he wanders into his room.

I slip the key into the lock when that other frequency, so faint and warm, the same boomerang in the meeting, races at me again then flashes down the hall. My body temperature rises. My gift snaps clear for a moment, but I'm still confused—that frequency is not attached to anyone or anything in the hotel. It lights up like a map pointing down the hall. The way it feels...like a warning, like an invitation, like I'm stuck in winter and summer is calling me.

I shrug off the feeling and step into my hotel room, glad to be safely locked in. Glad everything is fine. No one is after me. But as I plop down in a chair by the window and look out over the lake, that warm frequency pulses again outside of my room. The desire to know what it is wins out. I decide to follow it like a phantom in the night.

It leads me away from my room in a path of wavelengths moving so fast I can't read the equations inside it.

My heart pounds as I sneak down the hall. The layout of the hotel is etched in my mind. At the end of the hall there's an emergency exit. I'm sure it leads to the roof. The door has an alarm that will be triggered if I don't dismantle it. I grit my teeth, use K2 to hack into the controls and turn off the door's sensors. Instantly the electrical system of the door goes down. The drop of the energy in the frequency around me is obvious.

I race up three flights of stairs, pushing through the roof door. I was sure that warm frequency led me here, but no one and nothing is in sight. I linger because the night is clear, and the roof reminds me of the first time I met Noble at the Bardo Museum. Calm settles over me.

I sit on the roof, my head piecing together puzzles made of stars, fractals and lightning. But the moment of calm dissolves as my body spikes with adrenaline shooting straight to my chest. A sharp tingle comes over me, carrying a massive surge of electrical frequencies—and a split second later, an all-consuming void of them. Soon I know why. Lights all over the city snap out.

I jolt forward, alert. Three minutes is like an eternity as I crouch on the pitch-dark roof. As suddenly as the lights come back on, I register the pounding of boots on stairs. A surge of human energy races toward me. Silent alarms are going off in the building. People are charging upstairs *toward me.* Paranoid or not, someone is coming.

Elevators. Footsteps, large and decisive; more footsteps, light and swift. Weapons buzzing. A massive tangle of frequencies is converging on the spot where I am.

I scramble over loose gravel to the west side of the roof. A series of ventilation ducts poke and twist out of the roof. One forms what looks like a U-shaped cave 78 centimeters tall. I crawl into its shadows. As I turn, the perpendicular ventilation duct flexes with a popping sound as I accidentally hit it with my elbow. Why didn't I calculate that?

K2 buzzes on my wrist like a swarm of mad hornets, spouting messages from Harrison. *"Do not go into your room! Get out of the hotel!"* But there's no time to respond. I flip it to silent.

The access door to the roof slams open. Figures spring through, boots scrambling across the grit. Breath is sucked from me. Nine pairs of feet.

I raise K2 ready to fire a taser, but the odds don't look good. I'm outnumbered and crammed into a mess of aluminum ventilation ducts. Trapped in a dead end.

Why did I follow that strange frequency up here? I scold myself for this obvious tactical error. Their feet move across the roof. From the sound of it, this is a well-trained team. Professionals. They're within eight and half feet of the duct. Frequencies crash through me like jackhammers, making it nearly impossible to calculate. Just then a pair of black boots steps in front of me and a voice calls out.

"Jo!"

My numbers jolt me back to reality. Familiar sizes, shapes, and sounds download like a faucet on full blast. I exhale. It's the three bodyguards. Ms. T. And the PSS team.

"Thank God you're safe. After I left you, it was minutes before an alarm went off," Tank pants, shaking his head in wonder. "How did you end up here?"

I flash to that warm frequency that now feels like a ghost, a delusion. "What's wrong?" I ask, utterly confused.

Ms. T wraps her arms around my shoulder. "Your hotel room was broken into after Tank dropped you off. We received an alert on the Gatekeeper tech Eddie set on our rooms."

Eddie leans in. "All your stuff was searched or stolen.

There's no sign of the perpetrators on any security cameras."

"They were gone before we got there," Ms. T says, trembling slightly. The look on her face is enough to steal my breath. "You were gone, too. We thought you were...*taken.*"

Interesting. I wasn't paranoid after all.

CHAPTER 1

∞

RIVERS RESIDENCE
SEATTLE, WASHINGTON

Thirty-four days after Tunisia...

This is a memory. But the absence of numbers is how I know it's also a dream. The other dead giveaway is that Red is in front of me, marking up the wall with Chinese characters written in white chalk.

I rubbed my cold arms and sat cross-legged on the thin floor mat, ready for the lecture he was sure to give me about my choices yesterday. I saw it on his face the moment I told him.

When I was out with King at the warehouse, there was a small chance I could learn something about the thugs he was working with, perhaps a small way to stop the deal, a way to change something, save someone. But I played it safe. I chose to do nothing.

"Is this a confession?" he asked me, an inquisitive look lingering behind the depth of his eyes. "I didn't ask you to intervene in King's business. Why do you feel you need to tell me this?"

"Because," I said, a strange weight sitting on my chest, "I calculated a brief window where King was far enough not to see me, but I chose not to act, and then the window closed. Ten minutes later, more cash than I'd seen in weeks flew out the door to do more evil than I can imagine. All because it was safer for me to do nothing."

He hummed at me then wrote out a new list of Chinese characters I didn't recognize on the wall. "Come back after you have learned these words." I jotted the characters down on a note then slid into my own cell.

After my work was finished with King the next night, I wandered over to Red. Most of the inmates were sleeping, but Red was still awake, writing on scrap paper that Guard San had gotten for him. The light was usually dim in Red's cell, but not so in the dream. It was bright, vibrant somehow, filling the space with a strange glow. It didn't make sense. It was a dream, after all.

I knelt on the mat before him. "I'm finished."

"Ah ha. Then, let's see." Red's ever-present voice resounded in my head like it was yesterday. "What is this word?" He pointed to two characters *wei* and *ji* that formed the word *Weiji* in Chinese.

"Crisis," I said confidently. Apart from the ten new words he asked me to learn, I memorized a hundred extra from an old magazine that an inmate had left behind.

He breathed in deeply three times, a measure of twenty-four seconds, and I knew I'd missed something. "Partially correct," he said. "What is a crisis?"

I shrugged. "Something terrible."

"Ah ha. I see you didn't do the homework." His face bunched up at me.

I shook my head. "I wrote every word you asked me to, thirty times each, as usual. I know all of their meanings and every stroke pattern." Of course, I had to do it in between countless stock reports for King and playing chess with Guard San. But still.

"I didn't ask you to write the words. I asked you to learn them. There is a difference, a gap between knowledge and wisdom. Since the beginning, I've instructed you to look beyond the obvious. To gain insight, you must go deeper and dig for understanding. Words change and lose meaning over time. Sometimes we have to go back and remember what they meant at their origin to make sense of today." He sighed, and pointed to the first character in the word crisis. "*Wei* means 'danger'. *Ji* means 'opportunity'."

"So a crisis is a dangerous opportunity?" I asked.

A small smile cracked on his wrinkled face. "Depends on you. In English, the word crisis comes from a Greek word—*a critical or decisive moment; a point in which change must come.* The word does not mean 'something terrible'. It means it is time to act. In every dangerous event, there is an opportunity for change for the one who sees and acts."

He pointed to the next word on the list, *an quan,* which means 'safe'.

"*An* is peace. *Quan* is complete. Likewise the word safe does not mean 'out of danger', but rather 'in complete peace'." He nodded his head slowly. His eyes that have become like blades into my soul, remained fixed on me. "We can be in danger, and also have complete peace. Peace reveals our safety. So then, we can follow peace no matter where it leads."

"Are you teaching me this because I did nothing to stop King?" I asked, my hand tapping on the cement.

He set down his chalk. "Because, granddaughter, the world doesn't need any more people to see the danger. Rather, what we need is for more people to see an opportunity."

CHAPTER 2

∞

DOE BAY, ORCAS ISLAND
SAN JUANS, WASHINGTON

Fifty-two days after Tunisia...

My father and I are in his boat two nautical miles offshore from the coast of the San Juan Islands. Dad hauled me out here before my next PSS assignment. He's worried about me. He says I spend too much time in the dark. He's not wrong.

My infinity is back, but with it, a thousand questions, endless equations, and one divided heart—and in the dark is where I'll get my answers. After I solve Noble's star code, I'll sort out the war inside me—why my heart dreams of one person and my mind another.

I'm lying on my back against the freezing deck floor as the boat gently rocks to the patterns of the sea, but my eyes are locked on the vast winter night sky. The PSS telescope that Eddie built works so well, I feel like I could reach up and comb my fingers through the Milky Way. I want to calculate a highway of stars and find out where it leads, but I can't because there's a frequency hovering ten feet below our boat—an equation my mind is fixated on.

Judging by the sound and vibrations of its movements, its estimated length is nearly as long as our boat—21 feet; weight—possibly 12,000 pounds. I'm guessing it's a minke whale, common in these waters. I don't know why it's alone or why it's hovering under our boat. It swam up under us 12 minutes ago and hasn't left. It's weird that I know that. It's not normal. But then again, nothing has been normal since I got my gift back.

Which is why, 52 days after my gift returned, I'm still in a zoo of barking numbers trying to tame them into a cage... at least the package includes whales. Yet, I'm no closer to cracking Noble's code in the stars because I have no idea what he's charting.

My skin tingles and a shock hits my stomach like live wires are snapping. I sit up alert. I know this feeling. Another blackout is coming. I watch for the interference in the frequencies around me.

As if on cue, lights snap out one by one leaving the entire shoreline of the island dark. My whole body goes rigid. Twenty-seven seconds pass before the lights blink back on. I exhale. It's just a blip in the power – not long enough to cause any damage. I lie back down, trying to ignore the itch under my skin induced by these mysterious blackouts that are still happening.

My dad climbs on deck from inside the cabin and comes to the bow. He drops a wool blanket over me. Although the temperature dropped ten degrees after midnight, I still don't want to go inside. The dark has become my refuge, like I'm closer to *him* at night.

"Are Mara and Lily asleep?" I ask him.

"Yep." He settles onto the bench beside me, knowing I won't sleep until I finish tonight's star charts. "Is the whale still under us?"

I close my eyes, wading through layers of pulsing measurements to find its frequency. At first, the whale's sheer size alarmed me, but after calculating its gentle rhythm, I knew it wasn't here to hurt us. Then the massive creature under the surface became mesmerizing, even if I couldn't see it. It's a beautiful reminder that not all things with power are threatening.

The whale, which hasn't surfaced once, moves slightly. I shiver.

"Yeah," I say, a flutter in my stomach when I feel its presence. "He's still hanging out."

"How do you know it's a *he*?" Dad asks, chuckling and giving me a look. "Don't tell me your numbers can predict that now?"

"Not yet." I crack a smile, then burst out laughing. I need to laugh. Learning to operate with this new lens has made me far too serious lately. My dad isn't the only one who worries. The PSS team has commented on it too. I wish I could be more present, but my brain is on a journey of its own. I can't explain it, but there's a path in the dark, lit up with numbers leading to a crossroads. I need to follow it.

Meanwhile, my search for Noble consumes me and my dreams of Kai are intensifying. Even the whale is a reminder of two worlds—one above and one below me, both teeming with unexplored life and mystery. My mind, like my heart, doesn't know what to calculate first—the sea or the sky.

My hand slides to the boat's floor like somehow the whale knows I'm reaching out to it. Maybe it does. Apart from darkness, everything has a frequency. It's distinguishing one from another that is the hard part. Like the *phantom frequency*—the unidentified frequency that comes and goes like a radio wave in every location I've been to since Geneva. The PSS team and I can't agree on what it is. Eddie, who's taken it upon himself to research it, believes the answer lies in quantum physics.

Tonight, it bolted over the water for seven seconds before it disappeared—as if I need another mystery to solve.

Dad opens his thermos and pours me a cup of hot tea. "I can't imagine knowing what's around you like that." He stares at me thoughtfully. He would've never known the whale was there if I hadn't told him.

I sit up and take the tea from him, watching the steam curl from the cup before I set it down and look away. Even that simple action makes my mind swirl in a string of numbers... with an outside temperature of 48 degrees the tea must be 190 degrees to steam for 3 minutes.

"It definitely takes some getting used to," I say finally. "I'm always filtering out what's a threat and what's not—like in Geneva."

"Threats," my dad repeats. "So is Geneva why you're playing it safe these days?"

His words dig into my heart in a way I'm sure he didn't intend. I've tried to forget what happened in Geneva, but it still bothers me. I ignored my gut for the first time since China and didn't investigate that black-haired man at the Summit, the one who held the leash to 14 other men with creepy frequencies—even after my room was broken into. But my dad is not talking about the break-in at the hotel.

I prop myself up on one elbow, facing him. "What do you mean?"

"Marigold told me that you turned down the Defense Intelligence Agency's offer to reactivate PSS's Special Cases Unit." He wrinkles his brow.

My eyes dart to his face, calculating his expressions. I'm surprised Ms. T—*Marigold*—told my dad about the DIA's offer. When we landed in Seattle after Tunisia, Ms. T explained how she had run a department that worked with the government to solve special cases but had shut it down after a job went wrong and a PSS prod, a girl named Rayne Carter, died. But now, because of me, she'd be willing to reopen it.

I turned her offer down. My gift had just re-emerged. I'd watched Kai almost die, then lost him. Discovered Noble was Mandel. I needed time to focus on my new gift and what was happening inside of me.

Regardless, Dad's response shocks me. He has to know the DIA special cases are anything but safe.

"Is this Ms. T's influence on you?" I ask, laughing. It's not a secret they've been spending a lot of time together. "Those special operations are definitely more dicey than the ones we do now. I thought you'd appreciate the assignments we've been taking on lately." On the whole, regular PSS jobs may not be ordinary, but they're relatively harmless—no fingertip bombs, no political or economic crises, or terrorists—just helping humanity, which is relaxing.

"Safe like Geneva?" My dad puckers his lips to one side. "Look. I appreciate that you're being as safe as is possible *for you.* You just haven't been yourself lately, even with the return of your math gift."

I wince at his words but there's no point in denying it. It's true—I've been holding back. But the word *safe* pricks me like a thorn as though it's a beautiful flower I'll never have without a little blood.

"Finding Noble is my priority right now," I say, hardening. I divert my eyes over the dark water. "The news circulating about him is getting worse."

After Tunisia, the media went ballistic with rumors of a dangerous hacker breaking into satellites, tampering with government files. With the International Space Collaboration about to launch their first Super Satellite in a month, space agencies and foreign governments began voicing concern about the true intentions of the NASA Tipper. There's now a mandate to find him. While I know Noble's just trying to help, the rest of the world isn't convinced anymore, which is why I need to find him first.

Along with unsettling press on the NASA Tipper, there's a new thorn in our side. Ms. Carry Mines—a very high-profile and pesky journalist determined to expose PSS. Since we returned from Tunisia, she's been tailing our trips and investigating our so-called *student exchanges*. I've never seen Ms. T so upset. Her highest priority is always to ensure PSS remains under the radar to protect the prods, which is why our student exchanges now include public lectures at local universities to establish a credible alibi.

Our number of bodyguards also went up. Two of them stick to me like glue when we're on a job. Their constant presence is wearing on me. Thankfully, I haven't had to taser any of them yet.

Dad zips up his jacket, then sips his tea. "This may be a very fatherly thing to say, but I still don't understand why Noble is making you do all this work to find him. If he cares for you, he should be here with you."

My chest tightens. My dad's voice isn't judgmental, just full of concern. He tries to remain unbiased when we chat about my relationships, but my numbers tell me he's totally Team Kai.

Honestly, I'm beyond hurt that Noble hasn't reached out—I'm angry. When we were kids, he made me feel understood. I didn't need to explain myself to him. Even if he never told me his real name, we were connected—*are connected.* The five days we spent together in Tunisia—the way it felt to examine each other with numbers, the encounters we shared in the simulations—play on repeat in my mind. I need to know what I feel for him, which is why I can't give up. Noble's heart is in the stars and he's wondering if I'll find it. I'm wondering, too.

"Noble cares," I finally say. "He's just taking things slow." And whether Noble said it or not, he's giving me time to get over Kai. If my dreams count for anything, I'm not sure I have yet. I still wonder where Kai is, what he's doing and if he's okay. For weeks, I scanned Harrison's international news reports to see if he might be involved in any busts.

Wherever Kai is, he's not playing it safe. He's risking everything to make the world a better place. Which is why my numbers made it clear that he had to take this job. I had to let him go. Now he'll be gone for up to three years.

Wind rocks our boat, jostling me from my thoughts. Dad reaches for another blanket. "You'll figure it out soon enough. If you saved a world economy and stopped a coup then you can work this out too. Remind me when you leave for the next job?"

"Tomorrow night," I say. "Our seventh PSS job—more power grids in Saudi Arabia. After that we'll go to Namibia."

I adjust the telescope, about to look up when a strong surge of frequencies coming from below me race toward the surface, making my mind go wild with calculations. I reach for the rail, gripping hard as I trace the change in energy around us.

To my dad's alarm, I jump up, and spring to the side of the boat. The water starts sloshing. The whale starts swirling wildly below us. Graphs pop up in my mind. Hundreds of numerical vibrations in the water rise like mad. As the water ripples faster, my brain measures the energy and frequency of the wavelengths.

The onslaught of equations is so abundant that I imagine a pod of whales coming to tip our boat until I settle down to untangle the mass of ever-increasing frequencies in the water. They're not sound waves. They're equations I've seen since my gift returned, since I started charting the stars. But instead of above me, they're below me. An idea hits.

"Dad, start the boat," I say, keeping my eyes glued to the sea. "Agitate the water."

My dad doesn't hesitate. The boat is moving within 36 seconds. He circles the area, and the motor causes a reaction. A magical phenomenon.

I marvel and laugh. "Dad, come here. You have to see this."

My dad jumps from the captain's seat. Looking overboard, he gives a hoot and makes a mad dash for his camera. All I do is stare. *Light* is everywhere. A blue glow pulses in the water with beautiful streams of energy. Bioluminescence. Along with it, brilliant equations unfold like waves all around us.

My dad snaps eighteen photos—*they won't turn out*—of the plankton before he stops to look up at me. "Beautiful."

"Light," I mumble. The phenomenon below me bubbles with frequencies, while my mind wildly calculates. "More than 90% of sea creatures have the ability to create light inside themselves, even at the bottom of the ocean."

I'm breathless as it dawns on me: light has a frequency. Frequencies can be identified and measured. The mystery equations I've tried to solve for fifty-two days were not voice or sound waves, nor were they star patterns or asteroids. They were frequencies on the electromagnetic spectrum—the unseen light waves all around us.

The whale was there to eat the plankton.

"Dad, can you pass me my bag? I need to adjust the setting on this telescope." I scramble through the gear looking for a lens that Eddie made that can detect X-rays, ultraviolet and infrared light beyond our atmosphere.

I laugh, looking at the patterns around me now. What I couldn't see before is so obvious. Equations around me measure different wavelengths. A map of coordinates appears in the sky. I have the first stepping-stone across a wide river. My heart skips.

"I just cracked Noble's code." I whip my head toward my dad. "It's light."

CHAPTER 3

∞

OTAVI SHIPWRECK, SPENCER BAY
SKELETON COAST, NAMIBIA

PRESENT

98 days after Tunisia...

Tonight I'm thinking about death.

It's appropriate for my location, I suppose. It's our last night in Namibia, one of the least populous countries in Africa, and the PSS team and I have set up camp on Skeleton Coast where hundreds of ships have run aground, and the hungry sand dunes have left ghost towns in their wake.

But the death that's on my mind is vastly different. Most often when something dies, its frequency dies too. But not so with a star. The minute a supernova explodes, radiant colors, brighter than the sun, blast out of it, emitting more energy and frequencies than we can imagine, and its light waves radiate for centuries, long after its death.

These frequencies are how I'll uncover a message in the sky—written by a boy who created the most complicated form of communication in the galaxy. Not that I expected any less from him.

After a day of exploring old shipwrecks, I'm anxious for sundown, to be under the stars. Everyone else is celebrating a job well done at Namibia United Energy, but after I received an ambiguous text from Rafael, an old friend who I haven't heard from since China, I can't stop calculating. Negative predictions haunt me just like those shipwrecks.

Mila. I need your help. It's urgent. Per favore. Call me.

It doesn't make sense for Rafael to contact me unless something is very wrong. He and his father, Cesare, entered a hyper-secure witness protection program called *Ghost Markers,* set up by Agent Bai through Private Global Forces, after Cesare spilled the beans on Madame's thugs in Italy last year. Irritation and worry simmer in my gut. Rafael promised me he would stay out of trouble.

I responded to his message right away, but every phone number I tried was a dead end. Rafael is nowhere to be found. Since we don't have the right tech in Namibia to find him, I texted Agent Bai, who hasn't called me back yet. Ever since Kai and I split ways, Bai takes his sweet time responding to my messages. So, like it or not, I have to wait. Which is fine because decoding Noble's message is my priority.

Harrison, Pens, Eddie, and Felicia are crouched by a crackling fire, chatting in low hums not ten feet from me. I'm not paying close attention, but my name is being tossed around. So is Noble's name, especially since the geomagnetic storms causing satellite failures and blackouts everywhere are worse than ever. The International Space Collaboration will send up their Super Satellite in eight days, and everyone's asking the same question: Why would the NASA Tipper stop dropping tips when the world needs him most? While the world debates Noble's intentions, I just need to know if he's okay—another reason I need to decipher this message tonight.

I set up my heat-activated sleeping bag on a padded lawn chair outside a very large campervan. A large telescope is to my right on a sand-deflecting-table, plugged into a computer, which is cross-referencing algorithms I've programmed into it and recording every possible pattern of energy and frequency 24/7. The light pollution here is the lowest I've seen anywhere in the world. Once tonight's equations are complete, I'll be able to decipher a message in the sky and pinpoint Noble's location.

My eyes adjust to the dark as the sun finally sinks completely into the sea and my ears perk up at the sounds around me. The wind circles on the dunes, beckoning my brain to trace its patterns; the ocean currents in the distance move counterclockwise to the Northern Hemisphere; the vastness of an unexplored land with missing sections on a map begs me to fill it in.

There's something alluring about being far away from home, tucked in so deep and nearly lost where no one could find you if they tried. Is this how Noble feels when he disappears to one of his refuges?

After three minutes, anticipation gets the better of me, and I take a peek through the telescope.

If my theory is right, Noble has been tracking high-energy events that generate prodigious quantities of X-rays, gamma rays, and ultraviolet rays, like supernovas. He's also charting solar activity and charged particles in the auroras. What everyone else called "star coding" is actually equations for a new way to harness energy from light. With his ideas, Noble could change space exploration, travel, communications, energy... history itself.

No wonder he's in hiding. If anyone knew what he could do, everyone would be hunting for him, to use him like his parents did and abuse his mathematical gift.

The telescope hasn't registered an equation yet, so I grab an old pair of PSS night vision goggles from my backpack that I've been using for research. Human eyes are too small to pick up larger light waves that hide in the dark, and night vision is a way around that, but they're heavy and awkward to use. I slip them on and eerie traces of hidden light start peeking out of unsuspected places. With the right lens, it's amazing what we can see.

A jolt in vibrations tells me the team is coming my way. Finally, after much work, I can identify multiple people all at once, like my team, just by their frequency. With Noble it was easy because he was only one person, but when I'm interpreting hundreds of frequencies from different locations—people's voices, breath, movement, heartbeats, the thrum of life flowing under their skin, blood pumping, electrons firing—it takes a lot of focus.

Pens crouches down beside me, tying her long red hair up in a knot. "Did you get everything back online after the blackout?"

I look up at her through the night vision goggles and I'm captivated by the colors of heat glowing on her face but I can't count the freckles on her cheeks. It's distracting, so I take them off.

"Yes. Our systems are back on," I say, pausing as an unsolved equation fizzes in my brain. The blackouts still don't make sense to me. There's no real pattern to them. Tonight's blackout was a minute long, but it took eight minutes to reboot everything. A lingering guilt from Geneva pinches me in the gut, like somehow, it's my fault the blackouts are still happening.

"Any luck on Noble's location?" Felicia asks, eagerly. Felicia's the best hacker on our team. She's even signed agreements with the government about what she is allowed to do. It bugs her that even she hasn't been able to locate Noble, but Noble claimed only I could crack his code.

My stomach knots up at her question. "Soon."

"So, what happens when you find him?" Pens asks, a challenge under her breath. "Will you leave PSS?" For months, Pens has tried to get me to open up about my feelings for Noble. It's not that simple. At least, not for me.

"I don't know." I turn to Harrison. "Any significant news?" Harrison knows I'm referring to articles around the NASA

Tipper.

"Nothing about *your man.* To the dismay of the entire space community, he's gone silent. In other tragic news, Scale Tech's CEO Dr. Juho Salonen announced that his wife has fallen into a sudden coma, and those three scientists working on the ISC Super Satellite are still missing." Harrison scratches his head and changes the subject. "I also learned something interesting about your missing Italian friend."

He pulls up a holo-screen on his watch with an article dated not long after I left China. "Prominent Italian Crime Boss Seized." The image of the man's face included in the article is hard to forget. Black hair combed straight back, a shady smirk on his face. The article is about Cesare di Susa, Rafael's sleazeball father who was caught in Madame's notorious smuggling crime web. Inwardly, I cringe. "This is old news."

"For you, maybe." Harrison snorts. "You failed to mention that your Italian friend was the son of an Italian crime boss." Pens and Felicia turn to me, looking for answers.

I shrug. "Sorry. It's a long story. Rafael is not like his father." *I think. I hope.* "I told you guys not to do any digging. Bai and his team are investigating his text right now. They're in charge of his case."

Harrison tucks his ultra-blond hair behind his ears, then pulls up his hoodie. "Jo. Looking into things is literally my job description. I'm the news guy. I'm supposed to find these things. To be honest, the Jo I know would have left Namibia to find him already."

His words sting. But I can't blame him. He's right. I flash to Rafael's green eyes, soft brown curls, and dimples—and guilt pokes me in the chest. In the Pratt, he brought hope into my life in a way even Red couldn't. Rafael trusted me and helped us take down King. What we share is embedded into a part of my history I can't ignore.

"How did you find this article?" I ask. "I didn't tell you their names and everything on them was supposed to be taken offline."

"It wasn't hard. Felicia and I hacked into a list of deleted searches on that Chinese crime ring with Madame. The article came up." He stops, and chews on his lip. "I'm guessing you noticed that the day Rafael and Cesare went missing was the same day your room was broken into in Geneva?"

A deep shiver runs through me. My team knows me well enough to know my numbers wouldn't miss a detail like that, especially after what happened that night. But I didn't mention it to them because I needed to focus on finding Noble. Thankfully, they're not upset.

I unzip my sleeping bag, and slide in. "I noticed. I'm waiting for Bai to call me back. His team can handle this," I say, averting my eyes. Rafael's message has me on edge, but my irritation is worse. I did everything I could to help them start a new life, and if Rafael's dad is getting into trouble again, it can't be good. On top of that, there's no reason for PSS to research criminal friends from my past again. We don't want to end up with another Tunisia incident on our hands.

Harrison exchanges glances with the others, then shrugs like it's no use to keep talking about it.

"Speaking of Bai," Felicia says, changing the subject. "Are you still doing your support group with Mr. Chan?"

I flinch, huffing out an awkward laugh. "It wasn't a support group." The team stares at me like I'm a child hiding a toy behind my back.

I roll my eyes. "Fine. Maybe a little, but that routine is over now." After Kai went undercover, Chan and I were each other's only link to him. Talking to Chan was the only thing that could quell the four tons of agony that hit me each time I relived our exchange at the safe house after Kai almost died. At first, our conversations were always the same—Chan worried about his son. I told him Kai would be ok. Chan got mad at his son's decision to go undercover long term. I told him Kai had to do it. Chan claimed Kai would never find another girl like me. I agreed. We felt better for about a week. Until the next phone call, when we needed to hear it all again. Now, we check in and talk business.

Harrison moves to sit on my lawn chair. "We get it. We miss Kai too." Harrison slaps a hand on my shoulder. "Who else can say they know a kung fu master spy? Then again, you've moved on to the NASA Tipper genius."

A devouring thought, almost as ferocious as this consuming desert, eats away at my gut. Have I really moved on? If I have, I can't tell. Everything I care about seems suspended in mid-air like I haven't set foot on stable ground for three months.

Eddie notices my expression and punches Harrison's shoulder. "Shut up, dude."

My eyes focus on the orange and blue flames flickering in the fire. I haven't talked to any of them about how I feel, except Eddie, who just listens and doesn't give opinions. Yes, I had to let Kai go, and yes, I need to find Noble. But there's more to finding Noble than my feelings. A numerical path is driving me forward, and the crossroads running through my mind are closer than ever. Noble is the key to understanding what's happening to my gift. I don't expect them to understand. But until I know what direction to choose, I can't make any wrong moves.

"It's ok. I'm fine," I say to Eddie.

"I guess you'll be sleeping—or not sleeping—outside with the scorpions again, huh?" Harrison asks. "The research we did on them is cool, but they still have one of the most venomous stings in the world."

The Namib scorpion exoskeleton glows under UV lights, so we studied it in hopes of creating a new tracking-tech, but Harrison doesn't like anything that crawls. I shake my head at him. "I've calculated the odds of me dying from a scorpion sting out here. Let's just say, I'm pretty sure that's not how my life will end. But thanks."

Pens rests her arm on my shoulder. "What Harrison means

is we know you haven't slept much since Tunisia. You spend most of your time at night studying the stars, or reading about a dead prod."

I glance up. "How did you know I was reading about her?"

They all look to Eddie, who chews his lip before he speaks. "Even Ms. T knows you took the file on Rayne Carter. To be honest, we've all wanted to ask Ms. T about her too, but she's never talked about it." Eddie pauses. "Ms. T also told us you declined her offer to activate the Special Cases Unit, but that you hacked Agent Ramos's DIA assignment list."

"I'm an open book." I shake my head. "I wasn't trying to hide anything."

"What's going on in your mind then?" Pens asks.

Kai's bloody face in the helicopter; Noble's body slammed to the ground in Douz; the danger the team faced in Tunis. Things could have been so much worse...a weight of responsibility hangs heavy on my shoulders.

Ever since China, a fight has simmered inside me. That part of me came out in Tunisia, which proved Kai right: I am trouble. Crisis follows me whether I willingly jump into it, or not. I want to know why every path leads to threats, to danger, to darkness. Truth is, I thought about the Special Cases Unit, but why would I willingly dive into what I spent years trying to escape? Why would I willingly follow in Rayne Carter's footsteps and end up dead?

"Nothing I can define," I say, shrugging my shoulders. "And there's no real information on Rayne Carter anyway." My eyes return to the stars.

"Wait a minute," Felicia says, her eyes brewing up another idea. "Is this because your dad is dating Ms. T?"

Wow. Of course they'd choose the night I'm so close to finding answers to corner me for an intervention.

"No," I say, shaking my head. "Ms. T and my dad are great together. I'll admit it was a bit strange when he joined the PSS board, but my dad's love life has made my life significantly easier. He hardly worries anymore. He's healthier than he's ever been, and he's absolutely crushing his new business. Guys, seriously, there's nothing to be worried about."

"All right," says Pens, standing. "The jet picks us up at Walvis Bay early tomorrow. So get some sleep because it's your turn to do the student lecture at the Rio Math Institute once we get to Brazil. I'm heading to bed."

"Thanks," I groan. I forgot it was my lecture rotation. I was actually looking forward to meeting their economists.

Felicia taps Harrison and they both stand. "Oh, and since you weren't listening earlier," Felicia says, yawning, "our crazy journalist-mascot was spotted in Luderitz. She's definitely following us, so we're taking the back roads to the airport."

"Ok." A protective side of me tightens. According to Harrison, this isn't the first time Ms. Mines has tried to destroy PSS. What problem does this journalist have with Ms. T? For weeks, I've wanted to ask Ms. T about how Rayne Carter died. Turns out, it's not an easy subject to broach.

The others stand and stretch. It's late. I don't expect them to spend as much time in the dark as I do.

"Goodnight," I say, my head full of thoughts.

Everyone heads to the PSS campervan to go to sleep, except Eddie.

He stands. "I'll get us some tea. Back in a minute." He's not gone three seconds before K2 announces Bai's call.

"Answer," I command.

"Jo," Bai grunts, his voice has an underlying disdain in his tone just like our last conversation.

"*Bai Ge*," I say, rattling off some Chinese pleasantries. "Thank you for calling me back. I assume you got my message." He's probably only calling back because PSS gifted Private Global Forces a whole new set of updated non-traceable biotrackers for their teams.

"I looked into the boy and his father after you texted me."

"And?"

He sighs like he's deciding whether to tell me now so that I won't have to press him later. "They've vanished. The *Ghost Marker* protection team has no idea where they are," he says bluntly. "It's concerning. Cesare Di Susa was involved with some pretty heavy players in Italy. Our best people are on it."

Per favore, Mila. The pestering weight on my heart gets heavier as my mind calculates different possibilities behind why he called me. I add up the number of weeks he's been missing with the probability of trouble because of his thug father, and what might happen if he isn't found soon. It's not good. I squeeze my eyes shut to focus and tiny sparks of light flash behind them. I need to let Bai do his job.

"Thanks for the information," I say.

"I'll let you know what we find, but it'll take a while. I'll be out on an assignment for a couple weeks. Ok?" He's about to hang up but I stop him.

"Bai Ge, wait. Where is *he* right now? Is he ok?" Bai knows I'm not talking about Rafael anymore, just like I know he won't answer my question. But I have to ask.

"He's fine. On the job, nowhere near you." His words are full of bite.

It's been months since we've had the unspoken issue of Kai between us. I can't handle it anymore. "Why don't you just tell me what you're really thinking and get it off your chest?"

He pauses, five, ten seconds. The silence is grueling. I can't feel his frequency clearly through this phone call, but if I could, it'd be all prime numbers multiplied with angst.

"You're a grown woman, Jo," he says finally. "You make your own decisions. But *jiche*! That boy would die a thousand times for you. And you had to go and wreck him. Drop him like a fly. Leave without a reason. Not even a phone call! There's no honor in the way you left him. It cut him deep... thankfully he's strong."

Pain slices into my chest that makes me doubt my decision. But the numbers were as clear as day...I had to let Kai go. "I never meant to hurt him. I thought—"

"Whatever you thought was wrong. Now my cousin is gone. For good."

A shiver of goosebumps creeps onto my skin, then slinks into my stomach like sloshing waves. "What do you mean?"

"I've seen that look before in other agents' eyes after something bad happens. A resignation, a determination. Now Kai's a *November Romeo!* He's never going to stop."

I tense up. "What's a *November Romeo*?" I ask, frustrated. "I don't speak your spy jargon."

"It means '*Never Returns*'. These guys never stop going from job to job. Their mission is their life and nothing more. They never come home. Before he left, he asked me to check up on you from time to time." He scoffs. "So do him a favor. Keep yourself out of trouble."

My eyes squeeze shut, as my hand reaches to my stomach. There's nothing more to say. "*Hao.* Thanks."

After we hang up, my gaze returns to the sky. The team wants to know why I refuse to activate the Special Cases Unit. If only I could show them the constant threats that surround us. Each disaster we miss by a millisecond, a millimeter. By keeping myself out of trouble, I'm protecting them. So far, no one has died, like Kai almost did in Tunisia. This time the numbers are clear. If I don't stick to the right path, those odds won't last.

CHAPTER 4

∞

Vibrations in the air shift and the footsteps of a 5'9" person head my way. Eddie is sauntering over with a cup of tea in his hands. Thank God he's a night owl. I could use a friend right now.

As Eddie swings up next to me, Miles, bodyguard number two, wanders to the edge of camp, giving us some room. Eddie slips into the seat beside me.

He hands me the warm cup of tea. "I made this for you. I know you'll be up awhile."

Steam curls from the cup. I lean my face into it, and breathe in its rich, sweet scent. It's rooibos, an herbal tea common to the region. "Thanks, Eddie." I glance back at the bodyguards doing their rounds. "How did you get number 2 to move from his post? Promise to make him some kind of new weapon?"

He pushes his silky black hair aside and smirks at my joke. "I told him your body has a higher radiation level because of your math gift and sitting beside you for long periods of time can be dangerous to his health." We laugh. "Nah, I actually used this crazy thing called the truth—I'm your friend and I wanted to talk with you alone."

"Easy, right? The truth." I must look disturbed because a

sympathetic look settles on his face.

"Don't mind the team, ok? They're just worried about you."

"I know."

I've gotten to know Eddie better these past few months. After the others go to sleep, we exchange stories and scars from our past. It's nice to have someone around who understands the clandestine part of me. Eddie's conquered a lot of demons. He's not at a point where he'd want to face his former captors, but he's one hundred percent about doing good when the opportunity rises.

The three bodyguards finish their last security rounds of our camping area, and Tank comes up to us. "Everything is clear, Jo. If we're in for the night you can employ the *BFG.*" He snorts at the name Harrison chose for Eddie's new invention.

"Thanks, Tank."

I hold out my right arm with my emp-bracelet made of twelve quarter-inch metal balls buzzing with electrical pulses. "K2," I command, "employ the BFG."

The tiny metal balls are mini drones filled with electromagnetic energy, much like an EMP. They also act as tasers if I need them to. The bracelet matches a larger metal ball on a chain hanging from my neck, which is 100 times more powerful than the ones on my wrist. For emergencies only, of course. It had a technical name, but then Harrison called it *The Squirrel's Chestnut.* We made fun of him for days, but the ridiculous name stuck.

On command, the tiny drones take off in perfect formation to create a perimeter of 500 feet around our camp. The Big Friendly Gate, *aka* the *BFG,* is not friendly at all. In essence, it's a fence that forms an electric barrier around us, or me, if I'm alone. Anything that crosses the perimeter will get a pretty hefty electrical shock. After my room was broken into in Geneva, Ms. T makes us use it everywhere, even though the bracelet is still in testing mode. The first time we used it, we could hear bugs being zapped all night. No one could sleep. We had to adjust the settings.

"So, you're sure about tonight?" Eddie says, fiddling with the telescope.

I nod. Elation spills out of me, even if my voice is shaky. "Tonight's the night. My patterns will be complete enough to know where he is and decipher the equations of light that he uses to communicate." I press my lips together to stop an ever-growing smile. I've waited 98 days for this message in the sky, to hear what he has to say.

A tide of emotion swells deep inside me. To see Mandel—*Noble*—face to face again has been my sole focus for so long. He gave me a treasure map to find him and I've finally made it to the 'X'. Now I get to uncover what is there. It's also scary. Numbers won't guide me past this part. Everything ahead is a cavern of mysteries that math cannot solve.

Eddie picks up the bulky night vision goggles. "Man, these are far from subtle," he says. We both laugh. "When we get back to Seattle, finishing my *bio-lens* will be my top priority." He tosses the goggles on my backpack. Eddie's latest nano-tech project is for night vision contact lenses that can enhance light waves even beyond infrared.

"All in good time, Eddie. No one short of a genius could have gotten as far as you."

"Nah." He smiles slightly. His modesty is refreshing. "Still having those dreams?"

"Yeah...they're getting more intense, too," I explain. Since my numbers returned, my dreams aren't dreams. They're memories. Ones that take days to recover from—the Pratt; the pool house; Kai's hands on my skin...I shiver. "My dad thinks the dreams are just processing trauma, you know, from getting my gift back...losing people I care about. Same thing happened to him when my mom passed."

"That might be true, but I think it's more than that," Eddie says. "The more I study your frequency ability, the more I believe it's activating dormant areas in your brain. According to my research, you're picking up higher frequencies that boost your brain waves into a 'gamma' state, which makes you more alert and better able to recall memories. This may be why your dream life is replaying reality. In the meantime, if you can home in on lower frequency waves linked to 'delta' and 'theta' states, they can boost relaxation and improve sleep. The effects of bioelectrical oscillations on the brain are huge, which is why your mind is working overtime."

"That's intense. I feel like a kid being studied at Harvard again." I set my tea down, musing at the human brain. Ms. T has a similar point of view. *It's not strange*, she concluded, after I told her about the ability to pick up frequencies. *After all, the human brain built the machines that detect frequencies today. Sometimes, we learn about things before we see them.*

After they appeared, it was easy to see they were always there, but that I just didn't have the lens to recognize them. I still don't understand why I lost my gift in China and why I gained it back in Tunisia. What does it mean?

After twenty-three minutes of shooting the breeze, Eddie yawns. "I'm heading in for the night." He smiles sympathetically and places a hand on my shoulder. "I know the others don't always get the things we've been through. But you taught me to jump back in the game. To be myself. Same goes for you."

"Thanks, Eddie. Goodnight." Eddie's fifteen footsteps leave half-inch deep prints in the sand heading to the campervan, but within seconds the wind erases them.

Finally I'm alone under the African night sky. My hand reaches down, grazing the cold grains of sand. It's finer here, but the way it gets stuck in everything—my shoes, hair, K2—reminds me of Tunisia.

The phantom frequency ricochets through the air, but it's too fast to calculate. Red believed, like Ms. T, that we're designed to discover what is unseen, even if he wasn't scientific about it. For a moment, I home in on that infinity and nothing else matters.

Concerns about Rafael and the PSS team drift away. After I find Noble, I'll focus on locating Rafael. After all, Noble could find anyone with his facial recognition software.

I peer up through my telescope. The stars are so dense and bright, it looks like milk poured out across the sky. The recent solar flares have triggered the most intense displays of auroras scientists have seen in years, which has helped speed my research.

Noble's communication code is beyond complex. It's like a new form of Morse code using the wavelengths and frequencies of these high-energy stellar events. Once I gather tonight's activity and coordinates, I'll use an alphabet affiliation sequence to transmute the measurements into letters.

My research has given me 87% of the coordinates I need to discover where Noble is hiding. Tonight, I'll have the rest.

As the earth rotates, the data appears painfully slowly, dripping one number at a time like a broken faucet. I write each one down, cross-examining it with other data. As I turn the dials on the telescope and meticulously check my notes, finally X marks the spot. The data has a match—in the polar auroras.

My heart speeds up. I now have latitude and longitude coordinates for a spot on the opposite side of the world. Noble is holed up in the region around the North Pole.

I should have guessed. The well-known Arctic Space Lab run by Scale Tech is in that area. Their satellites and data centers have made ripples through scientific communities across the world. Not to mention the ISC headquarters is in Helsinki, Finland. He must be tapping into their satellites for his own research. Everyone is looking for him, and he's right under their noses.

My stomach explodes into jitters. After the PSS job in Brazil is finished, I could hop on a plane and find him. The location isn't exact, but there's enough data to decipher the general area.

My fingers tremble so much I can hardly hold the pen as I decipher the equations that tumble in like shooting stars. Ninety-eight nights of searching in the dark for this message, and finally a candle has been lit. My smile is so wide it hurts.

One by one numbers recalibrate in my head. I decode the final layer of data and breathe. Equations become letters and a message appears. When I read it, my smile fades.

It can't be right. A racing in my chest starts again. I double, then triple check to see if I've decoded the equations incorrectly. But I haven't.

Hope vanishes as a black hole opens in my chest, tearing down the last defenses of my heart.

The message is clear:

DON'T FIND ME.

CHAPTER 5

∞

There are no frequencies in this dream, but light, like particles, floats between layers of darkness, and rolls into the room like thin sets of waves, like the auroras or the supernova from earlier in the night.

I didn't want to dream tonight. I wanted to retreat into a world where numbers didn't rule me, a place where I could rest with the unknown. My dreams aren't like that anymore. Not since my gift returned.

In front of me Red is coughing so hard even my chest hurts listening to him. The memory is clear. This is the night Red died.

I flit my head right and left, looking for a way out, a way to wake up because I'm not sure I can relive this night. At the same time, I can't walk away from him. That night I cried until I was numb, begging to have just one more hour with him, to look at him once more before the light in his eyes went out.

"Granddaughter... What have I taught you?"

His voice is hoarse and echoing like it's not in the room but coming from down the hall. I want to respond, to say the right things this time but I just stand there, staring. There's a flame burning in his eyes. I can't concentrate because he's dying. The light should be growing dimmer. Instead, it's getting brighter, blinding, almost tangible—just like a supernova after it dies. I'll go blind if I keep looking. But I can't look away.

His words in the background are like a script I know well. He's telling me that I'll be kidnapped; then he gives me my new name. I hold eye contact like it's a tether.

"Phoenix."

"Red."

I want Red to know I'm there. That he is everything to me. That I'd be dead if it weren't for him. He pulled my soul out of the darkest of nights and transformed me into who I am.

Now he's dying all over again in front of me. Tears I can't feel stream down my face, but I can't concentrate on that because of the light coming from his face. I need to get closer to him.

I inch forward until my fingers touch his metal cot. I rest my head on his chest, listening to his heartbeat slow down. His chest rises and falls until it's so faint, I don't know if the dream is over. I hold on to him, mourning for myself, for the world that couldn't meet him.

My eyes squint open. The light is warm like a fire. Even in my dream, my cold body heats up. I want to sit next to him as long as I can, but even more I want to look at him one last time. I'm terrified the dream will end too soon.

I lean in closer. As the light goes out in his eyes, I feel colder. I start shaking. I'm close enough to turn his dying face to mine just as his last breath leaves his mouth, and the light fades. When I meet his eyes, I drop my hands and gasp—Red is not the one on the cot.

It's Kai.

I jolt awake as the phantom frequency races past me heading eastward. The coolness of the dawn tears in on me like a traitor as I sit up, limbs shaking. My first thought is that I am back in

Geneva. There are two frequencies in the air that are hauntingly familiar, but the elusive light filtering over the dunes confirms I'm still in Namibia.

I follow the phantom frequency toward a faint rumble in the east...a vehicle and at least two people. We're so far out and off road it'd be hard for anyone to randomly bump into us. I close my eyes and focus.

I'm still on the lawn chair twelve feet from the PSS van, still cocooned in my heat-activated sleeping bag—but it's far below the temperature it should be. It must have malfunctioned in the night. Which would explain why I'm shaking. Apparently, we still have more bugs to fix on this tech, but what I fumble for is the BFG. It didn't alert me to the people nearby. I tap K2 to see it's working. It's offline too. Another blackout must have caused it.

Slipping out of the bag, I bolt up over to my bodyguard, who flies up the moment he hears movement. "Tank, wake up. People are nearby and the BFG's not working."

He's up in a flash.

By the time Tank returns, I have the BFG back online and working.

"Not to worry," he says. "They were tourists. Came here to see the Spencer Bay wreck. I think I scared them. They got in their van and left pretty quickly."

My throat goes dry. Tourists to see the wreck before dawn? Or is someone still looking for whatever they didn't find in Geneva?

"Thanks." Shivering, I slink over to the van to get warm, assessing the situation. It's not like anyone attacked us. But what if I hadn't woken up? Thanks to the phantom frequency, I did.

Everyone is sleeping as I step inside the warm camper. The telescope, which I packed away last night, is on the table. The moment I see it, my eyes sting.

A shift in the van draws my attention. Eddie's eyes blink open at me from the bunk in the camper. "You get his message? Planning your romantic getaway?"

I shake my head, my jaw tightening to hide the emotion rising in my throat.

"Not quite."

CHAPTER 6

∞

INSTITUTO NACIONAL DE MATEMÁTICA PURA E APLICADA
RIO DE JANEIRO, BRAZIL

Two days later...

Today I am a decoy. I'm undercover. Taking a hit for the team. That is what I tell myself as I stand in this foreign lecture hall.

Out of 481 students, 94 are half-sleeping, 139 are playing with their phones, 98 are taking notes or doodling, 144 are genuinely paying attention, and 6 boys are attempting to flirt with me—while I'm lecturing. One is actually winking. In addition to all this, each person in this room has a frequency. And one of these frequencies shouldn't be here.

In an effort to concentrate and finish the lecture, I close my eyes and give in to my gift, which is like a waterfall in spring, cascading buckets of information. There is no way to stop what is happening, so I let it rush over me—every equation in the room, while I focus on the words coming out of my mouth.

"Light," I continue, "has a noteworthy history. Over the centuries, humanity has had new revelations and breakthroughs about what light actually is. We're still far from being truly able to define it. Light can function in more ways than one—waves, particles, photons, and rays."

I take a deep breath and point to the screen. "Generally speaking, light is a scientific troublemaker that continues to break *our* rules of the universe. It moves at its own speed—we can never catch up to it and nothing can slow it down in free space. Newton was the first to claim that the colors of the rainbow were from the same light that arrives from the sun. With a prism, he proved that we could *bend*, or refract, light to see its color, as through water." I point to the next slide.

"William Herschel then discovered each color in the rainbow had a different temperature, or energy level. After this, we discovered that outside of these visible colors are more invisible rays of light, all with different wavelengths and frequencies, all around us. You've come to know them as X-ray, infrared, ultraviolet, gamma ray, and even radio and microwaves, which you may relate to household items but are actually light waves on the electromagnetic spectrum. The good news is the universe is not as dark as it appears. We've finally learned that *what and how* we see depends on the lens through which we see it."

My eyes move over the crowd looking for one face. When you can count and record every person and their frequency in the room, you notice when a new one walks in.

I lock eyes instantly with the older man, dressed in a sports jacket and loafers. He glances from me to his smart watch—a gift from PSS—giving me a slight head nod.

Agent Ramos. PSS's overseer from the Defense Intelligence Agency, the head of the Special Cases Unit, and Ms. Taylor's good friend. *Wow.* He's always proposing new jobs to PSS, which I turn down. I wonder if he thinks my answer will be different if he meets me somewhere other than Seattle.

I drone on as the clock ticks by. "Why do they say light operates in 5-D? Why does most marine life emit blue and green light? Can humans produce light? In fact, we can. Our bodies produce infrared light waves just like the sun."

My voice bounces off the walls of the room as I speak and is either ignored or received. Once my lecture finishes, I'll join the team who is spearheading a new economic project with some of the top economists in South America aimed at regulating crypto currencies in their region.

Since PSS only operates covertly, it's vital we make a good show of these alibi-lectures while we're on a job. In Tunisia, we were technically exchange students until the coup got worse, and we were caught on camera going into the National Guard's office instead of visiting Carthage. It's becoming more apparent that we have to cover our tracks if we want to continue doing what we do.

"In conclusion," I say, "there's nothing on this earth or in our universe that can function without the full spectrum of light. Each time humanity has a breakthrough with light, we literally change the world. Just think: space travel, medicine, communications. How we perceive math, science, new dimensions. Even our own reality. Do your research this weekend. Press in deep. If you have any questions for me, direct them to the University of Washington. *Obrigado a todos.*"

Mr. Ramos waits patiently for 784 footsteps to march past him before he stands and walks over to me. Students thank me as they pass. The boys, who were winking earlier, step in my direction, but reconsider when Tank hovers around me. That's one perk of the bodyguards, I suppose.

"Professor Rivers." Mr. Ramos gives me a head nod. He is super fit, with broad shoulders and a solid physique. He is also much older than he looks. His brown hair has very few grays, and his brown eyes shine with strength.

"Agent Ramos. Flying to South America just to get a personal meeting with me? My answer hasn't changed, if that's why you're here," I say, collecting my notes.

As he is the DIA's current director, I should be kind. He

generously allows PSS to fly under his department's banner. They also review PSS tech and approve it for public and private use, or send it to the blacklist. Everything we do goes through them.

"Nah, I came for the lecture. Fascinating by the way." He motions to the black board where my scribbles depict solar radiation and the equation for the speed of light.

"Really?" I ask, narrowing my eyes on him. "I didn't know you had an interest in Geometrical Optics."

He laughs. "Oh, I do. More than you know." He's playing with me now. But he can't hide anything at all. His body language and expressions practically scream his secrets. On one hand, it looks intentional. Maybe that's why he's not a field agent anymore.

I draw in a breath. "You know something. Do you want to tell me?"

He considers me for a moment. "Do you want to finally hear about a job we could use you on?"

I smirk. He's tried this several times. I always give him the same answer. "I'll listen at the right time."

"That time may be sooner than you think." He shakes his head. Whatever he knows, he's working really hard to hold back. "You know, Marigold has given us lots of leads over the years. Together, we solved countless cases. We want to see PSS do it again."

I pack my satchel, keeping my eyes on him. "PSS deactivated that department for a reason."

"It was deactivated out of fear."

"Or out of protection?" Our eyes meet in a three-second stare down. But I've got him read.

He clears his throat. "Marigold is a good leader but after she lost her prodigy, she shut it down, and in the process, missed out on countless opportunities to save lives. Somehow, she's ready to open it again. I think it's because of you."

"You don't know me."

"I know your type."

"What type is that?"

"It's not just about feeding the hungry for you. It's more than that. It's shifting a balance. Tipping scales." He looks me over. "You could stop wars, if you choose to."

My lips tighten. A flood of heat rises within me like an itch I can't reach. So I rein in my control, and let my numbers gauge his voice, and read his movements. The ten ways he flexes his muscles then relaxes them as he talks. The calming way he has control over his actions. 84% of me wants to ask what he's up against. Reading his frequency tells me there's something in it for him...and maybe something for me. But the other 16% of me stands down. Because for the past 48 hours Noble's message keeps hitting me like a maglev train aimed at a brick wall.

"Wish I could." The words spit out of me like sour milk. "After being kidnapped, I just want to lay low, help where I can, take care of my dad, and teach math."

He gestures with his hand to my board still marked up with equations. "Teaching about photons. Like your student exchange in Tunisia?"

Hmm. So he knows about that. I swallow my pride. "Yeah. Photons. There's still a lot we need to learn about light." And we're back to our game.

"Studying Newton's law and prisms is ok, but I prefer Snell's law."

"Nice. Did your daughter teach you that? She's studying material physics at Columbia, right?" I smile, all teeth.

He raises his eyebrows. He keeps his daughter very well hidden. Separate name. Unlisted phone number. "That's why we'll get along, Jo. We both like homework. So...Marigold and your father, huh?"

He's baiting me. Showing me how much he knows in return.

"Perfect matches are made every day."

"It's not surprising," he says. "He's a great man. His health has never been better. Within months of getting back into the saddle, his high-risk investments have proved fruitful. He's turning heads from the biggest ventures in the world. Doesn't look like he needs much caring for."

"All people need caring for. And his success is well deserved. He's a visionary. Perhaps like you are." I pause. "So how was your vacation in the Maldives? Surprising it was at the same time as a Scale Tech event. Or was that a coincidence? Funny, how I recommended Scale Tech to Private Global Forces, and a week later, your DIA team was all over it too."

"You realize you're proving my point?" he says, smiling.

And he's caught me. There's something there. Something I want to deny. Part of me wants to pick a fight. Dive in headfirst. Charge to the front of the line. But even now, I hold back.

He snorts. "Agent Bai is a good friend, but PGF doesn't have all the intel we do." He takes out his card, holds it out to me. I don't take it. "Not that it's our business, but we do get intel on your boyfriend—excuse me, ex-boyfriend—from time to time. Chan Dao Kai, right?"

A trigger of explosions goes off in my heart after hearing his full name. My dreams won't be nice to me tonight.

My stomach knots and before I know it, I snatch the card out of his hand. Apparently, Mr. Ramos does know just how to bait me.

I shove it in my pocket. "You can tell me why you're really here now."

"I'm escorting you home."

"Home? We just got here. Our job is a week long."

"A replacement team has already arrived. You all need to be back in Seattle tonight."

Harrison pushes the door open to the now empty lecture hall, followed by a harried team and the other bodyguards.

They have my stuff. Must have been easy. I didn't even have time to unpack.

"What's going on?" I ask Harrison. "He said we need to leave?"

"It's true. Ms. T called an hour ago. Our plane is ready to go."

"Why?" I stare at them both. Mr. Ramos doesn't respond, and this time I can't yank the answers from his eyes.

Harrison cocks his head, and shrugs. "We're not sure. She's never done this before."

As I grab my bag, an undeniable force inside me flares like a dose of oxygen given to a dying flame. "Well then," I say, "let's go find out."

CHAPTER 7

∞

RIVERS RESIDENCE
WEST SEATTLE, WASHINGTON

I sleep, but my heart is awake.

After 34 hours and 58 minutes of travel by plane and van from Brazil, I collapsed in my own bed in Seattle—but in the dream world, the memory unfolds like a movie, like it was yesterday. I'm on the other side of the planet, in Shanghai with Kai, the night before we flew to Seattle for the first time after I'd been kidnapped.

The dream does not surprise me. I've replayed it many times in my head, especially after 98 nights of stargazing. That night was the first time I looked at the stars after I lost my gift. How could I forget it?

Vroom.

A motorcycle purred beneath me. My arms tightened around Kai's waist and my legs fastened close to the bike. A helmet was snug on my head, but the wind whipped through my hair down my back as Kai and I raced out of town.

The bike bent with every curve of the road. Without my gift every turn sent a spike of fear through my heart. I was unprotected, exposed to danger without my precious calculations. If I'd had my numbers, I would've seen the road ahead of me through dials, meters, angles, speed, direction, and force. I would've known whether he was driving safely or not. But my gift had been gone for over two weeks and the battle of learning how to function without it hadn't been won yet, not to mention the additional emotions I was feeling after gaining my family back. Tonight, all I could do was trust Kai, the one steady person in my life since Red. And in that moment, I felt safe.

"Where are you taking me?" I yelled into the wind.

His head flicked to the right. "You'll see. We're almost there."

The mountains outside of Shanghai were not tall, but they provided fresh air and a variety of trees to help us imagine we were far from the city. He parked the bike and took my hand. His touch flooded me with warmth. It was only the third time we'd gone out without worrying about Madame or King and my stomach flipped each time we were alone.

I climbed off as Kai stashed our helmets. "Welcome to *Xi She Shan*. West Sheshan Mountain." He breathed in deep, ingesting the fresh piney air.

At the path entrance, a sign was posted. "An observatory?" I ask, eyebrows raised. Kai always surprised me.

"Not just any observatory. This is the oldest one in China. People have come here to watch meteor showers for centuries." His smile drilled into me, so confident and yet so thoughtful. "Your last memories here should be happy ones."

My heart swelled like I was a kid who'd been stuck inside all week with rainy days, and suddenly he made the sun come out. It was a treat I didn't know I needed. I wanted to throw my arms around him, but I held back. The fluttering in my belly was still foreign. It teetered on a fine line of pure joy and losing control. I redirected it.

"Are you saying that our dates in derelict factories and hole in the wall restaurants discussing economic disasters and smugglers weren't happy?" I joked.

He laughs. "Every moment with you is happy, but I'm not sure they counted as dates. We were getting to know each other...in a very interesting way," he bantered back.

"What about when we went to meet the Masters in Song Valley?" I asked. "That was sort of a date."

"It could have been a date up until the point we almost got caught in King's warehouse and had to flee, after which you stopped talking to me for two weeks." He shook his head at me, laughing.

I blushed and cleared my throat. "Right. So this is our first official date?"

"Call it what you want. From now on, I just want to do everything with you." Kai slid his hand into mine. "Tonight is also sort of a gift. You told me once that you avoided the stars when you had your numbers, so now's your chance to see them in a new way. Like us normal people. I want to be there for that." He drew me closer to him, wrapping an arm around me as we walked.

Shanghai's summer was still warm and unlike in the city, out here pollution was at a minimum. The night was clear enough to see the stars. Kai spread out a blanket and we laid down. Then, I went breathless.

There was no gift instantly counting the constellations or calculating the axis of the earth and its rotations. No math to remind me of the time ticking ever forward. There was just a feeling. A heavy, beautifully crushing feeling. The weight of majesty. Of mystery. Of wonder.

As I stared at the sky for the first time without numbers, the immensity of it all hit me. I'd never imagined that the numbers had blinded me before to extraordinary beauty. But now I could see unfiltered. Red had told me once that beauty had a way of unzipping one's soul. He was right.

Maybe it was the loss of my gift. Maybe it was the threat of the economic crash being over or even leaving China, but a wet trail tickled down my cheek. So. This was what it was like to look at the stars—how did normal people handle its beauty?

Kai couldn't have seen my eyes brimming with emotion in the dark, but he felt it and moved in closer. He put his arms around me and tucked my head close to his chest.

"Incredible, huh?" His voice washed over me like endless waves. "Even the stars prove that we're meant to be together."

I perked up. It was not what I expected him to say. "Really," I asked, my heartbeat tripling in pace. "How do you figure?"

"It's simple," he said, his voice ever confident. "Billions of stars and planets, and we ended up on the same one. In a country of a billion people, we ended up in the same city, same company, same property, and as impossible as it sounds, your surrogate grandfather happened to be my uncle." He smirked. "Odds are, we'll always end up in the same place."

I almost agreed until I thought about the new job that Kai just accepted with Private Global Forces.

"Even as you train to become a field agent?" I asked. "Those odds don't look too good."

He moved in closer, his heat radiating like a blanket of warmth around me. "When it comes to you, I'll always find a way to beat the odds."

∞

A group of seagulls screeching outside my window startles me awake. My whole body is tense, holding the last two days in like a breath. With eyes closed, I'm already calculating what time it is, how little I actually slept, and how many times that memory has come back to haunt me as a dream. This is the fifth time. After Noble's message, the dream feels worse.

I rip the night off like a Band-Aid and remind myself we were called home for an important meeting at PSS. The prospect of a new challenge fuels me.

I breathe in the fresh lavender scent of clean linen as my legs brush against flannel sheets. So different to the scaly sleeping bag I was wrapped up in last week in the desert on a folding lawn chair.

My jet-lagged eyes open to soft winter light filtering in from my bedroom window. My mind captures a faint heat wave for 2.3 seconds before it fades. My duffel bag is still unopened on the floor but the desk beside me has all I need: my trusty PSS computer and a journal where I've been recording lessons and sayings Red taught me.

One night, I feared I'd forget him. The horrible thought sent me reeling. It was Kai's idea that I write everything down. *I won't let you forget Red*, he promised. The words rub against me like clothes on a fresh scrape.

Kai can't help me anymore. He is gone. He *wanted* to be gone. Even before Tunisia, he left Seattle earlier each time he came to visit, eager to be doing what he was meant to do.

The scent of dark roast coffee slips into my room along with a rhythmic pounding. Dad must be awake. I glance at my watch. It's not even 6 am. I push myself up. If I don't get moving the barrage of memories that have slayed my mind all night will surely return with a vengeance. I need to focus on the reason we're home.

In Rio, Agent Ramos was confident I'd be interested in whatever Ms. T called us home for. The challenge in his voice was tempting. But I've hacked his database. I know that most of the DIA operations revolve around some kind of crisis. I hate that my numbers skyrocketed when I read through them, like I'm drawn to problems.

I pull on a sweatshirt and slip into thick wool socks. After being in the southern hemisphere for weeks where it was sunny and warm, the gray, damp winter of the Pacific Northwest brings an even greater chill to the room, despite the heater running at 73 degrees.

I sneak out of the room. Mara's and Lily's doors are still closed. A humming of their sleeping frequency lingers in the air. I'm eager to see them when they wake up.

The window downstairs in the kitchen is cracked open just enough for the crisp salty air to sneak in. I stare out at the gray waves of the Puget Sound and breathe deeply. It's good to be home.

I pour myself a cup of hot coffee and follow a familiar pounding sound past the den to the garage. Inside, my father is still going strong practicing the kung fu exercises that Kai taught him. Why are there reminders of Kai everywhere? Ignoring that prick of pain in my chest, I head over to sit on a workbench.

A covered Ducati motorcycle is stashed in the corner of the garage. I'm not sure why I bought it. If my old sims were any indicator, motorcycles are hardly safe. But maybe that's why I wanted it. To prove to myself that if I can fly a helicopter, a motorcycle would be a kid's toy now that my gift is back. Or maybe I bought it because it reminds me of Kai. Either way, it's just been sitting there untouched.

My dad whips his head toward me as the door clicks shut. "Morning, Jo. You're back." His face is bright and cheery, a sight for sore eyes. It's refreshing not to have my bodyguards be the first people I see when I wake up.

"Morning, Dad." I study him. The numbers defining him have drastically changed. His arms, strong and taut now, glisten with sweat. I wouldn't bet on him winning in a street fight, but he's definitely got the moves down. I'm really proud of him. He eats well, works out daily, and is more active than I've seen him in years. The new woman in his life may have something to do with it. Love is an energy of its own.

"Don't mind me," I say, motioning for him to keep working out. "I'm not awake enough to talk yet."

"Just a few more minutes until I'll be done," he promises. "Then we can make breakfast. We still have a couple hours before the big meeting."

We. It's still strange that he comes to our PSS meetings now, even if he is one of our strongest investors. But his presence in the office is always positive. So I accept it as a good thing. I'm learning to trust the process.

"You knew I'd be coming home early, didn't you?" I ask, noticing the high tech, yet classy replica of K2, fastened to his wrist. His watch, D3, was a gift from Ms. T after my first official PSS trip. D3 has a feature connected to K2 that reports my vitals. I can turn that feature off if I want to, but I don't. He rarely checks it anyway.

"Yep." Dad nods, then once again pounds and kicks into the bag.

My mind streams with calculations as his body turns into equations of force and acceleration. Laws of motion coupled with his mass are multiplied into his movements. The way his strength is poured out of him and directed into the punching bag; how the force collides with the bag to move the weight. The way numbers calculate the position his leg bends into a stance that allows maximum power to his kick, how often his breath exits his body. The momentum is familiar, relaxing. The frequencies in the garage heave with energy, causing ripples of impulse in the air. The release in my dad is evident and empowering. My body leans forward, yearning for the same release.

After a long night of travel, it's the last thing my body wants to do right now, but my mind is threatening to pull itself apart. Pushing physical limits is a good way to release endorphins, clear the mind, and release tension. Then maybe I can calm down and make sense of the last few months.

I set my coffee down and pop off the bench. "Can I try?"

Dad looks up at me, examining my face, like he knows I'm after more than just exercise. "Sure, Jojo. The striking dummy is too hard though. I'll hold the kick pads for you." He moves aside, grabbing a towel.

I get into a position that Kai and the Sang brothers taught me. I'm no fighter but I've done a few practices with Kai before, and I've watched him do these a hundred times. I bend my knees and focus on the bag. Then, closing my eyes, the exercises play out in my mind. A mathematical rhythm turns on inside me where every movement is an equation. I'm reading a screenplay of body mechanics. A set of movements and a routine is planned out in my head.

My eyes snap open, and I attack the bag. My arms and legs slip into a cadence of their own like I have been practicing for years—or like I've watched someone else practice for years.

The memory of Kai's body is sharp and clear. My mind focuses on him while outwardly my body executes the movements. My fist, my forearm, my legs hit the bag in perfect formation. Even if my hits are weak, even if pain is registering, my body is screaming yes. More. This is the release I need.

The last 101 days since Tunisia pour out of me. All the confusion. The unidentified patterns and crossroads. The unsolved calculations and endless frequencies. Losing Kai. Searching for Noble. Everything goes out through my fists and legs and into the bag.

Memories jab through my mind—Noble revealing that he was Mandel in the desert. Noble telling me not to find him. Kai fighting the world so I can sleep. I don't stop hitting the bag.

My mind spirals. Kai's face replacing Red's in the Pratt; his bloody body in the desert in Tunisia; his voice in the helicopter telling me he loves me. I don't stop hitting. Noble's back is turned to me. He's walking away. Months of decoding the stars. Rejection... Soon, Madame and King are laughing at me. The Successor and the Loyalists are there, too. The scar on my neck is burning hot. My mouth is filled with water. All the threats that surround us every day bombard me and I need to stop them all.

Over and over and over I hit, kick, repeat. My body heats up. Pain registers in every knuckle, but even then I don't stop until a frequency, sharp and warm, slams into me. I stop mid-swing. The heat fueling the frequency is not my body temperature. Hands come down on my shoulder, triggering a reaction that is already in motion.

My fist flies around to stop the assailant before I can pull back. A split second later it cracks as it connects with flesh and bone.

"Ow!"

I spin around to my dad stumbling back a step. His head is tilted down. He's pinching his nose. Blood gushing on his shirt. "That really, really hurt, Jo."

I jump forward, alarmed. "Dad. I'm so sorry. You scared me. I don't... Are you ok?"

"I was going to ask you the same thing," he says, grabbing a towel for his nose. My dad studies me, eyes alert, but also full of concern and patience. There's a break in the skin on the ridge of his nose. If I know anything about fights, it's going to leave a bruise, even blackened eyes. "What's going on?"

I pant for air, but I don't answer because the heat draws me back to the original reason I stopped hitting the bag. The phantom frequency is close, boomeranging into me. Its patterns make no sense, like they operate out of time, space and distance.

"K2," I command my smart watch, "sensor everything within fifteen feet of me—temperature, sound, heat, energy, frequencies, and vibrations."

K2 instantly responds. "Systems monitoring." It's so faint it's hard to calculate.

My dad looks around the garage, still holding the small towel to his nose. "What is it?" he asks, his voice nasally.

I ignore the question, racing out the garage and down the grassy path leading to the backyard and beach, where a misty cold air comes off the water. Dad follows me. My neck twists around, investigating. Three cars pass in the distance. Two boats out on the water. One ferry horn in the distance. Three seagulls. Six people, a hundred feet away chatting; nothing threatening about them. Then the frequency begins to fade. Gone. Just like always.

I turn to my dad, letting out a large sigh. "That weird frequency again."

"The phantom one?" he asks, shivering in the winter air.

I nod, still slightly out of breath.

"Was it in Brazil too?" he asks.

"Yes." I keep my eyes up, towards the bend of the beach 402 feet away. "And in Geneva, Yangon, Santiago, and every day in Namibia. It's faster and its temperature is higher than most frequencies. I still don't know what it is."

I bend down, gripping a handful of sand, and squeeze it. The grains fall like an hourglass from my palm. My body relaxes. I feel better until I remember I punched my dad.

"I'm so sorry I hit you," I groan.

My dad crouches down beside me, a bloody towel in his hands. "It's ok. I shouldn't have interrupted you. And actually, I've been wondering what it would feel like to be in a real fight for months. Thanks for giving me a taste of it." He chuckles. I'm thankful he's being so gracious after his daughter socked him. "So are you going to tell me what that was all about back there in the garage?"

He's not talking about the phantom frequency. By the tone in his voice, he's about to do his "heart check-in" with me. Some kids might shrink back from talking to their dad about relationships and feelings. At first, I did too. But the way he sat there so quietly, listening and valuing everything I told him, convinced me to open up even more. He also shares stories about my mom that I've never heard before. The small things he loved about her seem to be never ending. Of course, we also talk about Marigold. They've grown really close fast, which is another reason I've delayed asking her about PSS's past. It feels weird to know more about my dad's girlfriend, especially when she's my boss.

I drop the sand and look up. "I just needed to work through some stuff, you know."

He breathes in. "Is this about cracking Noble's code? Because after the meeting today, Marigold is coming for dinner, and even if it's still cold out, it's going to be crystal clear. We can bring out the telescope. Cross reference patterns in the cosmos together. Tonight could be the night you find him."

My body stiffens as a deep pain grips my chest. "It's over, Dad," I choke out, facing the beach.

"What happened?" Dad's voice is calming. Numbers form around him like a roof in the storm.

"In Namibia, I got a message from Noble..." I stop, a lump rising in my throat. It still sends chills down my spine when I think about Noble telling me he was Mandel in Ksar Douz. For three months my mind has been consumed with snowflakes, fractals, seahorses, and this blasted connection we've shared since we were kids. After all we've been through, I thought he'd want to know what was between us as much as I do. To know what it feels like to be truly known by someone who sees you so completely. Maybe he changed his mind. Or maybe he knows something I don't.

Apart from that, I have a hundred questions to ask him about my gift. Who else can explain what is happening to me?

"Jo?" Dad scoots closer, wrapping a warm arm over my shoulders. "What was the message?"

I grab another handful of sand, squeezing down hard as I

answer. "He told me to stop looking for him." Saying it out loud makes it real. A sharp pain digs into me, but I push it away. I've learned to rise from hardship. I'll do it again.

"Funny right?" I shake my head. "I thought I had two boy problems. Turns out I have none."

My dad hugs me tight. "Impossible, sweetie. Although I don't know Noble, it doesn't make any sense. If he was a real genius, he'd have to know letting a girl like you go is a huge mistake."

"Is it though?" I ask. "Last time I was with him, he was almost taken in by the authorities after he followed me into a potentially fatal situation where my ex-boyfriend almost died—and Kai would have, if my gift hadn't returned." I groan, holding my head. "Besides, like you said, he's a prodigy like me. We count possibilities that others can't. He calculated something that doesn't work. I just wish he'd tell me what he's seeing and why. He didn't even give us a chance."

I don't say it out loud, but I wonder if Noble knows I still think about Kai.

"I know your experience with him in Tunisia was intense," he says. "You met your childhood friend. You lost Kai. Your gift came back. But high stakes situations aren't exactly a reflection of everyday relationships. You were together five days. It's not long enough to make life-changing decisions."

"I know," I sigh.

There's certainly more to Noble than what he showed me in Tunisia. More to his past. More to his future. But I also don't want anything to happen to him. With the launch of the International Space Collaboration Super Satellite so close, everyone is focused on him.

A cold wind shakes me out of my thoughts. I run my fingers over sore knuckles, and look at my dad. "We should go in."

I expect my dad to encourage me to let it go, but his face changes, and he slaps his hands down on his knees.

"I don't think you should give up on finding Noble."

I perk up. "I'm surprised to hear you say that," I say, "it's no secret which team you're rooting for."

He puts his hands up like he's been caught. "Not going to lie, I like and trust Kai. He was always open and honest with you. I liked who you were together. To be fair, I don't know Noble. But it's clear you feel something for him. You said it yourself, Noble is an equation you need to solve. If getting the answer is important to you, don't back down so easily." He smiles. "And for the record, I'm team Jo."

I'm touched but backing down isn't the problem for me. It's walking away. "Thanks, Dad." I shake my head. "But maybe I have to let him go. Like I let Kai go. I've held back for three months, and for what? From now on, I need to focus on what is in front of me. Like the meeting today."

Waves roll in, set after set. My mind, as fast as light, travels east to Shanghai. Some days, it feels like just yesterday that I was on that side of the ocean, dreaming of being here. Then without beckoning, every plane ride I've had since Tunisia tears through my mind. Every mile. Every route. I'm all over the map, but there's no obvious place to stay or go.

A biting wind from the Puget Sound rushes over me. I don't shiver. I let it remind my body of colder days in the Pratt. I toughen up instantly. A person or place has never defined me. It shouldn't start to now.

"Let's get ready for the meeting," I say standing, pulling my dad up. "Did Ms. T tell you why she called us home?"

"No. She doesn't tell me everything...yet." A dreamy smile slides on his face.

As we slip back inside the garage, K2 announces a call from Harrison, who's already at the PSS headquarters.

"You're at the office early," I answer.

"Been here since 4 am. Jetlag and hyper-excitement for the mystery meeting. Can you come in ASAP? We need to talk. I found more info on your Italian friend that we need to discuss...everyone else is on their way. Jo, you really need to tell us more about the kind of company you keep..."

I hang up and look at the punching bag, then down on at my purple knuckles. I even examine the tiny scars on my fingertips from the bombs I used in Tunisia. The release I felt with the punching bag felt so good. I didn't realize how much I'd been holding back for the past three months. Well, not anymore. Before I go in to get dressed, I uncover the Ducati, and grab the keys.

I look at my dad. "I've got to get to PSS early. Looks like I have more than one surprise waiting for me."

CHAPTER 8

∞

UNIVERSITY OF WASHINGTON
SEATTLE, WASHINGTON

There's a distinct feeling when you're being followed or watched—even more so when you can literally count every possible threat within a radius of 500 feet.

I park the Ducati in a campus garage. Apart from the numbers and frequencies alerting me to the encroaching presence, there's a heightening of my senses. An eerie feeling in the air—like whoever is lurking is not 108 feet across the road but right behind me.

My equations add up sixty new people arriving in the area, four cars driving by and 22 electrical devices. But as I walk to PSS, only one falls in line with my direction. The frequency is following me from the parking lot to the Quad. Paranoia is still a possibility I consider, but today I couldn't care less.

Before I cross the red brick cobblestone walkway that leads up to Savery Hall, I stop. I check my earrings and my emp-taser bracelet to make sure they're all functional if needed. Then I command my watch. "K2, perform a facial scan of people within 120 feet. Anyone significant."

A picture pops up on K2's screen. I groan. Ms. Carry Mines,

the pesky journalist who has followed us to five countries now. I should have known. Unfortunately for her, today is not the day to mess with me.

Ms. T told us if we bumped into her to ignore her. But if she is following me or stalking PSS that means she is on my territory. I'm not ok with it. Especially after being called home from a job.

Instead of ignoring her, a protective surge flares up inside me and I march towards her to where she thinks she is unseen. However, when she sees me coming, she doesn't walk away but boldly exits the shadows to meet me. A stubborn one, I see.

I storm up to her, my numbers performing a full, intrusive scan. Her stature, though short, is confident. The electrical tech on her body is low profile, but she's probably recording as we speak, so I make a note to be careful with my words.

"Ms. Mines. Trailing a bunch of kids, again? Prize worthy stuff. What do you think you will find?" I ask her.

"Ms. Josephine Rivers. The former prodigy who lost her gift in China." Ms. Mines looks me up and down with a smug look on her face. "You know that Ms. Taylor claims that her prodigy gig was shut down a long time ago. So I suppose you don't work for her and you're not arriving at the office right now." Her tone isn't vindictive but reminds me of a spoiled child who always gets what she wants.

"As usual, Ms. Taylor's right. I'm a professor of math here and organize student exchange lectures around the world with fellow STEM programs," I say with complete confidence. After all, it's true. PSS balances quite an act.

"You know," Ms. Mines says, ruffling her coat. "I'm not sure your guise of the student lectures is working."

I pretend I'm bored. "They've been written up and praised in over twelve countries."

With a wave of her hand she dismisses everything I've just said. "I suppose your student exchange in Tunisia, during the coup and elections which took a last-minute turn for the better, was just a fluke, or your STEM lectures that coincided with Chile's new earthquake tech, Myanmar's economic upswing, and Namibia's sudden breakthrough with natural resources were just coincidence. I could go on." She studies me. "You've read my articles. You know my theories. You prodigies are behind some fantastic breakthroughs. Don't you want the credit you're due?"

I have read her articles. She can make some pretty hefty assumptions with her *facts.*

"Well, now I'm just offended." I laugh, my hands on my hips. "Or maybe you're not doing your research. There were more than 30 significant scientific breakthroughs around the world in the past few months that were more noteworthy than the ones you mentioned. The medical discoveries happening right now are astounding. Life changing peace accords in the Middle East. Environmental phenomena. Genetic enhancements. Breakthroughs in magnetic physics and optical science. I'd much rather be associated with those if you write another article about us." I shake my head. "We're flattered, Ms. Mines. We may be smart, but we're not superheroes, and we can't be everywhere. If you'd like to do a story about our STEM program, we're happy to share more."

She doesn't speak, but her body language roots in position. She has certainly not given up her stance. I roll my eyes. I don't have time for her. "Goodbye, Ms. Mines."

"Want to hear another theory?" she calls out. "Your math gift returned. Or maybe it never left? Experts were confounded by how Chan Huang Long discovered China's near economic crisis and then planned a genius solution to prevent it. Shortly after this, you appeared dating his son, and claiming your math gift was lost. Sounds a bit fishy, don't you think?"

For a moment, the only words I hear are *dating his son.* I turn, staring at the woman. Willing her not to say his name. She doesn't.

From a news angle, Chan was the one who stepped in to

save the economy. He was praised for his 'super bond' solution. He didn't like taking all the credit, but he did it for me. To protect me. Like Ms. T does everything to protect the prods.

"I did lose my gift." That is the truth. She doesn't need to know it's returned. No one apart from Noble, my family, Kai, and PSS knows my gift came back.

"Well, I don't believe it. I think your gift is functional. I think you help governments. I'm going to prove that PSS is very much still operational and Ms. Taylor is a danger to gifted kids because of her own agendas." She swings a purse over her shoulder. "I won't stop."

My numbers say Ms. Mines is just guessing. She doesn't have proof. I stare at her, my gift tracing every angle of her eyes and frequency. She backs up like I'm going to hit her. The memory of the punching bag comes to mind.

I stand firm and sigh. "What do you really want, Ms. Mines?"

"The truth," she spits out like venom. "People can't see the world clearly if we don't show it to them."

"The world has bigger problems," I say thinking about Cesare Di Susa on the loose, Geneva, and the blackouts. "If you really cared, you'd be chasing after worse people."

She scoffs. "*Worse people* is a perspective. If Ms. Taylor is putting a bunch of kids in danger to solve the world's problems, people need to know." She pauses like she's convinced me.

I check my watch. "Sorry, I'm out of time." I give her a polite smile goodbye. "Ms. Mines."

I walk away, my numbers like antennas turned on high. If Ms. Mines suspects my gift is back, then others could too. My mind drifts back to Geneva on the night my room was broken into and Rafael and his father went missing. A prospect I've been avoiding buzzes across my mind—if those two events are connected, we have much bigger problems than Ms. Mines.

CHAPTER 9

∞

PSS HEADQUARTERS
SEATTLE, WASHINGTON

The PSS headquarters' door swings open to a frequency of chaos. The usual nerdy buzz of brain activity is gone. You'd think they were expecting a movie star. Whatever news is coming at today's meeting must be big if it's got all of PSS spinning.

A dozen new electrical frequencies, heightened protocols, and jittery conversations are going on in every corner. Even the analyst team, who by this hour usually have their faces quietly glued to a screen, are nervously chatting away. Mr. Barrios, PSS's counselor and tech manager, is with Ms. Yin, the secretary, laying out what looks like Veil over campus security. I make my way over to Ledger, our robotic coffee machine, eager to see my team.

"Morning, Jo." A few of the teen analysts greet me. "So unprecedented that you guys were called home. Do you know what it's about?"

"Not yet." Ledger pours a strong, triple shot espresso with a spot of milk. The amount of fidgeting in the room makes my own fingers tap. The anticipation must be killing them.

Harrison pops his blond ruffled head out of a room down the hall, waving to me to hurry up. I grab my coffee and head that way.

I step in. Everyone is dressed up. But it doesn't look like they got any sleep.

"Wow. You all clean up well." I nod hello to the team.

Harrison's research and newsroom area is an intersection of frequencies. Three screens full of information are streaming, recording, and searching for whatever Harrison has programmed into it for the day, or week. Once I'm inside, Harrison shuts the door.

"Ok," Pens says. "What is so important that we had to give up two extra hours of sleep?"

"How can you ask that?" Harrison says excitedly. "Whatever mission Ms. T called us back for has to be mega important. It's rare that we've ever had to abort an operation."

Pens groans. "They're not missions or operations. We call them *jobs*, Harrison. Ever since Tunisia you think we're all some kind of secret agents."

Harrison has that boyish, army-mode look in his eyes. "Pens. Seriously. With Jo Rivers in our midst, we're basically spies. Or at least we'd be branded as such purely by association. Especially after finding this." He clicks on a button, and another article pops up on the screen about Rafael's father, Cesare di Susa—his beady brown eyes pooling with corruption. "Cesare is related to Palermo Ricci, a very influential man in Italy and Asia. He's a tycoon behind some of the largest medical tourism centers in Asia and tele-communications companies in Europe. Similar to Chan."

I tilt my head forward. "I've heard the name. Why is he important?"

"Turns out, Cesare and Palermo are heirs of the most legendary Italian Mafia network the world has ever seen, formerly known as *Italia Liberata*. Cesare was supposed to be the next boss. The organization was busted before Cesare could take over, but a new and very secretive network has popped up on our radar, *Terra Liberata.* We think they're connected. Now through you, we have a link to it. So what does that make us? The coolest prodigy team I know of."

Pens curls her lip to the side of her mouth. "Or the sketchiest."

I fold my arms across my chest, hoping he's wrong. "Cesare gave up all his criminal contacts. He went into a witness protection program. He can't be operating *Terra Liberata.* You've got to give me more evidence if you want me to believe that."

"Ok. Cesare's old comrades were spotted in Geneva the same week as us." Harrison says. "And oddly enough, Rafael and his dad went missing at roughly the same time as the three prominent ISC scientists working on the Super Satellite didn't show up for work. Jo, two of the scientists' bodies were just discovered yesterday in a field outside of Helsinki." Harrison grows more serious. "How's that for more proof?" He snaps his fingers in the air.

That was disturbing news. The other events have been cross-referencing in my head since receiving Rafael's message—there's a definite connection but the string of numbers leading to Noble was stronger. Obviously, my focus on him blinded me to more important things. I'm about to chime in when the look on their faces tells me there's more. "What else?"

Felicia leans in. "We hacked Scale Tech's financial records. Cesare di Susa and his son are the largest shareholders at the company. Not only that, Cesare also owns shares in dozens of private space labs around the world. Several years ago, Palermo Ricci tried to buy Cesare's shares in Scale Tech. Cesare refused. After that, he moved to China." She hands me the list of companies. "Don't you always say you don't believe in coincidences?"

Queasiness creeps over me. A new set of variables is calculated in my head. A man like Cesare doesn't invest in satellites and space technology then move to China to help King with mindless petty crime. "What about Palermo Ricci? Does Cesare have any contact with him now?"

"Palermo's clean. He cut ties with Cesare long ago. He does all of his banking offshore in Asia where his most prominent medical tourism centers are based. But recently, Palermo has been courting Dr. Juho Salonen to buy Scale Tech. It's all over the news."

I pinch the bridge of my nose. Something is very wrong. My numbers highlighted Dr. Salonen and Scale Tech in Geneva, which isn't too surprising since the International Space Collaboration exists because of his funding. Whatever Cesare's interest is in Scale Tech, it can't be good. Now, he's on the run and he's gotten Rafael involved again—it makes my blood boil.

"Jo, I may not know a lot about Italian crime bosses," Felicia says, "but I have a rule: if someone owns huge shares in a company and goes missing right before a massive event in that company's interest...the two things have to be connected."

I nod. Negative calculations pile up, the black-haired man and those fourteen frequencies in Geneva on the top of the stack. "Any leads on Rafael's present location?" I ask, my mind spiraling through a number of possibilities.

Harrison shakes his head. "Nothing at all."

"They were supposed to be off the radar under the new *Ghost Marker* program starting a new life." I inwardly curse myself for vouching for Cesare. The only way he got a plea bargain was because of me. He testified against King and gave up Madame's contacts in Italy. He claimed he wanted out and I believed him.

"Or they could already be swimming with the fishes..." He makes a sour face. "Sorry."

Harrison is right. I should have looked harder for Rafael when I got his message. I should have looked into Scale Tech and what happened in Geneva too. Maybe I still can.

"Next steps?" Harrison asks.

"Bai's out of town, but I'll call PGF after our meeting. We'd better hope Cesare is not connected with Geneva. Right now, we have to focus. Our meeting starts in three minutes."

Pens looks at her watch. "Jo's right."

We remerge into the sleek office as a jittery group of teens. My dad is here, sitting at the coffee table by Ledger.

Felicia squeals. "Oh, Mr. Rivers!" She waves a hand at him, then whispers to me, "I need to thank him for his advice for this thing between Harrison and me last week. It totally worked. Now, we're even closer than before. Your dad is like the relationship doctor. You're so lucky."

"Yeah," I mumble. Glad every other relationship is working out. I glance over at him as he talks with Felicia. Then his face brightens. I don't even have to look to know why. Ms. T has entered the room. Her frequency mixes with my dad's. I look over. Her hair is styled up, and her clothes boast much bolder colors since she started dating my dad. She straightens her pencil skirt and they steal a secret glance at each other before she turns to us, instantly transforming into the commanding leader we know her to be.

"Team, it's time," Ms. Taylor says, tapping her watch. "Let's head over to Com-Hall. Our guests have arrived."

Everyone walks twice as fast as usual down the hall, squirming with anticipation. One by one the team enters. Harrison's jaw drops, as he falls into star-struck mode. Felicia elbows him, and his jaw closes. Eddie and Pens are speechless. Entering the room, I instantly start scanning the faces of the four people waiting for us.

My heart skips a beat as numbers explode—but not for the same reasons as the team. The guests in the room are not who I expected, which means, whatever I thought about this meeting was wrong. Apparently, the intel on Kai that Agent Ramos dangled in Rio wasn't his only bait.

CHAPTER 10

∞

The International Space Collaboration Administration should not be sitting in Com-Hall right now, but here they are. These people don't just show up at anyone's doorstep, especially when a massive event—the launch of their Super Satellite—is in a few days, which means, there's a problem. A big one.

Around the table are Chief Scientist Dr. Bernard from NASA, and two systems engineers—Dr. Kivi, from the ESA, the European Space Agency, and Dr. Sato from JAXA, the Japan Aerospace Exploration Agency, and a fourth man who has a less than friendly face on, one that says he's all business. I'd bet money, he's their lawyer.

"Welcome," Ms. Taylor says. Although we all know who they are, the visitors introduce themselves one by one, finally getting to the fourth man, who is, to no surprise, one of NASA's hundred attorneys, Mr. Frank Kelley, their lead counsel.

Their muted mannerisms and rigid bodies try to cover up worn out nerves. The way they look at each other and touch their watches indicates that they're eager to get the meeting started. They obviously have too much to do and not enough time.

Any job regarding NASA is US government business, specifically DIA. Agent Ramos isn't here, but apparently he really wants us to activate the Special Cases Unit. I hope he hasn't wasted his time. Agent Ramos knows astrophysics and aerospace engineering aren't our specialty. Sure, we're prodigies, but we're primarily a think-tank. So why is he bringing the ISC to us? What can we offer them?

Everyone else on the team is wondering the same thing. Except Harrison, a true fan boy, who is still drooling. Harrison is one hundred percent space-obsessed. Which is why he idolizes Noble. Today will likely go down as his favorite day since he was born.

Ms. T gets down to business. "I think I speak for all of us when I say we're humbled at your presence, especially at a time like this. Anything we have is at your disposal. Please begin."

"Thank you for adjusting your schedule to accommodate us." Dr. Sato takes a deep breath. She brushes her long black hair behind her shoulder and pushes up her wide rimmed glasses. "We know this is highly unusual, but we're looking for answers beyond our normal networks, considering the crisis of the recent blackouts."

My hand starts tapping my knee under the table. *Crisis—a dangerous opportunity.* The challenge lights a spark and a caution inside me.

"What we're about to disclose is a matter of international security," Dr. Kivi explains, a weight coming over the room. Ms. Taylor listens intently but her frequency buzzes in my direction, like she feels my numbers shoot up.

Dr. Kivi clicks a button, and up pops a virtual screen. "As you know the geomagnetic storms are still disrupting satellite communications and power grids around the world," Dr. Bernard explains. "If a solar flare is big enough, it could permanently damage a power grid, and electricity for entire cities or regions could be wiped out. Hundreds of millions of people could be without power for days or weeks, even months. You can imagine how this would affect health and safety, education and commerce. The economy could take years to recover. Just one day without power in New York City would cost one billion dollars. Imagine what would happen after weeks or months without electricity. The results would be catastrophic."

I shiver at the possibilities.

Dr. Kivi displays another graph. "Which is why the upcoming ISC satellite launch is so important. Our Super Satellite is designed to maintain a balance of electrical currents to the power grids, while also withstanding extreme solar flares and geomagnetic storms. Although we're restricted from divulging much, we can tell you that our satellite is not powered like other satellites, and it won't be compromised by these natural phenomena, as other satellites have been recently. However, new challenges have arrived." She sighs and looks to Dr. Sato.

"Our Super Satellite seems to have developed an unusual glitch in its programming, almost like its control software has been hacked. Although that should be nearly impossible, especially since everything checks out as normal. ISC scientists from all over the world have been looking into this for weeks without success."

"When did the glitch start?" Eddie asks.

"Soon after the blackouts started."

My mind skitters. Noble is so close to this. Too close. Is this why he told me to stay away? Is he in trouble?

I dig my fingernails into my thigh as my mind spins through memories like a dial. My numbers don't bring up specific details without a reason and in Geneva, both Scale Tech and the black-haired man were highlighted, and I didn't make a move. Now I'm regretting my inaction even more.

Dr. Kivi leans her hands on the table. "We don't know if the two are connected. Despite the glitch, the ISC board will not allow us to reschedule the launch. Which is why we came to you. We'd like to rule out any potential complications before the launch so that ISC efforts won't fail." She motions to a timeline. They have four days.

Ms. T's eyes flash to mine, steady and serious.

Dr. Sato clicks a button and the screen flashes to a live-view of the ISC headquarters in Helsinki, Finland. There are banners and people are everywhere outside the building.

"This is the busiest week in history. Helsinki is already packed. The ISC will host a banquet with world-renowned scientists and innovators, and its largest event ever, the ISC Celebration. There will be thousands of civilians coming to Helsinki to be part of this historic moment, and hundreds of international journalists flying in to cover the event."

At her mention of the banquet, my numbers light up like street lamps on a dark road. The numerical crossroads that have been streaming in my head for the last three months appear, too, like the banquet is leading me in the right direction.

Dr. Bernard hands us a small flier with the ISC logo on it. It's promoting the 'Celebration Rocket'. Because the Super Satellite launch is at their remote spaceport near the equator in French Guiana, a symbolic, three-foot civilian-safe, miniature rocket will be shot off a shielded stage in Senate Square in the center of Helsinki once the Super Satellite hits orbit. The mini rocket will auto-disintegrate at 5000 feet.

"Have you asked Scale Tech's Dr. Salonen for insight into the glitch?" Pens asks.

They stiffen at the question.

"Dr. Salonen has examined the satellite's programming and he is not concerned. He's convinced we have total control of the satellite. Scale Tech is insisting that the launch proceeds as planned," Dr. Sato says.

"That doesn't make sense," I say.

"Due to budget cuts, many space agencies have been forced to partner with private companies for funding. Scale Tech is our majority financial partner, so we can't force their hand.

We used to have a good relationship with Dr. Salonen. Unfortunately, since his wife became comatose and the two missing scientists were found dead, much has changed," Dr. Bernard confesses. "Dr. Salonen will, however, attend the ISC Banquet as the head of the Super Satellite project."

Dr. Salonen's name loops in my mind—if Palermo Ricci is courting Dr. Salonen—the ties to Cesare are even stronger.

"Who else will be at the ISC Banquet?" I ask, perhaps a bit too forcefully. My numbers are keeping me honest right now. If I don't ask, I know I'll regret it.

They exchange furtive glances. "It is an exclusive event. Many of our private investors and high-profile scientists and government officials are taking the opportunity to network with international companies who will be in town. The ISC Banquet will bring together the greatest scientific minds and private companies working in the space industry. The day after the banquet is the Remote Launch and Celebration, which is why we need answers before then."

"Of course," I say. I smile but inside my numbers are dismantling months of puzzles. The fluctuating and hyper frequencies in the room are so urgent I almost can't stay in my seat. My team recognizes my agitation right away.

Pens is writing furiously with both hands. Eddie pretends he isn't psycho-analyzing every word they say. Felicia winks and is already texting me from under the table: *On it. Finding out who is going to that banquet.*

Internally, my mind is reeling—why does Cesare own shares in Scale Tech?

Harrison clears his throat. "So just to be clear, you want us to figure out the glitch in the satellites so you can go forward with the launch?"

Dr. Kivi turns, the weight in the room shifting. "Not exactly. We need your assistance to find someone who we are certain can help us. We came here because we heard you had been in contact and it's imperative that we speak to him."

My gut lurches. They don't even have to say his name. Everyone is searching for the same guy. I avoid the team's glances as they turn my way. Instead I focus on our guests and the probability that they know more than they're letting on.

Dr. Kivi looks directly at me. "We'd like you to help us find the NASA Tipper."

CHAPTER 11

∞

Fractals erupt behind my eyes. Maybe it's destiny, or disaster, but a path in the dark is lighting up in front of me. I can't escape the numbers that say I need to find him.

When Agent Ramos dangled an offer in front of me in Brazil, this is not what I expected. A job to find Noble. I almost laugh. Regardless, it means finding him isn't just about me and our relationship anymore.

But how did Agent Ramos trace Noble to PSS in the first place?

My eyes flit to Ms. T. Her gaze is steady, not giving away a thing. Ms. T sent out the request to the Tunisian police claiming she had found a dangerous hacker, and the story of him getting away did spread past the local police, but there were no names or specific details. I don't think she saw this coming.

Honestly, neither did I. There's only one person who could have leaked the information to Ramos that I know who the NASA Tipper is. *Bai.* He met Noble in Tunisia. Not that Bai told Ramos who Noble was, but there must have been enough clues for him to figure it out. But that's not my concern right now. If the DIA is involved in this, it means that every person in this room is holding back intel.

Everyone on the team—apart from Ms. Taylor—turns to look at me. That's not obvious or anything. Definitely going to have to teach them about guarding their body language.

Of course, the ISC scientists' gazes turn to me as well.

"Is it true, then?" Dr. Sato asks me directly. "You've had personal contact with him?"

"How do you know it's a him?" I ask, almost protectively. I don't care who they are. I won't give anything away about Noble that could harm him.

Dr. Kivi looks embarrassed. "Our analysts deciphered he was male by use of language. We could be wrong."

If I help them, I'll be putting Noble at risk once again. Except, Noble would want to help if he knew what was happening. This is his expertise, and helping humanity is important to him, after all. But if Noble already knows about the situation and hasn't stepped in to help, there must be a reason. Either way, I need to find him.

A memory of his family's tents in Tunisia flashes before me—Qadar laughing with the older men, the gentle hospitality of Farah serving warm tea with a bright smile, the playful children vying for Noble's attention, the trust I thought we'd begun to share...but then his message in the stars tears through my mind.

Don't find me.

My stomach locks up. "We've been in contact before," I admit, rubbing the creases in my forehead. "I may know how to get in touch, but I can't make any promises. The NASA Tipper is very hard to find when he doesn't want to be found."

"We understand. The NASA Tipper was actively providing crucial information until recently," says Dr. Kivi. "Frankly, we've never seen a brain like his. We've offered him several jobs. He's never responded. If it's a matter of money, we'd compensate him as much as he asks, if that could persuade him."

I think about Noble accepting money and feel sick. "I doubt he cares about compensation." That's just not how he thinks.

"How about not facing over thirty lawsuits and five years in prison for breaking into government satellites and protected files?" Mr. Frank Kelley, the lawyer pipes in, a hard line on his lips. "Would that be a strong enough motivator?"

The room goes silent.

"That's not why we came here," Dr. Kivi says, softening. "But Mr. Kelley does have a point. The NASA Tipper has probed almost every satellite in the sky. He couldn't have done that without hacking into governmental agencies and private companies, which is an international criminal offense. We've evaluated his actions and while he accessed our systems without authorization, he did not exploit our data, but rather improved it."

Dr. Bernard speaks up. "After discussion with the scientific community, we've held back on lawsuits because he's advancing prototypes, designs and trouble-shooting for no compensation. So far, nothing has been misused or sold on the black-market."

"Regardless," Mr. Kelley cuts in, "he's a liability and has broken numerous laws. If he doesn't help the ISC and something goes wrong with the launch, he could face some serious consequences."

My dad looks up at me, drawing my attention. I had nearly forgotten he was in the room. I wonder what he thinks of Noble now.

"There is some speculation among our colleagues that he could be the one hacking the Super Satellite," Dr. Sato says. "There are only a few people in the world who have the technical knowledge to hack or reprogram such a multi-functional satellite. The NASA Tipper is one of them."

I straighten my back, hiding the emotion that is puncturing

me as I listen to their accusations. I swallow back an image of Noble in Tunisia, teaching kids, and shake my head. "He wouldn't do that."

"Are you sure? How well do you know him?" The attorney's sharp eyes corner me. An alarm goes off under my skin. Red says that those who steal honey will eventually get stung, and in this attorney's mind, he's already prosecuting Noble for that list of broken laws.

I shrug it off, like I don't care. Under a spotlight, too much emotion can betray you. Truth is, I don't know everything about Noble. I just know he isn't out to hurt anyone.

"No one can be sure of anything," I say in the tone I'd use in a business meeting. "But his patterns don't suggest anything of the sort."

Ms. Taylor comes to my rescue. "Agreed," she says, a bit stiffly. "Yes, he's upheld a certain code, which may be another reason he's unresponsive. Half the American media has demonized the NASA Tipper for not finding solutions for the blackouts."

Dr. Bernard turns on a screen. "Maybe we can turn that around, if he can help us. Which is why we're here. PSS is the only lead we have to locate him."

The coordinates in Finland have been burning a hole in my mind. Not for much longer.

Dr. Kivi shakes her head, eyeing the lawyer with a facial expression that wills him to stay quiet. "We're not here to accuse him of anything. Honestly, everyone wants to meet him. But now, it's imperative that we find him."

The ISC's scientists seem genuine in their admiration of Noble, but if their lawyer is any indicator, other parties won't hesitate to condemn his actions.

I look up at Dr. Sato. "There's no guarantee the NASA Tipper will help the ISC. At least in the way that you might expect," I say with a heavy heart. My stomach twists in pain.

I thought it'd be different with me. Three months of waiting and searching for him, only to be turned away.

"We understand."

I reach out my right hand. "Then it's a deal. I'll do what I can to find the NASA Tipper." My other hand taps my knee under the table—assessing uncharted territory. I need more information that I'm sure Agent Ramos knows.

If my calculations are correct, the blackouts aren't just a result of geomagnetic storms, power grids, and satellite breakdowns. Someone is trying to sabotage the Super Satellite. And someone has to stop whoever is behind this before it's too late.

So even if Noble hates it, I'm coming for him.

CHAPTER 12

∞

Ms. T and my father escort the ISC scientists out as the team hangs back. We silently eye each other until the door closes.

"Mind blown, anyone?" Harrison asks, still starry-eyed and shell-shocked. "NASA, JAXA, and the ESA in *our* living room asking *us* to take on a super top-secret mission. Just wish it were under slightly better conditions, not the potential loss of years of scientific breakthroughs and the future prosperity of numerous nations." He grimaces.

"This is a disaster." Eddie moans. He and I can smell corruption from a mile away.

"This is why PSS exists." Felicia straightens her back and cracks her knuckles. "Of course, they want Jo to find Noble, but I think we all know there's something else going on. What's our game plan?"

My brows knit tight together. I want to dash to Noble on the first plane I can find, but the events in Geneva and the intel on Scale Tech and the connection to Cesare Di Susa are eating a hole in my mind—I can't ignore it anymore. Rafael sent me that message for a reason, which means I need to locate Cesare.

Dr. Kivi said prominent people and companies from around the world will attend the ISC Helsinki Banquet. At the banquet, everyone will be in one room. If my predictions are correct, there's a high chance Palermo Ricci will be there too, since he's so keenly interested in Scale Tech. He and Cesare are family, and I'm betting he knows where Cesare is. I'll also be able to scope out Dr. Salonen. Not a bad strategy. Looks like I'll have to make a quick stop in Helsinki first.

"Did you hack the guest list for the banquet?" I ask Felicia.

"Of course, I did." She pops up a holo-screen, and we read through the names.

"Yikes!" Harrison hoots. "They weren't kidding. Exclusive with a capital E."

"Yeah...except for one problem," Felicia says, full of surprise. "I've been running background checks on everyone and it doesn't look pretty. A quarter of the list are unsavory characters with criminal records. How did they get invited?"

"Jo?" Eddie groans. "Several of the names match Cesare di Susa's former associates."

My brow furrows in thought. That only reinforces why I have to go. "Will Palermo Ricci be there?" I ask. Eddie nods. "Good. Between Palermo Ricci and Juho Salonen, I'll find Cesare, Rafael, and Noble."

The question becomes: how much do I involve the team in this?

I look up at them, so eager to help. But this job is mine. "Listen, everyone. Noble can solve the satellite glitch—but I have to find him first."

"Let's not forget that he doesn't want you to find him," Pens says, awkwardly.

"He doesn't get a choice," I say, defensively.

"What if the reason he doesn't want to be found isn't because of you?" Pens counters.

"What does that mean?" I ask, heat rising to my face.

Pens bites her lip nervously. "There's no way he doesn't know about the problems the ISC are facing. The guy keeps tabs on every satellite in the sky."

"Right now, it doesn't matter if he knows or not. There's more at stake. Noble will understand once I explain how dire the situation is." I tap my leg. For the first time in three months, the path in my mind is clearly leading me to this place on the map. To Finland. To a crossroads, where I'll find answers.

Every moment I've spent searching the night sky is now validated. If I hadn't cracked Noble's code, I wouldn't have been able to help the ISC. Except that's not entirely true. If I had followed my gut in Geneva, maybe we wouldn't be here. My jaw clenches tight. I messed up and it's my responsibility to make up for that now.

"Spill it," Pens says, her eyes trained on me. "We know you well enough by now to see something is brewing in that mind of yours."

I'm silent, evaluating. This is much bigger than just a malfunctioning satellite. My numbers point to something terrible. Do I really drag them into another mess?

Harrison sucks in a deep breath. "Jo, you promised after Tunisia to tell us the truth about what you see."

I release a heavy breath. "Noble is in Finland, and so is the cause of the blackouts. Cesare Di Susa is somehow involved in all this, and I need to find out how. In Geneva, I saw something while we were at the Energy Summit—a web of men, all connected somehow to one man in the audience. I don't know who he is. I calculated a subtle but malicious behavior, and I should have said something but..." I hesitate. "I didn't. After my room was broken into, I still did nothing. I'm pretty sure I felt the same frequency in Namibia too." I shake my head. "So, I need to get to Finland as soon as possible. I'll attend that banquet and locate Cesare Di Susa. And then, I'll find Noble." My gut swirls at the mention of Noble's name. Finding him scares me even more than broken satellites and Cesare on the loose.

Felicia rubs her hands together. "Trip time!"

I fold my hands on the desk, paling as I look at them.

"Wait. Just you?" Pens says, reading my expression. "Did you forget we're a team?"

I swallow hard, calculating. "You're the best reconnaissance team I could have, but this doesn't involve you."

"We talked about this, Jo," Harrison says. "You don't get to make decisions for us."

"Jo," Eddie chimes in, "you're not the only one who has regrets. If there's anything foul at play, I want a chance to stop it."

"If you go, we go," Felicia agrees.

I gauge them. "If we all go, you know what that means. I don't have time for a student exchange."

"Actually," Harrison says, pushing back in his chair, scratching his chin, "it's the perfect cover while you're at the banquet."

"Why?"

"The Helsinki University STEM team is one of the most innovative tech teams in Europe. I read about them last year. They're geniuses. They created a super high tech nanosatellite. Even partnered with Scale Tech in the past. They could be a resource. We could tap into their systems. At the very least, doing an exchange with them would be a great alibi and they would be fun to meet." He raises his eyebrows.

I study them all. They're ready to fight me on this. I sigh. "Fine. Contact them," I say. "Ms. T will appreciate a cover story in case anyone is watching." Harrison pumps his fist and everyone else smiles victoriously.

"So you think Cesare will be in Helsinki?" Eddie asks, doubtfully.

Naturally, Eddie is on my wavelength of thinking because of our similar pasts.

"No," I say, my resolve hardening. "But everyone I need

to find him will be there."

Harrison whistles. "Uh, guys. This may be harder than we think." He shows me his phone. "The cost for a ticket to the banquet is in the upper six figures per person, but that's actually the least of our problems. They're only allowing prominent investors, businesspeople, and industry professionals to purchase tickets."

"I have been all of those things in my past, and money isn't an issue right now," I say. This will be a little different. But I'm sure I can handle it.

"There's more. Attendees must be elite individuals with revenues of millions or billions and own or lead a Fortune 500 business. Exclusive with a capital E, remember?" he says. "However, they do allow a 'plus one'."

Eddie cracks his neck, pointing to the list of invitees. "Jo, this isn't an ordinary banquet, if you know what I mean." He's referring to the names on the list with a shady past or a persuasion to corruption.

The door opens. Ms. T and my father walk back into the room.

"Perfect," I say, glancing at the door. "I happen to know a guy who fits this description who we can partner with."

"Huh?" Harrison squints his eyes. "Who?"

I turn to my dad, who's wide-eyed with a Band-aid covering his nose. "Our new board member."

CHAPTER 13

∞

When I was younger, I was my dad's best business partner. We'd go into important meetings and during negotiations, if I calculated a way to land a better deal, I'd signal discreetly to him. He'd catch my small signs perfectly and with one small move, we'd come out on top. The same went for the stock market. Back then we didn't know he'd be accused of insider trading, sued, and even put on trial. Even though the courts eventually ruled out insider trading, there's still slander around his name. As it turns out, that experience could serve us well in Helsinki.

"Okay," he says with an awkward chuckle, "why is everyone looking at me?"

We explain the plan to Ms. T and my father, both listening with the look of a restrained parent trying to remain calm.

"So, how about it?" I ask. "A little father-daughter team up? Like the old days?"

"The old days almost landed me in prison, if you've forgotten." He doesn't look convinced.

I glance at Ms. T and back to my dad. "This is different."

My dad shifts in his chair. "You think I'll be effective in a meeting with criminal masterminds who could be planning an international sabotage? I don't know much about satellites."

"You don't need to. This banquet isn't about satellites. It's about control. There's more to these blackouts than meets the eye. But if we can find Cesare, I know he'll lead us to the answers." I look around at everyone, but they aren't convinced. I know it's hard for them because they don't see the things I do. It doesn't ever get easier trying to explain my mind to people, which makes me want to find Noble even more. He would understand what I'm seeing. He would trust me. I've longed for someone like that my whole life. "Look, Dad, it's not like we haven't fooled the crowds before. We're a great team. You're a high-risk investor. That's what they're looking for."

"Jo, as much as I love working alongside you, I just rebuilt my reputation. Don't you think showing up at a banquet full of crooks will reflect badly for me? And what if something goes wrong? I mean, come on, tell me the odds."

"That's why it'll work. You're back on the radar again. Everyone is talking about your comeback. And...you have a questionable financial past. If they're crooked, then whoever it is we're looking for will be attracted to you. No offense, but the odds in your favor are good."

I don't move my eyes off my dad because I can feel the team staring at me like heat beating down on a summer day. But that's not all. If I step in, I go all in. There's a tingle beneath my skin and I finger my sore knuckles from this morning. The desire to make the wrongs right, like Red taught me, bubbles inside me. I square my shoulders, leaning into the part of me that sees every King and Madame in this world as a target. If they're out there, then that's where I need to be too.

Dad's eyes meet Ms. T's. "What do you think, Marigold?"

Ms. T shrugs. "It's actually not a bad plan." Her strong eyes soften as she considers him. It can't be easy now that she's romantically involved with him, but Ms. T is one step ahead of my dad. "Jason, you know I'm a believer in taking risks, but I'm also strategic. You're not exactly trained for this type of operation. The ISC didn't approach us to attend a banquet. They asked us to find the NASA Tipper." She looks at my father. "The DIA who set up our meeting with the ISC didn't enlist us for anything else. We could be overstepping boundaries." She purses her lips. "But your daughter did ask, which leads me to another side of the same coin. I've come to trust my prods. Jo hasn't said yes to any assignment like this in three months. If she says we need to go, then I think we need to listen." Her voice is strong, but behind her eyes is a new kind of concern—one for my dad. "However, Jason, you need to be prepared that you and Jo are taking a serious risk."

His expression changes to one I know well—the determination I used to see so often when I was young. The man who knew what he wanted. He runs a hand through his hair. He's considering it.

Ms. T places a hand on his shoulder. "She's an expert at this. Jo will do the work; you're the cover."

"Here is a list of some of the other investors attending," Eddie says. "Not everyone has a questionable background. There are some very reputable people attending."

My dad looks it over. "Actually, I know a couple of people on here. Wow. Even Palermo Ricci will be there." My dad nods, impressed, but the team's faces go pale because of our earlier conversation about Palermo. What I don't expect is the horror written on Ms. Taylor's face at the mention of the last name.

Ms. T knows a lot of classified information, but she usually has a better poker face. Looks like that *heart to heart* conversation I've been putting off needs to happen sooner than I thought.

She resumes her poker face, but then says, "Maybe we need to think more about this." An emotion is in her voice that I rarely hear: fear.

"We don't have time," I say. I hate bullies, but fear is the bully I hate the worst.

A dangerous opportunity. The words flicker in me. Red trained me the way he did for a reason. He understood that part of me. Even Agent Ramos said, *I know your type...* Red never saw what I accomplished outside of the Pratt. But Kai saw it. He knew all about that itch, which is why he called me Trouble. My dad, too, recognizes that look in my eyes.

"You know what? She's right," he says, puffing out his chest with a large breath. "I'm in. I'll do it."

Pens is clicking away. "Ok. So practically speaking, does this mean we fly to Helsinki tomorrow? Because the banquet is in less than 48 hours."

Everyone is in agreement. "Let's do this."

"On separate flights. Ms. Mines is watching our every move." Ms. T taps her lip.

My father looks at me. "When I register for the ISC Banquet, you'll attend with me, right? So should I book two spots?"

I pause, the possibilities playing out in my head. How to get close to the inner circles. To Palermo and Rafael. To finding Noble. There are so many moving parts, it's hard to see all the variations of how this could play out. My dad might not succeed. "Book another party. Just in case."

They all cock their heads. "Who's the third guest?"

"Backup," I say, deep in thought. "Oh, and don't use my real name for the banquet. I won't be going as your daughter. I'll be going as your assistant. Under an alias."

"Which is?" Pens asks.

"The first name is *Mila.*"

CHAPTER 14

∞

RIVERS RESIDENCE
ALKI BEACH, SEATTLE

Dinner is over, and I'm sitting in the dark again.

Dad, Marigold, and my sisters are inside relaxing by a warm fire while I'm on the beachside balcony watching the last of the Northwest's winter sun head west over the Pacific. West leads to Asia, 5736 miles to Shanghai. Add an extra 26 miles and I'd arrive at the Villa. To think there was once a time I was on the other side of this ocean looking East. To this coastline.

The phantom frequency crests on the waves with a burst of heat before it dissipates in a flash over the sea. It ricochets so fast that for a nanosecond, it haunts me. But I steady myself, breathing in salt air, and taking in all the numbers until I sense Mara's frequency.

The door slides open. "Hey," she says, stepping outside holding out a cup of hot tea.

"Thanks."

She cuddles up beside me. "I'm guessing you calculated how many times Dad gazed into Marigold's eyes tonight." She gives me a playful bump with her shoulder. "We haven't seen him this happy in a long time, huh?"

"Only 32 times." I laugh. "Yeah, it's really nice." A lump rises in my throat as a large set of waves rolls in from the East.

"So you and Dad head to Helsinki tomorrow?" Mara asks.

I glance through the window at Dad and Marigold talking on the couch with Lily, then back to Mara. So much peace and safety. Which makes me wonder why I'm sitting alone on the balcony in the cold, mentally preparing for a trip to the Arctic Circle to search for Italian crime bosses and a boy who doesn't want me to find him.

I sigh and give my attention to Mara. "How do you feel about us going?" I ask. "I should have talked to you first."

Mara pulls my blanket over herself. "After China and Tunisia, I've learned to trust your *numerical* instincts." She laughs. "Except when it comes to how little sleep you get." She gives me a strong look.

"I can sleep on the plane."

"That doesn't sound promising." She pauses, biting her lower lip. She doesn't know how to say what's coming next. "Dad told me about Noble's message. I'm sorry."

A brittle cold digs into me. "I was going to tell you..." Once it stopped hurting so much. Matters of the heart are like waves in the sea—sometimes they are fierce and sometimes calm, but they never stop moving, even at night.

"So he's in Finland?" she asks. "How do you feel about seeing him now?"

I look up. Because of him, the night sky is no longer stars and galaxies. It's light and languages and codes and hearts; and lingering in the masses are millions of messages. I sigh. There's no balance in my heart, but a teetering between two people. "Have you ever felt as much pain for someone as you do love?"

"Aren't love and pain intertwined?" She gives me a hard look, similar to her expression when she faced me in Shanghai for the first time after my kidnapping. "What's going on with you, Jo? And don't give me a dumb answer. You're a genius, remember?"

I may be a genius, but when it comes to the heart, I'm a fool.

"Finding Noble means the end of Kai." It's all I can say without getting choked up. Since my gift returned, I've felt Kai's pain...and he's felt mine. I'm not sure how I know this, but I do. I swallow, gaining back my voice. "As soon as I realized I loved him, I had to let him go."

His love-stricken face in the Tunisia safe house flashes before me. *"If you don't love me now, I'll wait..."* he'd said. The kiss we shared after I confessed I loved him—not knowing it'd be our last. It's joy or pain he won't remember because of the SWAY I used on him. It's a memory and scar only I bear. He probably hates me right now. At least he won't regret his choices because of me.

"You didn't have to let him go," Mara says sharply. "You chose to."

"Mara, every number in me said Kai needed to accept this job. Lives depended on it. *His life* depended on it. This is what he's meant to do. I saw it every time he came to Seattle, he found a reason to leave earlier, and stay away longer. He was antsy. I didn't want to be the reason he missed his chance." I look up. "But that's only one side of the story...you know how I felt about Noble when I was younger. Mara, you said it yourself when we were kids—we were made for each other. Meeting him in Tunisia changed everything."

"So you love Noble?" she asks, so soft it's a whisper.

"Yes? Maybe? I don't know. Love isn't that simple for me," I tell her. Even saying the word out loud makes me tremble. All I know is everything is leading me to him.

Mara sighs. "Then you find Noble and get your answers." Mara squeezes my hand. I squeeze back.

Marigold walks out on the balcony, her warm long jacket

around her. "Mara, can I have a minute with Jo?"

"Of course, Marigold." Mara winks at me and walks inside.

Ms. T. stares down at me. Her eyes don't make it hard to interpret what's coming. Time for that heart to heart.

CHAPTER 15

∞

Ms. T settles beside me and lifts some of my blanket. "Mind if I have some?"

"Course." I extend it over her. My heart warms, but also locks up. The feeling of a mother is so close, yet there's a part of me that hesitates with her. Jumping into close relationships isn't easy for me. Especially after she started dating my dad.

"All right, I know you have questions for me," she says, softly. It's nothing like the tone she uses in the office. "It's best we tackle them before Helsinki."

The first time I knew there was something going on between her and my dad, I avoided talking to her about it. But after our Myanmar job, Marigold took me to Greenlake for a walk. The fractals on the lake's shoreline are still imprinted on my mind.

"Jo, your father and I have grown really close," she started as we made our way around the loop.

My face flooded with heat. "He's told me."

"I know, but you need to hear it from me too." She straightened. "I admire and respect your dad immensely. He's innovative, generous, kind, *handsome.*" She looked caringly at me. "I respect you too, Jo. I chose you to be part of the team because I believe in you. I certainly didn't know then that this relationship would develop. I don't want anything to compromise my relationship with you."

I swallowed dryly. Many of our formalities had slipped away, yet there was still a gap between us. Regardless of my unclear feelings, I responded with an answer that was true. "You're the first woman he's let into his life since my mom died. He wouldn't choose just anyone. I'm pretty sure you wouldn't either."

Now, here she is on my balcony, practically a part of my family and I'm the only one who hasn't stopped calling her "Ms. T".

But that's not why she's sitting on this balcony with me, and we're out of time for anything less than the truth.

"I want to know about Rayne Carter and why that journalist Ms. Mines is intent on shutting us down." The look on her face earlier also comes sharply to mind. "You also know Palermo Ricci, don't you?"

She exhales hard. "Yes. But I'll answer your other questions first." She takes a deep breath. "Prodigy Stealth Solution didn't always have the 'stealth' in its name. When I first started, it was called Prodigy Solution. We operated publicly and, as you know, we partnered with the DIA. A brilliant girl named Rayne Carter was one of the reasons I started PS. She was one of the many prodigies I worked with on a daily basis. But Rayne was special. An expert in human anatomy, biology, stem research, brain function, and inventing cutting edge medical and bio-tech. She was giving advice to doctors before she was 12." She pauses. "Rayne also had no home life, which made her desperate in ways I ignored."

"You said *she* didn't follow protocols. What happened?"

"As news spread about PS, the publicity started to compromise our projects and the prodigies' identities. Rayne was pulled in too many directions." She breathed in. "I don't choose just any gifted kid to be part of the team. The prods

I choose are smart, but they're also agents of change—bold, independent, and strong." She looks out over the water. "But the attention and pressure were too much. When I consulted Rayne about operating under the radar, she strongly disagreed. Despite her wishes, I moved forward with my plans to go private. Our relationship grew tense. She claimed I didn't trust her. She grew even more restless. I should have sidelined her right when I noticed. But before my plans were finalized, a medical technology research group at one of Palermo Ricci's medical centers approached us with a case. Rayne wanted the assignment. The job was outside our established protocols. Palermo's security team refused to accommodate my requirements. I said no to the job. But Palermo contacted Rayne privately. She was convinced she could do the job, so she agreed to the assignment without permission. A week later there was a fatal explosion in the medical lab. Three people didn't make it. She was one of them." Ms. T shakes her head. "When the police questioned Palermo, he showed proof that the explosion in the lab was Rayne's fault. That was three years ago. She was 15."

She sighs. "Ms. Mines was a journalist assigned to the story on PS and Rayne's death, and she ripped me apart for allowing teens to take on such jobs." She's quiet. "I loved Rayne like my own daughter. I practically raised her for five years. She would have revolutionized medicine. Changed the world. But she's gone because of me. I never want to make the same mistake again."

Devastation graffitis her face. Her movements are regretful and pensive. Her arms fold in, as if there's someone missing between them.

"Much like your dad, I spent many nights regretting my choices." Her voice hitches. "Jo, I won't lie. I've never met anyone who could compete with Rayne until I met you. That's why I need you to be especially careful. Palermo Ricci is ruthless when he wants something. To this day, I know there's more to the story of what happened to Rayne." She looks at me. "But where she failed, I know you'll succeed."

Her words cut into the vast trenches of my past. A fire tingling in my heart as I close my eyes. I didn't know Rayne, but I grieve for her. Ms. T's reasons for moving Prodigy *Stealth* Solution under the radar, with a ton of protocols and parents who knew the risks, makes sense. But a question rises.

"Would you ever choose a boy like Noble?" I ask.

"Noble is an interesting prod. Brilliant, generous. Not lured by fame, but I'm not sure he'd follow the rules. Let's see what happens in Helsinki." She looks over at me, her facial expression softening. "You stretch me at times, Jo. I'll admit that. But whatever we do, we stay safe. I can't handle seeing another prod lost or dead."

A lump rises in my throat. "I won't let that happen," I say, but I can't promise my definition of safe matches hers. Likewise, my definition of dead is different too. From my experience, being dead isn't all it's cracked up to be.

CHAPTER 16

∞

In my bedroom, my bag is packed in eight minutes. My body vibrates with so many nerves I'm not sure I'll get any sleep. In roughly 12 hours and 36 minutes, I'll be in the same country as Noble.

My hair is now blonde and two inches shorter. Straight edge bangs hang just below my eyebrows, and the contacts that Eddie made me are a shade of blue that reminds me of glaciers. Appropriate, since I'll be in sub-zero weather in the Arctic Circle. Eddie will bring all the other gear I need with the team.

My thoughts bounce from the height of the stars to the bottom of the ocean as I sit on my bed. It's got me reaching for something like that whale slowly gliding beneath the surface of my heart, following a current I can't calculate. Kai. He's always there.

I close my eyes, emotions rising like a flood. After I sent Kai my goodbye letter, I never looked back. He called countless times, but I couldn't bear to hear his voice. Every equation confirmed that if I talked to him, I'd take everything back. There's no honor in the way I ended our relationship, which is why Bai hates me, too.

What made things worse was that the frequencies I picked up increased my ability to feel things I couldn't before. His pain vibrated through me for weeks, and even worse, somehow I knew he felt mine, too. *Goodbyes are painful*, I told myself. It took me years to recover after losing my mom.

But if finding Noble is the final act of letting go of Kai, it makes me wonder—has Kai reached out to me? I've resisted the desire to even look at a picture of Kai, but now I want to know. Does he have any last message for me?

I sneak over to my PSS computer at the desk and pull up our old secret portal behind Wall Street's stock exchange, and my heart starts racing. For months, even though I knew Kai had left on his mission, I refused to open this portal because Kai always broke the rules to contact me.

Now, I slip past our layers of code and into our inbox, expectant. It clicks open and my stomach sinks. It's not just that there are no signs of him reaching out. Everything has been deleted.

Error pages replace our old chats. Websites replace our backdoors. He deleted it all. I dig a bit deeper. His accounts with his father's company are gone. In fact, he has no records in this forum at all. Not even a trace of him on any digital platform he once was associated with. I can't find anything with his name at all. Even my PSS radar search is useless. Anything that is related to him is all gone. Online, he doesn't exist.

Like Bai said. November Romeo. *A never return.*

I shiver and a lock of blonde hair I don't recognize falls over my shoulder. I brush it behind my ear and close my eyes. Maybe Bai was right. Kai is gone for good. I have to accept that. Kai and I were never meant to be together anyway. Two worlds that could never be one.

I close the computer and climb into bed, sinking down into the warm sheets and burying my face into the pillow. A frequency outside my window sweeps off the sea, promising me sleep if I give into it. But I know my dreams won't be nice.

I think one last time of Kai. Long ago, I made him a promise. Now it's time to break it.

CHAPTER 17

∞

Even in the dream, the knocking scared me. It was almost dawn in Shanghai. I was in the Villa, in my bed, not awake, not asleep—when whoever was at the back door had me jumping up, breathless. Without numbers, my sleepy disorientation was far worse.

My feet hit the cold floor as I scrambled to check the window, phone in hand. Three more knocks, then a soft, but distraught voice sent my heart thumping. "Jo? Are you there?"

It was Kai. Relief flooded me, but immediately all my sensors were up again. Why was he knocking at dawn? What was wrong?

I raced to the door, unlocking three bolts, and swung it open. The dream flickered as the first ray of light crashed through the door. Kai was there, disheveled hair and bloodshot eyes. Looking like he hadn't slept all night. He threw his arms around me, pulling me close to him. He exhaled strongly. "You're here. Good. Are you ok?" His chest vibrated slightly. I couldn't tell if he was shivering because there was dew on the grass and he was barefoot and wearing short sleeves, or if something else had happened.

"I'm fine. What's wrong?" My fingers ran through his silky

black hair and I breathed in the scent of his skin.

"A bad dream. You were..." he mumbled in a delirious way. "I just needed to make sure you were safe. I'll let you get back to sleep. Sorry for waking you."

Kai had seen a lot in the last few months because of me. The Pratt. Madame. King. The Expo. Golden Alley. I wonder what images went through his mind now.

"Don't go," I said, pulling him inside. "You can tell me about your nightmare in here."

We settled onto the couch, snuggling under warm blankets. As the sun rose, light snuck through the window, fanning with vibrant colors. Kai had not let go of my hand. When he'd calmed down, unexpected words tumbled out of his mouth.

"It's scary loving you."

His words startled me because Kai was always so brave. Madame and King were gone. There were no threats. We had just planned out our next few months in Seattle. What was bringing this on?

My fingers slid under his chin and tipped it down so our eyes would meet. He stared at me with his big brown eyes, loving, open, but with a hint of something I recognized all too well. *Fear.*

"Why would you say that?" I asked. "What happened?"

He shook his head and sat up. "It's stupid. Forget it. I'm just tired. It was just a bad dream."

The light of dawn grew brighter behind Kai, and I squinted to see his face. "It's not stupid. If it's fear, you need to speak it out so it has no power. Don't let it grow bigger in the dark."

He leaned in, his strong arms wrapping around me again. I sank into the safety of them. His scent, the freshness of a mountain peak, filled my senses. Even in the dream, my stomach lurched.

He cleared his throat. "I keep thinking I'm going to lose you like I lost my mom. Like one day I'm going to wake up and you'll be gone." He closed his eyes, breathed in deep, then confessed, "You're the only other woman I've ever loved." His jaw tightens and his emotion feels like exposed wires. Since I met Kai, he's feared nothing. The boy Chan talked about who lost his mom, who grew angry, who then grew strong... who then met me. This is what he feared? That one day I'd disappear again or die like his mom?

My arms snuck around his waist. The sun brightened in the living room, so much so that it felt like truth. I tucked my face into the curve of his neck. "I'm not going to disappear or die anytime soon."

"No one plans on dying, Jo. I've seen it. It just happens, whether bad guys make bad decisions or good guys make good decisions. You're not the safest person I know."

"I'll be safe in Seattle," I said, playing with a strand of his hair. "I'm not putting myself in danger anymore. I'm done with that. I survived the fire. I'm not going to jump back into one."

"Maybe not in the way you'd think." His face was lined with concern.

"Besides, my numbers are gone," I whispered. "It doesn't make sense for me to get into trouble."

"Your numbers are not what make you *trouble*," he said with a straight face. "Jo, I know you. You don't back down from a fight. And darkness doesn't scare you. That's why I love you. But just promise me whenever we're apart, whatever you do, you'll be safe."

Sun poured into the living room like blood coursing in veins, alive and powerful. Kai's heartbeat pounded in his chest as he waited for a response.

"I promise," I said, but the light was so bright now that I couldn't see and when I reached for him, he was gone.

CHAPTER 18

∞

THE LION BLOCK
HELSINKI, FINLAND

Helsinki is a city of lampposts and cathedrals draped in a beautiful white gown.

After driving by calm stretches of snow-laden trees from the airport, we arrive at Helsinki's city center, where classic European architecture mixes with a hip, urban atmosphere. Through a lens of snowflakes, I absorb it all—bustling department stores and city parks with fountains; a Ferris wheel standing against a backdrop of pastel-colored townhouses with their windows lit up. Boats on an icy harbor near Market Square remind its inhabitants that summer will come again.

K2, my smart watch, alerts me that we have arrived at our location just as the driver confirms it. "Welcome to the Lion Block." We pull on to a side road off one of the main squares in Helsinki.

Senate Square is roughly 59 by 116 meters and located in the most iconic part of Helsinki's center. The Lion Block, one of the unique Empire style buildings bordering the square, forms an entire city block where the most important administrative meetings in Finland take place. The Government Palace, Helsinki University, the National Library of Finland, and the Helsinki Cathedral line the square, which is now dusted in a perfect white glow.

Our bodyguards get out of the van first, then open the door for my father and me. As I step out, my nose tingles at the icy two-degree air temperature, making my eyes water. I tighten my jacket and slip on my gloves and hat. Frequencies hit me from all directions and my numbers take over.

My gift bounces from the number of exterior pillars on the buildings—18—to the lampposts lining the square—22—to the speed at which trams and cars traverse the streets, and the vibrations of bundled up people tromping across the square. Out of the 475 windows facing in the square—*and the number goes up as my mind wraps around each building*—there are only 188 that have lights on inside.

The square is wondrous and beautiful, but it also unsettles me, because the snow is muffling what would be accurate dimensions. It makes me feel unsure like a child, especially as I calculate the 8 by 8 meter shielded stage set up for the ISC Celebration Rocket surrounded by five policemen. It jars my numbers, though I can't calculate why.

My dad, however, is beaming. He's just happy to be here. He steps out beside me with wide, excited eyes. "It's freezing here. I love it!" he says like a kid. "Look at that." He pulls his hat over his ears and points to Helsinki Cathedral, an icon of the capital. "Beautiful, huh? Everything looks so pristine in white."

The grand church sits majestically on top of a set of stairs on the north side of Senate Square. The cathedral's exterior matches the stainless white of the snow, making it even more radiant under the winter sky. But I can't count the number of stairs—46? 47? I can't quite tell because they're covered in snow. It's not a terrible problem, but it puts me on edge.

"Yeah," I say, agreeing with my dad. Snow transforms an everyday dullness into a magical wonderland, but there's another aspect to it that my numb cheeks have already calculated—snow also has a dangerous side, like the ocean, like a wild animal. Just when you think it's safe, it bites or pulls you under. Still, I admit, it's charming here.

A frequency, like a slice of wind racing through the streets, soars into my chest like a sudden heat wave. The phantom frequency. It's stronger here. I crane my head, searching for its source. It's gone before my ability can trace it, but even in its wake, my senses are heightened.

Six feet away from us, a twelve-foot tall street lamp turns on as the dusk hits. The light illuminates every snowflake falling from the sky. I take off my glove and let the small fractals fall on my hand, melting into my palm. My stomach swirls like a flurry in a snowstorm. No wonder Noble's base is here. In the wintertime, he can study the auroras and fractals.

I'm eager to get inside to meet the PSS team. They flew in late last night on a red-eye flight to avoid being seen with me. They were tasked with setting up everything for today's plan—the STEM lecture at the university as well as the surveillance for the ISC Banquet. But my father beckons me to follow him down the street leading to the harbor. So I follow.

As I walk, my mind creates new maps and puzzles as I take note of shops, people and the urban life around me. Street signs are written in both Finnish and Swedish. The Finnish words are so long, sparking my curiosity. Instantly, a pattern emerges with how the words end, how they carry a direction. It never fails to amaze me that humans think and build languages so differently in every part of the world, and yet, here we are, able to work together on a project.

"Look," he says in awe, pointing to the harbor, which is frozen in certain places. "It's almost below zero and people are still walking around and shopping. Winter doesn't shut anyone down in this place. Not like home, huh?"

I shake my head. While my dad is thinking about weather, I'm thinking about how Helsinki's harbor reminds me of Seattle, Shanghai and Tunis. All of them are settled on the sea. What's up with me and ports? Maybe it's comforting knowing there is always a way in and a way out of a city, like my mind is always planning an escape route.

We walk back to the square, grabbing our luggage from the van when a flurry of frequencies stops me in my tracks. I trace it to a group of men standing near two cars. They must have just arrived and someone from Geneva is among them.

There's more than the usual electrical energy coming from them—at least I think so. I can't be sure because of interference from the weather.

"You coming?" my father asks.

My body stiffens, and an acute focus takes over. "Dad, give me a minute."

I crank my head until numbers shoot out in all directions, mapping out each person and angle. On the north side of the Lion Block six men dressed in thick coats, too thick for their stature, linger as if on patrol. I might be paranoid, but could they be carrying weapons under those jackets? Everything about their behavior is wrong. On the east side of the square, four parked cars don't have Finnish license plates. On the west side of the block by Helsinki University, three people stand around outside of a windowless van. Heading south toward a back alley, five more people in similar winter gear post themselves around the building. This block is surrounded. I know what that means. Whoever is in charge doesn't want their plan to fail.

Maybe what I'm picking up on is just security for the ISC Banquet or extra cautious tycoons with bodyguards, or just plain low-life criminals you'd find in any big city. But the arrangement of each out-of-place group feels too strategic, like

I'm walking into a trap. If they're Cesare's shady comrades attending the banquet, I need to know.

I focus on the men getting out of two black town cars. They walk toward a closed shack in the square. Soon the other groups surrounding the square begin to gather there too. I've definitely felt their presence before, but thankfully, they can't pick up frequencies like I can. They don't know I'm here. Likewise, I'm only concerned with one of the frequencies: a person talking into a phone behind the small shack—the black-haired man from the Summit in Geneva.

I march forward, heart pounding, while Tank and Miles trail a few feet behind me. A countdown begins as I cross the cobblestone street to the closed shack with letters spelling out *kioski* on the side of it.

Time to see who's holding the leash.

CHAPTER 19

∞

SENATE SQUARE
HELSINKI, FINLAND

Before I make it ten meters, I'm intercepted like a would-be touchdown pass in a football game. A man I suspected we'd run into is standing right in front of me, blocking me from reaching the *kioski.* His outstretched arms stop me, like a bar across my chest. My father and bodyguards are close behind me.

"Believe me," he says. "That's not the direction you want to go. Especially alone."

I push his hands off me. "Agent Ramos," I say, irritated, "you're in Helsinki. What a surprise." My eyes flit to the *kioski.* The men are now walking away, my chance gone.

Agent Ramos stands back, giving me room. "I'd say the same, but I already saw your team slip in last night. Weren't you supposed to be finding the NASA Tipper? What brings you here?"

"A banquet." My numbers drill into his eyes, which are brimming with secrets. He squirms like he's under a hot light. Most people do when my numbers intrude like this. "I couldn't miss the event of the century, could I?"

Agent Ramos laughs. "Funny. I didn't want to miss the banquet either, but they were out of tickets. I see you managed a way." He motions to my dad, who stands by, surely freezing as the temperature drops. Agent Ramos greets him, and escorts us toward the building where the car is parked.

"So if the banquet is important to the DIA," I say, "I assume you know more than what the International Space Collaboration engineers told us."

He smiles smugly. "Naturally. It's my job to know more. But it's classified. What I tell you is on a need-to-know basis." He looks at me. "But I have a feeling you know more too."

"I gather information through mathematical deduction," I point out. "You know more because Agent Bai tells you. Thanks for the job to find the NASA Tipper, by the way."

His lips quirk up. "Bai's a peer. He and I also work on a need-to-know basis. This is need-to-know. The NASA Tipper is a wanted man." He cracks his neck. "But I'm confident you'll find him. Just like I'm confident you already know his name and where he is."

"Even if I find him, that won't be enough, will it?" I ask.

"Does that mean you're finally ready to activate the PSS Special Cases Unit?" he asks. "Anything to do with NASA's security is a US government priority, which means DIA jurisdiction."

As a rule, no matter what is going on in my head, I keep my mouth closed and listen to all sides. Red used to say it was a simple way to prevent looking like a fool. Besides, Agent Ramos knows my position on partnering with the Defense Intelligence Agency.

"Don't get excited," he says to reduce the sizzling tension. "I've already bumped into Ms. Taylor. They're expecting us. And for those not keen on the DIA, I may have found a loophole for you to operate as PSS while assisting us on this assignment."

Loopholes can be handy.

"Ok, then I need your intel on Cesare di Susa and Scale Tech," I say, testing the waters.

"Wow," says Agent Ramos. "You kids do know a lot."

"Naturally, it's our job," I say, mimicking him.

"I suppose if we're going to work together, I'll need to brief you and the team." He eyes me seriously. "Let's meet in the Empire Room in the Lion Block 20 minutes before the banquet. There's a lot more you need to know."

CHAPTER 20

∞

SISU DEN
SOFIANKATU STREET, HELSINKI

A Finnish host with dark brown hair waits for us at a tall gate leading into an inner complex attached to luxury apartments. Ms. T arranged to rent a private flat, called *Sisu Den*, for the team. Apparently *sisu* means a special inner strength or resilience in the face of adversity. Ms. T liked the sound of it. Plus, numerous famous musicians have stayed here, and the owners are savvy with the security requests that Ms. T requires. Conveniently, the Lion Block and Helsinki University are also just across the square.

"*Paivää. Tervetuloa.* Welcome," our host says. "I hope you brought warm clothes. This is the coldest winter we have had in 50 years."

As the door to the building swings open, heat sweeps over us and there is a collective sigh of appreciation. Tank walks in front of me while the other two bodyguards, Miles and Alex, hover so close behind me it's suffocating.

"Guys, ease up a bit?" I unintentionally snap.

"Sorry, Ms. Rivers," Miles says, unapologetically. "Just

doing our job."

"This is one of the most secure countries in the world," I point out, "and we've done our homework on this apartment and the Lion Block. It's the safest place to stay in Helsinki. Especially this week, when security is high around Senate Square."

Even though I'm sure the team has swept this place for every kind of bug, I want to do my own calculations, inspect each hallway, and home in on any frequencies, but my bodyguards bumping into me keep interfering. I sigh. I'm so tired of these new bodyguards trailing my every move. The kind of bodyguard I really want is one who takes time to study me, to know who I am, which is sort of impossible at the moment. And if I want to keep doing this job, which I do, bodyguards are what I've signed up for.

Thankfully, Ms. T agreed that I didn't have to bring a bodyguard to the Arctic with me. Just my father will accompany me. Noble wouldn't appreciate someone he didn't know or trust showing up on his doorstep. I'm betting he'll make an exception for my dad.

As we enter *Sisu Den*, the private apartment proves to be a comfortable base. Six large bedrooms, two common living rooms, 3 bathrooms, and lots of windows overlooking the square. There is even a *villasukat* gift basket with an assortment of colorful woolen socks all nicely wrapped.

PSS Tech is already set up in the living room and I recognize my team's belongings on the couches.

As I wander back to a spare bedroom, a floral, earthy scent tickles my nose. On the dresser sits a vase of purple orchids. A flicker of heat tiptoes through me. Apart from my dad, Kai is the only boy who ever gave me flowers.

I move away from the purple blossoms and set my stuff down. After my dad and I freshen up and change clothes, we head back out into the hall where our bodyguards wait to escort us to the Empire Room in the Lion Block.

A clerk meets us in the entry and leads us down hallways. Inside the Lion Block, the rooms reflect an Empire style era. The beauty of the 1800 and 1900s is seen in every sparkling chandelier, the ten-foot tall windows draped in expensive linens, and vaulted ceilings with beautiful white crown molding. The antique charm doesn't cancel out the massive electrical buzz everywhere. From what I sense, the building is wired with high-end tech and security systems.

As we enter the Empire Room, the luxury goes up a notch—gold-framed mirrors, large paintings, candelabras on the walls, fireplaces with intricate moldings, and a long table where the team is gathered.

Ms. T is speaking with a blonde-haired woman privately in the corner. My dad wanders over to her, while I head to the table.

Tech is sprawled across its surface. The prods have brought our regular gear plus a lot of extra nano-surveillance tech.

"Hey." They turn toward my voice, and gasp. I flip my blonde hair with straight bangs. The clothing I'm wearing is far from what I'd choose. But I'm not Jo right now. I'm Mila Avola.

Harrison does a double take. "Whoa. Your hair and make-up—I barely recognized you."

"You made it," Eddie stands to greet me. "How are you feeling?"

He's referring to Noble. "Ready to see him." I breathe in.

Harrison waves his hand at me to sit down. "We're doing recon on Finland. Join us." Harrison's idea of recon on a new city is spouting off random facts that usually don't help us, but everyone likes it. I listen, too. I haven't had time for K2 to give me a run down.

"Apparently Finland is famous for being the happiest country in the world. Also, it has a nickname, "The Country of a

Thousand Lakes" —187,888 of them to be exact." Harrison gives me a wink. "It's also known for its excellent education system, super clean air, having more saunas than cars, Santa and a heck-ton of reindeer. It's also the birthplace of Nokia, which was a pioneer in technology far ahead of Microsoft back in the day, which is why Microsoft bought it out." He flips through his presentation.

"Get this." Harrison laughs. "Helsinki's SkyWheel is the first Ferris wheel ever to have a sauna as one of its cabins. Fits five people—should we do it?"

"We definitely need to try that sauna," Pens says. Felicia agrees.

I snap my head over to them. "Maybe after we help the ISC?" I say. "So, what do you know about Lapland?"

"Let's see." Harrison scrolls through a few pages. "A quarter of Finland is in the Arctic circle. In summer, Lapland has 73 consecutive nights where the sun doesn't set, and in winter the sun doesn't *rise* for 51 days. They call it *the polar night.* Almost two months of darkness. What a trip on your mind." He rubs his arms like he's cold. "You ready for that, Jo?"

"Ready or not, I'm going," I say, but I shiver just thinking about it. By tomorrow morning, I'll be in the most freezing, remote, and dark place I've ever been. Noble likes remote places so that he's not easily detected. Maybe that's why Scale Tech has their Space Lab based there. It would be largely off the radar, isolated and away from prying eyes.

"We've got an hour until the banquet," I say. "Agent Ramos is on his way right now. Anything we need to go over before he gets here?"

"Yeah. Our pesky tail is in Helsinki," Felicia says. Everyone groans.

"Oh, no. Ms. Mines?" I ask, my face puckering.

"She's outside," Eddie says. "No ticket to the banquet, but she's prowling the halls with other journalists. We have to be really careful she doesn't see us." He points to the PSS team and Ms. T.

"That's why we set up the lecture to be at the same time as the banquet," says Felicia. "Jo, you have to make an appearance at the lecture for our diversion to work. Just five, ten minutes; we get your face up on the panel, then you can return to the banquet. Conveniently, the university is right across the street."

"Got it. The banquet will be several hours long, with three distinct segments, basically appetizers and mingling, dinner, and dessert. It should be no problem to sneak out for a bit." I'm about to mention the frequencies surrounding the buildings when Agent Ramos walks in, calling me to the door. "Apparently, you came with a backup plan, Jo. And that back up plan is here." His eyes tell me he's impressed.

A split second later K2 alerts me that my guest is in the hall. Deep emotion rises in my throat. I stand up, and walk toward the door.

The PSS team follows me outside where a powerhouse of a man moves toward me. His stride is confident, never in a hurry, always aware of his surroundings. Perhaps that's where his son gets it.

A flood of memories skips through my mind: heated discussions; battles for trust and growth; economic spirals and super bonds, chess pawns and gangsters. Now his face reminds me of another home. He's a man I respect, even consider family. After months, I get to see him face to face, and the racing of emotion in my chest proves how overwhelming this moment is. For me, this man was an integral part of gaining my freedom, even if he was stubborn about it at first.

Harrison is easily star-struck and he instantly loses his composure. His mouth drops and he blurts out, "No way! Double score for PSS this week. I...I..." Harrison shakes his head incredibly. He's always been a groupie. "You invited Asia's leading billionaire to Helsinki for our super-undercover job?"

Everyone gawks. Apparently my guest was not who they were expecting.

I walk toward the man, who no longer has a flower in his lapel, but a ring on his finger and a sparkle in his eye. Similar to my dad, he's all vitality and sunshine since Dr. Ling came into his life.

Chan ignores Harrison, ignores my blonde hair, and comes up to me. Our eyes meet, and a million moments pass through us as we give each other a smile that has been built through fire.

"*Hao jiu bu jian.* Long time no see, Little Phoenix."

After months of long-distance calls, I didn't realize how much I missed him, how good it would be to see him. In some ways, he was almost another father to me. "It's good to see you, too, Chan."

CHAPTER 21

∞

Chan and I have both changed so much, but one thing hasn't: he and I are not huggers. But for some reason, we do it anyway. It's not as awkward as I expect.

Chan clears his throat and the softness in his gaze soon morphs into his usual business self. But underneath it, I know the truth. After hours of conversation on the phone, we understand each other in a new way. Kai's absence still hangs between us, but we've promised each other to believe in his job and in him even while he's gone.

He still uses the name that Red gave me, with my permission. In Mandarin, the "little" is not patronizing but simply implies that I'm younger than he is and that we are close enough to use friendly titles rather than professional ones.

My dad walks up, hand outstretched. "Nice to see you again, Mr. Chan."

"Ah, Mr. Rivers. Good to see you." Chan says, firmly gripping his hand. He glances at the bandage on his nose. "What happened?"

My dad looks at me, and back to Chan. I gulp and look away. Mr. Chan, on the other hand, touches his own nose—that I broke once—and waves his hand in the air, dismissing the question. "No need to explain."

My face reddens.

Chan clears his throat, then glances around the room. After the superbond secured his place as the richest man in Asia for years to come, he's been deemed a hero. More importantly, Chan knows what I can do.

Now, seeing Chan and my father by my side makes my numbers do flips. It also begins to worry me. "Did anyone see you come in?" I ask.

"No. I was escorted through a side entrance. But I can't promise they won't publicize my presence at the ISC Banquet."

I nod. Chan, too, has become braver. With Dr. Ling's new practice in Shanghai up and running, the safe house has helped countless trafficked women get back on their feet. They've become quite the team.

Chan turns his attention to the PSS team who are staring at him from the other side of the meeting room. "Is this the A-team you have told me so much about?" he asks.

I glance over at them and inwardly groan. Harrison is smiling wide, fidgeting, dying for an introduction. Pens, who doesn't know we're looking at her now, is taking selfies with Chan in the background. Felicia gives him an awkward bow that is more Korean than Chinese. Eddie is practically standing at attention as if Chan is the Chinese president. On top of that, they're all just gawking at him like groupies at a rockstar. "Yep. That's them."

Chan gets down to business. "What do I need to know?"

"A lot. First off, I should warn you—I've got a new name. You have to call me Mila this week."

"Why am I not surprised?" he grunts and turns to Harrison who is bouncing up to him like a kid approaching Superman.

"Sir, it's an honor to meet you. You're a powerhouse in the business world and it was incredible what you did with Asia Bank and the economy. You're a rock star. I mean, you're brilliant."

"Thank you," Chan says, modestly. "Nice to meet you."

"I know your son, Kai, too," Harrison continues. "When he came to Seattle, he taught me a little kung fu." Harrison beams, punching his hands in the air.

"Did he? That's nice." Chan's face falls slightly. I understand his thoughts. Always missing Kai, always wondering if he's alive. Chan gives his attention to Ms. T. "You must be Ms. Taylor. *Jiuyang, xinghui*, a pleasure to meet you."

"Likewise. Thank you for coming. Please have a seat. We were just about to begin." Ms. T moves to the head of the table, calling to the team. "Security please. We're on a clock."

Eddie sweeps the room with *Scatter*—a new tech that throws off any electrical frequency that isn't ours. Thanks to my strange ability, we came up with new ways to scatter frequencies like throwing a pile of gravel into the water—the ultimate bug scrambler. In the Bardo when I asked Noble how he scrambled his tech, it all came down to frequencies. I figured out how to create my own a few weeks after getting my gift back.

"We're clean." Eddie sits.

Agent Ramos catches my eye. "As you know, we're investigating the possibility that the recent blackouts and the satellites going offline aren't just a result of geomagnetic storms." He pauses. "But we have no proof. What we do know is that a whole bunch of players who are on our radar are in Helsinki now and will be inside the ISC Banquet—including former members of organized crime syndicates. Whatever is going on, the ISC seems to be in the middle of it." His eyes narrow on me. "Our first goal is to ensure the safety and success of the ISC launch, which is in two days. Our second goal is to root out what or who is behind the blackouts."

"So what's the game plan for the banquet?" I ask.

"Our two strongest leads lie with Scale Tech CEO, Dr. Juho

Salonen and Palermo Ricci. Dr. Salonen helped build the ISC Super Satellite, then stepped away from the public because of his wife's coma. Mr. Ricci has been aggressively trying to take control of Scale Tech. Palermo Ricci has a track record of ruthless corporate takeovers. If companies don't want to work with him, he buries them financially."

Harrison and I exchange glances.

"If Palermo has an interest in this launch beyond advancing science for the good of humanity, we need to know why," Agent Ramos sighs. "All cards on the table, there are billions of dollars at stake and if the mafia is involved, they'll do whatever it takes for the opportunity to cash in. We have intel that Palermo is arranging a private meeting tomorrow morning with some of the biggest players at the banquet. Only very special, very powerful people get invited into Palermo's meetings. We don't have any names. This may be our one chance to uncover his web and any potential threats. Unfortunately, our guys have been unsuccessful at getting a foot in the door. Now that we know you two are here," he motions to Chan and my dad, "we may have a chance of getting inside that meeting. But it's still risky."

My father scratches his chin as he once did in meetings. But Chan considers the situation with a straight face. He casts a sideways glance at me. "As Jo's former boss, I learned a valuable lesson. Life is too short not to do all we can to help people." He locks eyes with Agent Ramos. "I can get into the meeting." Chan's eyes dart to me again. "I've also come prepared. After speaking with my *advisor*, I had a sudden urge to invest in Scale Tech and several other space and tele-communication companies. I've seen enough greed to know what it looks like. With these people, only money will talk."

Chan's words fill me with pride. If only Kai could hear him talk like this. Chan is living proof that if we keep our feet planted on a path that honors truth, and keep doing what we know is right, the world can actually change.

And I'm glad he got my message about the stocks—another small backup plan.

My dad's face tightens. "I'm with Chan. I'll do what I can."

"You're both forgetting that I will be in the room. You guys are my cover. I don't want you getting too involved," I say. "And if I can find Cesare Di Susa, he just may have the information we need."

"Ok," Agent Ramos says, checking his watch. "I know you're all working together, but I advise you to enter the banquet and operate separately." He looks primarily at me.

Chan rises from his chair, his eye on the door. Harrison moves in quickly. "Not so fast, Mr. Chan. We have to tech you up!"

CHAPTER 22

∞

Eddie strides over to Chan. "Our team is going to outfit you with the most sophisticated surveillance tech on the planet. There is almost zero chance that anyone will be able to detect what we're putting in you."

"*In* me?" Chan asks, horrified. "I thought I'd be wearing a wire or something."

"That's old school. No one does that anymore," Eddie says. "This is micro-tech that will fit into your ear and eyes. It blends with the human body temperature and the frequency coming from you. It's nearly impossible to detect, unless you're Jo."

Chan glances up at Eddie with a look of utter amazement but shoots a concerned glance at me.

"It's totally safe," I confirm. "You won't even know it's there. It's mostly just for our team to follow what you're seeing and hearing. If you don't mind."

"*Hao.*" He sits up straighter. "Eh. I've agreed to this, so go ahead." As they fiddle with the tech, Chan leans over to my dad, who is getting the same treatment. "Never thought I'd see the day where I go undercover. *Huo dao lao, xue dao lao.* Live until you're old, learn until you're old. Who says old dogs can't learn new tricks?" He laughs softly. "What would Kai say if he saw me now?" He shakes his head at me.

My dad raises his eyebrows at Chan. "Hey. I'm in the same boat, Chan. There's always room for firsts. Jo claims we're her cover, that she'll do all the work. What do you think? Can we believe her?"

"Believe her? Not sure. Do I trust her?" He looks over at me. "Yes."

"Trusting me will cost you," I say back with a sly smile.

"It already has. I've been trading stocks all night because of one of your *theories.*"

"Then let's hope my intuition is right. You might even make a buck or two in the end, and you can reserve your first trip to space."

He laughs. "*Hao de.* I expected no less." He sits up straight, that solid determination pulsing out of him. "With you, I never know what I'm going to get. I once obtained a global shipping company, and now space technology and satellites." He grows serious for a moment. "It's ok even if I lose money, Little Phoenix. I have peace."

Once Chan is teched-up, he checks his watch then straightens and becomes the hard-hitting businessman I worked for in Shanghai. The one who always knows exactly what he is doing. The one his son watched and got his confidence from. "Ready, Jason and Mila?"

We both nod.

Every path has led me here. To Finland and this crisis. To where Noble is hiding. Now it's time to find out why.

Finally, we're all ready. I feel as if I've stepped into an alternate universe as I look at the two men in front of me. I can't believe it—I'm going undercover with Chan Huang Long and my dad.

CHAPTER 23

∞

BANQUET HALL, THE LION BLOCK
HELSINKI, FINLAND

Time to mingle with the mafia.

I apply bold red to my lips to match my red gown before walking down the corridor, ever aware of the tech vibrating with unseen frequencies off my body. At the entrance, a host in black attire opens the door, and I enter.

The opulent banquet hall is nothing short of magic. Elaborately decorated tables are lined with Finnish delicacies. Baltic herring seasoned with mustard. Smoked pike with Finnish malt bread and fresh pickled cucumbers. Plates of reindeer and salmon and fancy cheeses with cloudberries.

On another table there are fine wines in abundance. Men in tuxedos clink gold-rimmed glasses with women in evening gowns standing around tall cocktail tables. Miniature ice sculptures decorate every table, but the most impressive of all are the enormous ice sculptures chiseled into rockets and satellites adorning the dinner section of the spacious hall.

My calculations produce a detailed accounting of the room—twelve security cameras sweep the room from the ceiling, 8 exits, 16 guards, 25 tables, 120 people and 108 pathways. Nineteen new pairs of feet shuffle through the door, and my numbers recalibrate.

At the creak of a door, the air shifts. My body suddenly feels hot and thirsty, like I've been lost in the desert and parched for months. As if I'm near water but I'm not allowed to drink. *The phantom frequency is here.* I filter out everything around me and try to capture the equation that is faster than light. But as usual, it boomerangs through the room, then vanishes before I can blink.

With the guest list in my head, I study the room and divide everyone into three categories: experts from space agencies around the world, elite businessmen and investors, and finally, the slimeballs who move around the room like sharks. My gift highlights them with surprising ease. I'm not sure if that's something I should be proud of or not.

My job should be easy. All I need to do is ask a few slimeballs if they know anything about Cesare, while Chan and my dad schmooze with Mr. Ricci and Dr. Salonen. I haven't seen Palermo Ricci yet, but the crowd is thicker toward the back of the room, and clustered in different corners. I spot a man oozing with jitters and suspicion, easy prey. I'm about to make my move when a woman chatting behind me drops two words that steal my attention: *NASA Tipper.*

I turn. Standing by the drink table is Dr. Kaisa Ranta, a Finnish scientist I recognize from the guest list who is also on the ISC committee. I decide to approach non-mafia first. I wander over and introduce myself to the group of ladies.

"Dr. Ranta," I say, in a flimsy Italian accent. "I'm Mila Avola. I'm a huge fan of your work."

"Thank you, Ms. Avola. Welcome to Helsinki." Her Finnish accent is soft and disarming. "And what do you do?"

"I'm an optical engineer, working in both the US and China." I'm careful not to flinch at my own words. Of course,

I'm not an expert but thanks to researching Noble's code I may have enough knowledge to bluff my way through this banquet. "I heard you mention the NASA Tipper. Is everyone here familiar with him?"

"Of course. Who isn't? I'm guessing everyone in this room has offered him jobs, money, who knows what else?" She leans in as if to share a secret. "I don't mean to boast, but the NASA Tipper has shared quite a few revolutionary tips with Finland's own Scale Tech. We must be a favorite of his. It would be a pity to find out he's a criminal." She greets people left and right as they pass. I fight a frown. To her, Noble is just a novelty.

"He's more enigma than criminal," I say using my fake accent. I'm about to ask when they last heard from him when Harrison whispers in my ear. "*Stop talking about Noble and find Cesare. We're leaving now for the lecture. Meet you there.*"

"Nice meeting you. Excuse me for a moment."

I navigate the crowd like a mathematical dance, eavesdropping and assessing until I'm close to five of the slimeballs in fancy suits and my gift singles out one of them.

Grabbing a flute of sparkling water, I wander over to one of them and introduce myself in a sickly sweet voice that Madame would approve of. "And you are?"

The man gives me a stern three-second examination from head to toe, then replies. "Matteo Bianco." He flinches, his pupils also dilate. He's lying. That's not his real name, so I'll just cut to the chase.

"*Ah, Italiano?* Just my luck, you're Italian," I say, eager to drop my bait and see his response. "Are you acquainted with Cesare di Susa by any chance? I've been looking for him. He's an old friend."

The man's face pales like a ghost has walked into the room. Then he shakes his head nervously. "The name doesn't ring a bell. *Scusa.*" He scurries to another part of the room. This is why I'm glad numbers are on my side. There's a 98% chance he knows exactly who Cesare is and his unwillingness to admit it strengthens our theory.

I approach slimeball number two, who has remarkably green eyes, and initiate several minutes of excruciating small talk on the Italian Space Agency. He too is bluffing his way through this night. So not wasting another minute, I drop the name. "Cesare Di Susa must be around here somewhere. He's very involved with Scale Tech, and I'm very interested in speaking with him."

The green-eyed man's body goes rigid, his eyes narrow, a flicker of discomfort inside them. "Sounds like someone I'd like to meet too," he growls. "Let me know if you find him." My numbers go crazy as he walks away. He, too, knows exactly who Cesare is. If my calculations are correct, he hasn't seen him possibly for years, but he wants to. He joins the other men, and whatever he says makes them turn their attention to me. Their hounding eyes send shivers down my back. But my calculations are clear—they won't do anything while I'm in this room; and asking the rest of them isn't worth my time. No one will talk. Which means, Palermo Ricci is my next option.

Using K2, I scan nametags and faces as I walk around the room. K2 spouts off information about each guest, including degrees in astrophysics, aerospace dynamics, optical physics, sonic-tech, and engineering of every sort. I've never seen so many geniuses in one room. Conversations about the Super Satellite Launch and blackouts abound.

I'm whirring with the desire to absorb everything. If Noble chose not to hide under a rock, he could be here now in this room. Not only would he fit in perfectly, he'd blow everyone away with what he's discovered.

Finally, I head back to Dr. Ranta for some help. "Are you associated with anyone who works for Scale Tech? Or Palermo Ricci, perhaps?" I ask her.

"Why, yes," she says, picking up on my hint. "There are

several people here who used to work for both."

Dr. Ranta leads me to an Asian woman in a form-fitting black and gold gown. "Dr. Hitomi, this is Ms. Avola, an expert in optics. Dr. Hitomi used to work for Scale Tech."

The Japanese engineer greets me. "Hello. How can I help you?"

"My associates and I are very interested in Scale Tech's future projects," I say. I would name drop Cesare in this conversation, but I can already tell it's a dead end. Every number tells me she knows nothing. I ask a few polite questions about Scale Tech and she gives me cookie-cutter answers. What I really need is an introduction to Mr. Ricci.

While she talks, a man in the far back corner catches my attention. His back is facing me and he's surrounded with too many people for my numbers to assess him properly, but frequencies shoot like arrows from him in a way I've never seen before. Is he also loaded up with tech that's emitting intense electrical signals?

I check K2—there's not much time before I have to sneak out to the lecture. I turn to Dr. Hitomi and bluntly ask, "Is Palermo Ricci here? If so, I'd love an introduction."

Ms. T told me to stay away from Palermo, but in every crisis, there's an opportunity. My numbers led me here for a reason. I won't make the same mistake I did in Geneva.

Dr. Hitomi frowns. "I just heard that Mr. Ricci won't arrive until the dinner segment of the banquet." I almost admit defeat until her face brightens. "But you're in luck. Mr. Ricci's assistant is right over there." She points to the man surrounded by people. Frequencies are beaming from him.

Bingo. Palermo's assistant. I smile at her and lay on a thick accent. "I'd love to meet him."

As we make our way to the back of the room, a warm sensation comes over me. The closer I get to the other side of the banquet hall, the more I feel I'm playing the children's game, *Hot and Cold.* I'm getting warmer with each step.

Dr. Hitomi stops to apply more lip-gloss, then pulls her mouth into a smile. As for me, I transform into Phoenix, a boldness coming over me. No matter what, I'll pull answers from this man.

"Just met him today," Dr. Hitomi says, excitedly. "He's brilliant and charming. Most companies come to boast of their own projects, but not him. He's very interested in everyone else's latest developments."

Or maybe he has an agenda—like I do. But I nod to her. "A true team player. Wonderful."

We slide through the crowd, and my numbers skyrocket, like there's a nuclear bomb in the room. A powerful energy courses all around me. Hundreds of frequencies appear out of nowhere and hit me like an explosion so bright my knees nearly give out until—*zap!* Every frequency in the room goes blurry, leaving only an indistinguishable haze, except for the one in front of me.

I don't know what's happening. My gift just had some major interference. Equations I've locked away resurface. They don't make any sense until the crowd parts and I get my first glimpse of Palermo's assistant.

Dr. Hitomi taps him lightly on the shoulder. "Mr. Ming. There is someone I'd like you to meet." The man turns toward me, controlled, confident. Dr. Hitomi extends her arm to me. "This is Ms. Mila Avola, an expert in optical engineering. She's very interested in Scale Tech and meeting Mr. Ricci. Perhaps you could answer a few questions for her?"

I stop hearing anything. Her words drop to the floor like lead. I try to remain upright—as in control as the man facing me, but I'm completely off balance because every frequency in the room goes silent except for ours. It's like a supernova is exploding into a billion rays of color between us. I always wondered what our frequency would look like, feel like. Now

I know and it nearly rips me apart.

But apparently he's unaffected. There is not one hint of recognition on his face. He acts like he's never seen me before.

"Nice to meet you." There's a nanosecond where he glances at my blonde hair before he stretches out his hand. "Please, call me Asher."

I swallow, my throat dry. I stretch out my hand and heat ignites at our touch, runs down into my heart and threatens to electrify my entire body. In this moment, his name might be Asher, like mine is Mila. But everything else is orchids and motorcycles and fights and poems. Can he feel it? The energy surging in the room?

Plan A might not work. Because Palermo's right-hand man is Kai.

CHAPTER 24

∞

To say this is unexpected is an understatement.

I should have guessed, but whenever I think of Kai going undercover, my mind always goes to thugs, underground crime, the Madams and coups of the world. I never envisioned Kai assigned to a business office like his dad's. It makes sense though. The billionaire's son with multiple degrees and languages under his belt was never just a pretty face who could fight. Kai was always smart, trading stocks at age 12. He was logical, at the top of his class in math and science, and he already had years of experience working for his dad. Of course they chose him for this job. But what exactly is his assignment as Palermo's assistant? If he's undercover here, what does that say about Palermo? Is Kai at the banquet for the same reasons we are?

I swallow down my shock and force a response. "Nice to meet you." My voice is sweet, but not my own. My heart is pounding. So I carry my accent even stronger.

Kai stands before me now and all I can do is stare. *Dang it.* I was prepared to walk into this room and nail every single person down in a heartbeat. But then one heartbeat changed it all.

The touch of his hand in mine is so familiar, so safe that I don't want to pull it away. But he does. Not only does he pull it away, but he shakes off his hand like it's dirty now. He even backs up a step, gauging me like he would an enemy. I flush with heat, and an echoing vacancy spreads through me like a disease. Once again, I'm speechless.

Kai smiles rigidly, taking control of the conversation. "Did you say your name was Mila, as in *1000* in Italian?" he asks. "Clever name. The *person* who named you must be very close to you." His tone is sharp and unfamiliar, as if he's wearing his voice like a mask.

Kai knows the story of how I got the name Mila. He's met Rafael. He's toying with me, fishing for why I'm here. Why else would I use this name? Does he know where Rafael is? Judging by his numbers, I'd say yes. Which means, I need to find out why Kai is here. Despite my feelings, two can play at this game.

I ignore the needles in my heart and give him a tight smile. "Thank you. I have a colorful past and my name fits that. Sadly, the person who named me is not nearly as close as I want him to be, but I hope to change that." The shake in my voice hardens, while his eyes twitch slightly. It bothers Kai that I'm looking for Rafael, but he sighs like he's bored with me. But there's nothing boring about this conversation. Palermo is Rafael's family, and Kai has every answer I need. "You obviously speak some Italian. Is that because you work with Mr. Ricci? Is he a good boss?"

I dig into his eyes for answers, but Kai ignores my indirect question about Palermo.

"I'm well-traveled," Kai says, "and yes, I've recently spent time in Italy for work. I don't recommend it this time of year. Nor would I recommend staying in Finland for too long. It's far too cold. You strike me as the type who'd enjoy a drier, warmer environment, perhaps like the *Sahara*." His tone drops an octave. My face flushes. "Now, was there something else you wanted to ask me? If so, please do. I'm quite busy."

I nearly choke. Dr. Hitomi seems utterly confused by our exchange. So am I. But this is Kai. I can cut to the chase, let him know what I'm after. Surely, he'll help if he can.

"I want to know more about Palermo Ricci's interest in buying Scale Tech," I say, bluntly. "There are certain investors I represent who seek an audience with him. I'm also looking for a Scale Tech shareholder who I believe is related to Mr. Ricci." Kai blinks twice, clearly understanding each message I'm trying to convey.

"Ms. Avola," he says, politely but with that same cold tone. "We don't discuss our business plans so openly. Especially with people we don't know or *trust*."

The word *trust* is an arrow directed at me, and it stings. My stomach drops into my feet, but I stand taller despite the sinking feeling.

"Of course not. But we may share mutual goals," I say, appealing to him. He must know I'm here for a common purpose. "Perhaps we could discuss some kind of partnership between our two parties?"

I stare into his face. His dark brown eyes remind me of safety and fearlessness. Like an old habit, I want to put on his numbers like a warm blanket, but for the first time since knowing him, I can't. His body language is like a ten-foot wall I can't climb over. With every word and gesture, it's clear he's operating with a new security system around me—I'm now locked on the outside of what used to be my refuge.

Pain assaults my chest. But I clear my head and reassess the situation. Is Kai doing this because we broke up or because of his job? He's undercover, and we are both surprised at each other's presence. But it doesn't feel that way. In Tunisia, we still communicated. He'd find a way to speak to me. He's clever. But this poker face is one I haven't seen. *November Romeo.* Bai's words come back to me.

Everything about him being a *never return* feels wrong. Like Red being locked in the Pratt, where the world couldn't see him.

"Unfortunately," he says, breaking my gaze, "we don't partner with just anyone. Once we make an alliance, we don't split easily as some are accustomed to. Now, if you'll excuse me, I have other engagements."

His temperature and heart rate are off the charts for Kai. It's like he's in a fight, but he's just standing there staring at me. Someone he loved. Someone who left him without a goodbye just like his nightmares. I've never seen him like this before.

But then his words hit me like an avalanche. *He has other engagements.* I gasp out loud. *His dad is here.* Kai will be livid. His father also won't be able to pretend as I do. If his dad sees him, it'll be game over. I need to let Kai know so he can avoid both Chan and my dad at all costs.

"Asher, please wait," I call after him. The strange name on my tongue tastes wrong. "Maybe you've heard of my boss, Chan Huang Long? He and his US business partner, Jason Rivers from *i*Vision have come to Helsinki for the banquet and the ISC Celebration of the launch. Scale Tech is making quite the buzz, and they are eager to invest. Perhaps we could meet up later to talk more about a potential partnership?"

His face turns a shade of red I've never seen. But he covers it up well.

He dips his head, like I mean nothing to him. "Thank you for your interest, but I'm afraid that isn't possible. This week we have our hands full. It was nice meeting you." His eyes narrow in on mine. An intense anger and hurt radiate from them. The smile on his face, however, continues to be ever charming. How can he do that? How can I not?

"Enjoy the rest of the banquet," he says. "I hope you find whatever it is you're looking for." Kai doesn't waste time. He makes his way through the crowd toward the door. The radiation of his frequency and that weird blurriness fades. Soon all the other frequencies in the room return. I shake my head and breathe.

Dr. Hitomi has witnessed our entire awkward exchange and gawks at me like I'm crazy.

I turn to her, face flushed. "Is he always like that?"

She offers a sympathetic look. "I'm not sure. He was very agreeable earlier," she says, eager to shift the conversation. "Between us, he's very handsome, don't you think? So strong."

"Yes. He's very strong," I say, watching him leave the room. His swagger suggests nothing is wrong at all, while the memory of his touch sends shivers down my arms. "Thank you for your help, Dr. Hitomi. Please excuse me – I have somewhere I need to be."

I head for the door, trying to catch my breath. The boy fighter who loves orchids and poems, who once loved me, is here. But nothing good can come from it.

I've got to find a way to talk with him alone before things get even more complicated. Or worse, we blow each other's cover.

CHAPTER 25

∞

My numbers run on auto-pilot as I walk quickly toward the exit of the Banquet Hall. I can't concentrate. My chest is pounding. I came here to find Noble—not Kai. Running into him wasn't a part of the plan and it's messing with my head. But all the numbers in the room can't cancel his calloused hand pulling away from mine, his dark eyes, so distant and cold. Every shield he had was up, ready for a fight. He guarded himself against me like I was a *threat.*

My calculations try to make sense of it. I didn't think our breakup would result in Kai raising his defenses against me. But every undercover job he does is extremely dangerous, and I'm jeopardizing his cover. Which is why I let him go in the first place. Lives depended on his success—they still do. It was the right choice. But no matter how angry with me he is, I still have to find Cesare and figure out what Palermo Ricci is up to. The ISC is counting on us.

As I pass by a group of cellists and violinists near the exit, I spot Chan talking easily with three men and one woman. If he knew his son was in the building, it would change everything. I can't tell him. Not until I talk to Kai in private. Chan may be a tough business player but there is no way he could control his reaction if he bumped into Kai. In time with the musicians, I tap a 16-8 beat rhythm on my leg. If Agent Ramos knew Kai would be here and didn't tell me, our partnership ends here and now. For me, that is "*need-to-know*" intel.

K2 alerts me of a message: *The lecture is starting soon. Get over here.*

I have 52 minutes until the dinner segment of the banquet begins. It's Eddie's turn to lecture, so all I have to do is show up for the meet and greet across the square at the University. I'll have just enough time to make an appearance and ask a few questions, but it's the last thing I want to do now. I need to talk to Kai before I leave for Lapland, not waste time at a student lecture. But for PSS's sake, I'll ensure our alibi is solid. Besides, I need to tell the team about Kai. I have no doubt that Felicia's hacking skills can help me locate him. If he's smart, he'll seek me out first.

As I head toward the door, Tank follows close behind. Miles is waiting outside with my change of clothes. I follow the numerical map in my head through the crowd, spying on my dad. The hair on my arm sticks up. Of course, he's talking to two of the men my gift highlighted. At least he looks like he's enjoying himself, even if he is talking to *mafiosi*. I sigh. He and Chan will be ok for 30 minutes without me. The room is full of security.

I slip into the hallway but stop abruptly. A familiar frequency accosts me. I grit my teeth. *Ms. Mines.* A crowd of journalists covering the ISC events are standing forty feet away in a roped off area outside the Banquet Hall. Ms. Mines is in a long emerald satin jacket, and I won't be able to pass her in the hall without her spotting me. I groan. Journalists are not allowed in the banquet, but apparently, they're still allowed in the building. Very annoying, but even more of a reason to slip away to the University.

I change course so I'm not in her line of sight. Two tall

Swedish men are drinking at a bar table set up in the hall, and I slide behind them. Tank immediately scans the hall and spots Ms. Mines. Her story-hungry eyes are trained on the Banquet Hall doors. There is no way she won't notice me. She's a journalist who is looking for a story in everything and everyone. But she's not looking for a blonde Josephine with thick-lined bangs and dark makeup. She's never seen me dressed up, but there is a 50% chance that she will recognize me. Not great odds.

A minute passes as I assess the situation. If only she would strike up a conversation with one of the other journalists, we could make our move. But she doesn't.

I'm running out of time when the phantom frequency darts into me and then through the hall, right past her. Immediately, I lean out of my hiding spot for a better view, but then the tall men I've been hiding behind start walking down the hall. My mind sharpens, and all my numbers recalibrate. My odds are now a 53% chance she won't recognize me. I crack my knuckles. Good enough.

"We're going," I say. "Now."

Tank shakes his head. "She'll see you."

"Only a 47% chance," I mumble.

"What?" he asks.

"Nothing." I walk confidently ahead, counting each step, watching her gaze land on the Swedish men, then on Tank and Miles, and finally on me. Tank's grip on my arm tenses as she looks our way. The bodyguards don't break their stride, even though their breathing quickens, and their frequencies intensify.

All I concentrate on is that extra 3% chance she won't recognize me. Because the moment I calculate her gaze on my dress, I know I'm safe. She takes five seconds too long evaluating the four men's faces, which minimizes her time to examine me. Then, she makes a poor choice: her eyes shoot straight to my dress and physique first, leaving less than one second to study my face before I'm past her. It's not enough time to recognize me. I lift my chin, passing her with confidence.

I sense her gaze lingering on my back like tentacles. But she doesn't move. A small victory, but I'll take it.

∞

When we reach the stairs, Tank leads me to the women's powder room. Miles hands me my bag, and I go in and change my clothes.

I slip into knee high boots and pull a thick gray sweater dress over my skinny red one. I put on a huge blue parka, a snowboarding beanie, and thread my arms through a backpack. Hopefully, I look just like a regular student decked out for winter.

I text Harrison. "Walking there now."

We slip out of the Banquet Hall, the crest of the lion glowing in the night. The stairs are scraped clean of snow, but they're still slick. It doesn't take long to realize there's an art to walking on icy ground. The streetlamps are all turned on, light reflecting off the glistening snow. It's so magical, yet here I am, sneaking around Helsinki in disguises.

As we head toward the university, the outdoor stage set up for the Celebration Rocket catches my eye again. The location of the stage doesn't make sense. It's too close to the street. There must be a reason it's set up there. I make a note to ask K2 for details of the square later.

The team and our Finnish contact, Minttu, are waiting for us at the main entrance. She is holding a sign, "Professor Jo Rivers." I wave, twenty feet to go.

She's dressed in a cool wine-colored winter coat, stylish boots and fuzzy hat. For being so bundled up, she looks fabulous. Apparently, our Seattle team knows nothing about winter fashion. She also knows how to maneuver in this snow and ice without slipping and breaking her neck.

"Professor Rivers," she says, smiling. Her accent is very faint, and her enthusiasm is greater than I expected. "The girl who graduated with her PhD at age 15. A huge pleasure to meet you."

"Thank you. Sadly, I'm not that girl anymore." In my mind, the statement refers to all I've gone through, but my goal is for her to associate it with the loss of my mathematical gift, which I announced at a press conference upon my return from China. Not everyone saw the video of my announcement, but there's a 92% chance that anyone who researches my name has seen it. Adding in Minttu's current expression, there's a 96% chance she has too.

Like clockwork, she responds. "We were briefed on your past. I'm sorry you lost such an incredible gift. Thankfully, you still love math and are passionately contributing to the sciences."

I nod, biting my lip. *Passionately contributing to science* is not exactly how I'd phrase the purpose of this trip. But it'll do.

"This way, please," she says, "the lecture will start in twenty minutes."

As she leads me past classrooms, I catch glimpses of student designs hanging on the walls—cutting-edge ideas for lighter rockets and smaller satellites.

As we turn a corner toward the lecture hall, we run into the rest of the PSS team. I pull Felicia, Eddie and Harrison over to the side, out of earshot of Minttu. "We've got a problem." Their eyes widen in question. "Kai is here. *At the banquet.* Undercover!"

"Ouch." Harrison grits his teeth. "Not good."

"On more than one level." I look at Felicia. "I need to locate his position." She nods, and hops on her PSS secure phone.

"Give me ten minutes."

We enter an impressive lecture hall with a neo-classical vibe. Thirty-foot ceilings, windows on all sides, pillars adorning the walls, six gorgeous chandeliers brightening up an already white room, and dark red seats with a capacity of 700 people.

Two students rush over to us as we enter. A tall brown-haired boy with big blue eyes and a girl with dyed red hair and big glasses stand eagerly waiting to be introduced.

"This is Kasperi," Minttu says, pointing to the boy whose dimples appear when he smiles. "He's working on hyperspectral imaging cameras on satellites and is also heavily involved with space robotics. This is Aada. She's finishing her thesis on space technology that could provide tools for mitigating climate change." We all exchange hellos.

Harrison wasn't kidding about this being a unique team. I look at Pens, who has turned to mush. She's practically drooling over Kasperi.

"Wow," Pens says to Kasperi in a breathy voice I've never heard her use before. "You must work on so many things simultaneously. How do you do it?" She bites her lower lip.

"I always have two projects going on at once in my head. I seem to work better like that," says Kasperi. Pens giggles, fidgeting with her hair. "After the lecture, I could show you a few other designs I've been fiddling with?" He smiles wide, and I'm pretty sure Pens has forgotten why we've come to Helsinki.

"Absolutely." Pens follows him to the front row.

I look over at Felicia asking with my eyes if she's found anything. She shakes her head no. I bite down, then smile at our host, playing the part. "We're excited for your team's lecture on the evolution of nanosatellites," I say, and although I won't get a chance to hear it, I am impressed by the research these students are doing.

She smiles. "We feel the same about Edward Joo's research on quantum physics."

"It is one of his favorite subjects," I say, looking over at

Eddie. He's busy speaking with Aada. "Eddie's research is extensive. He's young, but he's an expert in the field."

Minttu leads us to our seats. Finnish students are wandering in and finding seats, too. We review the schedule. The lectures will start in ten minutes. Eddie will speak for 45 minutes, while the rest of the team will continue surveillance. I will slip out while Eddie is speaking and get back to the banquet for dinner and dessert.

Minttu leans over to me. "I must admit, your proposal for an exchange was so unexpected. Is it because the International Space Collaboration is happening this week?"

"In part. Everyone's excited about the Super Satellite launch, but that's not our only reason. We've been impressed with your team for a while," I say repeating Harrison's intel. "Designing your own nanosatellites and launching them into space? That is no small feat."

"Thank you," she says in a polite, soft tone. "We could never have done it without Scale Tech. Our department worked with them closely for years. Unfortunately, after the blackouts started, the partnership with Scale Tech was shut down."

I perk up. "Scale Tech has intrigued me for quite some time. How did such a small Arctic Space Lab focused on Arctic data and weather satellites become so powerful?"

She laughs. "From the outside Scale Tech may appear mundane, but it's anything but small. They have 100 acres of labs, data centers, telescopes and radio towers—all protected with an Infinity Dome."

"A what dome?" I ask, my numbers constructing an image in my head.

"The Infinity Dome is an electromagnetically charged field that acts as their fence over the entire 100 acres. It's totally impenetrable, unbreakable. No way in without permission." She shakes her head proudly. "Finns may be soft spoken, but our designs are not. Certainly not Scale Tech's designs. Even the NASA Tipper has given Dr. Salonen tips." She smiles as she repeats the same information as the scientist from the banquet. "Dr. Salonen believes in mentoring the next generation, which is why our team helped design the dome with his team. We were there the day he turned it on for the first time. To say we were devastated the nanosatellite program ended is an understatement."

One hundred acres of protected labs is a curious thing. "I can imagine," I say, the clock ticking in my head—seven more minutes before the meet and greet is over. "Do you mind if I ask you a few more questions about Scale Tech?"

"Sure," she says. "Ask me anything you'd like."

I smile. Maybe attending this lecture wasn't a waste of my time after all.

CHAPTER 26

∞

SENATE SQUARE
UNIVERSITY OF HELSINKI

Eddie walks out on stage and the lecture begins. The team and I are seated in a row with other professors and students. I sit on the end seat, next to Felicia. In two minutes, I'll need to slip out.

My numbers analyze the auditorium until every person and angle of the room is accounted for. Felicia's ten minutes to locate Kai on any Helsinki CCTV security monitors are nearly up. If she doesn't have any leads, I'll make my move. But for the moment, I'm feeling more optimistic than I have all evening, even if I haven't located Cesare yet. In less than seven minutes together, Minttu spilled a whole bunch of free intel about Scale Tech and Dr. Salonen. The Finnish STEM team has access to Scale Tech's system, which means, if Felicia can hack their department's files with Scale Tech's data, she'll have enough information to hack Scale Tech, which may come in handy.

Apart from sharing information about the Scale Tech's Arctic labs, the University STEM Team will also assist with the Celebration Rocket. Before the blackouts, Dr. Salonen encouraged the ISC to adopt the theme of 'raising up' the next generation as part of the ceremony. If Dr. Salonen wasn't in cahoots with Cesare and Palermo, I may have liked him.

As the lecture starts, my skin warms. The phantom frequency. It's close. I glance out the windows overlooking a dark courtyard. Equations for wavelengths of things unseen spin like a dial faster than the speed of light, and then they vanish. It's so fast that anyone looking would think it was the wind in the tree branches. It reminds me that I need to get back to the banquet.

I lean over to Felicia. "Time's up."

"I found something just now. You'll never believe it. Kai's outside this building. South side, near a parking garage exit." She shows me the map. Tiny shocks erupt all over my body. He found me.

"Thanks," I say, grabbing my hat. "One last task. Find a way into the University STEM department database and trace any files from Scale Tech. We need access to their main systems. I'll meet you guys back at the Lion Block after the banquet." She nods.

I slide out of my seat and slip out from the lecture hall. I get three steps before Tank and Miles are behind me. "Ms. Rivers, you know we have to accompany you back to the Banquet Hall."

"Of course," I say, but my numbers are welling up inside me. I may not have another chance to meet Kai before my father and I leave for the Arctic to find Noble tomorrow morning. This is my chance. But Kai can't be seen with me *and* my two bodyguards. Meeting him at all in public is risky. But that's Kai.

As we walk to the front entrance, I analyze the building. My bodyguards are close behind me. I track the different vibrations around me and filter everything else out. There's movement below me. Cars—at least thirty feet below. Is there a garage below the university? If so, I can sneak out to meet Kai and then get back to the banquet—without tasering my guards.

At the top of a staircase, I stop at the sign with "WC" with a woman in a dress printed on it. It's pointing downstairs. Perfect—a bathroom. If there is a way into the garage, this will not lead to a dead-end.

"Can you wait here?" I ask. "The ladies' room is downstairs. I have to change back into my dress."

Tank and Miles look at the sign, and nod. "Sure thing, Miss Rivers."

I feel bad about what I'm about to do, but I'll text them the moment I'm heading to the banquet to let them know where I am. "Be back soon." I slip down the stairwell.

"K2, I need a way to the garage." My smartwatch responds with a map of the building, and bingo—a path leading down another set of stairs.

I end up in a parking garage with only a few cars. There are signs everywhere that I can't read. Heavily locked doors line the tunnels every 100 feet. My numbers predict the doors lead to even lower levels. I shiver.

"K2, what's going on under this city?" I ask as I move toward the south entrance.

K2 runs a report: "Helsinki, built on granite, has more than 40 kilometers of underground tunnels, garages, malls, walkways and bunkers. Made during a time of war, now remodeled and equipped to hold more than 750 thousand people in case of an emergency."

Forty kilometers of underground tunnels. A dart of panic hits my chest. I've overcome many of the triggers from my previous trauma but going underground is one thing that still trips me up. I need to get above ground soon—but I also have to find Kai, and Felicia said he was somewhere around here.

Before I can move, a stone wall of a man, with a long wool overcoat and a furrowed brow to match is in front of me.

"I thought you were going to change clothes?" Tank says. Miles shows up a second later.

I chuckle. Apparently, my reputation precedes me. I'm about

to explain when a flood of frequencies rushes our way.

Numbers crawl through the enclosed concrete tunnels with a feeling of dread, quickly followed by the tapping of feet. Two men appear, make that four, ok six. These guys are multiplying out of the darkness—and they don't look like good news. Tank and Miles tense up behind me, drawing bandana masks up over their noses.

It's clear this pack of guys in black is heading straight towards us and their frequencies aren't warm and fuzzy.

As they approach, three of the frequencies stand out—one is from Senate Square, where Agent Ramos blocked me from reaching the kioski; the second is one of the slimeballs from the banquet; a third is from Geneva. The other three are new, but they all have one thing in common. *Danger.*

A desire to investigate them pounds like a door that needs to be opened. But now is not the time. I have to find Kai.

Tank gently guides me behind him with a hand that feels as big as a dinner plate. We retreat to the entrance of another tunnel. "Stay right here."

Miles takes another four steps before stopping, creating space between them and us. He has a wide stance, with a posture that clearly states: *You have to get through me first.*

The pack slowly fans out as they approach. They reach under their jackets and pull out retractable batons. With a flick of their wrists the metal sticks extend clicking into place. This isn't going to be pretty. But it's also the perfect time for me to slip away. Tank and Miles will be fine. PSS security doesn't mess around—they will most likely taser, zip tie them, and be done—all without showing their faces.

The exit sign indicates a way out and I quietly speed that direction while Tank and Miles are occupied.

Before the tunnel makes a hard left, I stop dead in my tracks. Another six men clad in the same dark jackets walk swiftly toward my part of the building. I dodge behind a car, carefully studying their faces. My numbers recalibrate, flashing a way out 20 more feet below me through one of the doors leading underground. I shake my head. Underground isn't where I want to go right now. My fingers start tapping furiously.

My mind counts the clap of their shoes, their heights, weights, sizes and other dimensions but that doesn't give me the information I need. I wish they would speak, so I can hear accents, language, the frequency in their voices. But the people coming toward me are silent. They're likely coming to get their car. This is a public place. People come in and out of garages all the time. Except they're dressed like the other six brutes who are all probably unconscious and zip-tied together right now.

I pull my hat low over my head, my jacket zipped up tight. The backpack hugs my shoulders. I look like a local student. Just like my odds of avoiding Ms. Mines, there's a 50% chance they won't recognize me—if they're searching for me. They're expecting to see a girl with her bodyguards.

Then they enter the garage, and my back is to them as I study them in the side mirror of a car. It's my play now. It's either walk right past them or go underground. I decide to risk it. I step out, and head their way, my eyes on the garage exit, moving toward the light. But unlike Ms. Mines, these men are staring at my face, one, two, three—at second four their stare is so intense, I glance up at them. Their eyes go wide. Mine, too. *They know who I am.*

I waste no time in turning around, then bolt into a run down the opposite tunnel.

The vibrations in the air shift as the men jump into action, serious and full of intent. The tilt of their bodies, the momentum they carry confirm that I'm not paranoid this time. They're chasing me.

Whether I like it or not, underground is my only option. I run over to one of the doors and turn the knob. *Locked.* The men now spread out blocking every driveway except one. I keep going.

Leaving behind my bodyguards may not have been a smart

idea after all. If all of these doors are locked, this direction will be a dead-end. My gift usually accounts for that. It rarely leads me into what could be a trap.

I race faster now, trying every door but they're all locked. *Gai-si!* My chances of escaping are narrowing by the second if I don't find an unlocked exit.

My father's fear that I'll be kidnapped again comes roaring to the forefront of my mind. I haven't felt that fear in a long time. It's trying to creep back in right now, but I hold it at bay. My numbers led me down this path—my math brain knows something I don't.

Frequencies bounce off everything. A part of my mind is screaming for help, but there's also a buzz in the air, maybe the phantom frequency? Whatever it is, it settles my nerves enough to drive me forward.

"Saw you at the banquet." One of them shouts. "We just want to talk with you for a minute."

"You got the wrong person," I shout back, sneaking behind another car as we play a game of cat and mouse. "I'm just an ordinary girl."

"Nothing ordinary about you," says a 6'1", 203-pound man in a thick Italian accent.

Twenty-five feet up ahead, there's one last door. The men are closing in on me. I'll be trapped if that door doesn't open. Numbers cover the door like graffiti. What they mean, I don't know. But if I don't risk it, I'm a goner.

I slide along with my back to the wall until a screech comes from the door, and it cracks open. Vibrations of air move below me, a pulsing frequency behind it. *Kai?*

I can't tell for sure, but it's better than sticking around here.

I run and pull open the door. A gloved hand mutes my scream and pulls me further into the underground abyss.

CHAPTER 27

∞

HELSINKI UNDERGROUND TUNNELS

Darkness doesn't have a frequency. But terror does. So does peace. Kai's pulse, the same as in the banquet, permeates the air.

Just as the men reach the door, his strong hands slam the door and lock it tight. I back up against the wall, still catching my breath.

Behind the door everything is pitch black. That's what I'm diving into—not just darkness, but darkness underground. My heart is racing, and I breathe deeply to calm it. I can do this.

Dull lights slowly come on. Kai's familiar frame, even in distorted light and even set on defense-mode, is comforting. He backs ten feet away.

"*Ni le!* Ugh. Where are your bodyguards?" Kai says, not hiding his frustration.

I bite my lip, thinking about Miles and Tank with fists out and zip ties in their pockets. "They had a few loose ends to tie up."

He shakes his head. "Whatever. It's none of my business." Kai's voice hardens. "This way."

We snake through a hallway, and then through another door that leads us once again down a level.

"Where are we going?" I ask.

"Down."

My throat tightens. "If you remember," I say, already choking on the stale air, "underground isn't much my thing."

"It's the safest way out," he says, and marches on.

I stare numbly in his direction and force myself to move—one foot after another, counting every centimeter as I do.

The moment we hit 40 feet below sea level, the musty air triggers me like I'm breathing water. I focus on one breath at a time, but it's no good. Old sounds of the Pratt buzz in my ear, and the panic spikes like a rocket in my chest. I stop, steadying myself on the wall. I just need a minute. Kai is marching forward. *Just move*, I tell myself. But panic isn't a guest you can tell when to come and go. One step at a time. After all, Kai is who I came to see, and he is leading me out.

"How did you know I was in this building?" I ask, trying to quell the shaky panic in my voice.

"Easy. I searched for a STEM lecture program in Helsinki. I was going to signal you when you came out, but when you didn't, and those men went in... Well, I went looking."

"Thanks." The tunnels are narrowing, and so are my thoughts. My breaths shorten. When my gait slows again, Kai stops and turns around, gauging me in the dull light. His eyes squeeze shut. Every muscle in his body is wound up tight, but he fights against it and walks up to me.

He puts his hands on my shoulders. "Look at me," he says. I want to do what he says but by now, I'm spinning. "Jo, look at me." His voice is stronger this time.

I lift my head. My eyes fall into his brown ones. For a moment I'm lost, and that weird explosion of energy happens again. The frequencies, like rapid fire, increase by a hundred percent, erupting like electrical bombs, then blur out completely, leaving the space between us silent except for his heartbeat and mine. I don't break eye contact.

"You're safe, Jo," he says, his voice is strong, but his eyes soften for a split second, a touch of the inner boy behind the tough façade. "This isn't the Pratt. This is how I get you back to the Lion Block. Ok?"

His voice. His heartbeat. His hands on my shoulders. The delusion of the Pratt shatters. My body relaxes and my thoughts clear like clouds burned away in the noonday sun. Back in Shanghai or Seattle, Kai always knew when things triggered my trauma.

Once, I saw a small girl get burned by a sidewalk street vendor. The smell of burnt flesh and her screams triggered me so bad I swore my neck was on fire again. Kai found me hiding behind the pool house, scratching at the scar on my neck. He'd even left work early to find me. He carried me into the Villa and held me until I was ok. Later when I asked him how he knew something was wrong or where to look for me, he shrugged. "I always know when something's wrong with you."

I look at his hands still on my shoulders now. The situation is vastly different from that night in the Villa. It's clearly taking him a lot of effort to touch me.

I nod. "Ok. I'm fine now. Thanks."

He snaps his hands away, and charges forward, leading me down a long exit into a large space. My numbers calculate a huge area much more modern and extensive than the Pratt. We're literally standing in a basketball court. Bunkers and lockers are up ahead. They're using geothermal heat down here.

His low voice sprinkles the air with sound waves and familiar numbers as they crash into me. "Helsinki has extensive tunnels and underground bunkers beneath the city for use in a disaster. They're state of the art, built to last through a war. Not all of them are public. This area is restricted."

I follow Kai in silence wondering how he knew about these tunnels and why. We navigate the passageways back to the Lion Block, passing extensive air and water filtration systems. I marvel. This place takes first prize for ingenuity and design. Like the Finnish STEM Team said, Finland's designs are not shy. If King had known about these underground wonders, he would have traded the Pratt in a heartbeat.

LED motion sensor lights flick on as we pass through. Within a few minutes, we arrive at stairs leading up. We climb them and end up in a private garage.

If my calculations are correct, we're not even 80 meters from the Lion Block, and almost directly under the stage for the Celebration Rocket. Kai turns to face me. He's in a thick, long black jacket and boots. I've never seen him in winter gear, ready for snow. But it has an adverse effect on me. Snow reminds me of Noble. Divisive equations split down my brain, creating even more distance between me and Kai.

We stand in silence for 12 seconds. The oscillations coming off him aren't good either. One part of his frequency is singing between us like a familiar song. The other part fluctuates with enough power to rival my emp-bracelet and necklace combined.

I step toward him.

"Don't come any closer." He holds up his hands. I stop at the warning in his voice. When did I become such a threat to him? Does he have cameras on his body? Either he is being watched or he really doesn't trust me. Numbers don't lie.

"Fine," I say. "Let's talk about the ISC and Palermo."

"You know I can't tell you anything." Kai's voice weaves into 2, 4, 6 unique frequencies before they all fade out again. *What is happening to my gift?* It's distracting.

"If you can't tell me anything, then why did you find me?" I ask.

"First off, to ask you to leave."

Staring at him now, it's obvious how truly angry he is at

me. My goodbye letter comes to mind, and heat flushes my face. "Kai, I'm sorry—"

"Don't start. We're not here to talk about us. That's over. People move on, *Mila*. I get it." His voice is distrusting and cold like an underwater current.

"That's not what happened—"

"Yeah, it's worse." He shakes his head, rubbing his forehead. "You brought my father to Helsinki."

"Someone is trying to sabotage the ISC's Super Satellite," I say.

"I already know that. Right now, I don't care about anything except my father." Kai looks around, then shakes his head. "How could you get him involved in this?" His tone is harsh. "I leave town and you put the last person I care about in danger?"

His words knock the air from me. *The last person I care about...* But he's right. I counted on Kai being far away for three years, so I didn't consider what he'd think.

"I'd never do anything to put your father in harm's way," I say. "The numbers checked out. He's working with us to investigate Scale Tech the same way we did with Global Shipping during the economic crash." I watch his face for any kind of mutual understanding, but he's all nerves. He knows if things go wrong here, anything could happen. Especially if anyone sees Kai and Chan in the same room. "I promise I won't let anything happen to him."

"Your promises... Am I supposed to count on those?" he says, his lips tight. His frequency shoots into me like a hundred balls of fire.

I'm silent, pretending I'm not hurt. Instead, my numbers dig up his pain and collect it like sand in a bottle. What can I say? I broke promises to him. I had to. It was my turn to make a sacrifice for him.

He shakes his head. "What tech do you have on right now?

It's distracting." His hands motion to something around me.

I look down at myself. Nothing is obvious. But I don't hesitate to tell him. "The usual. Plus a bit of emp-taser jewelry." I shake my new bracelet, K2, and pull up my hat to show him my earrings. My necklace with the Squirrel's Chestnut is under too many clothes. "Why?"

He backs up, giving me a confused glance, examining me. "It's obvious you have tech on." He gives me a very odd look. "You'd better fix that if you don't want people to be suspicious, and believe me, people are watching everywhere." He grunts, swinging his hands down. "Do you even know who those guys were?"

"Not exactly," I say, "but they've followed me before."

Kai flinches. "They're a very elite and evolved mafia. There's an all-out war between two sides about to take place."

"Is Scale Tech involved?" I ask.

"Scale Tech is in the middle of it. And so am I unless my cover is blown because our fathers—*and you*—showed up at the banquet."

"I wouldn't have attended if I'd known you were here." His attitude toward me in the banquet clouds my judgment, and my voice hardens. "And if it compromised your mission so much, you didn't have to save me from those men just now."

He snaps his head up. "Yes, I did. You think doing this job can stop who *I am?* I wouldn't let anyone fall into their clutches if I could help it. That's a part of me that will never change." Our eyes connect, and oh boy. This is a Kai I've never seen before. A glimmer of the boy Chan described after his mother died. This goes deeper than hurt. I recognize this emotion—it's betrayal. That's how Kai views me now, like I betrayed him. What Bai said comes ringing to my ears. *There is no honor in leaving him like that.* There are some things my math cannot calculate...like other people's emotions. I had calculated the hurt, just not the betrayal. Guilt sinks its teeth into me.

Maybe I should've talked with him when I stopped our relationship. Instead of freeing him for his destiny, I embodied his greatest fear of me leaving him just like his nightmares foreshadowed I would. One day he'd woken up and I was gone, just like his mother.

The thought of Kai's nightmares makes me want to draw closer to him, but I can't. This is exactly why I chose not to see him after our breakup. It's not fair to Kai. A part of me wants to run to him, talk it out, but then Noble strikes at the back of my mind like lightning, flooding me with memories from childhood to Tunisia that stir a whole new set of desires. I am divided. Bai talked about honor. Well, I couldn't honor Kai while having thoughts of Noble. I can't do it now either.

I step back, even though it's counterintuitive. Kai's mission is his priority. He's made that clear. And my mission is clear too. The ISC is counting on me. I came to find Cesare, Rafael and Noble. And if I can help prevent whatever mafia war Kai is talking about, I will.

Kai checks his watch. "Look *Mila*. I don't have a lot of time. Right now, we need to agree on some things before everything goes horribly wrong." He pauses. "As you probably know, this is far bigger than just Scale Tech and the International Space Collaboration. Palermo is about to show off what he can do in the banquet, and more wealthy, crooked patrons will join his side. I know what you're capable of, so do whatever you came for but get my dad out of this mess immediately. I don't care what Agent Ramos is telling you. Don't let my father go to any private meetings with Palermo. He'll be tagged for life. And he cannot know I'm here until it's over. He won't be able to handle it. As for you, leave as soon as you can." Visible tremors go through him. This undercover job is harder than he thought it would be. Or seeing us is messing with him in a more serious way than I anticipated. Kai was always so resilient. But now...

I fix my eyes on him, numbers pounding out calculations, predictions. On top of that, my internal clock has told me I've already missed half of the dinner segment.

"Did you hear me?" he asks, his stare cold.

I nod. "Yes. I'll get your father out. But we can't leave yet. My dad and I are heading north tomorrow morning. There's something I have to do." If he has any intel about Scale Tech's Arctic Labs, I'll know it by his reaction.

His eyes snap up at me, wild. "North? No." He shakes his head. "That's worse than Helsinki. Don't go. Not this week."

"Sorry. I can't back out of this one," I say, realizing how much more important finding Noble is. All the crossroads point there. The numbers...if I don't go north, I can't guarantee things will work out for this mission.

He groans, his fists tightening. "Right. I forgot who else is up there." His jaw clenches. Whatever he wants to say, he's not saying it.

Heat floods my face. He knows Noble is there? I want to ask how, but I can't. Not now.

Under a clenched jaw, his eyes plead with me. "Listen, you don't need to be involved. Palermo is not what you think. He's much worse."

My numbers whir. Kai is mentioning Palermo, but what about Cesare? I'm about to ask when I sense two frequencies heading this way. I become alert.

"Someone's coming," I say. "Less than 12 seconds before they turn the corner." Out of habit, I step toward him again, but he backs up.

"*Not* within five feet."

"Why?" It's a painful whisper.

His eyes turn glacial. "I don't trust you anymore."

A splash of numbers hits cold and heavy, but his words are ten times worse.

"Get back in the shadows, then take the door on the right.

It'll lead back to the Lion Block."

I retreat into the darkness, and I squeeze through the closing door, just as a guy and girl step into the garage. The guy lingers by the entrance while the girl runs inside the garage. Didn't Kai say this area was restricted? How did they get inside?

"Asher?" A girl's voice, anxious.

"Over here." Kai walks out from in between the cars.

"There you are." The girl is breathless. "You left the banquet. What were you thinking? I was worried when I couldn't find you."

"I'm ok. There was a bit of trouble I had to take care of. But it's *over*," Kai says. "Are we still on schedule?"

"Yes. It's almost ready." The girl slides her arm around his, resting her head on his shoulder. My body goes rigid.

"I can't go back to the banquet," he tells her.

"Why?" she asks. Kai is silent for a moment, considering his plan. She softly pulls on his jacket. "Asher, you can trust me."

Reading Kai's numbers is like second nature to me. I expect calculations that hide his true intentions, like the ones I saw when Kai was undercover with the Successor in Tunisia, but I'm wrong. His body is relaxed, relieved to see her. My hand flies to my mouth as he answers her.

"I do."

CHAPTER 28

∞

BANQUET HALL
THE LION BLOCK

Kai's directions get me back safely to the Lion Block. Not even Ms. Mines is around. But even after I stash my other dress and reapply my make-up to head back into the Banquet Hall, Kai's words are still ringing in my ears.

I don't trust you anymore.

They are the worst words I've heard since Madame told me my father didn't love me. Especially after what Kai said to that girl.

Words have weight, spine, texture and frequency. Red always said that if the wrong words come into our heads, only truth could supplant them. But in this moment, I have no idea what it is I need to hear.

I reenter the Banquet Hall's main dining room with a new focus, juggling what Kai just told me about the mafia wars, Scale Tech and Palermo. It bothers me that Kai didn't give me more information. To make matters worse, Cesare's whereabouts are still a mystery and Palermo will apparently show off what he can do tonight at the banquet. Whatever it is, it can't be good.

Suddenly, the ISC's visit to the PSS office feels far more urgent: if I can't find Noble, I can't be sure the ISC's launch will succeed, and I still have no idea what Kai's role in this is.

It's down to plan B. First get my dad and Chan out of the Banquet Hall as fast as possible before their presence here messes up Kai's cover and blows his operation. Second, find Agent Ramos, and wring his neck.

Where are they?

As my numbers rain down on the room, the remaining mafiosi circling the room are even easier to spot. Only this time, their movements make me pause. Their master is in the room. The black-haired man. Kai would have warned me to get out of the banquet if it was dangerous. But he didn't. He only said Palermo was going to show off his power. Now it's clear. Palermo is the one who holds the leash.

Predictions in my head say I can't stop everything Agent Ramos and I have set in motion—not yet. I ruffle my bangs, hiding my eyes, and let my numbers go to work.

Jason Rivers was supposed to approach Dr. Salonen and Chan Huang Long was going to meet with Palermo Ricci. Chan and my father don't mess around. They've likely made life-long impressions and are up to their necks in negotiations. I grit my teeth, and my fist swings downward. How could I put our fathers in danger like this? Why didn't I leave immediately for the north to find Noble? I should have gone straight there—alone. But then, I remember the path in my head, which led me here. I have to trust that.

Instead of people gathered around tall cocktail tables, they are now seated around circular banquet tables for dinner, admiring the grand ice sculptures while eating. Tank is also back in the room. He's relieved to see me, but that doesn't stop him from giving me a dirty look. I avert my eyes. I'll apologize later.

I weave through the tables, obeying the numbers popping in

my head, which navigate a path for me. A waiter with a sharp angular jaw and broad shoulders approaches me.

"Miss, may I help you find your seat?" he says, his accent floating in the room like music.

"*Kiitos*," I thank him. It's not the moment to draw attention to myself, especially after the men in the tunnels recognized me. The waiter seats me at a round table draped in linen next to eight other people. I'm served roasted guinea fowl, braised red cabbage and creamy pepper sauce on one plate, and fried arctic char with stewed beluga lentils and purée of Lappish potatoes on another. It's quite the feast.

Friendly conversations about the Super Satellite and Celebration Rocket take place around me.

The frequency in the Banquet Hall has shifted since I left to make my appearance at the university lecture. It now carries a threat. What can Palermo demonstrate here that will turn people to his side? And whose side is he on? A bad feeling swirls in my gut.

When I finally locate Chan, he is already face to face with the black-haired man. Palermo Ricci sits across from him at his dinner table and the two men lock onto each other. Their body language is like two alpha male dogs—scoping each other out. A mutual respect is passed back and forth. They understand one another.

As I situate my napkin, I touch my earring discreetly. "Harrison," I whisper. "Access to Chan's audio, please."

Instantly Chan's voice crashes through the mic into my ear in a tone I've heard many times in China during some of our more intense meetings.

"Mr. Ricci, now here's a man I've wanted to meet for a long time." Chan dips his head. "You exceed everyone around you. In China, we call that a man who knows the future."

Palermo laughs, slowly and methodically. His lips curl up in a knowing grin. "The honor is mine. Chan Huang Long is also a name with a reputation that precedes itself. So tell me, Mr. Chan," Palermo says, studying him. "What brought you to the ISC Banquet?"

Chan offers a stately smile. "The future, of course. The ISC launch will be a vitally important event in history...if it succeeds..." Chan moves his head, as if in thought. "The ISC does fair work, but Scale Tech's future vision for satellites is far more impressive. When I see companies that are creating the future, I want in. Coming out on top is all about knowing how to get in before the door is open. How do you think I got where I am today?" A smile twists on his lips.

No... I tense up. Chan is far better at bluffing than I remember. He's also pushing through those doors far more aggressively than I calculated. Which is what I asked him to do. I still remember what he said: *I've dealt with men like this before. Either you get in and get on top, or they crush you.*

I sit back and force myself to trust Chan's instincts. He clearly knows what he's doing. Even if this is a game, if he plays it the way I instructed him, he'll likely still come out on top. Unless they suspect him. Kai's worried face comes to mind. I wince.

Palermo narrows his eyes. "Companies like mine require much more than just money," he says plainly. "My vision for Scale Tech is global, revolutionary, and long term, which is why my partnership with my company is very selective. Once you're in, you're in for life."

"Live together, succeed together, die together," Chan laughs. "Often it takes all of them for a real vision to be achieved."

Palermo grunts a laugh. "*Si. Vero.* Tell me, Mr. Chan, how long are you in town?"

"After the Celebration Rocket, I return to Shanghai. Enough time, I'd say." Chan's offer is on the table.

Palermo's head barely nods, but his eyes are calculating Chan's next move. Then a bend in his frequency tells me he's buying it. He leans forward. "We're having a private meeting tomorrow with some other investors before the ISC launch." Palermo pulls out a card. "You should join us."

All the blood drains from my face as Chan receives the card respectfully with two hands. "Tomorrow it is."

His eyebrows rise ever so discreetly. He's done exactly what he's supposed to do, just like I asked, and the exact opposite of what Kai asked. If Kai hated me earlier, he'll never forgive me now. If Chan attends that meeting, he'll be marked for life. I've put him in more danger than ever before.

Palermo offers a tainted smile. "Enjoy your dessert...and the show. It should be what sweetens the night." He stands and walks to another table at the back of the room.

Snapping around, I spot my father and my heart nearly fails for the second time this evening. Just like Mr. Chan, he's talking with his intended target: Dr. Juho Salonen, and dominating the conversation. My confidence in what they could accomplish wasn't misplaced, but now, we're in much more of a jam than before.

Dinner plates are being cleared, and platters of desserts are being placed at every table. Rich mousse with gooseberries; chocolate tartlets with salted caramel and cranberries. I bite into a tartlet, while keeping an eye on my dad. Harrison tunes into my visual cue, and a second later I have my father's audio in my ear.

My father is primarily talking innovation and vision—the things he loves. He poses new questions to Dr. Salonen, while everyone around the table listens. His passion is envisioning everyone. Dad's not the least bit nervous—which makes me nervous—because he may have forgotten why he's here.

But the way he watches Dr. Salonen, I decide that's not true. As Dr. Salonen explains new projects, my father listens attentively. They, too, are connecting on a deeper level—but completely different to Chan and Palermo.

My father has always believed in other people's visions. It reminds me of the Infinity Dome, and I wonder if Noble knows about it. Cracking his code on electromagnetic frequency manipulation was how I designed my emp-bracelet, the BFG. I sigh. Noble should be here right now. Not holed up in some refuge in the middle of nowhere.

"...*i*Vision always seeks out the right partners..." My dad explains to Dr. Salonen. "We're not so much interested in money as we are supporting true visionaries."

"Agreed." Dr. Salonen nods his head. "You have an impressive background, Jason, and have resurfaced in miraculous ways."

Off to the side, waiters come in serving coffee and tea, wine and champagne. Everyone is in high spirits eating dessert. But I'm on high alert, watching. Waiting.

"After the ISC launch, Scale Tech will launch its own constellation of super satellites, am I right?" my dad asks Mr. Salonen. "What is Scale Tech's true vision?"

Dr. Salonen frowns slightly, a knot bobbing in his throat. He considers my father then his voice drops an octave. "That's complicated."

After a minute, Pens is in my ear. "What do you need us to do? Call the dads out? By the way, Ms. T is livid you ditched Tank and Miles."

I touch my earring, about to say yes, when I change my mind. "No." We need to stay just a bit longer. We pull out after dessert.

Seven men shift in the room all at once. It grabs my attention. They're getting themselves into place. I tense up, as if a countdown has begun. But for what?

A moment later, the Banquet Hall's chandelier lights dim to black, then bright colors of red and green, gold and blue flash on the ice rocket sculptures, dancing with rainbows of light.

Gasps of delight ripple through the room. "A light show!"

People clap as the beautiful strobe lights unfold a magnificent performance.

But to me, everything about it feels wrong. My skin tingles, my numbers go berserk. First, there's a drop in temperature. Then, a loss of energy. Frequencies in the air go haywire, spiking in all directions—until they snap. I know what's coming, but no one else does.

I slip off my chair, heading to the wall, memorizing the room before the room is engulfed in darkness. The lights begin to flicker.

I brace myself.

Three.

Two.

One.

A tidal wave of electricity sweeps the room, and all power goes out in a zap. The room is swallowed in darkness, an unsteady pause where the light used to be. A thousand frequencies fade away.

Applause erupts all over the room, a stunning end to the performance they think. They have no idea what this is. But I do.

Numbers storm my mind, a heart-hammering trail of dangerous threats...Kai was right. Palermo sure knows how to put on a show.

CHAPTER 29

∞

Everything is black and silent.

It takes two minutes for people to understand the power outage is not part of the show. But this blackout is not caused by a solar flare. It was planned, and a deliberate demonstration of power. If Palermo can cause a blackout anywhere, anytime and make it look natural, then he controls a weapon that is far more dangerous than I ever imagined.

"Please remain calm," a voice in the room repeats in three languages. "Lights will be back on in a minute."

I doubt it. If Palermo is using this moment as a demonstration, then he will drag this out just long enough to be uncomfortable. In the dark, each passing minute feels like an eternity.

Everyone in the room stays in their seats except me. Although my tech has also blipped, my numbers are alive and well. I've already mapped out the room. I maneuver in the dark around tables and people fidgeting nervously, sneaking closer to Chan and my father. I need to talk to Agent Ramos immediately. My father and Chan, however, will have to stay here. If they leave now, it would look suspicious.

The room rumbles with hushed and panicked whispers.

"Look! Not even my phone is working."

"The solar flares are getting worse." A woman's voice is distressed.

As I pick my way across the room, I spot ten faint electrical frequencies, which means certain people didn't lose their power.

I pull Chan over to my dad. "After the lights come on, finish eating dessert, then regroup in the Empire Room. I have to leave. Do not make deals with anyone else, ok? Be careful." My voice shakes thinking of Kai. He knew this was going to happen.

"You don't sound like yourself," my dad observes, worried.

Chan leans down, too. "What's wrong?"

If Chan is this concerned about me, what would he do if he knew his son was working with Palermo?

"I'm fine. I just need to talk to Agent Ramos," I say.

After I help them back to their seats, I slip out of the Banquet Hall. Still in the dark, I weave my way through hallways where people are plastered in place, afraid to move in the inky blackness.

An ISC host's voice rings out from an intercom in the wall. "Apologies everyone," she says. "Solar flares have been causing temporary blackouts all week. This is why the Super Satellite launch is so important. Thank you for your patience." How much do they know, I wonder?

Regardless of what the ISC knows, when their chief scientists came to PSS they made it clear—the Super Satellite can't afford to fail.

CHAPTER 30

∞

EMPIRE ROOM
THE LION BLOCK

When I enter the Empire Room, the lights flicker and external frequencies return. With an audible zap, electricity is restored. Lights and tech blink back on.

The team is gathered with Agent Ramos, Ms. T and two bodyguards, who are hyper vigilant.

Agent Ramos is speaking to Ms. T. "I just got an update. Another satellite went down. Three more are malfunctioning. Telecommunications are being hit hard. Iran is blaming England now. It wasn't just in Finland. Blackouts are happening in six countries right now. Russia's northwestern minor power grid is fried."

Ms. T nods solemnly, then glances my way. "Josephine. You're back." She gives me a tight smile. "I heard you ditched your bodyguards. You had a good reason?" She's not happy.

Teeth clenched, my eyes seek out Agent Ramos. "A very good reason. One that I hope wasn't on a need-to-know basis." My eyes are weapons. "Kai's here. With Palermo, who just effectively demonstrated what he's capable of."

Ms. T's face goes white. Agent Ramos, however, doesn't look too surprised.

My heart is pounding as I stomp over to him. "If you knew he would be here when you invited me—"

Agent Ramos throws up his hands. "Whoa, calm down. I found out the moment you did. I sent an agent to stop you from meeting him in the garage—by the time he arrived, you were nowhere to be found."

"Why would you stop me from meeting him?" I snap. "If he's here, we'd better know why, or it could jeopardize everything and everyone. He has intel about the blackouts, about Scale Tech!"

Agent Ramos stands, surprise flickering on his face. "He told you what he knows? He was willing to work with you?"

My eyes dart to the table circling three knots in the wood grain. "Not exactly."

Agent Ramos goes still. "I suspected as much from what Bai told me." His jaw locks as he studies me. He's considering his next words.

He's dangled that info long enough. Now I press him. "It's now or never, Ramos."

Agent Ramos looks me square in the eyes. "Bai's not convinced Kai can make it through this job."

"What do you mean *make it through*?" I ask. Those words could mean anything.

"Kai has always been extremely focused during every other mission, except this one. His head is not in the game. He's been making small mistakes. Whatever kept him balanced and laser-focused before isn't there." He folds his arms across his chest, and breathes in. "I've been at this game a long time, Jo. Kai's good, but to thrive in an undercover environment, you have to be hard, totally in control of your emotions. Harder than Kai is. Seeing you again might unbalance him even more, which could do two things: he'll be caught or he'll break. If he breaks, he turns into someone else. Vicious. Violent. Paranoid. Someone you won't recognize. The real him won't surface for a long time, if ever. If he's caught, they won't let him live. If he makes any more mistakes, Director Kane will pull him out."

Kai, the November Romeo...a never return...

This is my fault. In Tunisia, he admitted to it, *"You're my center. You're what keeps me alive out there..."* The blurry frequencies pulsing around Kai's chest scrape my insides.

"Kai doesn't fail." I've said it many times with confidence, but now, there's a stain of doubt. Kai isn't himself. That much is clear. And I'm the reason.

I push my feelings aside and numbly explain what Kai told me in the underground about Palermo, Scale Tech and the coming mafia war. Though I'm not ready to disclose what he said about going north. They might not let me go if I do.

No one speaks while I talk. Pens takes notes. Eddie watches me with concern. Harrison pulls up several mafia thugs' mug shots on his screen. The innocent twist on Felicia's lips tells me she's hacking into something illegal.

Ms. T paces the room. Agent Ramos is still trained on me.

"Kai made a request," I say. "Chan can't know he's here. It would blow his cover."

"Agreed." Agent Ramos says. Then he moves in close, his voice low and stern. "If you see Kai again, you walk away. You let him do his job. Don't interfere or get involved. Don't bring up the past. Let him conquer this, ok?"

Kai's voice rings in my head. *People move on, Mila...* A bit late to walk away, but the reasons behind Ramos' command are clear. "Understood," I say.

A walkie-talkie type device in Agent Ramos' hand buzzes. He speaks into it. "Let them through." He clears his throat. "Chan and your father are back."

The room goes silent as my dad struts in with a big smile. Chan, less obvious than my dad, follows with the same victorious grin. Their swagger can only mean one thing.

"We've done it," my dad says. "I have a personal invitation to visit Scale Tech from Juho."

"And I have been invited into the private meeting with Palermo. It's tomorrow," Chan says. They give each other another victory grin while my stomach sinks.

Agent Ramos sucks in a large breath. "You've done what no other agent could do."

Any other agent except Kai, I think to myself.

"Jason?" Ms. T says, folding her arms on the desk. "What was your impression of Dr. Salonen?"

"Nice guy." My dad sighs. "Dr. Salonen may be the CEO, but he's not running the show. He's a man who's lost his vision and his company. He's powerless. If he's involved with anything illegal, it's not voluntary."

"Are you sure?" I ask.

"Jo, I know what a man looks like when he's lost everything." The frequency in my dad's voice shakes. He doesn't need to remind me of when he lost *i*Vision, his reputation, and me. My heart sinks.

I nod.

Ms. T turns to Chan. "And your impression of Mr. Ricci?"

"Eyes of a shark, tongue of a snake." Chan declares. "Everyone is below him in the room. But not their money. He is a man of much power. Tonight was his night."

I cringe. Kai asked me to get his father out of here, but I just helped him get deeper in. I stand. "You've both done an excellent job. Now we should consider someone else taking over from here. These guys are far more dangerous than we thought."

"No, it has to be done," Chan says, a solid resolve in his voice. "I know a strategic deal when I see one. I looked in Palermo's eyes. Whatever he is doing needs to be stopped. We have until tomorrow to prepare."

Dad nods, clapping Chan on the back. "I agree with Chan. Someone stole Dr. Salonen's company from him. I want to steal it back."

Jiche. I mentally slip into Chinese, my jaw clenching so hard it hurts. Now both of our dads are in trouble. They've been invited into a deal with the mafia and nothing I say can stop them.

CHAPTER 31

∞

SISU DEN
SOFIANKATU, HELSINKI

A path of light shifts between the shadows in my mind. My equations led me here. To Helsinki. To the Mafia. To Kai. Into a mess...a mess I hope can be resolved when I find Noble.

The window in our private suite faces north. With bare feet, I pad over the heated floors to look outside. Fractional dimensions and proportions spill out over everything going on in the square above and below it. Now that I've been in the tunnels, my mind pairs them with the square's dimensions above, giving me a multi-dimensional perspective, as if I can see through the ground. The position of the Celebration Rocket stage still boggles me. Kai and I passed right under it tonight. The crossroads of numbers that intersects in my mind is always present, but for now, all I see clearly is another dot on the path leading me to the Arctic.

I let out a large sigh and grab a cup of hot tea and my maps. Sitting on the couch, I study the Arctic Circle and the remote wilderness we are about to fly into. A helicopter would be nice right now.

Dad knocks on my door before peeking in. "Our flight to Lapland is set. We leave bright and early."

"Thanks, Dad." I say, setting an internal wake-up call in my head. He's still standing there. "Anything else?"

He folds his hands. "I talked to Marigold...Kai being here definitely throws a wrench into things, huh? I can't imagine. How was it seeing him?"

I put my tea down. The blurry frequencies buzzing between Kai and me flood my mind. His distant eyes, a frequency of pain. *How was it?* Colossal. Comforting. Confusing. I'm about to answer when my father stops me. "Actually, tell me later. Eddie's here."

My father and I walk out into the apartment's living area. Eddie's spreading all the usual gear out on the table. "Tech time for your trip up north."

I offer a weak smile. "My favorite part." I want to tell Eddie about Kai's frequency, get his take on what I saw, but I don't know how to summarize all that I'm thinking into a few minutes. I'll tell him when I get back, depending on what I find.

"First things first," Eddie says. "A contact of Ms. T's claims to have critical information on the NASA Tipper. She's trying to contact this person. When we know anything, you'll know. Second, Ms. Mines spotted your dad and Chan. If she sees our team, she's likely to fabricate yet another theory."

I groan.

"Alright, let's get started."

Eddie has brought us Arctic gear: insulated boots with extra grip for icy conditions. Arctic suits—made with the same thin, but brilliant, material as my sleeping bag in Namibia. They are water and windproof, designed to keep the wearer comfortable in sub-zero weather. Goggles, facemasks, gloves, hats, and sleeping bags complete the kit.

"Be aware of the wind chill factor. It can take you out within minutes. Take your tranq-earrings out, too. The metal can cause frostbite on your lobes. Wear your facemask. In very low temperatures, it's painful to breathe the air. Oh, and keep your drones warm. This gear is good," Eddie says, "but I'll admit, this was a rush job. We didn't have time to do the final tests in arctic weather yet. These are all prototypes, and cold weather can shut down tech. I've done my best, but I don't know how the weather will affect everything."

My sleeping bag in Namibia comes to mind.

Eddie continues. "If you make sure the sensors are plugged into the batteries, it should all work correctly." He points to the sleeve compartment. "There's a charger in here if you need it. But I lined these with a new special-forces bio-tech grade insulation, which is ten times warmer and lighter than what's available to civilians, so at least if it breaks, you won't die right away." He laughs awkwardly.

My dad snorts. "That's comforting." He thanks Eddie, and leaves to find Ms. T.

"Last of all, a gift for you." Eddie opens the case. Two small contact lenses with subtle graph-like markings on them.

"Bio-lens?" I ask. "Are they really ready?"

"They're still a prototype, but they may come in handy. Be careful though, it's a step past night vision and the downside is that any bright light can blind you temporarily, so only activate them when necessary."

"Thank you, Eddie." I smile. "Pens said your lecture was great. Can't wait to hear about it when I get back."

Eddie's face straightens. "Ms. T is really stretching her faith letting you go alone with your dad and no bodyguards—especially after what happened in the tunnels."

I groan. "Bodyguards can't join me on this one. I've calculated it." I don't use that as an excuse. I'm aware of the danger but in the middle of it, I have peace. "I'm just going to find Noble. That's it."

Eddie sighs. "How do you feel about finding him?"

I shrug. “Right now, it’s the only thing that feels right.” I glance up at the window. When I find Noble, the path in my head will finally make sense.

Eddie packs up the gear. “We’ll be available through K2. Just let us know whatever you need. Okay?” He half smiles. “The rest is up to you. Find Noble and get answers...for everyone else too.” He smirks.

I smile back even though my stomach crunches into a ball. It doesn’t feel like it will be solved that easily. “There’s a reason Noble went dark,” I say. “I don’t know why now, but I will soon.”

“Be safe.”

Knock. Knock.

I open the door, and it’s Chan. “Can we talk?”

CHAPTER 32

∞

Chan is just who I needed to see—to convince him to leave immediately. I have to do this for Kai—he'll never forgive me if something happens to his father.

After Eddie leaves, I pour hot water for a cup of tea, and Chan and I slide into two chairs. Chan folds his hands into his lap.

"Thank you for today," he says. "For a chance to do something."

My heart squeezes. Great. How can I ask him to leave now?

He continues. "What I saw in that room, I haven't seen in a long time. Palermo Ricci is not desperate. He's confident in his plan. Which is why we have to stop him."

"Which is why you should head home," I say. "My numbers are showing this is far more dangerous than we originally thought. I want you to be safe. Dr. Ling and Kai need you to be safe. I can't let anything happen to you."

A determined look burns in his eyes. The same look was in them the day he told me about Red, sitting in the Villa. "You didn't make this choice for me. I made it. I already counted the cost." He clears his throat. "This is what I do, Phoenix." His use of my old name makes it worse. "Do you remember what

I've had to face in my company? These men are no different. If anything, they are intimidated by me. I am your best chance at getting on the inside. Secretly, I've always wanted in on the action."

I raise my eyebrows.

He laughs. "Just once. Don't get excited. I have Dr. Ling at home. I'm not Kai and I won't take an unnecessary risk. But if I can stop another disaster, I will."

"What if something happens to you?" I say. "We should let the DIA handle it."

"The DIA came to you," Chan says. "I trust you will work it out."

My eyes plead with him. "Kai would never forgive me. You called me trouble for a reason. Just like he did. You're both right. I am."

Chan lowers his eyes. "You're in good company. Kai's mother and Red were also trouble. Kai's trouble too. But you're all the good kind of trouble, as Kai always says."

He's trying to make me feel better, but now I feel worse. He's here because I invited him into this web of danger and he's thanking me. He doesn't even know the worst part. That Kai is here.

Kai's face in the ballroom causes my head to spin. *Call me Asher.* Kai's voice echoes like a song underwater—deep and beautiful, but hard to reach. He's a sunken ship full of treasure but guarded by sharks. Chan notices.

"*Zenme le?* What's wrong?" Chan voice is low. "You look upset, just like the day you had to tell me about the crash."

I squeeze my eyes closed. I sigh. "Kai hates me."

Chan shakes his head. "What nonsense are you saying? He could never hate you. Believe me. I tried to set up my son with many nice girls. He never had an interest in anyone until you came along. I should have known he'd choose someone like his mother. I'm not sure why Kai agreed to such a long mission, but Kai makes his own choices."

I never even told Chan the truth. That Kai didn't just choose to leave, but I broke up with him. Left him a petty note. Blocked his calls...I expected Kai to tell Chan, but he didn't. After Kai left on his assignment, that detail didn't seem to matter, but it bothers me now.

"What if he never comes back?" I ask. "Kai loves this job, this life. To be honest, he got bored visiting me in Seattle. With each trip, he wanted to leave earlier and stay away longer. His assignments got longer too. A normal life just isn't for him."

"And a normal life is what you want? Look at you here in Helsinki—last week you had brown hair. Today you're blonde. Tomorrow you leave for the Arctic Circle." He waves his hands at the gear on the table. "Then there's Tunisia."

My cheeks go red. "You know about that?"

"I know my kids. You and Kai in the same region during a coup with a miraculous turn around? I guessed you had something to do with it. Thankfully, not many people know the real you or Kai. Why do you think your father and I are here? We're doing our part to protect our kids."

My heart warms, but I'm not sure Kai would see it that way. If Chan only knew how close Kai was...I grow silent.

"Here. This is why I came to see you. To give you a gift." Chan pulls out a box from within the bag he was carrying.

"Kai wasn't bored when he visited you in Seattle. He wasn't leaving early either. He was working on a surprise for you." He smiles, putting the box in front of me. "In fact, he wanted to move there to be with you, but I wasn't ready to be without him just yet. He stayed in China out of respect for me, which gave him an idea. He told us that you were collecting memories and sayings from Red in a journal. So, he grilled Dr. Ling for information. Turns out, all of their family belongings were hidden in Song Valley after they fled their home, including Red's old things before he went into the Pratt. Kai went to look through everything hoping to find something meaningful that he could make into a gift for you."

Chan hands me the box. Inside there are old letters, a traditional red Endless Knot, and a dirty old chess set. Below that, a large leather journal next to a small white one, and a small handwritten note that says, *To Josephine Rivers, from Chan Dao Kai.* My heart almost breaks in half.

"It's Red's old journal from before he was taken, and some of his old things. The small white journal is Kai's. He was compiling something for you. I didn't read it."

I take the box into my hands. The scent of wrong assumptions accosts my senses.

"While he was at home, Kai worked on this. I think it was for your birthday or your anniversary of getting out of the Pratt. I can't remember. Before he left, I asked him about it." Chan exhales and I predict what he's going to say. "Kai told me to throw his journal away and keep Red's stuff for Dr. Ling. But I couldn't. I knew it was for you, no matter what had happened in your relationship. Kai always was a bit extreme, even in his loyalty and love. He's like me in that way..." He shrugs. I remember the picture in his wallet. He held on to Moli, his wife, for years. "But you're right. There is no telling when we will see him again." He sighs.

My eyes shoot to the gray fuzzy floor mat. Kai could be in the next room for all I know. But Bai could be right, too. Judging by the look I saw in Kai's eyes tonight he just may be a November Romeo.

"What if I'm the reason you don't get to see your son?" I ask.

"Kai is a grown man. He makes his own decisions, Jo. If your numbers agree, then trust them, even if it doesn't make sense. Do you remember when you asked me to trust you, when I couldn't see it?" He's referring to the economic crash.

"How could I forget? It took you forever."

He laughs. "I have learned a lot since then. We need to trust each other, and sometimes it might get worse before it gets better. But second chances do come around." He smiles, eyeing the ring on his finger. I think of him and Dr. Ling. Regardless of what tomorrow might bring, right now I feel lighter.

"*Xiexie.* Thank you."

"Okay." He touches my shoulder. "I have to call Dr. Ling now. She's waiting for me." I walk him to the door and say goodnight.

I stare at the box. Inside, I rub my fingers over Red's journal, feeling the leather, inhaling the scent. Then I pick up the small white journal, counting the cost of opening it. Considering where I'm headed tomorrow, and who I'm trying to find, even I know I'm not ready to open either of these books tonight.

I stuff the two journals into my bag, then climb into soft sheets, eyes heavy and closing. I drift off to sleep, afraid of what my dreams will bring.

CHAPTER 33

∞

"The secrets of the sun are endless."

The dream carries me back to a rare day in the Pratt when Red and I were allowed outside together. It had rained earlier in the day, but the sun decided to show up and was breaking through the gray, misty clouds. We sat on flattened cardboard boxes in the dirt, caring about nothing but the sun on our backs and fresh air.

Red mused like always and I happily listened. "We can't look directly into the sun, yet without it we see nothing. Much of its power is working beyond our vision but it still leaves room for us to discover its secrets." Then he flattened his hand like a brim above his forehead, intently searching the sky.

"What are you looking for?" I asked him.

"Paths of light I haven't seen in a long time. A secret that can be revealed with our back against the sun and water in the air." Red laughed. Then his finger shot out like an arrow. *"Ah ha. Kan kan! Yi* dao *caihong gaogua tiankong.* Aha! Look! A *path* of a rainbow hangs in the sky."

I leaned forward, squinting until I finally saw the faint colors above the Pratt's derelict buildings and lighthouse. The rainbow was pretty, but I was more intrigued by the language Red used to construct the sentence, especially since he had been grilling me all week with new grammar lessons. "Why does Mandarin use *dao* to describe a rainbow?"

"*Dao* means 'the way' or 'the path'. Everything has a path. Even a rainbow." He crossed his legs, breathing deeply of the rain-scented air, and stared up at the sky contentedly.

His words should have brought me hope, but they made me grumpy instead. When King returned, I'd be off to a meeting at the Port. I looked down, shoving my worn boot into the dirt.

"A rainbow is just part of the electromagnetic spectrum," I told him, brushing off whatever deep meaning he wanted to convey. "It's not a secret. It's refracted light that bends in water which makes us see the colors."

Red laughed at me. "Yes, science helps to explain what is in front of us. But light was there long before they gave it a name. Just sit back, granddaughter, and enjoy the sun while we have it."

I looked at him. His eyes were closed now. The light breaking through the clouds outlined his features. He was still while my hand tapped restlessly at my side.

"It's not that simple," I replied. "You see a path of color. All I see are numbers."

Red hummed at me, his dark eyes finding mine. "Your math is a gift, but it will not always help you understand your path. Light can. You see, light reveals the way. Therefore, the light will lead you. But just like a rainbow, you may need to bend a little to see what is already in front of you."

I exhaled, pulling my knees to my chest, examining all the colors from red to violet. "So, what about you?" I asked, still cross and wallowing in self-pity. "Did the light lead you to the Pratt?" All week I'd tried to get him to tell me about his past—to no avail.

Red sighed deeply. "Light is a dangerous thing to follow. Before you know it, it'll drive you to the darkest corners of the earth."

CHAPTER 34

∞

ARCTIC CIRCLE, LAPLAND
ROVANIEMI, FINLAND

Flying into Lapland, Rovaniemi is lit up like a Christmas tree in a dark winter world. We shuttle into town mid-morning. I zone in on the powdered snow landscape and realize how very few frequencies there are compared to Helsinki. But that's not really where my thoughts are rooted. I am in the north. A place where two boys I care about asked me not to come.

As my father and I walk to meet our contact, an icy wind snakes through the streets, howling wildly. I pull my hat lower and yank my scarf up. Twenty-one degrees below zero sure does a number on the eyes and nose. But inside my heat-activated suit, my core is warm and toasty, zinging with heat even down to my toes.

Surprisingly, the town is bustling with tourists who don't seem to mind the cold at all. They're tromping toward the various advertised expeditions for snowmobiles and reindeer sleigh rides, aurora light tours and Arctic sauna experiences.

Numbers fuse with frequencies and footprints in the snow. But on the whole, the town is relatively peaceful.

The cabin we rented is fifty miles from here, and in an area I've calculated to be close to where Noble is hiding. Of course, he had to choose one of the most remote and extreme locations anywhere on earth. Our plan is to drive to the cabin, then explore the area on snowmobiles. Even though it's mid-morning, we only have three hours of daylight to find him. And the ISC launch is tomorrow.

"The driver is just around the corner," my dad says, half distracted. His eyes dart left and right. "Oh, look. Ice castles and dog sledding and Santa Claus's Village! Too bad we didn't come in December. Maybe next year, all four of us can come back."

I return an awkward smile. This is my dad's first international trip since China. So far, I've managed to introduce him to the Mafia, then drag him to a place with such extreme weather that it might kill us both, all to uncover a plot against the ISC while hopefully avoiding a mafia war. At least he's having fun.

Snow squeaks under each step as we pass festive streets and well-lit cafes with the scent of warm cinnamon rolls wafting out. The arctic sky is wide above me, but clouded over, much like my mind.

At the corner, a tall Finnish guide dressed in sub-zero gear, steps out. "*Päivää.* I'm Teemu," he says in that disarming Finnish accent. "Are you the two who have rented our *Sami House* cabin? Are you photographers?"

"That's us. But we're just regular tourists." My dad puffs out his chest, giddy.

"I hope you came prepared," the man says, spying our thin-looking suits. "The Sami House is our most remote cabin. The snow is quite deep out there. The auroras will be beautiful, but if you need help, it will be a while before anyone can get to you."

My dad casts a check-in glance at me, then back to the guide. "We're fully prepared." My father tugs on his heating suit.

"*Hyvä.* Good." He smiles. "Everything you requested, snowmobiles included, is already there, plus a bunch of extra wood to burn. The auroras are moving in strong tonight. Those geomagnetic storms may bring tourists, but they're causing quite a scare this winter. A big snow may come too this week, but tonight's sky should give you a great show. We'd better hurry."

I flinch when he mentions the geomagnetic storms, which aren't—in this case— causing the blackout crisis. Around the world, where certain power grids have already been damaged, people are panicking; seeking out churches, hoarding supplies, changing to wood burning stoves for heat. We have one more day to figure this out.

As Teemu loads our gear into the SUV, my mind spins off in different directions searching for any threats. So far, I don't sense anything dangerous. But it's still early. Off to the left, excited groups of tourists board a snow-bus plastered with an advertisement for the Ice Hotel. In the span of ten minutes, I've already registered 21 different languages.

In the vehicle, I look at the brochure for the *Sami House.* There's a picture of a herd of reindeer and a man dressed in colorful traditional garb.

"What does *Sami* mean?" I ask Teemu, my curiosity about different cultures overtaking my worries.

"The Sami are an ethnic people that live in the North of Finland. They used to be nomadic reindeer herders. Today, many tourists love to take a sleigh ride with them."

Along the way, our guide converses with my dad about Arctic survival. "There are shelters called *Laavu* scattered through the entire Arctic region in Finland if you are ever caught out in the elements," he explains. "They have all the basic facilities. Some even have a sauna."

"A sauna is a basic need?" I laugh.

"In Finland, we have a saying, '*if sauna, tar, or alcohol*

can't cure it, the illness is fatal.'" He smirks. "The number one threat in the Arctic is freezing, so yes, saunas are important."

The car is warm, but I press my nose against the cold glass, letting the sensation reset my nerves. With every hour, we're getting closer to Noble, and yet, this trip isn't to entertain my heart. Time is ticking. The ISC needs Noble's help. Cesare and Rafael are still missing. But I've also waited for three months to see him. My stomach tightens.

After another hour, the clouds split apart. We pass a private road, and a surge of frequencies crash and slosh like waves in an ocean. Adrenaline mixes with the frequencies in the icy air. Threats. Are. Everywhere.

My head twists from left to right as we cruise through the area. Hidden within the trees are cameras and sensors. Glints of unnatural light bounce with frequencies. This place is heavily patrolled. But Teemu and my dad are totally unaware.

I lean forward. "Teemu, what's this area known for?"

"Scale Tech's Arctic labs and data centers are in this area. At one time, they were open to visitors, but not anymore," he says with a sigh.

The abuse of power arouses a lion in me, alive and awake. Ready to pounce. Bodyguards may call me rash, but where others see impulse, I see a path of numbers that carves a way through it all.

I think of Helsinki. Kai gets it. He knows the risks—no job is without them. No day is without them. But he also knew who he was and what he wanted. Me? It's been three months since we broke up and I still don't know what I want. Which reminds me, I need to know if Chan is back from his meeting. I text Harrison for answers.

Harrison: *He's not back yet. Hold tight.*

Me: *Okay.*

I steel myself and take a deep breath. Chan wouldn't have taken this on unless he was sure about it. I have to trust that.

Our driver turns down a narrow tree-lined road into a recently cleared driveway in front of a log cabin in the woods. I tap my leg furiously as we get our equipment from the car and Teemu explains the basics about the house. After we assure him that we don't need anything else, he drives away.

My mind is a hornet's nest of thoughts. We drop our things inside, except a backpack of supplies we'll bring with us on our expedition. Then I open the garage where the snowmobiles are parked. "Come on, Dad. According to my calculations we either find his house in the next hour, or we sleep in the snow tonight."

"Thank God for our heat-activated suits," he says.

I check my coordinates then we hop on the snowmobiles and speed away.

The vehicle beneath me is a ghost moving over the ice as my numbers completely take over. As the sky darkens and the temperature drops further, the phantom frequency boomerangs around us in the forest, whizzing through the crisp fresh air. However, that is not what I'm tapping into—a melancholic hum trails in the air and it's getting stronger. After a while, I slow down. My internal compass goes wild.

I feel his frequency. I feel him.

I slow down and my dad pulls up beside me. "Let's stop," I say to my dad. "Ditch the snowmobiles. We go on foot from here." I don't want to alert Noble.

"Jo, it's getting dark. We may need them."

"We're close enough," I say, tightening my backpack. "We'll come back for them. Let's keep going."

I trek through the snow, warmer than ever. But I'm shaking. My dad comes up beside me. "Are you okay? You look..."

"I'm fine," I say, even though I'm not. I'm confused, hurt—I'm about to see Noble and on top of that, a negative frequency lingers in the distance.

We tromp through the woods and reach a clearing up ahead

surrounded by trees. My memory starts to spark. I've been here. In the snowflake simulation. The area behind the trees that I wanted to reach in the simulation is now spread out before me. I can even make out a group of structures.

I did it. I found Noble's refuge.

CHAPTER 35

∞

I track the path like a wolf.

Darkness changes the landscape, but it's nearly the same as the sim Noble created for me. My stomach buzzes with warmth and fear.

We carefully climb down the snowy hill, past the trees until we enter the clearing. Tucked behind a row of trees, there are a few tiny outbuildings off to the side, but in the middle, there's a beautiful wood cabin connected to a large Aurora Dome, a glass structure with a dome shaped like an igloo.

I shake my head. Of course Noble wouldn't have anything less than an Aurora Dome. A strange smoke-like substance curls from the chimney. Biofuel, I'd bet. Solar panels line the roof. From just a glance, everything on this property is custom made, upgraded and built to withstand a blizzard of a hundred years.

We trudge through the snow, passing the first structure. When my dad pushes open the doors, it's hot and steamy inside. "Look at this," he says. "If nothing else, we can sleep in here."

I step over and glance in. Scents of basil and tomatoes fill my senses. It's a greenhouse...in the Arctic. But it's like no greenhouse I've ever seen. A unique heat lamp is radiating a variety of colors. He's experimenting, mimicking vegetation growth in space—and it's working. There are vegetables, fruits and herbs of all kinds.

I continue toward the house. The fresh snowfall has blurred the tracks on the ground, but I swear the outlines indicate two different sized footprints. Thankfully I don't need footprints to know this is Noble's house. I approach the front door. A large piece of stony coral sits dusted with snow on the doorstep.

I knock. No one answers.

I'm tempted to imagine he sensed I was coming and fled the premises. But I don't believe that. He's here, waiting for me.

I try the door—it's locked. Knowing Noble, I already tripped his security system, but judging by the door handle, there's a way in without a key.

Although he could be in any of the structures, this house is where he spends his time. I want to enter this place alone.

"Locked," I tell my father. "Can you look for a key in the other buildings? I'll look for a way in here."

My dad agrees. He has the same idea I do. It's dark now and we have to get inside one of these buildings before nightfall, or we'll freeze.

I'm fairly certain Noble won't mind if I break in. He broke into my sims—he certainly shouldn't be angry about this. Besides, I'm going to have to recharge my suit soon.

I pick up the largest piece of coral. I have an inkling of what his style of key would be like. Turning the coral over, it's obvious he's done something to magnetize it. I set it against the doorknob and smile at the buzz. With an electrical pop, it opens. I step inside, ready.

First, there's a mudroom where a picture of the Sahara hangs near a chair covered in a pattern of fractals. Then there's another door. It's not locked, which means he could be nearby. He probably doesn't get many visitors.

Weaving through the cabin, I laugh quietly. It reminds me of the tents in Douz. Beautiful wooden walls and tables. Plush rugs and soft wool blankets. Everything is luxurious and beautiful and useful.

The living room is warm. There's a skylight in the ceiling, built to watch the northern lights, the stars, and the moon. My skin tingles inside this home. It's so familiar and yet otherworldly. Noble's created something brilliant. He always does. I wish I could sink into the couch, wrap up in a warm blanket and watch the aurora borealis through the glass dome. Teemu said there'd be a show of auroras tonight...but then reality comes crashing back. The ISC launch is tomorrow. If Palermo is planning something, we don't have long to avert a potentially deadly crisis.

Thoughts trickle through my head as I make my way deeper inside. What if Noble won't help us? What if he's angry that I'm here? After all, he told me not to come.

I pass a bedroom. His scent is there but his frequency is not. His belongings are few. Mostly books, lots of tech, journals.

I wander further into the house. Another small room is outfitted as a gym. Martial arts books lay open on the floor. Kung fu training bars are stacked on the ground. *Dear God.* Apparently, I have a type.

Finally, I find the equivalent of the tech tent, but far beyond what I saw in the tents in Tunisia. Videos. Plans. Blueprints. Charts of frequencies. Pages of equations. Telescopes and lenses of all kinds. The facial recognition software is also set up. Five screens of surveillance are going at once. Audio recordings, too.

Tucked into one screen is a picture of me in Tunisia. I'm sitting in the desert on a sand dune at dawn, gazing toward the horizon. That was before I knew who he was. Before my life got complicated.

I close my eyes. There is no sound, but a frequency enters the room, followed by the scent of fire smoke and cardamom.

Numbers cascade down my back. I turn around slowly as a figure appears in the shadows across the room.

A voice I've longed to hear speaks into the darkness.

"Hi, Digits."

CHAPTER 36

∞

After 3 months, 5 days, 28 minutes, 41 seconds of waiting, the boy I've longed to see—since he dropped me off at the freeway entrance with Qadar—is in front of me.

I expect him to come to me, but he doesn't. He stays in the dark corner, as he did in the Bardo Museum. Shadows affect our ability to use numbers to read people. Is he hiding something?

"You found me." He stands still across the room, the dark shrouding him like a curtain. His feet shuffle on the rug, taking in my new appearance. "You shouldn't have. I told you not to."

My numbers glitch like I don't know if I should scream or cry or laugh. I want to ask why he's hiding. I want to ask him a hundred things. Instead, I blush. I didn't realize how embarrassed I'd be, standing here. How vulnerable it is to seek someone out. Especially when they don't want you to. No matter how smart or strong we are, our hearts don't always follow the rules.

Even if I don't know what I truly feel for him—I came here because I thought I could be truly known by him. Or I came because the world needs him. Either way, I step closer to the light where my face is fully exposed. "I came a long way to find you."

His breath hitches, but he doesn't move.

Another step closer. "Why don't you come out?" I ask. He doesn't answer. I steady my eyes on the shadow. "We need to talk. There's something wrong. I was sent to find you. We need your help."

I sense the motion before he moves. Then, his voice again. "Is that the only reason you came?"

"No..." My voice trails out. In two seconds, the vibrations in the room shift.

"No surprises after this..." he says, the shadows fade as his figure emerges. Soon, we're facing each other, standing in the light.

Then, we see each other. *Really see each other.* In a way only we can do. His skin is not suntanned like the last time we met, but a pale brown, making his mahogany eyes seem darker. His brown hair has grown out, sweeping against his jawline. He's just as striking as the first time we met, but this time his beautiful full lips hold a sadness that wasn't present in Tunisia.

Our numbers trace each other's movements, gauging each other's intentions and reactions. He's right. There is no surprising each other anymore. He'll know before I take a step. I'll know which part of him will move first, his arms or legs. Right now, all I can think about is how his whole body is focused on me. His posture longs to lean into mine. The mystery of us is real, even if our emotions are tinged with fear.

The warm house is such a stark contrast from outside that soon, I'll need to take off this suit. The phantom frequency skitters across my mind. It pulses a warm heat inside me before it vanishes. Noble doesn't seem to notice it.

I had believed that the phantom frequency could be of Noble's making, but standing in front of him, I know it's not him. I'd see the equations from him or in this room. But there's nothing except Noble's familiar frequency I saw in Tunisia.

He steps closer the moment I do. I extend my hand but his reaches mine first. It's like a game. A game we've never played. We laugh shakily.

But even with numbers in the room, Noble is hiding everything he can. He's pushing against my ability that he knows is assessing him even as he moves closer. A whirlwind of equations, a storm of emotions, a hint of sadness—he holds it all back as if building numerical walls around himself. *What is wrong?*

As kids, our gift is what drew us to each other. Two people who could read each other in ways no one else could, holding nothing back, accepting each other.

He senses my dilemma, and shakes off whatever fear lurks inside him, and stands straighter. Despite the heat from my suit, I'm trembling again.

My dad is outside. I should go find him, tell him that I found Noble. Instead, I step closer. As I do, thoughts of Kai war somewhere in the back of my head until Noble brushes away the hair that falls in his face. His numbers are loud and clear now.

His gaze trails my face from my eyelashes to my lips. A girl doesn't need numbers to know what his next move is. He wants to kiss me. My heart hammers in my chest just knowing he's thinking about it.

We're face-to-face now, but both of us are cautious like we're stepping onto thin ice. He touches my lips gently with his finger. Frequencies of lightning and starlight strike me, just like his lightning tore up my life in Tunisia.

He moves in so close, my back is now against the wall.

"I'm glad you came anyway," he says, nearly out of breath.

"Me too." My voice is a whisper. "I need to ask about the satellites..." A chaotic burst of numbers fly at me, warning me of approaching footsteps, but I don't respond because I'm too lost inside Noble's numbers.

He tilts up my chin. "I've waited a long time to do this."

His warm hands are on my face, totally disregarding the numbers charging at us. Kai's voice rings somewhere in the back of my head, along with a creaking floor in the other room...but for the moment, it's just us.

He leans down, his lips so close to mine. I close my eyes—then numbers hit me. *Hit us.*

Our eyes barely snap open. Two men barge into the room along with a cold breeze. *Two men?*

The man I know races to my side. "Jo!" My father's hands fly to Noble's shoulders, yanking him away. For a second, I think my dad is going to try Kai's kung fu moves on him. I groan. The moment is shattered like thin ice. To be fair, all my dad could see was that I was pinned to the wall...

"Are you okay?" he asks me. Noble backs away.

"Yes, Dad." My face burns red.

My father assesses the situation, understanding crossing his face. "Oh, um, right." He narrows his eyes on the boy now standing at attention. "You must be Noble."

Noble clears his throat, his face flushed. "Yes, sir. Nice to meet you."

I'm about to speak when the man behind my father emerges, and my jaw drops.

I almost don't recognize him. His black hair is loose—not slicked back like the last time I saw him—but much thinner now. The mustache is gone. His jaw is clean-shaven. His green eyes are the same, though lacking the chilling gleam I remember. He gives me a crooked grin, then spreads his hands wide open in front of him—to show he's got all cards on the table.

"*Ciao, Mila.* King's lucky girl. We meet again," the man says in a thick accent.

I stumble back, my mind flipping through memories of underground conversations with this man's son in the Pratt.

My gaze shoots up toward Noble. "What is *he* doing here?"

It's Cesare Di Susa.

CHAPTER 37

∞

The first night I met Cesare, the Shanghai wharf had reeked of everything foul, but Cesare was the worst of all. Angry numbers oozed from his pores and tension fueled the air. He agreed to every wicked scheme King proposed without flinching, but never asked questions. I thought Cesare was a coward looking for fast cash, but looking at him tonight, it's clearly not the case.

Cesare's sharp brown eyes fix on me now with the same resolute gleam as the night we took down King at the Pratt. We'd had an intense conversation with the international police. In exchange for a plea deal, he'd give up his contacts and agreed to never again touch a life of crime. At the time, I believed him. Bai took him into custody and has been in charge of his case ever since. I'll give him one chance to explain.

Cesare removes his gloves while my numbers attack him for information. His orange parka and rubber boots have snow on them, which means he was already outside when my father found him. In a bright orange expedition suit that's puffed out like a marshmallow, he looks more like a sour grapefruit than the menacing crime boss I met in China. But it's hard to care when the weather outside can kill you in less than a few minutes without the right clothes. A smile curls up on his chapped lips. I've never seen any form of joy on this man's face before. It's the first time this piece of slime reminds me of his son, Rafael.

I march up to him. "Cesare Di Susa," I say without hiding my irritation, "you're not where you're supposed to be. Neither is your son."

"An unfortunate hazard of my past," Cesare says, tightening his lips. "Despite the unlucky circumstances, I'm glad to see you. I assume you got my son's message?"

"Where is Rafael?" I demand as my mind calculates for any immediate danger or traps, like a cop searching for weapons, but I detect nothing but ill-wrought ideas brewing and bitter regret.

His eyes flit to Noble's, then he huffs a regretful laugh. "Let's sit by the fire," he says nervously. "I'll prepare some coffee. We'll talk."

"I don't want coffee. I want answers," I say, in his face now. "Your son asked me for help. And we had a deal—one that you broke. From what I can tell, you're about to break it even more. I should call Bai right now."

Cesare's eyes narrow on mine. "If you call him now, Rafael's blood and many others will be on your hands."

The tension in the room is as thick as the darkness outside until my dad intervenes. "Hi, there. *Piacere.* You're obviously *Mila's* Italian friend's father," he says. "Let's start over. I'm Jason Rivers."

Cesare regains his calm, a gentleman taking over. "*Si.* I know who you are. *Mila's* father. Famous businessman. Nailed for insider trading." Cesare gives him a wink.

Dad clears his throat and gives me a sideways glance. "That's right. Glad that's out there." Then he turns to Noble, making it obvious that he's examining him thoroughly again. "My daughter has told me a lot about you. Thank you for helping her and Kai in Tunisia."

Blood drains from my face and Noble's eye twitches when my dad mentions Kai. Both Noble and my frequencies skip, as if even Kai's name is an unspoken barrier between us. I can't believe my dad just did that.

Noble shrugs it off and smiles at my dad. "Of course. Your daughter means a lot to me." He pauses, folding his hands behind his back. "Welcome to Lapland. I, um...didn't count on you coming here."

"So I noticed." My dad's face is straight as a nail, the warning clear. *Oh, great.*

Noble's lack of trust for older men shows in how he tightens up his posture. His numbers evaluate my dad, but it's over within a couple seconds. He's recorded enough to know he's not a threat, no matter how he postures. Noble won't find anything except a loving father, who never turns away a kid who needs a friend. He's much like Qadar in that way.

On the contrary, Noble is very comfortable around Cesare, which means this isn't their first meeting. They've already exchanged two glances where an understanding passed between them. This is a string worth unraveling. It also makes my insides boil. Noble, who confessed his feelings for me and then fled, told me to find him. Once I did, he told me not to come. After three months in the dark, an international crisis, and a trip to the North Pole to reach him, now he wants to kiss me. To top it all off, he's housing Cesare, who is most likely the root of the problem.

"I don't like secrets," I say, my voice sharp. "There's a lot of explaining that needs to happen and not a lot of time. Who's first?"

Noble's hand shifts. He'll reach for my arm, if I don't move. I soften when his touch clamps down on my elbow. His face is apologetic. "Things are more complicated than you know. And they just got worse."

"Worse? You mean now that I'm here?" I ask, the hurt mixing with urgency. "Because out there, in Helsinki, and in the rest of the world there are blackouts and mafia stalking the ISC Banquet. Two things no one wants. The whole world is looking for you Noble...and you're hanging around with a criminal."

Cesare shoots me a dirty look. "Ex-criminal," he mumbles.

I raise my eyebrows at him. "We'll see about that. Private Global Forces is looking for you and Rafael. So are Palermo's men. And I've been looking for you." My face is heating up as the words keep coming out. "You don't just run away without telling anyone where you're going!" My words are directed to Cesare—but the emotion isn't. Noble feels it loud and clear.

His grip on my arm tightens into a plea. I turn, not ready for what I see. The desert skies are hidden in his eyes, vast and endless. I had definitely imagined this moment differently. What's worse is I can read his body language and he can read mine. He didn't imagine our reunion like this either. Unspoken words still hang between us. It's clear we want to be alone—to talk, to fill the silence with numbers and catch up on three wasted months. But it's not possible when my father is standing to my left and a former Italian crime boss is standing to my right.

Three seconds pass before my dad elbows me lightly, breaking off our staring contest. "Things to do, remember?"

I linger for a moment longer before I tear my gaze away. My dad is right. The ISC launch can't afford to wait for two teen geniuses to solve their relationship problems. And I finally found Cesare. My team is waiting on me, and Kai—who's not waiting for me—is out there, mixed up in this too.

My dad pats Noble on the shoulder. "Great house you have here. Hope you have room for two more tonight?"

"Of course." Noble relaxes.

My father then turns to Cesare. "You mentioned coffee?

I, for one, could definitely use a cup. Please, lead the way."

"*Bene.* Finally someone with a little sense." Cesare steers him off in the direction of the kitchen.

Noble, still a bit hesitant, finally forces a grin. "Maybe it's a good thing you brought your dad." He shakes his head as he leads me into the kitchen.

CHAPTER 38

∞

NOBLE'S REFUGE
ARCTIC CIRCLE, FINLAND

Noble's coffee effuses an aroma of cardamom throughout the house, but not Cesare's. His coffee is short, bitter, and dark, like the amount of daylight here in winter.

Noble serves my dad and me a cup, and we settle by the fireplace in the living room under a darkening sky. Noble eyes the place beside me on the couch then glances at my father. He chooses a spot in the corner on a stack of pillows that reminds me of Tunisia.

The tension in the room is four-sided.

I set my coffee down. "I learned something about you recently that I'd love a bit of insight on," I say to Cesare. "You're the largest share-holder in Scale Tech. You also failed to mention that you are Palermo Ricci's cousin and were in line to be the next boss in your mafia family before that alliance was taken down. An alliance that has now resurfaced."

Cesare clears his throat. "*Sì.* Everything is a big mess. My family has a long and complex history. Which is why I moved to China in the first place—to escape it all. My reputation, however, got around and I wound up with King. An old life doesn't like to let go, which is why I need to deal with my past once and for all."

I pause. "You were supposed to be starting a new life with Ghost Markers," I say.

"You don't know my family like I do," he says. "A legacy doesn't die easily. Palermo found us within weeks after the trial. He offered to free us as if we were prisoners. Offered me partnership. It was time to begin phase one of renewing our family's great legacy."

"Which is?" I ask.

"My grandfather knew his reign was coming to an end, so he made a plan to move forward in a new way. He called it Terra Liberata, *a free earth.* An elite and evolved mafia that would monopolize industries and gain power from within. A five-phase operation. One day, he promised, we'd own it all—military, medical, environmental, digital, communications. Then, power and domination would be ours. It was terrorism, but in a legal form."

"When did your grandfather have this vision?" I ask.

"Years before he was caught," he explains. "He collected secrets to blackmail politicians and used blood money to invest in everything. In his will, he divided it up amongst us, but on his deathbed, he chose me to carry out his legacy because I was the rule breaker in the family. The risk taker. The black sheep. He thought I'd be more ruthless because of it. Turns out, the only rules I wanted to break were his." He sighs. "The vision was too much for me, but not too much for Palermo." He sips his coffee.

"Tell me about your cousin," I say. My father leans in, but Noble has evidently heard this before.

"*Brillante e brutale.* Like my grandfather, Palermo is obsessed with power, and he is smart like you. When I declared that Terra Liberata would end with me, Palermo declared himself the next boss. Half of the family followed him. Half remained loyal to me—but not for long. Phase one started with communications, satellites, and electricity. But most of my grandfather's wealth is in my name. Palermo only had stocks in medical companies, so he approached me about buying my shares of Scale Tech. He wanted to gain influence in the technology industry and use it to advance Terra Liberata. I refused." Cesare shakes his head "Palermo doesn't take no for an answer. A year later, he asked again. When I said no, he killed my wife and threatened my son. After that I was done. I moved to China." He rubs his hands on his legs. The anger I felt in him in China now makes sense.

"For years, I tried to ignore him," Cesare continued. "To look away, not get involved. But after the blackouts started and news got around that Palermo's acquisition of Scale Tech was turning hostile, I told Agent Bai. He looked into it, but Palermo has a spotless record. Thankfully, PGF believed me anyway and sent in an agent."

"Kai..." I whisper.

Noble's eyes dart to mine. "You saw Kai?" Noble asks, his face turning a shade darker.

I nod. "In Helsinki," I say, flustered. "We bumped into each other. He was undercover with Palermo."

"I see," Noble says, masking an emotion I can't pinpoint. "What did he say?"

"He advised me not to come north," I say. Noble goes rigid again, hiding his numbers. Whatever he's thinking, he doesn't want me to know. "He said there's a mafia war coming."

Cesare grits his teeth. "I'm the only thing standing in Palermo's way, which is why he took Rafael. That's what he does. He kidnaps and threatens people. You may have read that Dr. Salonen's wife is in a coma? Palermo put her there using a drug he created in his medical labs. As for the three scientists that went missing? Palermo forced them to work for him at the cost of their spouses, and then had two of them killed. Rafael and the third scientist are being held hostage at Scale Tech's Arctic Lab until the scientist completes the weapon and positions the Super Satellite for use. Palermo's blackout weapon is not quite complete. Up until now, he's been using an experimental nanosatellite with a faulty design. His real weapon is in the Super Satellite."

He exhales. "If I had stayed in Croatia or talked—I'd be dead. In our world, we deal with these things within *la famiglia*, which is why I called men who used to be loyal to me to come here. Together we will stop him."

Aha. Back up mafia is about to arrive. Great.

"What is Terra Liberata's plan?" My mind is computing, memorizing, forming predictions but I need more information.

"The ISC Super Satellite Launch will be used to create the largest blackout in history. It will cause unrivaled chaos. Evidence will show that a massive geomagnetic storm was the culprit, but that is not the truth. Using the Super Satellite as a weapon, Palermo will destroy over 200 satellites orbiting the earth and wreak havoc like wolves in a sheep pen. Terra Liberata will gain access to an enormous amount of data—bank accounts, missile codes, government files and secrets. Their power will be unrivaled. Not to mention the disruption and deaths caused by the blackout itself. The consequences will be unfathomable—unless we stop them."

His words are a thousand tons of water.

"How do you plan to get into Scale Tech?" I ask, my mind buzzing with numbers. "The entire area is loaded with surveillance and armed security, and apparently Scale Tech has an impenetrable electromagnetic dome protecting the labs."

"This is why I'm here with him." He points to Noble. "This boy knows how to get us inside."

Noble's frequency spikes, but he avoids my gaze. I harden my emotions, so I can focus.

"So, what's the plan once you're inside?" I ask.

"My men will meet us there after Noble opens the southern gates. The patrols are fewer there. We go in and stop Palermo. Rescue Rafael. Noble will access the programming of the Super Satellite and set everything straight, preventing the blackout before they activate it. *Finito.*"

"You make it sound easy," I say. "Kai called it a war. Palermo must know you're coming."

"He suspects I'm up to something, but he doesn't have proof. Regardless, you're right. There will be blood." He rubs his belly as it growls. "Dinner?"

CHAPTER 39

∞

While Cesare prepares a pasta dinner with herbs and vegetables from Noble's greenhouse, we continue discussing the plan for tomorrow.

I wrinkle my nose at Cesare. "You seriously want to talk about blood and stopping a mafia war and international terrorism while sautéing garlic?"

"What, do you think the mafia discusses everything with a cigar and grappa in a dark basement?" he laughs. "We still eat dinner. I'm hungry. I bet you are too; you just didn't say anything."

If I wasn't before, the garlic wafting in the air makes me hungry now. "Fine. What were you saying about *blood*?"

"That it's inevitable. In my family, there are two types of blood—one that is loyal, and one that is shed. Growing up, I didn't know anything different. When men you respect live like this, it's hard to see the truth. That's why there will be blood—I'm betraying Palermo, who is family. But if we're smart, we can reduce the amount." He throws in the onions.

The word *blood* should scare me, but it doesn't. I'm compelled to prevent it. I'm relieved that Cesare and Noble have a plan to stop the satellite takeover and the blackouts. But the plan is too simple, and my numbers scream it's not enough.

"When is this break-in at Scale Tech happening?" I ask, thinking about the meeting Chan has with Palermo.

"We will meet my men at first light at the gates," he says. "Palermo doesn't arrive there until the afternoon."

I bite my lip. "Do you have a map of Scale Tech's facility? I need to see it."

Noble clenches his jaw, reluctant to show me. He knows what happens when our minds see a map. But he hands over a device that has a detailed map of the area including the entire one hundred acres of Scale Tech Labs. My mind sets everything to scale. The roads, rivers, and lakes; the small homes and *laavus*; Scale Tech's massive property and dozens of lab buildings.

I point to the map. "The Infinity Dome covers this whole area?" I ask in wonder. Noble nods. "There's no way to disable it?"

Noble shakes his head. "No safe or easy way—it would require too much power."

After factoring in the snow and temperatures, my mind has a clear idea of where and what everything is. There's still one question plaguing my mind.

"How did you two meet?" I ask Noble, motioning to Cesare at the stove.

Noble jumps to answer. "The short version is I've had my eye on Scale Tech for a while, which led me to him." It's a half-truth. He knows how to get around lying, which he did to me in Tunisia. I let it go. It's a question for later.

"What's important," Noble continues, "is that I can get Cesare's men through the Infinity Dome without blood."

There are holes in this plan, and my gut feels it. "I don't know what you're seeing," I say, referring to his numbers, "but I think you're going to need our help."

Noble's brow tightens. "No. That's not what my calculations say. You're not going anywhere near that place." Noble's eyes harbor a thousand secrets and an undetermined amount of pain. His eyes flick to my father.

"Don't look at me," my dad says. "She's the head of this operation." My dad looks like he wants to help too but we both know our job was to find Noble, who's agreed to help the ISC debug the satellite. We didn't come to stop a mafia war. Ms. T, who's waiting for an update, won't be pleased. But the numbers keep pointing in that direction.

I look at Noble. "The ISC mentioned the Super Satellite had a glitch. What do you know about it?"

He narrows his eyes for a split second. "It's a hidden program that I'll disable tomorrow." His answers are too short, too vague. Something doesn't add up.

"I'm sorry, but we have to come with you," I say, thinking it over. "Rafael contacted me for a reason."

"Yes, and Palermo's men know who you are because of that," Noble says indignantly. "He should never have called you." Noble looks out the window. I look at Cesare.

"Don't worry," Cesare says. "I already told Noble about you and my son." He winks, and I'm horrified.

"There wasn't much to tell," I say, inwardly cringing. "We were just friends."

"Friends?" He laughs. "You two were so...*carino*. Cute. Fumbling over words. Awkward stares. Ha!"

I hold a steady smile to hide the pure embarrassment thumping inside me. It was partly true anyway. I never knew what I could or could not say in the Pratt. But we developed trust, a bond, a friendship I needed—one that brought hope to my life that it could be normal.

Cesare daintily pours a buttery herb sauce over the pasta, divvying it out onto four white plates. He removes his apron. "*La cena è pronta.* Dinner is served."

We sit around a small wooden table with a glass skylight

above us. Stars abound.

"Usually, I'd serve wine," Cesare apologizes. "But he—" motioning to Noble "—doesn't drink."

Taking my fork in hand, I realize I'm parched. Before I can reach for the carafe on the table, Noble is pouring me a glass of lemon water. He sets it in front of me, a shy smile on his lips.

"Thank you," I say, my numbers heightening.

I bite into a forkful of pasta, which is surprisingly delicious then turn to Cesare. "What else can I do to help?"

"Protect Rafael. He's a good kid. I don't want him mixed up in this life." Cesare sighs.

Noble frowns, his expression like crossed out equations. "Jo, please," he says, concerned, "don't go anywhere near Scale Tech."

"Noble, we can do this. Just like Tunisia," I say. "You could never have delivered the holothumb to Kai without me, remember?"

He sets his fork down. "Tunisia?" He doesn't look happy. He's calculating something. "The circumstances here are much worse than Tunisia. Impenetrable electromagnetic security. A mafia battle. A crime boss bent on finding you. Global blackouts that could last for months. You can't just walk into Scale Tech with a fancy watch and fingertip bombs and stop the bad guys. That won't work here."

I finger my emp-bracelet. "That's because you're not factoring in new variables. Including the fact that my dad and I are joining forces with you and Cesare, and my knowing about Kai's involvement."

"I considered that, but you're also not familiar with the Infinity Dome or Scale Tech's security system, which I've been studying for months. There's only one way to solve this. You can't see everything I'm seeing."

I lean in, my voice stronger. "Then show me."

"I wish I could," Noble says, frustrated. "You have to trust me on this."

"Well, you have to trust me too," I snap, hurt dripping in my tone. "Maybe if you had told me about all of this sooner, we wouldn't be in this mess." The table goes silent for a full five minutes...

"More pasta anyone?" my father says, breaking the silence. "It's delicious, Cesare."

The vegetables on my plate are now lukewarm and the spaghetti is all stuck together, but I slowly start to eat anyway.

Soon Noble's numbers are micromanaging the dinner table. He reads my thirst again and pours more water. I want the pepper—he reaches for it a split second before I do. "Here," he says, eyeing me through his hair.

"Thanks." I take the pepper, not sure if this is his way of apologizing or proving he's right. But my numbers jump in like it's a game of chess.

The next time he wants more bread, I push over the basket. "Butter with that?" Later when he's about to reach for pasta, I jump up awkwardly to serve him.

"It's okay," he says, quietly. "I can reach it." He turns away, his frequency erratically dropping up and down.

My heart sinks. In Tunisia, my gift only turned on a few times around him—only for a minute or two. This is intense. It's almost a battle for who sees more—me or Noble. The constant flow of my numbers counteracting his is dizzying.

The two dads at the table notice our obvious ability to counter each other's moves and watch us as if we're a spectacle. I didn't realize it would be like this. Noble said there'd be no more surprises. Learning how to help each other when we know too much is harder than I thought.

Noble and I finish dinner with awkward glances, listening to Cesare and my father happily talk about Rovaniemi and the Arctic. They're actually enjoying each other's company, which is what I want to be doing with Noble and I'm pretty sure he wants to do with me.

After dinner, Noble thanks Cesare, then bends down to me, his voice soft again. "Will you take a walk with me?" His eyes lock onto mine like a promise. "I want to show you something."

My stomach flips thinking of being alone with him. After all, this is why I came. To find out what he means to me. I nod, setting down my napkin, and stand.

"Dad," I say, and he looks up, "I'll be back. Noble and I are going to take a walk."

"Now? In the dark?" My father squirms in his chair. "It's 28 degrees below zero."

Cesare stifles a laugh. "*Ragazzi* never get cold when they are *alone*."

"Alone?" my dad repeats.

"It's safe, sir." Noble swallows. "It's not far from the house, and we have to keep our face masks on..." He clears his throat. My cheeks burn again.

"I'll be fine," I say, patting him on the shoulder.

Trust melts onto my dad's face. He knows I've waited months for this moment.

While Noble grabs his gear, I slip into my white snowsuit, which is at 50%. More than enough time for a walk.

We meet at the front door. He's decked out in gear that looks made to survive a nuclear winter. A thick hat is pulled down on his head. He stretches out a polar-gloved hand. "How about that hot chocolate in a field of fractals?"

I take his hand. "I'd like that."

CHAPTER 40

∞

The full moon gleams on the white landscape, brightening the dark terrain. The arctic air rushes at my eyes, making them water. A resounding silence echoes through a frozen land.

"This way," Noble says, leading me by the hand past the house and dome and onto a trail between the trees.

Shadows shift on the path as the breeze moves the branches. It's strange having been here before in a simulation. The trail is familiar but also absolutely new. Unlike the sim, the dark changes the landscape. There's also a squeak in the snow as we walk, which means the snow must be cold and dry.

We follow a trail, passing snow-laden trees stooped over like old men, while others—covered in hoar frost crystalized designs—are like decorated women at a winter gala. My numbers hum.

After four minutes, we round the hill. As in the simulation, a table and two chairs are set up next to a small metal encased fire pit. Noble pulls a miniature device from his pocket, points it at the fire pit, and up blazes a smokeless fire. Then, he pulls a small thermos and two cups from one of his many pockets.

"Welcome to my Arctic home." He points to a small frozen pond, the ice refracting into brilliant patterns in the moonlight.

He brushes snow from the chairs. "As you can see, there are as many fractals as I could want here and an even better view." He looks up at a night sky untouched by city lights.

My head tips up. The sky is so bright it looks like it will fall under the weight of so many stars. "It's beautiful."

"Yeah," he says, pulling down my face mask, followed by his. "It is." The shy grin on his face, coupled with the freckles on his nose, make my breath come out in faster puffs—or it could be the cold air.

"I thought we were supposed to keep our masks on," I say, a lighthearted challenge in my voice. His numbers, now that we are alone, are even more attentive. They make me flutter nervously.

"We were..." he says, "until we arrived at the fire pit." He cracks a playful smile.

We each settle into a chair, knowing which one the other would pick. I stifle a laugh. "This is new, right?" I say, pointing out the obvious. "Being around each other like this."

"It's what I predicted. No surprises." He smirks, growing silent. It's not like in the Sahara Desert where things felt more understood...natural. Here, it's like we're high school students forced to dance together after we just met. Only, the dance will be over all too soon. Red claims time isn't our enemy, that it helps us see what's ahead. But with Scale Tech and Palermo nearby, what's ahead doesn't look promising.

The fire flickers heat onto my cheeks, but an entirely separate pulse of energy spikes in me. The phantom frequency flashes its familiar equation like a ghost in the wind boomeranging into me, then vanishes. It's jarring, but also reminds me of all the questions I need to ask Noble about my gift, the crescendo of numbers building up inside me.

Noble pours me a cup of hot chocolate. I take it. He drops his defenses a bit, and there's a shift in both of us. There is nothing stopping our numbers now. I've waited days to see how our numbers would interact. To solve these feelings dividing up my heart. I push Kai's face from my thoughts, and focus on Noble, a boy who can understand me in a way no one else can. But as soon as I do, Noble tightens up, like he did in the house. I think I know why. Real questions have to be answered. Maybe we aren't sure what the answers are.

I rub the tip of my freezing nose. "This is silly," I say. "Let's just be a normal boy and girl for a minute, asking normal questions, okay?"

"Is normal possible for us?" he jokes, then gives me a look that implies he'll try until he sips his hot chocolate and an odd expression crosses his face. "So first question. Are you over Kai?"

If the weather doesn't freeze me, the question does. "What?" I avert my eyes, stunned, not even sure how to answer him, not even sure what he'll see if he looks at me. I swallow the lump in my throat trying to come up with an answer.

Noble groans. "I'm sorry, Jo. That wasn't fair. Forget I asked." He shakes his head like he screwed up. "As I said, I suck at normal." He shakes it off and changes the subject. "New question. I've wondered for a long time about your gift—if it's taken a parallel journey to mine."

I breathe, relieved he's talking about our gift, a subject I'm eager to discuss. "Let's see. If you mean picking up on new frequencies every day, even if I can't identify what they are; my brain processing at the speed of light; a path of numbers, scrambling dates and equations that just keep building and thickening like it's going to erupt? Sound familiar?"

Noble nods knowingly. "Very familiar. I went through it too."

"Good to know I'm not crazy," I say, thankful I'm not alone in this. "Eddie says the frequencies are activating dormant areas in our brain."

"Eddie's a smart guy," Noble says. "Our brains are able

to pick up on much more than what we see with our eyes. These dormant areas are turning on like light bulbs, activating abilities we've only dreamed of and they're pairing with the math gift we share."

"Does it go on increasing forever?" I ask.

"It didn't for me. There was a period of build-up which led to a very clear intensification, then after '*an eruption*' as you called it, the frequencies balanced out."

"What do you mean intensification?" I ask.

His eyebrows shoot up. "For me, I heard something that made my gift skyrocket into a blurry, crazy amount of energy. After that, it was a day or two before it erupted into a vision I'll never forget. It was as if the photoreceptors in my eyes partnered with my math gift. For a few minutes I could pick up what only nocturnal animals or machines could see, even the light we emit as humans. The phenomenon ended minutes later and balanced out. If it hasn't happened to you yet, it's probably coming."

"What did you hear that triggered it?" I ask, remembering what happened when I ran into Kai in the Banquet Hall. I avert my eyes.

"A voice." His tone is solemn.

"Whose?" I ask.

He tightens his lips, a darkened expression on his brow. "Not one I was expecting." His frequency curls into clouds of mist like a hiding child. "My father's."

A protective surge rises in me. "He contacted you?" I ask, shivering not from the cold but from his stories from years ago of his parents' abuse and the way they never understood him and manipulated his prodigy gift.

"Both my mom and dad did. Audio messages on an old app I previously used." His eyes dart to the fire. "Turns out, they were looking for me."

"Noble...that's huge..." I say, calculating the weight in his eyes. "Did you respond?"

"Not yet. But my numbers say that if I don't soon, I may not get another chance." His boot kicks a pile of ice. We're both silent. He's lost in his thoughts, which are clearly as heavy as me showing up on his doorstep. "I'll think about them more clearly after this business with Palermo is over." The tone of his voice is all wrong. He squeezes his eyes shut, clearly wanting to change the subject. "I've always wanted you to see this place. Not the best timing though, huh?"

"If you had invited me instead of making me decipher your code, I would have come sooner." My voice shakes with emotion.

His lips turn up. "I knew you'd crack it," Noble says, staring into the fire.

I study the beautiful enigma in front of me. He's holding so much in, even I hurt because of it. So I drive the conversation forward.

"Why, Noble? Why did you let me search for you for so long? What held you back? What was more important?" I grow embarrassed at what I want to say next, but I push the words out anyway. "You made some pretty big confessions in Tunisia..." My face burns at this admission. If he sucks at normal, I suck at all things love. "But now that I'm in front of you, it's like you don't even want me here."

He looks up at me. "I'm sorry. That's not it at all. I do want you here. But things just didn't work out the way I wanted them to." He stares back into the fire. "I'm sure you know I'm trying really hard to hide things." His tone drips with remorse.

"Please don't," I whisper. "You've already hidden enough."

He lowers his eyes. "There are reasons I didn't want you coming right now. Reasons you might not understand." He inhales slowly, considering how much to say. "Everything is so complicated. Out of control. Blackouts started happening two weeks after Tunisia...and I need to fix that first. No one will understand the choices I've had to make. But after it's done, if things don't get worse, I'll need to leave again."

"Already?" I ask.

He raises his eyebrows at me. "Jo. There's a mafia boss in my kitchen. This place is obviously compromised," he says with a huff. "Too many things have gone wrong. I have to fix it all. But I've done the math, and even I don't know how it ends."

"Forget math, Noble. This isn't your fault. Palermo's men are causing this chaos. You're not the only one who has to help solve this."

"You're wrong, Jo," he says. "This is my fault." Regret pools in his eyes. "Everyone is blaming me for the satellite failures and blackouts, because they're right. The tech Palermo is using to cause them is mine."

CHAPTER 41

∞

Fifty-two headlines buzz through my head where the NASA Tipper was blamed, and now I learn it's all true. But that can't be the whole story. Noble wouldn't create anything that hurts people.

"What do you mean?" I ask him.

He stands, his hand outstretched once more. "Come on. I'll show you." We walk back toward the house, entering the side door into the glass igloo-like structure, the Aurora Dome.

There are computers and tech everywhere, along with multiple telescopes. The desk is littered with hand-drawn diagrams, blueprints, a map of the Arctic and another piece of stony coral. Noble's surveillance program and facial recognition software is actively scanning on two different computer screens. There's also a futon covered in brightly colored pillows, the perfect spot for looking up at the stars through the dome.

"This is the soul of the property, where the magic happens," he says, attempting a smile. He sits at a computer and gestures to me to sit in the chair next to him as he pulls up images and files with equations and formulas from the code I cracked, then points the screen my way.

Looking closely, I scan through pages of designs for a Super

Satellite design that looks hauntingly familiar.

"You see?" he says. "I figured out how to harness and convert a lot of light energy that we've never been able to tap into before." He brings up a screen showing the design for a new giant folding solar panel. "As a kid, I thought it was amazing that the sun was always at work, even at night, even in the darkest times and seasons. Its power is evident in the auroras, activating the most beautiful energy, but it's totally untapped. So why not use that?" He smiles wide. "Today, we can only harness a small percentage of light waves out there. But with this design, I can activate *and* harness the energy in auroras and other stellar explosions, as well sunlight beyond the visible spectrum. Imagine a massive solar and stellar panel that could convert all of these phenomena into energy. I know you already understand some of this stuff because you cracked my code," he says, with gratitude in his eyes. "I've worked on these designs since I was a kid, but they weren't fully complete. I hadn't yet discovered what material I needed to use for the panel in order to convert the energy or figured out what would work as a conductor to send it back to earth. After my gift resurfaced and the frequencies started, I finished my research. Just think, now we can have sustainable energy even in polar regions all winter, even at night, all the time."

I scan his notes and spot the key to his design—radium—the 88th element. I can never seem to escape that number.

I'm silent for a beat, lost in awe. "Noble...this is amazing. It'll change the world."

"I thought so too. Until my designs got into the wrong hands, and my ideas for harnessing this energy were turned into a weapon. That's how Palermo will wipe out power grids and satellites. Instead of using the energy of auroras to power homes and cities, they're pointing it like a gun to take out grids and satellites. They've been experimenting with my designs in a nanosatellite they launched three months ago. So far, it hasn't been able to create the amount of damage they were hoping for. So Palermo's scientists built my technology into the Super Satellite. Thankfully, the weapon's programming isn't complete yet. That's what the last scientist who Palermo is holding captive is trying to finish."

"How did they get your designs in the first place?" I ask. "Did they figure this out from one of your tips to Scale Tech?"

"No." He shakes his head, a hard expression on his face. "They got it from someone who saw my designs long ago." Pain is written across his face. "If they finish the weapon, no nation will be safe." His entire body tenses up, until something distracts him. "Look." Noble points up.

Above us, a light show is taking place. Bright greens and reds swirl in the sky. The aurora borealis is dancing a waltz and my numbers go wild calculating frequencies of all kinds, within this room and above us. I stop looking up at the lights. Like magnets, my eyes are drawn irresistibly to Noble.

"I'm going to miss this place." He notices me and moves closer, an intensity burning in his eyes. "Jo, I have a refuge for every season hidden around the world. This time when I leave, I want you to come with me."

"What?" Ripples of shock shoot through me, though I don't know why. This is Noble. Complicated, brilliant, enigmatic Noble. Of course, it would come to this. This is how he lives.

The offer hangs like icicles, frozen and suspended in front of us, sharp and breakable. His eyes radiate light and fire like stormy nebulas worlds away. A part of me wants to cut this string keeping me tied to earth and float away with him. To see what we could do, what we could have, what we could be.

"I'm serious." He takes both of my hands. "I was going to ask you after this was over. But now that you're here, there's no point in waiting. After tomorrow, if you're ready, I want you to run away with me."

Another part of me is calculating—the threats, the responsibility, the billions of lives hanging in the balance, my father, Rafael, Kai... If I leave with him, I'd be throwing water on a fire that burns inside me...the equivalent of letting Madame go free and letting the darkness win. But isn't Noble the reason I came here? And what if tomorrow we can fix everything? Then could I go with him?

"If you were ready right now," he says, "I'd even leave tonight." He picks up the stony coral covered in infinite designs, and hands it to me. It feels like he's handing me the moon, the stars and his heart...but the particles of the night are also woven between us, dark and unseen.

"Jo." His voice is gentle. Our frequency sparks like tiny shocks of lightning and the connection we experienced in Tunisia moves in like a storm. The way he understands how I think hits me on so many levels that I don't know what I want. I don't know how to answer him.

He moves in so quickly, my mind is racing with thoughts. His fingers touch my cheek, his eyes are on my lips. Equations fly at me clouding my judgment. I have so many questions. Do I want this? Do I want *him*? Kai's face and the words we exchanged in the tunnels beneath Helsinki are still pounding in the back of my mind. I need more time to process everything. But time was never in our favor. Not in Tunisia, not here. There's a ticking clock in our heads and equations dictating our actions, too many to keep track of, and I already know I'm a fool in these matters.

His nose is touching mine, our breath mingling, numbers dancing in the centimeters between us. "We can try that kiss again," he says. "If you want."

My heart pounds against my ribcage like drums as he closes the space between us. My eyes close, then his lips are on mine.

CHAPTER 42

∞

The kiss is lightning, striking fast and powerful. A tornado of numbers and frequencies and a million memories caught up into one stolen night. It's chaotic and beautiful...at first.

But soon it's a melting snowflake. Fractals breaking apart. With each twist and breath, he pulls me closer, but it feels like he's far away. For a moment I'm lost in the wilderness of his frequency that dances like the auroras in the sky, but everything else is endless rolling hills of snow that melt in spring, a sunset in winter. His lips are on mine, but he's holding back something precious. Am I too? I'm not sure, but I feel like he's thinking of something, or *someone* else. Whatever has captured his mind is more powerful. I pull away.

He pulls back too, his warm fingers still on my cheeks. "I've wanted to do that since I was 13," he says sweetly. He smiles at me, but it's obvious he's still fighting whatever is on his mind.

"Me too," I say, but I'm confused. My mind is turning with more possibilities. It's true that I wanted to enjoy that kiss. But I couldn't. Something is in the way.

"So," he says, quietly. "How about it? Want to roam the world with me, making maps and writing books?" The reference to our childhood dream tears at me.

An avalanche of emotion buries me where all I see is Mandel, the boy who shares my numbers, the boy I made plans with long ago—until the events of the past few days snap like reality checks inside me. I grab his hand and squeeze. "Noble, I can't answer that yet. Not until tomorrow is over. People are depending on us."

Noble's eyelids snap closed. A disappointed exhale escapes his lips. "I know. It's a fool's wish in the midst of a storm." Then he pulls my chin up, giving me another small peck on the lips. "Fine. Tomorrow, we'll figure this out."

"That's why I came here, but..." I trail off.

Noble wrinkles his brow. "But what?"

I don't let go of his hand but squeeze tighter. "You're still hiding something. Your mind isn't on me. Noble, what's wrong? What are you planning?"

"This is why you shouldn't have come." He looks away. "My tech is going to ruin everything."

I pick up one of his star charts. "No, it's not. I've never seen anything more revolutionary in all of my life. Noble, you can't hide from the world anymore."

"I'm not hiding from the world, Jo."

"Then who are you hiding from?" I ask. "Your parents? Me?"

He doesn't answer the question.

"When the ISC came to ask for help from PSS," I say, "all those brilliant scientists wanted to meet you, to learn from you."

"Or to arrest me," he scoffs.

"So show the world who you really are," I say. "Offer yourself in a real way."

"Like you? You're hiding behind PSS. Jo... I was showing them what I discovered," he says. "I tipped off everyone I could. Gave away everything I could. Look what happened." He sighs. "The truth is, I broke every law they're accusing me of, even though my intention was to help. Either way, they're going to find out the blackouts were caused by my designs. I'll be blamed. I refuse to be a slave to another person's agenda."

I shake my head. "You don't get it. They don't get to influence us, we get to influence them. Light doesn't follow the rules, Noble—it shatters rules, it reveals new rules. No one else could crack your code, but I did." I set my eyes on him. "I'm not hiding at PSS, I'm supported. There's a world of difference. Instead of hiding out here alone, I have a whole team who look out for me, who create tech to help me, who do the things I can't, all so we can help the world together. You can be a part of that."

Noble rubs his forehead like he has a headache. "Jo, after tomorrow you might not think the same way." He sets his hand on my cheek, a plot brewing behind his eyes, straining to hold in everything he's hiding. "It's late, and your dad made it pretty clear that he's not going to sleep until I do. We have to leave at first daylight." A sad smile is on his face.

"Noble," I say, "Please tell me you know what you're doing."

"Everything will be fine," he says, his numbers creating a wall between us. "I promise."

"Ok," I say, but now I'm hiding the truth too. I'm not sure I believe him.

CHAPTER 43

∞

When we return to the living room, Noble shows my dad and me to the guest bedrooms in the cabin. The two rooms both have glass skylights, a heating system threading through the floors, and photos of the auroras and arctic wildlife on the walls.

The bedroom I choose has a fuzzy white carpet like mine back home and a large bed. Next to it is a wall-sized window boasting a view of hundreds of trees rolling out across snowy acres. The room is aglow with flickering firelight.

Noble's cabin has a rugged beauty inside and out, and certainly gets the prize for *coziest winter nest ever* all wrapped in a cold white bow.

I collapse on the bed and try to stop the numbers swirling in my mind, but resting never works. I text Harrison about Chan. Finally there's a message back.

Harrison: *Chan had his meeting with the mafia lords, and he's back in one piece. Thanks to Chan we have info on everyone in the meeting and all the numerous companies Palermo owns that will benefit from the blackout. Did you find the prize?*

Me: *Yep. And the crime lord.* Then I text what I learned from Cesare and our plan: that we're going to the Scale Tech labs tomorrow. Noble will hack the Super Satellite and disable the programming for the blackout weapon. The launch should succeed. Cesare will stop Palermo and his men.

Harrison: *Sounds like it's going to be a bloodbath.*

Me: *What? No. That's not the plan.*

Harrison: *Mafia, Jo... Keep your tech on at all times.*

Me: *Did Ms. T ever get that intel on the NASA Tipper?*

Harrison: *Not yet. I'll call when I have it.*

Me: *How is Chan?*

Harrison: *Surprisingly calm.*

Me: *Did you scan him for any tech? Did he eat or drink anything at the meeting?*

Harrison: *He checked out fine. He said they toasted with champagne at the end of their meeting.*

The meeting with Palermo sounds too easy. I don't like it.

Me: *Ok. Protect him tomorrow at all costs. I'll be in touch.*

After we're done, my dad comes into my room, taking a seat beside me on the bed. He clears his throat. "You and Noble were gone awhile. Everything okay?"

Our conversation *and kiss* move in like a cloud-covered sky. "Not sure. Something's wrong, but he won't tell me until after tomorrow."

"That's probably why he told you not to come," my dad says. "Tomorrow won't be a walk in the park. He may not know how to handle it. Even if Noble shares your mathematical abilities, he's not you."

I nod slowly. "What do you think of him?"

"It's strange watching the way he looks at everything—that part is like you. Never thought in a million years I'd see another mind flying at the speed of light the way yours does. But he's guarded, like you were after China. He has had very different experiences, Jo. The boy you knew as a child is now a man. It's clear he has some hard choices to make."

Choices. I don't mention that Noble invited me to leave with him—my dad would fly us back to Helsinki right now. Instead, I say, "I thought I'd know how I felt about him after coming here and talking with him, but now I'm even more confused. I need more time...seeing Kai in Helsinki didn't help." I groan. "How can I have such strong feelings for two people?"

Dad's hand runs against my cheek. "There are many different kinds of love. Sometimes, it's hard to understand exactly what you're feeling. You know, before I met your mom, there was another woman."

"What?" I say, shocked. "You've never mentioned her."

"I never needed to. After I chose Candace, I never thought about the other girl. For me, the experience wasn't as extreme as seeing frequencies and saving the world, even if both girls were smart, talented, and beautiful."

"How did you choose?" I ask.

"The Continental Divide." He smiles.

My brow wrinkles. "And that means?"

"At the Continental Divide, the earth has chosen which rivers flow into which seas. Everything west of the Divide flows to the Pacific. Everything east of the Divide flows into the Atlantic. It all clicked the day I had that thought. It wasn't about which path had the least resistance. Both directions had their mountains and valleys. But my choice was about who I wanted to face those mountains and valleys with, and whether we were both headed in the same direction. I realized that not only was I head-over-heels for your mom, but we wanted the same things. Our destination was clear. We were flowing the same direction, so no matter what stood in our way, I knew we'd make it to the sea."

Dad wraps his arm around me, gently squeezing. There's a brief pause in which I know we're both thinking of her. "You keep saying those numbers in your head are leading you to a crossroads. When you get there, you have to believe you're going to make the right choice." He leans down and kisses my forehead. "Be patient. Let's get through tomorrow first. After that, things will be clearer. Besides, we need to sleep so we're in tip-top shape for our clandestine rescue mission. This is my first *assignment*, you know, and I don't want to mess it up." He smirks. "I'm right through that door if you need anything."

"Thanks, Dad," I say. "Goodnight."

I climb into the large bed with Noble's offer playing on repeat in my mind.

Run away with me.

I calculate everything in the room twice, four times, then ten, trying to calm my mind, trying to fall asleep.

The phantom frequency is somewhere lurking in the distance, its equations howling at the moon. It's following me, but I'm used to it now and it comforts me. Soon, I'm fast asleep.

CHAPTER 44

∞

In my dream, the light is more brilliant than it was in real life on that day, shimmering through the windows like a curtain of gold.

It was three in the afternoon in Shanghai, and sunlight poured in through the huge windows of the factory. The former X girls were upstairs doing laundry with Dr. Ling. I sat on a brown leather couch in the back room trying to focus on work, while Kai exercised on the mats in front of me. I wasn't getting much done.

The deadline was quickly approaching for the JJ Bond, but I couldn't focus. Couldn't tear my eyes away from the boy in front of me. I studied his movements – the way he bent his knee, the angle of his arm when he hit the bag, the subtle shifts of his feet. Every angle was perfectly in balance, but there was more.

As I watched him cycle through a series of moves, the sun shifted and shone directly through a chipped and distorted piece of glass in the window. The dust in the air sparkled with a prism of rainbows, bathing Kai in magical light. My numbers galloped like horses, chasing the numerical refractions on his golden-brown skin. I was in awe of the boy bathed in light and numbers.

As if some power in the sunlight fueled him, his pace quickened, his feet moved faster. The focus in his eyes was solid, unshaken, balanced. In that moment, I believed that if he were thrown into a fire, he could walk right through it, unharmed. If there was a storm, he could calm it. He seemed completely unaware of the light shifting in the room, yet it was a part of him. Infinity traced his arms and legs as they swung in the air.

He was like Red, I thought. That's how Red could endure the Pratt. He carried the light inside him.

I often referred to Red as my light in the darkness. His eyes that first night were a beacon, calling me out of the shadows. What Red started in the Pratt, Kai was continuing.

My body flooded with warmth. I wanted to explore everything about the boy in front of me. To find the hidden colors hiding in his rays of light. The tight rein I kept on my numbers dropped and my equations charged at him.

They uncovered layer after layer, exposing everything in and around Kai, both beautiful and painful. While I usually controlled this part of my gift, this time I didn't stop the numbers. I couldn't.

The room froze, like we were suspended out of time, as if we were the only two people on earth.

The equations kept digging, tearing down all his walls. My numbers zipped up and down every scar and imperfection, the shape of his eyes and lips, burning every inch of him into my consciousness. It was deeply personal, knowing someone this way. Almost too deep to calculate at all.

But I went too far. My numbers were too invasive, an unchecked power. I took a piece of his privacy away from him.

Kai must have picked up on it because he stopped exercising, and his eyes latched onto mine. He set down his weights and came closer. Every step made my heart race.

As he approached, his eyes were steady, still locked onto mine, bright and brilliant. A fire coursed inside me and I couldn't look away if I tried. The day we met, his expression was so confident, but it was not one of surrender like it was right now.

He stood in front of me, skin damp from exercise. He took my hand, always so careful with how he touched me, then sat next to me on the couch.

"I know what you're doing right now." His fingers skimmed my cheek.

"Oh yeah?" I squeaked. An equation I didn't understand ricocheted in the room.

"You're examining me with all those numbers in your head. Marking out my every move. My every habit and trait. Every strength...every weakness." He laughed. "Soon I'll have no secrets left."

My face turned bright pink. I was caught red-handed, sneaking into a place only two souls were meant to crack open together, a place where mystery spilled its secrets.

He was right. I had stripped him of his defenses. The way my mind calculated people revealed too much. My sisters hated it when I dug too deep. Even my dad would squirm and get nervous. I never wanted to use it against anyone. I usually stopped my gift before it went too far. I tore my eyes away from him.

"I'm sorry," I said. "I didn't mean to. I know it makes people uncomfortable. I'll stop."

"No. Don't stop," he said, shaking his head. He leaned in, his lips against my ear. "I like it...a lot."

I pulled back, shocked. Never in my house—or life—had I heard anything like this. My eyes met his, searching for what he meant, but there was nothing in his face but peace.

"You like it?" I asked, unbelieving. "Why?"

He peered down at me, his brown eyes like an open highway, a soldier laying his weapons at my feet.

"I want to be known by you." It was a whisper, but it could

have been thunder for how it made my heart tremble. I felt a crumbling sensation as my own walls fell too. With sunlight beaming all around us, he took my face in his hands. "Count me all you like, Josephine. Memorize all of me. I've got nothing to hide from you."

∞

I startle awake. The phantom frequency boomerangs around the room like a numerical light show. I sit up, breathless, a deep ache in my chest.

I check K2. It's midnight. I'm about to go back to sleep when I perk up—something feels wrong. There's an itch, as though I forgot to turn off the stove.

We still have seven hours before we leave for Scale Tech. I should get some sleep, but I can't—my mind is spinning with residue from my dream and all the questions I have for Noble. I go to the window. The beautiful green light show is over. A thick layer of clouds covers the sky, and the moon's glow is replaced by darkness. Snow begins to fall.

I pull on a sweater, rubbing my arms, trying to identify what is missing. Closing my eyes, I dig into the frequencies, reviewing the yard, the house. Suddenly I stop, chills running down my back—there's a void in the house. Noble. I can't feel his frequency anymore.

I snatch my suit and socks, dressing as quickly as possible. My stomach tightens. In the dark, I make my way to his bedroom. Empty. He's not there—neither is the winter gear he was wearing earlier.

I rush through the cabin searching every room, pressing my ability as far as it can go to locate his frequency. I speed down the hall and into the Aurora Dome. A lamp on the desk flickers to life when I enter, but he's not there either. All the papers on the desk have been put away, save a small note sitting under the stony coral by the buzzing surveillance screens.

His frequency is not within a mile, or I'd be able to pick up on it.

Noble is gone.

CHAPTER 45

∞

I almost don't want to touch the white note under the stony coral because all I hear in my mind is *I'm sure you know I'm hiding something...*but he's given me no other choice.

I open the letter under the lamp and read it.

Digits,

I'm sorry. I asked you not to find me because of what I have to do. Please forgive me. I'm not sure what the outcome will be, but I see no other way. You asked how they got my designs...the audio recordings on the screen will help you understand. Please don't come follow me this time. Tell Cesare I'll help Rafael.

After this is over, we'll figure out everything else. I'll make one promise I know I can keep—I'll never ask you to crack another code to find me.

Yours, Mandel

Fingers shaking, I set the note down. On the desk are two black flat screens with four windows open, all set up for the audio voice messages to be played. A set of earbuds is laid out. I'm hyper aware that the photo of me in Tunisia sitting on sand dunes is missing from the background.

A feeling of dread and curiosity stirs in my chest as I sit in the desk chair, then push play.

The first audio recording hits me like a shock wave to the chest. It's my voice—and Kai's.

Me: Well, you're on brand sacrificing yourself for others...

Kai: For you...

It's a recording of our conversation in the Tozeur Safe House in Tunisia after he almost died. I've pushed this memory away long enough, but now that it's here, it consumes me like a flood.

...

Kai: Trouble, what'd you do? The room is spinning.

Me: Of course it is, I kissed you...

Kai: Laughs. *That would do it...*

...

Me: Can I ask you a question?

Listening to our dialogue feels like I'm back in that room again. My throat goes completely dry.

Kai: Jo, maybe you don't see it but you're the one who has to make a choice...

...if you don't love me now, I'll wait...

I swallow hard...Here it comes...I slump against the desk.

Me: Truth is, Kai, I love you...so much...I love you.

Kai: That's all I've ever wanted to hear...

The recording ends but I'm drowning in the sound of his voice. Noble's question at the fire pit. *"Are you over Kai?"* He was letting me know he heard my confession. My eyes close tight. What is Noble thinking?

My finger hovers over the keyboard before hitting play on the second recording because now I'm almost afraid of what I'll find. But there's no time to spare, so after two seconds, I press play, and a man's voice—deep, stern, and emotional—starts speaking.

Audio 2: *Son? Are you out there? Are you okay?*

Shaky, a crack of emotion. A long pause. Regaining composure.

It's been too long. Your mom and I want you to come home... I know you're alive. The NASA Tipper can only be you. I know my son... Long pause. *I haven't been the best father... I regret many things.*

Trembling breath. Large inhale and exhale. *I hope you'll give me another chance. Please contact us.*

I choke up even before the recording ends, rushing to press play on the third message. This time, it's a woman's voice, strained like she's been crying.

Audio 3: *Noble, honey? It's your mom...we miss you so much...*

Tears. Sniffling. Choking back sobs.

"Please come home, son. I'm so sorry for everything. Your dad and I both love you... I miss my boy." More sobbing.

End recording.

Hot tears trickle down my cheeks, blurring my vision. I don't know if I can bear to hear anymore. But Noble asked me to listen to all four audio recordings, so I will. It wasn't easy for Noble to share his parents' messages with me. But he did because he knew I would understand. My heart is dashed to pieces. I can only imagine what Noble felt—anger, pain, hate—but if I know anything about him, he probably also felt a spark of forgiveness, and even love for his family. I've been there. After Madame stole me away, I knew what it felt like to be unloved, unwanted—even if it was a lie. I also knew what hope felt like, and that new beginnings were possible. A lump bottles up in my throat.

The fourth audio message pulls at me. My finger presses play. It's Noble's father again. But this time, the message is ten times worse, each word like a knife.

Audio 4: *"Noble..."*

The same regret is in his voice—but this time, there's something else—fear, dread. *"Son, something terrible has happened. Your mom and I are in danger. Awhile back, I sold some of your old unfinished designs. The buyer contacted us, offering my colleagues and me a lot of money to finish it. Turns out, we can't finish it by ourselves…my colleagues are already de—"* He chokes up. Voice trembles.

"I don't know what will happen to me if I can't finish it. Your mom and I have been threatened. I'm sorry, Noble. If I could do it all over again, I'd choose you instead…"

End recording.

Numbers rip open my mind, flipping through files and memories and news articles. *"How did they get your designs?"*
"Through a person who saw them long ago…"

No. My head drops to my chest as everything becomes clear. I know where Noble is and what he's doing. It makes sense now why he didn't contact me, why his kiss was distant and sad. He was thinking of his parents who need his help; calculating the choices he has to make, even through all the pain he's already endured.

K2 alerts me of messages from PSS. *"Call us now. News about the NASA Tipper is in. FYI—it's disturbing."*

I command K2 to call immediately. Harrison picks up on the first ring. "Jo?"

"Tell me everything," I say, although I already know what he's going to say.

"Ms. T's contact at NASA gave us classified information on the three scientists who went missing. One of them is a man named Dr. James Adams, former NSA, then later NASA. Seventy-five days ago, he went missing with his three colleagues…" Harrison continues, his voice shaky now. "Jo—you're not going to believe this—we're 99% sure he's Noble's father."

Noble Adams. My eye shut tight as I force the lump in my throat down. When Noble was thirteen his father forced him to finish a formula for the NSA. He locked him in his room until it was finished, manipulated his gift over and over... I grit my teeth.

In the silence, numbers explode around me, calculating. The last remaining scientist who Palermo is holding captive is Noble's father—and the stakes are now clear. Cesare said it himself: if the last scientist can't get the weapon to work, both he and Rafael will be disposed of.

The thudding in my chest is so loud I can barely think. Even if Noble's parents treated him horribly, of course he would save them—that's just who he is. Predictions unfold before me. It's clear why Noble held back his plan, why he kept the Infinity Dome details to himself, why he pushed me away. *You may not think the same thing tomorrow...* His plan is clear, and darker than the night. I gasp out loud. He's going to finish what his father couldn't.

If he fails, he won't make it out of there alive, and if he succeeds...my throat closes at the chaos he plans to inflict on the world. The conclusions are drawn, the odds clear.

Noble isn't breaking into Scale Tech to stop a blackout. He's going there to cause one.

CHAPTER 46

∞

Crisis. Danger. Opportunity.

My numbers led me to a land of darkness. An operation of darkness. But I don't believe they led me here to fail. Even now, I strain to find that small path lit up before me—anything to fix this.

"Jo? Jo!" Harrison is yelling at me.

I forgot I was on the phone. I snap back, mind clear. "I'm here," I say. I explain what I know—that Noble is going to Scale Tech to finish the blackout weapon and save his dad. If he succeeds, the world will suffer, if he fails, his dad will die. There's no good answer.

"What do you need from us?" Harrison asks.

My hands and feet tap frantically against the floor and desk, as a thousand possibilities spin through my head—I've got to get to Scale Tech to stop Noble. The dome has to be opened for Cesare's men. We've got to prevent this blackout and ensure that the ISC launch succeeds and Super Satellite is safe to use.

My mind crashes against the biggest obstacle in my way: The Infinity Dome. Noble knows the only way in. *No safe or easy way...too much power...*

Second obstacle: the area is heavily patrolled. With Noble's maps in mind, I count and refigure, count and recalibrate.

"The Finns," I say to Harrison. "If anyone will know a way past the Infinity Dome, it's them. Get the Helsinki University STEM team on the phone. Find a weakness in the Infinity Dome. And, Harrison, keep your eyes on me tonight."

I hang up and go back to my room. I check on my suit. It's still hovering at 50%. It hasn't charged at all. My eyes grow wide when I see why: it's unplugged. My palm slaps the floor. Noble really was tricky. He unplugged it so I wouldn't have enough battery to follow him. I plug it back in and begin packing everything I'll need.

After thirty minutes, K2 alerts me to a call from Eddie. "Answer."

"Jo, we found the weakness, but Noble is right. There's no safe and easy way to do this—especially with a limited amount of time." His voice is faux-calm as he explains. "It's going to take a lot of firepower. We can't get it to you fast enough."

I finger my necklace, thankful for the backup. "Eddie, you're forgetting a piece of tech hanging around my neck."

"You brought The Squirrel's Chestnut?" he asks, surprised.

"Emergencies, remember?" My numbers calculate every ounce of energy in my weapon and the schematics of the Infinity Dome until a path emerges. It's a dangerous plan, but in the slim inches between every factor I've considered, there is an opportunity.

As far as plans go however, my dad's going to hate it.

CHAPTER 47

∞

It's 1:00 a.m. when I wake my father and Cesare and tell them to meet in the kitchen in five minutes. I race back to my room to pop the bio-lens in my eyes, remove my earrings and place them in a pocket, then hurry back.

In the kitchen, Cesare's sipping chamomile tea in fuzzy slippers. His eyes are bloodshot, and his hair is messy. The view jars me. He doesn't look like a crime boss any more than Harrison looks like a genius. Cesare looks like my dad. A man who gets tired, who needs his sleep, a man who will do anything for his son. Red told me once that he often reminded himself that every criminal in the Pratt was once a little kid who needed hugs and someone to believe in them. He said it helped him remember they were still people with needs who could change. Here's one more example. I hope.

"*Buon giorno*," I say, greeting him with the few Italian words I know from Rafael.

Cesare rubs his bloodshot eyes and turns to me with a sour look. "It is not *giorno*, Mila. It is *notte*. Why did you wake us?"

My dad skitters into the kitchen fully dressed and ready to go. "Yeah, what happened?"

"Plans have changed." Noble's letter is like ice in my hands.

I stuff it into my pocket and glance out at the dark sky, where snow is falling softly now. "Noble is gone. He left roughly an hour ago."

Cesare sets his tea down. "*Lo sapevo.* I knew something was wrong. He was too nervous."

My dad wrinkles his brow. "Where and why?"

"He's helping Palermo and Scale Tech." My stomach binds up into a knot, remembering the way he hid his numbers so I couldn't come to this conclusion earlier. "The third scientist who Palermo took captive is Noble's father. Palermo also threatened his mother, as he did with Dr. Salonen's wife. Scale Tech has been using Noble's research this whole time. Noble's father sold the original designs to Palermo but now his life is being threatened if he doesn't get the weapon to work, so Noble's going there to finish the job..."

My dad's shoulders droop. "That's terrible," he says, his face full of concern. "And it certainly changes things."

Cesare slams his hands down on the table. "What about my son?" Cesare says, an angry line on his lips.

"He has a plan to help Rafael," I say. It doesn't comfort Cesare, but he softens a bit.

"How can I blame him? Double-crossing us to save his parents? It's a mafia move." Cesare sighs. "But now, there's no way for us to get past the dome. Our plan is ruined..." Cesare rubs the creases on his forehead.

"No," I say, my resolve hardening. "The plan is still on. You and your men will arrive at the southern gates at first daylight. They'll be open."

"How?" My dad asks, his eyes widening. "Noble said it was nearly impossible."

"I just got some new intel. I'm going to dismantle the dome myself. Alone." An apologetic smile spreads on my face, hoping he won't ask any more details. What Eddie told me about the Infinity Dome would only worry him more. "I need to leave right now."

"What?" my father gasps. "No! I don't think so."

Even Cesare puts his hands together as if in prayer, shaking them at me. "Mila, *fa un freddo cane*—it's freezing, extremely dark, and Palermo's men are everywhere."

"That's why you two can't come. I'm the only one with night vision and numbers to guide me past the threats, which at this hour, will be fewer. They won't expect me. Three people tromping in the woods will cause too much commotion. I've already calculated it all out." I show them the map. "See? I've already memorized this whole area. I have a plan. The Infinity Dome has a weakness. Right here. I'm going to disable it. Then, there's a *laavu*—over here. I'll hide out there until daylight, then meet you. I have nine hours. It's plenty of time."

My dad is shaking his head. "I'm supposed to let my daughter go out into extreme weather alone while mafia brutes roam the land and wish her good luck? No, thank you."

"Dad, we have our suits. I have all the right gear. And weapons. If I get into any trouble at all, I'll turn back. I promise."

"You? Back away?" He scoffs. He sounds like Kai... *You don't back down from a fight...*and maybe they're right.

"I'm sorry to put you in this position, Dad," I say. "But I've got to stop Noble before it's too late. The Super Satellite launch is tomorrow morning, and we can't let it go into orbit weaponized." I rub my forehead. Noble must have another trick up his sleeve. The boy I know wouldn't help Palermo and risk lives without a backup. Even to save his dad. But there's no twist to his plan that I can predict.

I turn to Cesare, handing him a slip of paper. "Take the snowmobiles and ditch them at these coordinates—a mile south of Scale Tech's Arctic labs. Dad, do you have the watch Ms. T gave you?" He shows me his wrist. "Okay. I'll be in touch. I'll meet you at the southern gates at first light."

His face wavers between support and worry. "Are you sure

you're going to be okay, out there by yourself?" I nod. My dad leans in. "Are you sure *I'll* be okay, with him? No offense—" he looks over to Cesare—"you seem like a good guy, but... how do I know you won't betray us if Palermo gives you a choice between us and your son."

Cesare's chest puffs up like a rooster about to fight. "My men and I are going as one family, and you're under our protection now. I won't betray your trust. Certainly not with my son's life on the line. We'll work together to the end, even to the *l'ultimo petalo.*"

"L'ultimo petalo?" My father asks.

"The last petal? 'Til roses run white? You've never heard these expressions before?" Cesare stares at him. My dad shakes his head. Cesare sighs. "In my family, it means to the last drop of blood."

My dad wrinkles his brow at me. "Nice. Last drop of blood. Great."

"If it helps, my numbers reveal that he's extra dramatic. But he's telling the truth," I say. "Noble and I have both assessed him. He won't betray us. You'll be fine."

"Alright, fine," my dad says. "There's no reason not to trust you, even if it's hard to do." They walk me to the door.

"Mila," Cesare stops me. "With Palermo and Terra Liberata involved, nothing is going to be safe. The lies have to be exposed but be sure of this—there will be repercussions. Be very careful."

The warning is clear. But the story in his eyes tells a similar tale to my own—we know all about repercussions, but we also know that there's a time to act in spite of them.

"I understand," I say, inhaling a deep breath. "Cesare, it will be up to you and your men to stop Palermo. I'm trusting you."

He gives me a curt nod, then wishes me good luck. *"In bocca al lupo."*

I pull on my facemask and step outside into the viciously

cold air, wondering when it was I started to trust men in the mafia.

My internal GPS sets my course. I have no clear view of what's ahead. But it's a path I have to take—even till the roses run white.

CHAPTER 48

∞

The night is silent as I head out to retrieve the snowmobile. The falling snow works in my favor—it swallows up all sound as I navigate through the trees, and with visibility obscured, I'll be harder to spot.

With the cloud cover above me, it should be dark, but after I activate the bio-lens, the world comes alive. The bio-lenses' light sensitivity is so high that even the smallest traces of light are enhanced, making it easy for me to move at a steady pace in the dark, maneuvering between the spruce and pine trees, while taking note of their height, width, and motion.

I reach the snowmobile, and ride as far as my numbers show I'm safe—five miles. After that, I ditch it. Scale Tech property is too close. There are thermal motion sensors planted in the trees—I can sense elevated electrical activity nearby. For the rest of the journey, I have to go on foot.

When I have 1.1 miles to go, I calculate my ETA—at normal walking speed on level ground without snow, it would take me roughly 15 minutes to arrive at my destination, but after factoring in the terrain and depth of the snow, combined with my heavy boots, the strong wind, and lower body energy, which is sapped by cold weather, I'm looking at around 30-35 minutes.

My drone bracelet is tucked under my jacket cuff. Pulling it out, I activate one drone to circle me as I walk, partly because I promised my dad I'd be safe, partly because I need to test how it operates in cold weather. It's flying well so far.

The only road through this area is 320 feet to my right. I follow its path, staying in the tree line. Apart from an occasional rustle in the branches or a small animal scurrying away, it's deathly silent in the woods. Thankfully, I've got everything I need to protect myself from the elements and wild animals. The suit has 45% battery left, giving me just enough time to get to the Infinity Dome, then to the shelter to charge my suit. For now, I'm warm and toasty.

Snowflakes land on my gloves reminding me of Noble's fractals and the choice he has to make. And how he chose not to trust me with it. I instantly compare it to the dream I had just two hours ago—Kai never hid anything from me. Thoughts of the Continental Divide fill my head until I notice my drone isn't stable.

Instead of circling me at an eight-foot diameter, it's staggering up and down. Eddie was right about the effects of extreme cold. I call it back, and it attaches to my bracelet. I need to keep it warm for what's ahead.

I recalculate the map in my head—0.5 miles north until I reach the Infinity Dome. Even now, the air has become thick with frequencies from antennas, telescopes, and surveillance technology of every kind. I chart a new path where I'm sure to avoid cameras and sensors.

Seven minutes later, the control tower of the Infinity Dome comes into view. The tower itself is unimpressive, just like Minttu described—it looks like any normal airport traffic control tower. It's 210 feet tall, peeking out above the tree line. But what the tower is projecting in the air is unlike anything I've sensed before—it's booming with electrical pulses. A dome of energy particles, sparking with electricity, encloses the property. If my calculations are correct, this electromagnetic force field can block solid matter—missiles, bullets, radiation. *Aiya.* My plan had better work.

I crouch and move closer to the boundary line, hiding as I move from tree to tree, alert and listening, gauging the sensors. Hopefully wild reindeer with a similar size and heat signature as humans have tripped them in the past and my movement will register as similar blips. Wind pushes against me harder.

Finally in place, I call Eddie. "I'm here."

"How's the suit?" he asks.

I glance down at my gauges. "Not great—32%," I say. "It isn't cooling down, but it's not heating up either." Now that he mentions it, my body temperature is lower. My feet and legs feel a bit stiff, too.

"Hmm. The low battery and weather are affecting it far more than I predicted," he says, worried.

"No problem, body-temperature wise, I'm good. I'll make it to the *laavu.*" If things go well. "Okay, ready."

When I'm within 200 feet of the dome, the buildings that comprise Scale Tech's campus appear. I squint. The lights from the tower, although dim, are too bright with my bio-lens. I sneak closer to the electric barrier. When I get within 100 feet of the tower, human frequencies whirl in the air. Six guards patrol the area. I pause mid-step—three of them are the same men who followed me in the tunnels under Helsinki. The air is permeated with bad intentions.

"Alright, Eddie, let's go over the plan once more."

"Okay. There is one weakness: the control tower. It operates like a power grid for the Dome. When detonated, the EMP in the Squirrel's Chestnut will produce a pulse powerful enough to short-circuit their control tower's grid, cutting off power to the Dome itself, which is protecting the labs. Take down the tower, take down the dome." He pauses. "Just make sure you're at least one hundred feet away from the dome when you launch the attack. We're not certain how it will react to the explosion and EMP. There could be an aftershock wave."

"Okay," I say. "Where's my target?"

"Program your drones to detonate the Squirrel's Chestnut over this location." Exact coordinates for an electrical panel connected to the Dome appear on K2.

"Got it." Minttu says it'll take 24 hours to reboot the Infinity Dome after it's disabled—and since there's no real way to disable it, damaging it will have to do.

I move closer. The massive amount of voltage is off the charts. I unzip the top of my jacket pulling out the cherry on top—the Squirrel's Chestnut. I detach the bullet-shaped metal cylinder from my necklace and calculate the energy in four drones plus the chestnut. I only have one chance. There are so many variables at play, and too much is at stake. One mistake could cost not just me, but Noble, his father...the world.

"Eddie, what if the energy in the EMP isn't enough to do damage?" I ask.

"It should be—if your drones all hit the panel at the exact same time. If not, we're screwed." He whistles. "Also, the EMP-bomb needs to be carried in at top speed. The blast won't hurt humans, but the sound of the explosion may alert everyone in the entire North Pole. Power off everything beforehand, just in case. It may take a while to reboot your tech."

"Okay." I recalculate the trajectory for my drones once more. Every equation adds up—this will work. After I launch the attack, I need to make it to the shelter a half-mile away in less than 20 minutes. My suit is losing battery fast. I crouch into position behind a line of trees.

"Okay, Eddie, wish me luck."

"Good luck, Jo."

I power off my suit, and the bio-lens; and K2 is set to power off the second the drones detonate. My focus pulls tight.

Praying my drones have enough power in them, I program the details of the panel target into K2. Then I connect the Squirrel's Chestnut to the four drones that will deliver it there. The blast will be like a strike of lightning and could send me flying backwards. But if I'm not within range, the plan won't work because the drones' power levels aren't consistent at these temperatures. I move into an open space with a bank of snow nearby to be safe.

My drones now hover in the air, creeping between the treetops, silently awaiting my command. They're buzzing with 12,000 volts of energy but flying three times slower than usual. The cold is slowing them down. The density of the air is too thick. *Curse this snow.* Eddie's plan might not work. Unless I get closer, breaching my range of safety, the drones' flight distance and accuracy may be too diminished to work.

I crawl 25 feet closer to the edge of the dome. I'm too visible, but there's no one in sight. I send up a fifth drone, adding another 3000 volts of energy to help the drones reach the tower with a punch. Finally, K2 confirms they're moving in sync. Out of 12, I have 7 drones left.

The drones are set to detonate on contact with the panel. My jaw locked tight I command K2: "Detonate." I send them flying at full speed and run for cover.

The drones race like missiles into the night air, arrows catapulting at their target.

5 seconds. A countdown begins in my head.

K2 switches to drone visual—right on target.

3 seconds.

I'm counting down the blast, but my mind is elsewhere. *How will the EMP affect Noble's plan? Does he know I'm coming?* I step back, boots crunching in the snow. A spike of energy pierces my senses. *Dang it!* I tripped a sensor. Frequencies spiral through the air a split second before an alarm sounds. But it's too late to care.

1 second.

The frequency of energy zaps me before the sound. Then a blast like a bomb detonates. My ears ring like bells.

The Squirrel's Chestnut works perfectly. The trees bend under a tsunami of energy, shaking their branches and dropping snow to the ground with a gust of power that rips me from my feet and sends me flying violently 15 feet through the air. I slam into the snowy bank and through a cluster of bushes with sharp leafless branches. I'm knocked to the ground, head spinning. The branches miss my eyes, and my suit material is tough enough to protect me, but my exposed cheeks and forehead are scraped and bleeding. My facemask is in shreds. The blood from my wounds freezes instantly on my face.

I rest my cheek against the snow, laughing breathlessly, slightly hysterical. I couldn't care less about the blood. I did it! I took out the Infinity Dome—its palpable energy pulsing in the air is gone.

I lie on my back, assessing myself. For three seconds, everything is black. My ears are ringing and I'm slightly disoriented—I'm experiencing loss of balance, nausea, soreness, a 38% chance I have a concussion.

My head is still spinning. The trees dance above me. Even my numbers are scrambling to balance. Despite all that, I have to get moving. I'm cold.

Get up, Josephine.

I roll to my stomach and push up to my knees. My head is pounding. I push to my feet and start walking. Then running.

Sound waves travel all around me like a warning bell. The electrical walls have fallen, even the surveillance around me is down, but while the Dome can't reboot for 24 hours, the simpler tech can. After two minutes, I power on K2, but it's glitching. Same with my drones. When my bio-lens twitches back on, the right lens is missing. It must have been knocked out of my eye in the blast. And my suit is dead.

I still have a good body temp reading with time to spare, but it's cooling down fast. My predictions look okay until they recalibrate with the roar of a two-stroke engine creeping through the trees. Snow mobiles. Six human frequencies charge in the direction of the sensor I tripped.

Well, I would've had plenty of time to make it to the *laavu* except now they know I'm here—and they're coming in fast.

CHAPTER 49

∞

I dash between the trees, numbers blazing a trail. Heading toward the *laavu* isn't an option now. The next possibility is a mile away—if I escape my pursuers.

I command my drone BFG to activate around me, but nothing happens. I rip off my glove, tapping the drones. They're freezing. Even though it's insulated inside the cuffs of my thermal suit, my body temperature is not high enough to keep their metal warm. I shove them back under my sleeves, hoping they won't freeze my wrist off. I wish I had those fingertip bombs right now. They'd be warm enough to use.

"K2," I command again, "get my drones working." I need protection fast.

"Drones are unable to activate at full power until the temperature rises 8-10 degrees for 4-6 minutes." K2 spouts off instructions with an unconcerned tone. "Then, they'll be operational."

Four to six minutes? Not possible in this weather—not unless I shove them in my armpit, which is sort of hard to do while on the run. A vehicle, big and clunky, veers off close behind me now. Its speed, however, is only two miles per hour faster than mine. Must be a snowcat of some sort.

I run a zig-zag pattern, predicting the snowcat's direction and dash the opposite way, but with headlights and tracks in the snow, they can see me darting through the forest. My only advantage is size. The snow cat is very large, and they have to maneuver around the trees.

Three men on snowmobiles round the corner plowing into the snowy glen, closing in around me. Their headlights are so bright that my eye with the bio-lens surges with light. The flash is so powerful that when I open my left eye again, there's only a strobe of blackness and splotchy colors.

Great. Now I'm down to seeing out of only one eye, temporarily. I run faster, harder, but my toes are cold now too, like I'm running on needles.

I need a vantage point where my numbers can plan an attack. Depending on the men, I could still use K2's tasers and my earrings if I can get them from my pocket in time.

The snow is coming down like puffs of cotton balls, scattering my dimensions. Am I going the wrong direction? I don't have much time and I cannot let them catch me.

I set my course to run east toward the frozen lakes, away from Scale Tech Labs. My mind runs through twelve immediate possibilities. I take the one with the best odds— there's a 56% chance they won't drive on the frozen lakes, and on the map the forest was thicker in the east. I can run, then hide.

I race in between the trees. The snowmobiles move slower, carefully dodging branches. But they're faster than me.

Violent frequencies buzz with intent as the whir of snowmobiles cuts through the forest. Palermo's men close in around me. The same men I always sensed were coming for me—in Geneva, in Helsinki, in Namibia—close in around me.

I dodge behind a cluster of snow-filled trees. But it's no use. I'm leaving footprints in the snow.

Three snowmobiles, followed by another vehicle, pull into the glen. Six pairs of feet trudge and plow after my tracks. I leap over piles of snow to set a course for the last half-mile to the frozen lakes, but the odds predict I'm not going to make it. Dread fills me.

"K2," I pant, "are the drones working?"

No response. Then, two seconds later, a static-filled reply. "Neg-a-tive." I prepare a taser, but it fizzles out. Palermo's men stalk the forest, in a circle surrounding me.

I have 19 seconds, but my body moves into swift action. As a last-ditch effort, I lie flat behind some bushes and bury myself with snow, hoping the white suit will hide me, but it's too late. A boot crunches beside my head, another at my feet. Any moment now.

Six flashlights create a ring of light around me. My drones don't work. K2 is down. I take off my gloves reaching for my earrings, but they're too deep inside my pockets and my fingers are too cold.

One of the men from the underground tunnels yanks me up by the arm and drags me over to another man. Snowflakes fall between them, and puffs of steam shoot from their mouths like dragon's breath.

"The girl everyone talks about." This guy shines a flashlight in my face and laughs. "No wonder the boss wanted you. Who would've thought a little girl could take out the Dome? Palermo won't be pleased—but he'll love that we finally caught you."

With my right eye, I glare at them, calculating. My dad's worst nightmare is happening. Once again, I've been taken.

CHAPTER 50

∞

The back of the snowcat is uncomfortable, but it's *warm*—which is exactly what I need according to the calculations forming a plan in my head.

The men, definitely Italian from their accents, secure my wrists with a nylon cord, pulling it tight. On instinct, rather than numbers, I scream. "*Ow!* You're hurting me. My wrists are nearly frozen." It's loud and squeaky, a poor ruse to get them to loosen it. So I start shaking, playing it up as best I can. They frown and pull some slack on the cords. I hide a smile as they shove me onto the floor of the snowcat. The advantage of being a woman.

I land on a rubber floor mat, my hands behind my back. I lean against the rear door of the snowcat cab. Thankfully, they didn't take any of my tech. Not that it matters...yet. Everything is malfunctioning because of the cold.

Three men sit with their eyes trained on me. The doors lock as we start moving through the snow in the wrong direction. They're driving up a hill toward the lakes—away from the dome, away from the labs where I need to be in seven hours. I can't let them take me too far in this direction. I need to stop Noble. I need to get there before my dad and Cesare.

"Where are you taking me?" I ask, my tone implying helplessness.

"To a safe place until our boss can meet you when he flies in," he says, his lip curling.

Palermo flies in after the main launch, Cesare reported, *to ensure the blackout weapon succeeds.* If I don't get out of this snowcat, I'll miss it all.

The map in my head is spread out, all the features popping up—lakes, cabins, *laavus*, another town thirty miles off. I scan the cab, factoring everything around me into the equations multiplying in my head, calculating a way free.

Three solutions come to me immediately, but the first one involves seriously hurting these men. King's dark influence lurks in the back of my mind tempting me like a siren, but I can't do it. Red wouldn't approve.

The second plan involves seriously hurting myself, which won't result in me arriving at the labs on time either. Which leaves me with the third plan: a fifty-fifty chance of success.

If I don't execute it correctly, I could break my neck. But if I execute it well, I can escape. I'm sure of it. After that, my odds depend on the elements and how fast I can run. My suit won't take me as far as I need to go. But it's a risk I have to take.

First, I need to change K2's operating language so I can communicate with K2 without these men understanding my commands. Odds are they don't speak Chinese.

I glance out the window, speaking low. *"88-gai yuyan—Hanyu."* K2 buzzes in confirmation that the operating language is changed.

"What did you say?" growls a man. His body language tells me he's annoyed, but relaxed. He doesn't see me as a real threat. Most men don't.

"Nothing." Next, I whisper another command to K2 in Chinese to bring up a blueprint of the snowcat's engine and circuiting system.

"*Smettila!* Stop talking," one of the men barks in a thick accent. "Or speak English or Italian."

"Sorry," I say. "I talk to myself when I get nervous." Thankfully, I don't need anything else except time. First, I wriggle my wrists to loosen the cords around them, thankful for the rubber floor mat below me. Then I pull my wrist to my hip and examine the blueprint of the engine on K2. After this, I check my drones. Still cold. Four more minutes to heat up.

"I'm not who you're looking for," I say, stalling.

"Sure," they laugh. "Then why are you out in the middle of night blowing up Scale Tech's security dome?"

"I told you. That wasn't me," I stare hard at him. "I was looking for the person who did it. He's still out there."

The cords on my wrists are almost loose. But if my plan is going to work, I'll need an open window. I tighten my jaw, embarrassed at what I have to do, but I suck it up and moan loudly with discomfort.

"*Cosa é successo?* What now?" The blond man with a blue hat snaps towards me.

"I'm sorry, but can you crack the window? I get carsick. The fresh air will help." My smile is pathetic. They erupt into frustrated Italian mumbling, but they crack the driver's window slightly—a half-inch. Just enough. "*Grazie.*"

Now I need to get them talking.

"What do you want with me?" We're heading northwest, nearly three miles off course. The map in my head is recalculating. Once we reach the top of the hill, I need to be ready. But my drones aren't back online yet.

"We have just a few questions for you, then we'll let you go...after the big event." They snicker. They don't plan on letting me go. The same as Noble or the missing scientists. Now for the shock factor.

"Palermo won't succeed," I say, working out the cords behind my back.

The big one leans over, a scowl on his face. "You don't know what you're talking about."

My next statement is a risk, but I have to take it. I felt it during the banquet, and definitely after talking with Cesare. I have to test my theory. "Scale Tech belongs to Cesare Di Susa."

They stiffen, turning their heads. Even in their body language you can tell there is a chain of command, and Cesare's name causes fear.

"You know *Cesare*?" one of them asks.

I nod. "He's coming for you. Calling the loyal to return. What happened to the Dome back there was only a taste of what he can do. Only those on his side will avoid the coming bloodshed. Return me to him, and I'll guarantee your safety."

The heavy-set guy in the passenger seat cranes his head back and laughs nervously. "Cesare's legacy died long ago." But he can't hide the shiver moving through him. They all shift in their seats, nervous expressions on their faces.

The driver gets on his phone and starts blabbering the news in Italian to someone. Let the news spread. The war is coming to them, no matter what. This way, Cesare might have some turn back to him.

My internal clock is ticking along with the internal GPS inside me. We'll pass one of the largest frozen lakes in approximately three minutes. My hands work free of the cords binding my wrists, and I pull off my cuff.

I count down. Two minutes until my drones should be back online. The snowcat climbs up a hill and my body tenses.

One minute to go but still nothing from my drones. *Come on,* I inwardly scream.

Thankfully, the men suspect nothing. In their eyes, I'm their hostage. But they're wrong. This time, I don't feel bad about what I have to do. The frequency in my drones zings to life as they power up. *Finally.* Operation short-circuit number two is a go.

The men are too busy conversing about Cesare in Italian to care about me anymore. I turn my head, chin in my shoulder and speak softly in Chinese. I tell K2 to upload the engine diagram for a snowcat into the drones, then program three tasers to target the fuse box, the main computer chip, and the starter cable. If the taser hits any of those areas where the electrical current is strongest, it will short-circuit the vehicle. That will leave me with four drones and one high risk of freezing to death out in the elements.

I peer out the window. The hill is covered in fresh snow, four to five inches at least, which will be my salvation. Kai has done this kind of roll before—the numerical diagrams are programmed inside me. Like the punching bag in my garage, I'm relying on my body to obey the mathematical example in my head to execute it. If I can do it well, I should avoid injury, depending on how I land. Knowing this only makes it slightly less frightening. And I can't factor how much it will hurt.

Time's up. Here goes.

Three.

Two.

One.

The drones break away from my bracelet and dart out the crack of the window, zooming under the snowcat. Two seconds later, an electrical pop makes the vehicle go berserk. The radio blares. The lights go out. The door locks snap open, and the snow cat rumbles to a stop. The men all start yelling.

I waste no time. I slam open the back door of the cab. Knowing the numbers involved doesn't make it much easier.

It's all downhill from here.

I don't think. I jump.

CHAPTER 51

∞

Slam!

My shoulder hits the snow with a thud, and I tuck into a roll I've watched Kai do many times. Snow splatters onto my face and my body tumbles two...four...five times downhill. Gravity carries me down. I hold tight to the pattern in my head, my back and shoulder smashing into the hill and other debris. The depth of the snow provides a forgiving cushion—but still, pain courses through me. I'll have some nice bruises to match my bloody face.

After I stop rolling, I carefully stand, dizzy again. Numbers, like a lasso, pull me back to my center. The world becomes clearer—32 trees and roughly 250 feet between me and the snowcat. Numbers stretch from my heart rate and breathing down to my legs. Then, a path unfolds before me through the wilderness—I need to get to the lakes. A quarter mile east of the lake is a *laavu.*

Above me, outside the snowcat, the men are yelling, arguing in Italian, which means the other drones didn't have enough energy to knock them out.

My legs buckle slightly at first, but I push forward and race toward the lake, growing stronger by the second. My body assesses itself as I set a fast pace through the snow. I'm not seriously injured; just stiff and getting colder every step. My suit isn't keeping me warm anymore, but adrenaline sure is. For now.

The map in my head warns me the lakes are close, whether I know it or not. *Ice is different on every lake...* Without the specific lake dimensions, ice thickness, and depth of the lake, it'll be like walking on the edge of a knife. Except numbers are on my side.

With the map in my head guiding me, I step out onto the largest of the lakes before me. Numbers cover the lake's surface, averaging the ice's thickness for this time of year. I calculate a path. If there was ever a time to trust my numbers, it's now. Unfortunately, the wind is picking up and my body temperature is dropping. No numbers can combat that reality.

The ice starts speaking immediately. Loud cracking and eerie popping sounds instantly send a lump of fear to my throat. Even if my mind knows the ice is safe, my body is freaking out. But I step forward, obeying my calculations—this is the nature of ice. It can be frozen solid with zero threats, but still make these sounds. I focus on taking small quick steps and move forward gambling on the odds that these Italian mobsters don't know as much about ice.

I'm halfway across the lake when one of the men attempts to follow me. My pace quickens. The cracking sounds become more frequent. If the ice were thinner, I'd lie down to distribute my weight across the ice and slide forward as fast as possible, but I have to trust the numbers right now. In temperatures this low, the ice should be solid no matter what sounds it's making and the odds I'm betting on—that Palermo's men don't know this—are much thinner than this ice. Palermo's man, braver than most, moves faster toward me in small but quick steps until the ice cracks louder under his weight. A yelp escapes him, and he drops to his knees, crawling back to the other side, cursing the whole way.

"*Non sono pazzo*!" he screams to the men on the bank. I breathe, and press forward, trembling with cold and nerves.

I make it across the lake. They can't see me now through the heavy snow falling between us. They'll have to drive around—when they get the snowcat working again, but they'll have no way to find me. No way to know where I'm headed.

I walk slowly, setting my course toward the shelter. I want to revel in my victory—I deactivated the dome; I escaped these men—but I can't. I'm too cold. I command K2, "Call my father."

"Stabilizing." K2 reports, then is quiet. My drones have lost power again too. Hopefully, my earrings can still pinpoint my location even if they are freezing. I have nothing. No tech. All my concentration goes into reaching the *laavu.*

I need light to see. I rub my bio-lens, but only a faint glimmer appears.

Eddie gave my suit forty-five minutes to maintain warmth in -28-degree weather, which was 15 minutes ago. Now that my adrenaline is wearing off, shaking takes over. My legs are throbbing—or I'm just now noticing. My lips, exposed from my shredded facemask, are splitting with pain, my eyelashes are nearly frozen together, and I'm far off track and tired. *Stupid.* A nasty judgment attacks me from the inside. *Why did you rely on your tech? Why didn't you plan this out better? Why...*

"K2," I command again. "Tell my father where I am." But my message is muffled under my jacket and K2 doesn't respond. The wind and my fingers are too stiff to take off my gloves. If I lose my gloves, I lose my fingers.

The snow is coming down harder. I can barely see. I need to make it to the shelter before hypothermia sets in. Although my tech is useless, the GPS in my head still works. A path of numbers lights the way, but my legs won't obey anymore. They're pulsing with pain. So is my cheekbone.

The phantom frequency rebounds through the area. Whatever it is, it gives me hope that I'm not alone. A mini burst of strength shoots into my tired muscles.

I need to get warm. The thought drives me forward. Six hours before the sun comes up.

I grit my teeth and take another step, then two, then thirty-six—749 more steps to go. All I focus on is the next step. If I can get there and warm up, my fingers will function enough to fix the suit, and I can stop the blackout. So why do I feel like I need to rest? At least for a minute?

Snow is insulating. It's a whisper of a thought. Animals bury themselves to keep warm. Pine branches are everywhere. If I build a shelter here, then I can sleep, warm up. But with hours to go before daylight, I know it's a death trap.

"K2!" I scream. Nothing. One more step—521 feet to go.

My thoughts grow dark. If I don't make it, it'll take days for someone to find me here in the wilds of Lapland. By the time Eddie or my father discovers I'm in trouble, it'll be too late. Scale Tech will have sabotaged the most important international space collaboration in history and Palermo's massive blackout will devastate Europe. Who knows what will happen to Rafael? Noble. Kai. My father. The team. And me? I'll most likely be...I can't feel my face. I can't breathe. 241 feet to go.

Exhausted, I fall in the snow and roll under a tree. The wind slices my jaw. Though I'm not an expert, I know that nerve damage from frostbite can happen within minutes of exposure, but my face is so numb it's hard to care. No. I do care. *Stay awake, Josephine.*

Under the tree, I close my eyes and focus my energy. My legs throb with numb pain, but it comforts me. Once the pain disappears, I'm a goner.

Why did I come out here? What did I think I could do? The light was supposed to lead me. Soon, a storm of delusional thoughts sinks its hooks into me. *Winter is a time to be dor-*

mant. You can rest now, like the earth below you. What better place to sleep than in an ocean of frozen fractals? The voices sound pretty, but they're not. I recognize that voice from the Pratt calling me into a pit of darkness, telling me to give up. I won't listen. *I won't.*

My bio-lens must be working again because light, like the auroras, moves all around me. Frequencies in the air hover and wave. I imagine I'm being wrapped in light, a blanket of warmth like in my dreams. Amidst the light waves is the phantom frequency. It's warm, and strange equations pump into the area faster than light. But soon everything blurs together—the snow, the light, the colors.

My eyes close to the silence of a white hooded forest, as snowflakes fall on my frozen face.

Snow crunches in the distance. Two legs, at a quickening pace, move toward me. I don't even care if Palermo's men find me because hypothermia is setting in and I'm starting to hallucinate. The dream of Red dying on the cot and the cell flooding with blinding light like a beautiful supernova is replaying now. It's almost like I can see his face flooding with light. But the dream doesn't end there.

I've heard when hypothermia sets in, you start to experience a weird calm and simultaneously feel really hot. It must be happening now because the hallucination becomes a frequency that rolls in like fire, potent as the rising sun.

Feet scuffle in the snow, trudging 16, 14, 12 feet from me. It's not an animal. It's not an enemy. Whatever it is explodes into a billion rays of light, blistering with heat in every color.

Warm hands touch my lips, checking for breath. I can't open my eyes. My body has shut down.

The dream of Red comes to an end and a familiar male voice speaks. Heat floods my body. "Hold on, Jo. I've got you."

CHAPTER 52

∞

My eyelashes are frozen shut, my eyelids as heavy as the grave—but I don't need my eyes to know who is with me now. For once, the city boy who smells like forests and rain and mountains, finds himself surrounded by them. But for me, it's déjà vu. It's not the first time he's shown up, hovering over me while I'm lying on the ground in a precarious situation. My whole being sighs with relief. If he's here, I'm safe.

"Kai," I puff out a whisper, my mouth chattering.

"Yes, Jo. It's me." His voice isn't distant like in the underground tunnels, but it's not soft either—it's laced with the boy I know who never loses a fight. Right now, that is what I need. His confidence sears life into me.

"I...can't...move." I don't feel my lips move as I speak. I can't even be sure he heard me.

"I'll get you warm, just hold on." Kai's frequency impresses upon me like a crown of light as he leans down—a torrent of numbers pouring into me. The pounding of his heart fuses to my frequency. My numb body surrenders to him as he scoops me up and holds me firmly against his chest.

Kai's familiar gait marches hard in the snow. In my blurry state, I attempt to visualize the path as Kai heads south, weaving between trees, up and over mounds of snow. I want to ask him where we are going but my mouth won't move. I'm dozing in and out, vaguely aware of random numbers crossing my mind—54 minutes to Noble's cabin—I'll freeze before we reach it. 422 feet ahead to the next *laavu.* We walk 237 feet, 346 feet, 505 feet. After we pass the *laavu,* I almost try to ask where we are headed, but Kai's pace is steady. He's not wandering. He has a destination.

A shivering spell hits me. My temperature is dropping again. Kai folds back his jacket collar and tucks my freezing face against his warm neck. Warmth shoots through me like a bullet. All my body screams for is to get warm.

He readjusts his arms and my body, pinning me tighter to his chest. His arms must be killing him, but his concentration is unbreakable. After two more minutes and fifty-one seconds, a door creaks open. Kai turns sideways as he carries me through. The door slaps closed behind us. The acoustics of the room bounce into numbers, drawing up a picture of a small shack. What is this place? A shed won't be enough to get me warm.

"Kai..." My head is heavy, my thoughts clouded and blurry.

He sets me down on a hard surface. My face is cold again. I want to nuzzle it back into his neck. It's only a few degrees warmer than outside but the wind and snow are gone. I want to ask what he's doing here. But I don't have enough energy to speak.

"I'm starting a fire. Stay still." He moves around the shack uncovering and rustling things around. A metal hinge creaks open followed by several dense thuds—logs are thrown into some sort of stove. A match is struck. Smoke and the smell of burning pine and pitch fills the room with a hiss and a crackle. *Fire.* I want its warmth, but I feel nothing.

Kai moves closer, assessing my body as a paramedic would, searching for broken bones. I barely feel anything.

"Does anything hurt?" he asks, his voice tender this time.

I muster up enough strength to speak. "Closer...to the... fire." My eyes try to open, but they're still frozen shut. I'm shaking more violently now, loosely aware that I can't stop it or make sense of anything.

"You're close enough. Does anything hurt?" he repeats.

I attempt to answer, but I can't. My mouth is uncontrollably shivering.

Kai's frequency is racing. That adrenaline I recognize from his fights takes over. Kai throws two more logs into the stove, then shuffles around pulling things out. His fingers press down on my wrist. Then he holds something—*a thermometer?*—over my forehead.

"Your temperature is 91 degrees—far too low. Your pulse is weak. You've got stage one hypothermia—your body can't heat itself. Hold on. I'll get you warm."

Kai's movements are swift. He's ripping something from his bag. Two sets of zippers are unzipped. *Mine? His?* His jacket falls to the floor. My suit is coming off me. My boots, too. His hands are careful as he touches me. My dad always made it pretty clear that a real man always protects a woman physically and emotionally, but there was never a reason to tell Kai. That's just how he operated.

I'm left in a tank-top and leggings, shivering violently without the ability to stop. Kai transfers me inside of a sleeping bag, which is even colder. *It's not going to help,* I want to say. But then he climbs in too and heat rushes at me.

His skin is a fire of its own. Warm arms wrap around me, holding me close to his bare chest, which is pulsing with life and heat. He's tense, but he pulls me closer, wrapping around me like a blanket. I completely fold into him. His hands rub my arms and back stroking heat back into me. My face presses into him, and I doze in and out with a state of peace I haven't experienced in months.

"Where...are...we?" I croak out, my mind a blotchy mess.

"Inside someone's lakeside sauna. Don't worry, they're not home," he says, holding me tighter. "The *laavu* was too risky. This place is small and will heat up quicker."

My eyes are still closed. As I'm wrapped up next to him, the frequency of his heartbeat mixing with his voice pours over me like it did in the Banquet Hall. These combine with brain fog from severe exposure, and words I shouldn't say tumble out. "You found me...you always find me."

There's a huge spike in his frequency—not necessarily a nice one. Silence. Two deep breaths. He clears his throat. "Don't talk, Jo. Just rest." Wrapped so close I feel his arms grow tense and his jaw harden.

His words hurt, but in my delirium I can't pinpoint why. My numbers detect a deep frustration sizzling in him too—he's worried or extremely upset. Kai always hated to see me in danger. Despite the circumstances, knowing he still might want to protect me makes me feel better.

The dry sauna air grows warmer—I know this from numbers alone. We stay like this for, 3, 12, 25 minutes until my shaking stops and my mind becomes clearer. My fingers are on his abdomen when slight feeling returns in them. Lines I don't recognize are on his skin. My finger traces it. Scar tissue runs from his ribs to his lower abs. I shudder. When I found him in Tunisia, they'd cut him open. The wound is much longer than I expected. I keep my hand over it, flashes of him in the helicopter returning in droves.

My eyes finally blink open. I tilt my head and look at him. My breath catches. His black hair falls against his cheekbone. His jaw is set tight. Every inch of his face pulses a memory I fall into; a story I want to read. My heart pounds against his chest. His lips are so close to mine. He peers down at me, his heart thudding in his chest too. He eyes my lips for one long second. I'd do anything to understand what he's thinking in this moment, but then he jerks away.

Reality hits me like a bat to the head. *What am I doing?* This can't be happening right now. I came here to end this war inside me. Not make it worse.

Whatever change just happened inside me, Kai feels it. He props himself up, finds my pulse, and checks my temperature again. He sighs with relief, then starts climbing out of the sleeping bag.

Before I can stop it, a word I shouldn't say rushes out of me. "Stay…" Then I cringe at my foolishness. He climbs out anyway leaving a huge void—in the sleeping bag and maybe my heart.

"Your body is warming up on its own now." His words should comfort me but all I hear is our conversation from the tunnels: *I don't trust you anymore…*

And he doesn't. Looking at him now, the numbers are painfully clear. A deep pain throbs inside me alongside the physical pain of my body thawing. I squeeze my eyes shut. Kai shouldn't even be here. He has a job to do—one I'm compromising. Again.

Agent Ramos's warning starts throbbing through my veins. *Stay away from Kai. Don't bring up the past. Let him survive this.* An ache I don't understand worsens. I pushed him away so he could do this job, but here he is, three feet from me. Why can't I escape him?

Kai fumbles for his shirt. I should look away but I don't. Instead, my numbers are pulled to him like magnets. Right before he pulls his shirt over his torso, a marking on his left side upper abdomen, which wasn't there 3 months ago, catches my eye. A razor thin black symbol of an infinity sign. I shiver again, this time not from the cold.

CHAPTER 53

∞

Kai pulls tight his jacket, hood and facemask. "I'll be right back. The rocks are getting hot, but I need more wood." The door closes behind him.

In the firelight, I survey the sauna. Rich pine wood lines the walls, floors, and benches. Small wooden buckets with ladles are stacked in the corner. A typical altar of rocks sits just five feet away. A round thermometer is nailed to the wall. Frequencies of heat move in small waves in the air. I imagine smoke pumping outside. Thankfully, the fire won't give our location away. In extreme cold, surface temperature inversion makes it so the smoke can't rise. It gets trapped between two layers of cold air making it travel horizontally and much harder to detect in a snowstorm.

Waiting for Kai to return, my thoughts hop around and blur together. *I almost just froze to death. What is happening with Noble right now? Are my dad and Cesare ok? Kai is here...* Restless calculations wrestle in my mind until an unforgiving blast of cold air rushes at me as the door reopens and Kai enters.

My eyes follow him. I'm aware my heart is picking up pace again, but I'm not sure why. Kai has more wood in his arms.

He sets down the logs then pulls off his facemask and his hood. Kai feels my stare. His dark brown eyes flick to mine for a moment, before he looks away. He's not happy, he's guarding himself—and he's not hiding it. He, too, is calculating what's ahead.

"You feeling a bit better?" he asks in a polite but distant manner. I nod. Feeling in my legs has returned and I can move my arms again. "Okay, just rest while I see to your wounds. You're covered in blood. Your lip is busted, and your right cheekbone is pretty banged up, too."

I push out more breathy words. "Thank you...for coming for me..."

Kai doesn't respond. Of course he doesn't. Just like in the tunnels, it's obvious how much I've hurt him. His numbers prove it. I left him without a proper goodbye. Now, by helping me, Kai is doing the exact opposite of what PGF ordered. *If he messes up again...he could lose his job or get killed.*

Kai hovers over me with a medical kit. I stay as still as I can, avoiding his eyes and focusing on the hissing and popping of wet wood as he works fast, but efficiently. His ungloved fingers wash and disinfect my cuts, and he sets a butterfly bandage on the edge of my eye. He slides an ointment over my cheekbone. My pain level reduces so quickly I must be delusional. More feeling returns. His hands are warm. I find myself wishing he would lean in closer, hold me to his chest again. But he doesn't. What makes it worse, Kai clenches his jaw with each touch of my body. I have to make it right. I've lived through enough fear and pain to know what I have to do.

"Where are you supposed to be right now, Kai?" I ask, my voice returning.

"Not here." His voice is low and stern.

"You can't stay," I say. Agent Ramos's warning is screaming in my ear. "You're putting yourself in danger. You should leave, now. The whole point of your job is so you can save lives."

His glance is deep and painful. "Whatever we *aren't* right now, I could never just do my job, knowing you might die out here." His voice breaks. "Palermo's men called in an alert that the girl who blew up the Dome escaped. Not hard to guess who. What was I supposed to do? Hope you'd make it? Unfortunately, I can't do that." He groans. His hand, which was applying a bandage, pauses but his fingers stay on my face, sending mini shock waves through me. "I asked you not to come, Jo. I also asked you to get my father out of this, which you didn't do either." I focus on his moving lips. He won't meet my eyes. He's as taut as a bowstring. Because he can't do his job properly knowing his father is in danger—and he despises me for it.

Silence...

I don't argue with him because he's right and I don't have any strength. Why does all of this feel so wrong? He was supposed to be happy in this job.

We should talk about a plan and what I can do to solve this. But he's upset and I can't think beyond this sauna. I never got to say goodbye to him. Never explained why I really left him. Maybe this is my chance.

I roll toward him. "I'm sorry, Kai...for everything."

My words are met with stark silence, and layers of numbers. Kai stiffens. Whatever he is feeling goes beyond hurt. He truly does not trust me. And it makes me feel so sick.

He finishes bandaging me. He removes his hand from me with as much determination as in the Banquet Hall. But for me, his touch unchains a beast I've held at bay since I wrote him my goodbye letter. Only now it mixes with the conversation I had with Chan replaying in my head. *Kai wasn't bored...he could never hate you...*

Ugh. Why am I debating this? Nothing has changed. Kai is technically still 'gone' for one to three years, and I came here to find Noble and see what is between us. I have to back off. Agent Ramos knows what he's talking about, and Kai is clearly not okay with me being close to him. Why is everything such a mess?

Kai looks at his watch. "Why don't you sleep, Jo. When it's light, I'll take you to wherever you need to go. Hopefully back to Helsinki."

I let out a sigh, knowing he won't like my destination. "That would be the Scale Tech Lab gates, where my father and Cesare will be waiting for me."

"Cesare and your dad?" He groans and runs a hand through his hair again.

I dart a glance to my gear lying on the floor. "I need to charge my suit so I can meet them. There are battery-powered heat panels built into the lining. But something malfunctioned..." I trail off.

"You're not going anywhere for a few hours." He picks up my suit jacket. "I'll try to fix whatever's wrong." He grabs a tool in his pack, and the part of him that loves tinkering takes over.

Kai doesn't look at me at all while he works. But my eyes stay on him, watching the light of the flames bounce off his cheeks until my gift surges and I nearly gasp.

His frequency brightens like in the Banquet Hall. Only this time, it's clear and it's pulsing side by side with mine, almost in tandem. I've never seen that happen before. But the characteristics of it are so familiar...

After a grueling 4 minutes and 28 seconds of silence he says. "It should charge now. I'll connect it to my battery." He plugs it in then puts the suit by the fire to dry. His face is red now from the heat. He peels off a layer of clothing until he's in a V-neck undershirt. Funny. He's starting to sweat, while I'm only now starting to feel warm. He drinks from a water bottle, and a thirst I didn't know I had rages in me. He notices, and bends down beside me, letting me drink then gets serious. "Who did you come here with?"

"My dad."

He narrows his eyes at me. "That's it? No bodyguards?"

"No." I keep my eyes on him since he's actually looking at me, and I can't stop staring at his frequency. And almost freezing to death must also have something to do with it because Agent Ramos's warnings are so faint I can barely hear them now.

Kai lets out a frustrated sigh. "Why not?"

A memory comes to mind, and I look at him square in the face. "I'm done with those bodyguards. I don't want them anymore," I say, my heart splitting and speeding up. "None of them are right for me."

Our eyes lock. Kai's heartbeat is off the charts but he's clearly not happy I said that—I'm not either. We're getting too personal. I need to stop, to bite my tongue and stop talking. But his frequency is doing strange things to me.

My numbers can't help but calculate him deeper. His heartbeat speeds up as my numbers streamline into him. He doesn't stop me, but he moves two feet away, taking more gear out of his pack, putting distance between us on purpose. In an eight by twelve-foot sauna, he can't get too far away. But I get the point. He's not here for me. He has a job to do. And so do I. Lives are at stake and no matter what, the sun will come up in a few hours. But I can't seem to hold my tongue.

"Kai, I wanted to talk to you before I came here, to Finland." My voice cracks. "I went to 'the street' but everything was—"

He cuts me off before I finish. "We have nothing to talk about, Josephine. Except tomorrow." My stomach collapses inside me like a black hole. "If you're not going to sleep, why don't you tell me what you're doing here?"

I nod, my eyes tearing apart the wood grain above me.

"Cesare, my dad, and I plan to find Rafael and stop Palermo," I say, mechanically. "...and help Noble."

"Noble, huh." Kai shakes his head. "I guess you know now that your new boyfriend is the one building their blackout weapon." Kai doesn't look up but speaks into the flames. "He ruined my perfectly good plan. Against my better judgment, I gave him the benefit of the doubt. Look how that turned out."

My head snaps over. "He's not my boyfriend," I say, perking up. "And what do you mean he ruined *your plan*?"

Kai scoffs. "It's not surprising he didn't tell you," he says, his voice low. "Jo, I'm the one who brought Cesare to him. The plan to let Cesare's men into Scale Tech to stop Palermo was mine."

CHAPTER 54

∞

The sauna feels much hotter and smaller now. This time, it's me who can't move far enough away. I asked Noble how he and Cesare met, but he wouldn't say.

Kai throws another log into the fire. "I saw him at the labs working with the scientist. I recognized his face. And he recognized mine." Kai tightens his jaw. "So I confronted him. He was not happy to see me."

Those two in the same room together? My thoughts tumble down an awkward road. "What did he say?"

"More than I cared to hear." Kai's frequency skips in fast waves. He doesn't look at me. "I knew what he was doing for Palermo. He claimed he was forced into it, so I offered him a way out. Rafael was there. Cesare was coming for Rafael no matter what. All he needed was a way past the Dome. It was the perfect way to stop Palermo's plan. But I couldn't be the one to help Cesare. I needed to maintain my cover." Kai sighs. "Eventually, Noble agreed to the plan. But he backed out. He'll be a prisoner now."

I roll to the side, my body obeying my commands again. "Kai, the scientist who Palermo is holding hostage is his father. Palermo threatened his mom too." I explain everything that

Noble told me in the note.

Kai breathes deep. "*Guaibude.* I've never seen Noble speak to the scientist. But his unease, his tension, his struggle with the man, made me wonder what was between them."

"Noble's never had it easy," I say, wondering how Noble is doing. "His gift is like mine, but his parents never nurtured it—they only manipulated him for their own gains. As kids, we were the only ones who could understand each other." My brows knit together. The thirteen-year-old me is balling up her fists, ready to fight. I loved him and hated to see him scared and unappreciated. I was glad when he told me he planned to run away. Right now, I hate that he's forced into this mess. Once again, his gifts are being manipulated. It makes me so mad and confused.

"I noticed his gift right away. Must be nice to have someone who can understand that part of you." Kai tightens his jaw, pausing in thought. His frequency thunders. "But Palermo won't stop. He's already forced Dr. Adams to work on other designs, some just as dangerous as the blackout weapon. When this is over, Palermo won't hesitate to get rid of Noble and his father if he thinks they won't be cooperative."

"Noble has another plan—a way to stop Palermo. I know he does. But my calculations don't look good. Either way, something will go wrong. Noble knows it too. I saw it in his eyes. I'm not sure he'll make it out." My voice trembles. "That's why I have to get into those labs. Noble needs—" I choose my words carefully "—*my gift.* I'm the only one who can help him."

Kai's face straightens as he stares into the fire, nodding slowly. His breathing slows down, moving into a deep and methodical pattern. It's the same way he prepares before he spars with his kung fu masters. He's planning, making decisions. He knows what he has to do and sets his mind to it. "Terra Liberata is far bigger than just Palermo's plan to gain a monopoly on telecommunications. We have to be careful with how this plays out, or we won't be able to stop everything Terra Liberata has set in motion." He folds his hands into fists. "But I think I have a plan. I'll get you into Scale Tech and to Noble. We'll stop this—no matter what."

Kai's eyes are distant as he says his name, but as always, his confidence wins out. Kai, the boy who does what is right, even at the cost of his own feelings.

"Okay...whatever your plan is, I trust you." My voice is a whisper.

The words visibly irritate him. He stands and adds another log to the fire, and the sauna blazes. I let dry heat tear into my core. He sits on the bench opposite me. His face is distant and hard, but his numbers are going wild.

I'm exhausted and should sleep, but my brain keeps assessing my body and going over the escape and severe exposure. According to my numbers, if Kai was even five minutes later, I might not have fingers or toes. Which makes me wonder. I turn to him.

"Kai? How did you find me?" I ask. "I was practically a corpse buried in snow, hidden beneath a tree. The odds are nearly impossible."

"I had night vision goggles on, but it was your tech glowing like a beacon that helped me find you. I told you to fix that in Helsinki," he says. "After I traced one of the men's phone locations to the lake where they lost you, it took less than 10 minutes to locate you. I saw you from fifty feet away, at least. No wonder Palermo's men caught you so easily."

I give him a puzzled look. My tech was deader than dead so I'm not sure what he was seeing. His night vision tech must be highly sensitive.

Kai blocks the door with logs and sits on the lower sauna bench monitoring the temperature of the sauna. He pulls a sweater over his head. His black hair is swept down on his face. I inwardly sigh; he's so close but so far away.

Kai pulls out his phone. His face softens as he reads whatever is on the screen. His thumb taps what I assume is a reply to whoever is communicating with him. A jolt in his frequency makes me think it's someone he trusts. He isn't supposed to be in touch with anyone else. Then I remember the girl in Helsinki. My stomach sinks, almost nauseous.

At the same moment, Kai looks up. "We have roughly four hours until we need to leave. We need to get some sleep while your suit is charging, then leave while it's still dark." He exhales, looking out the window into the storm. "You sleep first. I'll stay awake for a bit and keep the fire going."

"Alright." I lie down and close my eyes.

My dad's speech about the Continental Divide percolates in my mind. "*It wasn't which path had least resistance. Both directions had their mountains and valleys. But it became about who I wanted to face those mountains and valleys with, and if we were both headed in the same direction...so no matter what stood in our way, I knew we'd make it to the sea.*"

Those crossroads in my head appear, a jumbled mess of dates and countries and memories and pasts and futures. Every path led me to Finland. I thought it was to find Noble, the one with my gift, who I believed could know me better than anyone, who could travel the same direction as me. What if I'm wrong?

My mind drifts to memories of Kai that I've not allowed myself to relive. I stare at the frequency coming off him, dancing in the firelight in time with mine. My eyes roam over him with waves of gratitude until they can't stay open anymore.

I succumb to sleep.

CHAPTER 55

∞

The dream flickers like the flames in the sauna as another memory pulls me under.

It was two months after I moved back to Seattle. Kai was in town for the third time, and even though I'd been getting along with my father and sisters, his presence made me feel like myself again. On that afternoon, I'd arranged a date in an area of downtown Seattle that wasn't exactly *safe*. Even the street gave me the creeps.

It was at some old-school hole-in-the-wall American diner that was supposed to be real American food. Upon arrival, the waiter encouraged us to order 'the blue-plate special'. So, we walked over the linoleum tiles, past the dozens of handwritten notes on the wall, and grabbed a booth as greasy smoke permeated the air.

My face puckered as I sipped on watery coffee wondering if it was yesterday's brew and forced a smile at Kai, who leaned across the table in the ripped up blue booth.

Kai choked down another piece of greasy meat—*we couldn't even be sure of what it was*—before he wiped his mouth and set down his fork. "Can we stop pretending now and do whatever you really came for in this neighborhood?"

My eyes widened with surprise. "What do you mean?" I asked innocently.

Kai cocked his eyebrows. "Come on, Jo. Admit it. Why are we really here? I have my suspicions, but I want to hear you say it."

I push the food around on my plate with my fork. I'd barely touched anything, either. "What? This is an American experience and I've missed a lot of those. And obviously spending time with you before you leave is my main priority."

"Right…" He wrinkled his brow, then looked at his plate. "If that's the real reason, we're going to regret this for the rest of the day." He holds his stomach like he's going to throw up.

I squirm in my seat. "Ok. Humor me, Chan Dao Kai," I say, our eyes connecting. "Since you know me so well. Why are we really here?"

"Alright." He pushed up his sleeves, never one to say no to a challenge. His gaze was deep, and full of mischief. "According to the news, a human trafficking ring in Seattle was busted on this street a few days ago, but they couldn't find the leader's righthand man *or woman.*" He tapped his fingers on the table, mimicking me. "If I'm correct, our lunch date is your way of checking things out." Our eyes connected over the nearly untouched greasy plates between us. I bit my lip, guiltily. He grinned. "I may not have math in my head, but it doesn't mean I don't calculate you in my own way. In fact, I've memorized enough of you so that soon you won't have to say a word and I'll know what you need. Right now, it's not hard to see that your mind is on the hunt." He laughed.

My heart swelled inside me. There was no end to him, I thought. Whatever I felt for him wasn't a trickle of a small brook or even a river passing through me—it was an ocean, deep and wide, surrounding my every shore.

"So, am I right?" he asked. "Or am I wrong, and this is your new favorite restaurant? In which case, I will beg you never to bring me here again."

My face bunched up. "It was pretty disgusting, huh?"

He laid money on the wrinkled bill. "Yeah, we're going to pay for it later...in a different way." He slipped his fingers into mine and pulled me to my feet. "But this is about you. What is it that you want?"

I squeezed his hand as we walked outside the diner and down the street that hauntingly reminded me of Golden Alley. "I don't know. I thought if I saw something useful I could tip off you or Bai. Maybe my gift would come back." I laughed, like it was a game. "The simulations have been doing weird things to me. I can't sit back and do nothing. You've vowed to never let the Madames or Kings of this world roam the streets. I don't want them to either."

I shook my head. Even I didn't understand what I really meant or even the choices ahead of me. My gift was gone. I was safe and home with my family. All I knew was something inside me was burning and I needed to find out what it was.

He stopped me mid-street. "Why didn't you just say so?" His eyes were so patient.

I peered up at him. "I promised my dad I'd take it easy, remember? And you always call me Trouble. That's why."

He laughed. "You are. Big trouble. I wouldn't have it any other way," he said, his voice doing strange things to me. "We can do anything you want. I think we've learned that we're stronger together, am I right? And if I remember correctly, I told you I never want to see you knocked down in another alley again."

I ran my hand down one strong forearm. His eyes were so sure of everything. When he was there, I never felt afraid. "Well, I was being safe about it," I said, my numbers racing from his eyes to his lips. Goosebumps shot up on his arm. "I brought my own personal bodyguard with me."

His arms swung down, latching onto my hips, pulling me

closer. I buzzed with excitement as we collided. "Is that what I am to you, just a bodyguard?"

I slid my arms around his waist, my insides flipping so hard I almost couldn't contain it. Hundreds of words I wanted to say to him were locked inside me. But none of them would come out, so I just laughed. "Maybe you are. Do you have a problem with that?"

He leaned down and pulled me into a kiss. "Never," he said in between breaths. "It's my favorite job."

∞

It's still dark when I wake to Kai's voice. *"Jo."*

I crack open my eyes. Kai is lying down three feet from me, his body between me and the door. I start to ask him what he wants but notice that his eyes are closed, his lips barely spread apart, his face painted with anguish and joy. He's not awake. Maybe I dreamed it.

I've only been asleep for 3 hours and 22 minutes. I lay my head back down, groggy. I'm surprised he can sleep around me since he doesn't trust me. Three minutes pass when I hear it again.

"Jo."

I wait two minutes for him to wake up and tell me something else has gone wrong or maybe that he wants to talk, but there's no mistaking it. He's whispering my name in his sleep—just like Noble heard him do in Tunisia. *Wherever Kai was, you were on his mind.*

I groan and check K2, which is functioning again. We have fifty minutes before we have to get moving to meet my father and Cesare. I should text Eddie to let him know I'm alive and the plan is still on, even if it's all a mess—Noble at the labs. The ISC launch. The mafia showdown. And...Kai, who is undercover, who I'm not supposed to have contact with, who is three feet away from me...

His breathing is even and steady. I crawl closer and prop myself up on an elbow, looking at him. Resisting the desire to touch his face nearly kills me. For three months I'd only seen him in dreams until I arrived in Finland. I lie back down. Still in Kai's sleeping bag, I scoot closer to him, my body three inches from his. Heat radiates off him. I close my eyes and count every second of this moment, knowing it won't last.

A new day is coming, and I'll face whatever it brings. But for the moment, I'm warm and safe, lying on a hard floor in a sauna, in the middle of Arctic Finland, in a blizzard, and somehow, I can't think of another place I'd rather be.

CHAPTER 56

∞

Thirty-one minutes later, the phantom frequency pulses through me. My eyes blink open. It's still dark outside the sauna windows. Kai is stirring awake, too. He must have moved even closer to me while we slept, because now we're face to face. I lie still, waiting.

"*Zao*, morning," I whisper as his eyes open. The softness in his gaze at seeing me close to him makes my cheeks flush. But then his brow knits together, and his expression folds into suspicion. Kai scoots away and sits up, assessing himself.

Out the sauna window, the arctic morning is still dark, but the white snow softens it. I sit up too, quietly watching him. The fire is burning low, the sauna still warm. Kai throws a small log on the fire, then checks my suit.

"It's at 100%." He unplugs it, and hands it to me. "Feeling ok?"

"Yeah. Fine," I say, moving different parts of my body that are sore but working properly. "Just hungry, and I have to call my dad."

"Here." He hands me some kind of dried jerky meat and a water bottle. A polite smile is on his face, but he's miles away from me. He checks something on his phone, and his lips purse together. He's contemplating, his thoughts running nonstop. I get it. Apart from the mission to stop the blackout, Chan met with Palermo, and the ISC launch is this morning. Not to mention I'm here.

While I chew on jerky, K2 connects to my dad. He answers after two rings, the engine of a snowmobile rumbles to a stop in the background.

"You really love stretching your old man, don't you?" he says. "Didn't you get any of my texts?"

"Sorry, K2 was dead." I do not mention that I almost was too. Now is not the time. "Where are you?"

"We already left, about 30 minutes away from the labs, we think. Is the Dome down?" my dad says.

"For at least 17 hours."

My dad relays the message to Cesare who says something in Italian.

"Cesare is eager to get inside. Apart from meeting up with his men, he is eager to confront Palermo's men and convince them to switch their loyalties to him before Palermo arrives."

My mind calculates his words. "I think you should lay low until we get there," I say. "It's crawling with trackers and patrols—so stay off the main roads. They're also hacking into tech, so don't use names." I look up at Kai. "We're setting out in a few minutes, and we'll be there soon."

"*We*?" my dad says a bit worried. "I thought you said *Noble* left and is inside the labs?"

"*He* is." I think of the right words to say to my father wondering how much to say about what happened after I left Noble's. "Last night, I got into a bit of trouble, and someone else helped me out. He's here with me now..."

"The person is a *he*?" he asks, suspiciously.

"Yes," I whisper, "*he's* a person I trust with my life."

Kai spins his head to look out the window then zips up his jacket. Kai—always on brand, risking his identity to help me.

"I see." My dad exhales with an audible sigh of relief. "Thank God. I didn't like the idea of you being out there alone—wait, he's been with you all night?"

I swallow. "Dad. We gotta go. See you soon." We hang up.

I pull on my snowsuit and set the gauge and temperature. Kai covered the wires and panel with an extra layer of insulation. Hopefully, the cold won't affect it as much. I zip up my suit then grab my boots. While I finish getting dressed, I calculate Kai's movements as he prepares.

Everything from Kai is humming. He's not totally in control, like he's fighting with himself. With a few hours of sleep in me, Agent Ramos's warning seems a bit more urgent. I'm tempted to blame myself, except I remember how the ISC came to PSS. Agent Ramos came to me. My numbers lined out a path for me to be here, in this time and place. Even if the reason isn't clear, I have a part to play in this. No one can stop that.

After two minutes of relative silence, Kai pulls out his facemask then an extra one for me. He holds it out. "Here," he says, his breath uneven. "Yours was ripped up."

I stand, taking the facemask from Kai's hand. Our eyes meet and the frequencies between us wrap into each other, swelling up and down. I can't identify which is his and which is mine. Heat surges between us. He can't see what I see, but none of the feeling is lost on him.

Looking at him now, I can't let this day pass without telling him why I really wrote that letter, why I let him go—even if I'm still confused about what is between Noble and me. Like my dad said, I have to trust myself to make the right decision when the time comes. My hesitation passes and I step toward him, but the moment I do, he briskly moves to the door, his body more tense than ever. A subtle warning lingers on his face.

"It stopped snowing," he says softly. "We should go. We'll discuss the plan on the way." He slides on his gloves and opens the sauna door.

I nod. "Alright."

His frequency bounces in all different directions. Outside, he takes a deep breath of the crisp air and centers himself.

I zip up my snowsuit, pull on the facemask, hood, and gloves. I take one last look at the sauna and memorize every detail, my numbers placing it into a sacred timeline and memory bank that will never be erased.

Then I step outside, joining him in the frigid air. "I'm ready."

CHAPTER 57

∞

The cold snaps at my few millimeters of exposed skin as we trudge through the trees. Our breath puffs as we trek through the fresh snow, my legs tired and sore from yesterday, but at least this time my thermal-reflective suit is functioning properly. I'm warm from head to toe. I hope Kai is too, because his body is as stiff as an icicle.

The snow feels like a physical sign that Kai isn't melting any time soon. Without meaning to, my thoughts turn to Noble and whatever drastic plan he concocted to save his parents who sold his research, who wanted money and status more than they wanted their own son. Noble only ever wanted them to love him for who he really was, not what he could do for them. His parents never really understood, until perhaps now. I think about his dad's audio message. "*If I could do it again, I'd choose you.*" But now it might be too late. Depending on what happens today, they might never see who Noble really is.

I step through the dry snow. Yesterday it was a baptism of fractals and today it's an assassin. So much can change in a day. I almost died out here, but I'm alive because of Kai. The moment doesn't pass lightly. I stare at him, a few feet in front of me. Even in the snow, he moves like a ghost, silent and smooth, just like when he's fighting. I think back to last night, my head on his chest. The scars on his abdomen. My mind drifts to when he found me. The brilliant light and frequencies—I was delusional for sure, but it didn't feel as though I was dreaming. My numbers play over him now, calculating new things. I've never seen him in snow gear or hiking through 14 inches of snow. We've never been in such extreme weather together. It's ridiculous, but even under these horrible circumstances, I'm thankful we get to do this together.

After 2.7 miles of tramping through the trees with no conversation apart from a 'watch out, there's a sensor there', a childish urge kicks up in me, and I bend down. I tell myself it's a way to break the ice with him so we can talk openly while we trek the remaining 2.3 miles, but maybe it's more than that. I dig underneath the dry fluffy snowflakes and grab a couple lumps of the snow's crust layer, then I launch a snowball at him. It smacks him in the center of his back.

He stops, and slowly turns around and pulls his mask down. "Did you just do what I think you did?" His face is puzzled.

I shake my head. "What? No..." I say innocently. "Snow must have fallen off a branch you walked under...or something." I point up. When he looks up, I launch a second, but he smacks it to the ground before it reaches him.

"Or something." He stands there, that same battle raging inside him. His numbers fly around me, humming a song I know well, but everything else in him is a torrent of confusion and mystery. His thoughts have changed about me so drastically. It's selfish, but I wish I could have the old Kai back, no matter what we are now.

I walk up to him, pulling my mask down a bit. "Sorry. You and I never got to play in the snow, so naturally I had to prove I could beat you." I smile up at him. Then, for just a moment, a smile cracks on his face.

"Ah, you already know who would win in a snow fight,"

he teases, that charming confidence surfacing. "In fact, I think I won last night." He steps toward me, clearly ignoring his own warnings.

"You're right," I say, locking eyes with his. "You win. I give up." The moment freezes. The heat of our breath escapes in small clouds and a storm of emotion flurries around us. "Kai...I—"

K2's emergency alarm goes off, breaking our gaze. "Urgent call from Harrison," K2 alerts.

Kai shakes his head, like he's coming out of a daze, and walks forward. His numbers go up like walls again.

I sigh. "Answer."

"You're alive! Thank God!" Harrison says. "Your sensors were scaring us last night. We didn't know if the weather was causing them to malfunction or if you were, you know... Uh, we're also picking up a life sign with you. Are you safe?"

Kai leads us down a winding path toward our goal. I catch up to him, and he slows down for me to walk side by side.

I glance at him. "Yes. It's—"

Harrison cuts me off. "No details over any device right now. We're scrambling our call with as many radio signals as we can but the whole area is heavily monitored. We'll *Veil* you as best we can, but they have military grade tech popping up all over the place, especially after the Dome went down." Harrison pauses. "What's your ETA?"

We're down to 1.5 miles. The sky is a dull blue around us. "Depending on the terrain, maybe 30 minutes. Did you inform the rest of the Helsinki team about today?" I ask, referring to Ramos.

"Of course."

"Did you get the other info I needed?" I ask.

"Take a look at your watch."

The security schematics of Scale Tech's Arctic labs pop into view, the buildings where they hold their central systems, the

Master Satellite Control Center, and storage warehouses. A digital rundown reveals how they secure each building; ID cards, keychain entries—my specialty—or voice signatures.

"Good." We come out of the dense woods into a stretch of land that has far fewer trees, and more frozen lakes. Kai pulls his phone out—I assume to pull up a map, but then he looks back at me. He knows the map is in my head. I point out the best path, and he leads on.

"Basically," Harrison continues, "with your gift, you should have no problem maneuvering the buildings. Now all you have to do is get past the guards, of which there are many. As for the launch and blackouts, better find *your man*, he's our only hope."

Kai tenses at Harrison reference to "your man". He must know it refers to Noble. I almost rip into him, but Harrison has no idea Kai is with me. It's safer that way anyway. "Thanks. I'll be in touch."

Kai speeds ahead leaving thick trails in the snow.

"Hey," I say, practically jumping to catch up with him. "Back there, we were about to talk." If we don't talk before we reach the labs, there may not be another chance. I messed up once, leaving him in a horrible way. I won't do it again.

"I told you. We have nothing to talk about." He darts his brown eyes at me, and electric arrows shoot into me. He winces, then softens. "Look. I've got to keep my head where it matters right now. Being with you is already messing with it. I'm in this game until it ends. You know that. If things go wrong today, I'll lose everything I worked for, and millions will suffer for it. Today we focus on stopping Palermo and getting everyone out of here alive—all without exposing me. Got it?"

"Of course. You're right." Kai is undercover. Not me. Ramos knew my proximity would mess with him, that he wouldn't be able to maintain his cover. "Okay, then tell me what you know."

CHAPTER 58

∞

Kai keeps his eyes on the path, as he huffs out information. "After years of planning, Terra Liberata is finally surfacing. It's run by Palermo Ricci and an elite group of foreign leaders, mostly all very successful businessmen, which you have now roped my father into." His lips tighten. "I guarantee he was marked for life in that meeting. Palermo doesn't let people in without some kind of insurance. Even his backup plans have insurance. He's always doubly prepared."

We're in the trees again. Kai holds a branch for me to pass. My gift is on high alert, picking up sounds and vibrations. As the sun rises, more frequencies are surfacing. I stop to gauge for sensors but many of them are far off, closer to the roads.

"Look, your dad wouldn't listen to me. So we made it as safe as possible. He got back in one piece, with information that helped us," I say, panting as we hike uphill now. "He even told me he wished you could have seen him. You would have been proud."

"I've always been proud of him. But I want him to be alive when I get back." Kai smacks a branch, and snow falls to the ground. "Cesare is coming to claim his throne, which I support. But Palermo is his own kind of insane genius. Launching this satellite with a weapon created by *your man* is his first step to controlling telecommunications, power grids, even the military. No country will be safe. Palermo will use the Super Satellite to take out other satellites one by one until the world is dependent on Terra Liberata. We can stop the blackout, and maybe even Palermo, but it's going to take much more to stop Terra Liberata."

We emerge from the trees into a large clearing and look downhill. Scale Tech's campus is in full view. From the outside, it looks rather mundane. But according to Minttu, it's a hidden city amidst the snow and trees. More than 75% of the campus is subsurface, like many aerospace facilities. The cell towers and antennas are the only giveaways, and what look like water towers surely conceal more antennas.

"Once I can talk to Noble and understand his plan," I say, "we can stop this blackout. Cesare can handle Palermo."

Kai barely glances back at me, then nods. "Fine. But we have to locate Noble and Rafael first. Some Scale Tech buildings go down 50 levels subsurface, and I don't know where they're holding them. Palermo has given Noble until the satellite reaches orbit to override its programming and start the blackout." Kai gives me a hard look.

"Ok. The ISC launch is happening in 30 minutes," I say, calculating.

"Cesare's deadline to hand over Scale Tech for Rafael's life is also the same time." Kai pushes forward. "Once we get inside the facility, we'll need to disable the cameras. In there, I'm Asher Ming. No matter what happens, I have to keep my cover." Kai is tense, all guards up. I can't stand it. The wall of distrust between us is so tall.

Kai's phone buzzes, and he stops to respond to someone, his demeanor turning tender. A pang of jealousy pricks me. I wonder who he's communicating with.

Despite the warnings in my head, something entirely stupid

rushes out of my mouth. "The girl I saw in Helsinki...is she undercover too or is she something else?"

Kai stops and pulls down his facemask. The look on his face is unmistakable. I've pushed him too far, crossed the line. I did the exact thing Agent Ramos warned me not to do.

"Jo, what are you doing?" he asks, his voice cold. "You left me, or don't you remember? I got home after Tunisia, not even fully recovered from almost dying, to a letter from you that said we're done. No explanation. No answering my calls. Done. Like we never existed. You don't get to ask these questions right now."

I'm the one who hurt him, and yet an avalanche of hurt falls on me. But he's right—except for one thing. I made a sacrifice. I gave him up so he could live his life without regrets. He doesn't know what I told him that night in the safe house. He doesn't know why I left or that if I had let him communicate with me, I would've changed my mind. And the fact that he doesn't trust me anymore is a knife tearing apart my insides. I have to tell him everything. I have to make this right before this day is over.

"Kai," I say, trembling as I remember the night he almost died, when I confessed that I loved him. "I want to explain." Even as I say this, Agent Ramos is screaming in my head. And Noble's face and offer is flashing there, too. *Run away with me.* The crossroads are coming to a point.

"Really? Right here and now? Not three months ago?" Kai motions to the trees. "It's not the right time, Jo."

"If not now, then when?" I ask. "I didn't know I'd get to see you, and I don't like how things are between us. After today, I..."

"We're not together anymore. You came here for Noble, remember? You told me that," he says, his tone is without feeling.

I glance up at the trees. The light is brighter now, but it

won't last for long. We have less than twenty minutes before we arrive. "I'll admit it. I came here for him. My past with Noble is complicated. He showed up at the same time you were offered that job. He shares my gift, and there were all kinds of unresolved feelings between us that I needed to understand." I walk closer to him. He backs up. "And I left you in the wrong way. I did. I'm sorry I hurt you. I had my reasons. And I'm sorry about your dad. Is this why you don't trust me?"

"No." He shakes his head. His eyes are burning holes through me. "All of that I understand, and I could forgive it all. Even bringing my dad into this. But that's not the problem." He swallows hard like there's a huge lump in his throat.

"Then what did I do that made you stop trusting me?" I ask, terribly confused.

"You really don't know? That makes it much worse," he says, his face deepening into the Kai I know who is ready to face whatever is coming. He's held it back, but now it's loose. "I stopped trusting you the moment you drugged me."

I stop breathing. The blood drains from my face. Hypothermia is better than this icy chasm between us—one that I created.

He knows about SWAY.

CHAPTER 59

∞

The truth is written on my face. I'm misunderstood, my intentions misconstrued, but I'm definitely guilty. Just as I couldn't stop the EMP shockwave launching me into a snowbank, neither can I prevent the blow from his words stealing my breath.

"Kai..." I gasp. "I didn't drug you."

He clenches his jaw. "Jo. That's exactly what you did. You put a chemical in my body, which took away my faculties. I'm a trained spy. I recognized it right away, the symptoms, the feeling. Everyone at PGF is familiar with the different brain-altering chemicals out there. We've built up immunities to some, me included. I just couldn't believe that you of all people would do that to me." His frequency is vibrating so powerfully I need to steady myself. "Jo, you used a weapon against me. As soon as you left, I asked them to check me for it, praying with everything in me that I was wrong. That you would never go that far." His face is distorted with the memory.

He shakes his head. "But the test came back positive. The girl I loved poisoned me. The girl I trusted with everything, with all of me—betrayed my trust." He looks at me with wild and mournful eyes. "How could I ever again be with someone who would do that? I trusted you completely, and you used it against me, with a kiss." Behind his eyes are mountains of pain and betrayal. It would be easier if they just fell and crushed me, instead of forcing me to try to stand under their weight.

My heart shatters to pieces inside me. I replay the memory in a completely different light, and he's right. What I thought I was doing out of love and sacrifice was done in foolishness. I believed I could get him to tell me the truth so he could take the job without hurting me. But I took away his choices. I took away his trust.

"Kai..." I can barely speak. "Let me explain—"

He cuts me off. "For three days I sat in Tunisia wondering how to live with the fact that my own girlfriend drugged me. Seeing you with your childhood friend didn't help either. I knew you had things to figure out, but I never needed you to be perfect. I believed we'd come far enough together to tell each other the truth. I broke rules for you. My loyalty was to you first. I believed in us...until that moment. After that, everything started to shake. I planned on confronting you but then I received your letter. The girl I knew, here one day and gone the next. No goodbyes. Just like my mom. *Phoenix. Jo. Mila. Whoever you are.* Maybe I never even knew the real you..."

"No." I shake my head, my eyes stinging now. "If anyone does, it's you."

"Not when I can't remember anything, Jo," he says angrily. "Not when you controlled an outcome between us without my knowledge."

If energy could crumble, it's doing it now. *His love for you is dangerous,* Agent Ramos said, *it can get him killed on the field.* Which is another reason I should have bit my tongue and let him do his job. But it's too late. Everything is out in the open.

"I never meant to betray you. I just needed to know the truth. You wanted the job, Kai, and you were made for it. You wouldn't have chosen it if I'd given you a choice."

"Why didn't you trust me to tell you the truth? I would

have." He squeezes his eyes, a cloud of his breath huffing between us. "But you still don't understand, do you?"

"What?" I ask.

"That you're right, I would've chosen you over the job. Because that is what people do when they've given themselves to each other." He grits his teeth. "I didn't want to make decisions for just myself anymore. I wanted to make decisions *for us.* We were supposed to talk about it. Don't you think we could have come up with a way to make it work? A way to do it *together.*" He eyes the path in front of us leading to the labs, rubbing his gloved hands together. "But that's over now. You came here for Noble. You should stick with that. Maybe you two are the only ones who can understand each other. I didn't always understand everything about you, but I did trust you, and I can't do that anymore. For me, a relationship without trust isn't worth having. Which means, we don't have a future."

After I sent him the letter, his pain tore at my own. Right now, everything is a thousand times worse. With the truth out in the open, our frequencies spike, as if to prevent drowning in a deluge of emotion.

There is nothing I can say right now that can take this hurt away.

My heart is frozen in the middle of the crossroads. Choices are hounding me on each side. Noble, the boy who has my gift, who I loved in my childhood, who's in danger right now, is on one side. On the other side, there's Kai, the boy who pulled me out of darkness after I escaped the Pratt, the boy I confessed my love to…the boy I drugged and lost. Everything is muddled. Too messed up. When I told him I loved him, it was true. It was real. We both felt it. But now…

I step closer to him. He doesn't move. The wind blows a dust of frozen fractals between us. Snowflakes are landing on his cheeks.

"You don't remember anything that I said to you in Tunisia," I say, panting in the freezing air.

"Obviously. Isn't that the point?" He's still and cold like a sculpture of ice.

"It was important..." My chest is rising and falling as if an ocean was swelling inside me. Another step closer. I look at his eyes, then his lips. The first lips I'd ever kissed. I move one-inch closer, so close that the trees and snow feel like a dream, like we're removed from the world all together.

His hurt vibrates like a pack of hungry wolves howling in the night, but the love pulsing from him is stronger. Almost tangible. It's racing in every muscle and tendon he has. It's wound up tight in the adrenaline that saves his life, a sacred place where he centers himself and holds all his treasure. He doesn't hide it from me. Even now, he lets it loose and I feel it all, both love and pain.

"It must have been," he quips, his tone hurt.

"I..." My breath catches. He deserves to know how I feel... but the words stick in the middle of my throat, like all the other times I wanted to tell him. I'm at the floodgates: if they swing open, I don't know if I'll be able to stop everything from rushing out. Why could I do it with SWAY but not now? What is wrong with me?

Kai's heart is racing. He's waiting for an answer, searching me for some explanation he's longed to hear. The hum inside him radiates with so much love he could light the whole forest on fire.

Kai's hard shell cracks, just for a moment. "What was so important?"

The crossroads of equations light up, brighter than ever before, but I'm trapped in the dark until I choose it. The phantom frequency is pulsing so close I swear it's inside me. I want it to wrap around me, lasso me away. My eyes squeeze shut. What am I doing? If Kai hears this now, won't it mess with his head even more? He'll never be able to finish this job. He needs to stay focused so he can live and save others. I'm once again repeating the same mistake that caused him pain in the first place. And yet, how can I not tell him?

My watch buzzes. My indecision is a second too long. K2's emergency comm-line blares with erratic shouts—my dad's frantic voice jars us back into reality.

"Jo!" My dad blares out. "We're in trouble. Come quick!"

CHAPTER 60

∞

SCALE TECH ARCTIC LABS
LAPLAND, FINLAND

Sounds of running. Yelling. Panting.

Panic creeps into my father's voice. "We're outnumbered!"

"Dad! How many are there?" I scream into K2. I need numbers to calculate. "Where are you?" Shuffling noises block my ability to hear clearly, but his comm-line is still open.

"Not sure," he shouts through the static. "Southern compound by a cell tower—"

The line drops.

Kai jumps into action, his body straightening into a mountain. A regretful look is in his eye as he pulls up his facemask. "Like I said, this isn't a good time to talk."

I nod, pulling up my mask too. "Let's go."

Kai and I dash down the hill, adrenaline racing through us. Our speed increases from four to six miles per hour with the downward momentum. The snow is thicker here. My legs burn as we bound through it. My sight is set on the labs and reaching my father. Equations race alongside me downhill: expended energy level up 310%; numbers of mass and acceleration computing my force of gravity; snow depth 18 inches; 6 more minutes to reach Scale Tech's southern compound. We could be too late. They could be dead by then. I ignore the odds.

As we run, the schematics Harrison sent unfold in my mind. Buildings. Labs. Sensors. Guards. Cameras—I calculate a path of least resistance to reach my dad at the southern gates. Fifteen patrols are stationed at the Dome Tower—a bonus from last night. Twelve other guards—that I can sense—patrol other buildings ahead of us. My mind runs through a set of scenarios...more than half pointing to Kai. His cover cannot be blown.

We slow down as we approach the entrance to the compound. Kai looks over at me, his eyes reaching into mine. "Tactical move? What's the map in your head saying?"

This nugget of trust—*if only in my gift*—fuels me. I evaluate the movements and patterns of the guards, and a path with significantly lower odds of getting caught is mapped out. "This way," I say, leading us through the maze of buildings. Daylight increases. So do the shadows.

The road is empty, but it won't be for long. We'll be spotted for sure if we're not strategic.

We weave through dozens of buildings and antennas. An electrical frequency is moving quickly toward us. A vehicle. We have two seconds to duck behind a snowbank. I grab Kai and pull him down, just before the SUV passes. When it's gone we pop back up and keep moving.

"There!" Kai shouts as the southern labs are in view.

Three large warehouses sit in a row. We don't have any visual on my father or Cesare yet, but behind an industrial roll-up garage door there are a plethora of human frequencies and the sound of commotion coming from inside is enough to tell us they're in there.

I groan, numbers flying through my mind. "I can't believe they went inside without us." We head that way.

"He is *your* dad. Maybe the trouble part comes from him?" Kai says, cracking his knuckles.

We sneak past a line of black vans parked in front of the warehouse, our backs against a wall. "Well, *your* dad effectively infiltrated the mafia," I retort, then bite my tongue at my stupidity.

Kai huffs. "Then I guess we have a chance. Ready?"

I nod.

We reach the building entrance, where a door is cracked open. Loud crashes come booming from a lower level. We fly in the direction of a set of metal stairs and the noises increase. Thirty-four feet scuffling. Smashing. Breaking. Grunts and thuds getting louder. I cringe.

At the top of the stairs, we look down into a storage room full of containers. A full-on fist fight is going on. Six security guards are throwing punches. Men are slammed up against racks and metal tubes. Glass casing is shattering on the ground. Cesare and my dad are mixed up in the fight. But I'm not close enough to see if they're okay.

Kai sighs with relief. "Thank God—they're not Palermo's men. They're Scale Tech security. They won't recognize me." Kai looks at me. "If you disable cameras before Palermo gets here, I can swing both ways, hopefully without getting caught."

"Okay."

Five more security guards arrive on the scene at the same time we do. My eyes dart to Kai. "You'd better get down there!"

A cocky smile spreads across his face. "With pleasure."

CHAPTER 61

∞

Kai pulls on his mask and storms into the storage level, vaulting over a row of boxes at a full sprint. I race after him, having no time to tell him that the odds of our plan working just dropped to single digits.

Kai targets those five security guards first. I slink behind racks of supplies, scanning the scene for my dad. My mouth drops. Cesare and my father are going fist to fist against four other men. Both of them are fighting...and not unsuccessfully.

My dad's legs and arms jolt through the air swiftly, his motions strong and concise. Even if he doesn't operate with Kai's elegance, he's executing all the kung fu moves that Kai taught him—actually holding his own—with a trained security guard. Technically, this is his first real fight. I'm impressed.

As I come around a corner, my dad catches sight of me just long enough to become distracted. I cringe at what's about to happen—*slam!* My dad is knocked down by a full body tackle. He flies backwards landing on his back with a hard thud, but somehow carries the momentum of his attacker and reverse rolls out of it and lands on his feet. He bounces up with intensity, blocking an incoming wild swing. The block definitely hurts my dad's arm but to his credit, he presses on.

His footwork is clean, moving in close, twisting from the hips and releasing three more heavy blows to another guard coming at him. There's a crunch and groan, and the guard actually goes down. I'm pretty sure that guy will wake up soon, but it'll be with a monster headache.

Kai taught my dad too well. I'm *speechless.*

My eyes move to Cesare. His face is already a bloody mess but there's a savage determination on it. A purple knot forming on Cesare's forehead tells me he used his head to incapacitate the man lying on the ground next to him.

Two more men come at him. Cesare curses, then spits blood on the ground. He tucks his chin and dives into the mix. His moves are fierce, messy, and dirty. He is a street fighter through and through. Kicks to the groin. Knees to the face. Elbows to the neck. He grabs for a piece of metal tubing and slams it into a man's chest. I cringe. *Ouch.* Okay. Definitely mafia training.

With Kai's frequency dancing to the side of me, I crouch behind the rack and text Harrison: *I need Felicia to get me into Scale Tech security. I need all camera security rerouted to me and access to the main computer systems.*

Harrison: *She's on it. Hold tight. The launch is happening right now on every news channel. I'm guessing you'll miss it?*

Me: *Too busy trying to stop it from blacking out Europe. How's Chan?*

Harrison: *Safe and sound. Our guards are with him 24/7. Pens is working on his intel now.*

I sigh with relief. Nothing can happen to Chan with PSS around.

Harrison: *How's it going there?*

I look at the beatdown happening in front of me and scratch my forehead.

Me: *Better than expected? Cesare's really starting to use his head.*

I turn back to the fight. My father and Cesare are now cornered but going strong, until one guard brings out a baton like they had in the tunnels in Helsinki. Kai hates weapons. He thinks using them is weak. Like a sixth sense, he sees the baton and hardens.

Barely out of breath, Kai takes down the two guards he's fighting, then races over to the guy with the baton headed for Cesare and my father. Kai slides into the middle of the brawl, between the legs of a guard in a wide stance. He simultaneously swings out his legs like a break-dancer, spinning around and taking down the guard. A quick elbow to the gut followed by a loud groan and that guy is finished. Jumping to his feet Kai pulls to a stop when he sees my father and jumps in alongside him. Kai grabs my father's arm and spins him around just in time to stop another attack. My dad uses the momentum to launch his next move. They're now fighting back-to-back, master and student.

"Hi, Mr. Rivers," Kai says, over his shoulder.

"Did I just hear K—?" My dad's relief tumbles out at the sound of Kai's voice, but there's no time. A massive kicking fest ensues—mostly involving Kai, who takes down twice the number of men as my father and Cesare.

A right hook, sweeping kicks, punches and jabs. Things I never could have imagined are happening before my eyes. My dad and ex-boyfriend fighting side by side—not to mention that they're both fighting on *Cesare Di Susa's* team, which makes the equation even more unbelievable.

Blood and bravery spill out from knuckles and lips as the fight continues, but I need to make sure these cameras go down before they discover Kai is fighting on the wrong side. We need to maneuver around this place unseen if I'm going to find Noble and Rafael.

I close my eyes, wondering if I can feel Noble's frequency anywhere close to me. But there's nothing. Scale Tech is massive, so I'll need access to the cameras to scan the property for Noble and Rafael—and fast.

A second later, Felicia's voice is in my ear: "I've got eyes on you. Move to the southeast part of the warehouse. On the back wall, there's a security panel. You need to plug K2 into it, or I can't shut the cameras down and you'll be tripping sensors everywhere."

"Got it."

Following Felicia's instructions, I plug K2 into the panel on the wall. Instantly it recognizes my watch as a threat and tries to lock me out, but Felicia is already inside.

"Ok, Jo," Felicia says. "You should have access. Just need one more minute to gain control."

While Felicia does her thing to reroute the camera feeds to K2 and our system, I work fast, scanning the footage from each room in the Scale Tech complex on K2's tiny screen, searching for two people. Fifty-five seconds later, Rafael's familiar frame pops up, pacing in a small lounge in lab 5, which a sign says is the Aerodynamics Research Lab. A camera in the hall outside the lounge shows three guards stationed at the door. *Found you.*

After 23 seconds of scanning each lab in the security cameras database, I locate Noble and my heart wrenches. He's crouched in front of four monitors, madly working on something. His body language is tenser than ever, like he's balancing two reactive substances about to combust.

A large, dark-haired man sits behind him in a folding chair holding his head in his hand. His clothes are wrinkled, his body a mess of anxious frequencies. He looks up every few seconds at Noble, his face an older version of the boy in front of him. Dark circles hang under his eyes and his face is so drowned with grief my stomach lurches. Dr. James Adams.

Noble's dad.

But his father is not what makes my calculations skyrocket

and our odds plummet.

Felicia's once again in my ear, her voice starting to tremble. "Scale Tech cameras are now under our control. K2 has full access. There's only one building I can't shut down..." She doesn't want to say it, "The Master Satellite Control Center. It's a completely different electrical and security system. It's totally rigged in every way. I'd warn you to steer clear of that building, but it doesn't look like that will be possible..."

I suck in a large breath, holding back a thousand numerical explosions. Noble is in the Master Satellite Control Center—and what Felicia means by 'rigged' is no small thing. Judging by the surging electrical frequency surrounding it, it's not just security sensors. The whole building is wired with bombs, and they're ticking.

CHAPTER 62

∞

The power pulsing from the Master Satellite Control Center is enough to take out the entire building and the lab connected to it. Palermo is taking no chances. He's covering all his tracks, which means that control center is where I need to be.

With the security sensors down and cameras re-routed to me, I run back to the fight. Sweaty and panting, the three victors stumble over. All the guards have been taken out, hands bound.

I make eye contact with Kai. "Cameras are down."

"Good." Kai pulls down his mask, and turns to my dad, impressed and nodding with approval. "Your moves aren't bad."

"I had a good teacher." My dad, bruised and purple, is glowing. He throws an arm over Kai's shoulder.

Cesare wipes his mouth, then cracks his neck. His hands spread open to Kai. "Ah, the real *Capo. Grazie.*"

"Cesare." Kai claps him on the back. I don't miss the look they exchange. They know each other much better than I think. What has happened in the three months after we broke up?

"Not exactly plan A, huh?" Kai says to Cesare, a shift of urgency in his voice. "Where are your men?"

"They should arrive any moment at the southern gates. Then I confront Palermo's men and call them back to me." He grunts, looking over his shoulder at the open door. Blood trickles from a cut on his hairline, but he combs his hair back in place like it's no big deal. He exhales. "But first, my son. Where is he?"

"I found him and Noble," I say.

"Then what are we waiting for?" Cesare says. "Let's go get Rafael."

The clock ticking in my mind compels me to stop him. "No, he's okay. He's not in danger yet. But we'll all be in trouble if we don't stop Palermo and help Noble." I look at Kai. "Rafael's safe. For the moment. But where they're holding Noble on the north side is wired with explosives. Doesn't look good. I don't have any other details."

"I need to get my son," Cesare says, fiercely.

Kai stops him. "Jo's right. It won't work. Not with the timeline. The launch is happening right now. You need to gather your men and prepare. Palermo is nearly here to ensure the blackout weapon is ready. If you need to confront his men before he arrives, that moment is now, or you'll be in far greater danger, and so will Rafael." Kai juts his chin to the north. "They're on the north side of the complex by the Master Satellite Control Center, where Palermo will arrive soon. They'll be ready with far more security."

"Cesare, I know you won't like this," I say, "but I'll get Rafael and bring him to you. Draw them into the Solar Power lab. We'll rendezvous there."

Frequencies scramble in the background, feet pounding and voices. I tense and look at Kai. "We don't have much time. More guards are on the way."

"You're not going alone, are you?" my dad asks.

Kai looks at me. His frequency wraps around mine with a fierce warmth. I shiver. "There will be guards at Rafael's door," he says. "I'll send your dad after I take care of the guards, okay?"

I look at my dad, then back at Kai. "I'll be fine. I have tasers and a map in my head. What we need is backup. We're outnumbered."

Reluctantly, they agree.

I look over at Cesare. "Your men better be loyal."

CHAPTER 63

∞

I sneak down the corridor, following the floor plan in my head to the lounge where Rafael is held. Frequencies of all kinds spit like grease in a pan, but none of them are human until I peek around the corner and spy on the door where Rafael is being held.

Kai was right. Three guards stand at the door. I pull out my bracelet and test a drone. They're at 65% capacity, but they should do the job long enough for me to get Rafael out.

I stay hidden behind the corner in the hallway as I prepare my drones—four left. The guards are 24 feet away. Like at the Infinity Dome, I'll need to get 12 feet closer before I fire the drones to ensure they're strong enough to take down each man. They'll see me, but causing confusion always buys time.

My fingers fumble to program the drones. The weight of the calculations coils around me as I think of Noble surrounded by explosives. But I can't dwell on that now. I ruffle my long blonde hair from my hood. The numbers aren't exactly in my favor, but I've always been good with low odds. With a smile on my face, I turn the corner in full view.

"*Moi*," I say, using a greeting from my phrasebook. The guards straighten at the sight of me, rattling off a string of sentences in Finnish.

Seven more feet to go. My chin is up. I stride confidently up to them. "Sorry. I don't speak Finnish," I say. "I'm looking for the propulsion research facility?" On the map, it's down the hall.

"Stop here, please." They put out their hands. "We need to validate your security level."

"What?" I ask innocently. Two more feet. I keep walking. They step forward, barricading the hall. But it's too late, three drones take off. They buzz off me like hornets, striking the guards' necks before they know what's happening. The men fall with a crackle of electricity.

I wince, though I'm grateful at how easily they went down. I don't want to see any more blood today, even if I know that's not possible.

"Sorry," I mutter as I step over them.

The lock on the door is not simple. It's an ultrasonic voice activated key. These aren't even on the market yet. They detect sound waves in voices as passwords. I groan. Thankfully, these devices are not foolproof yet. I just despise what I have to do.

"K2," I order, "Record."

I stand over the guard, who is temporarily knocked out and drop my knees into his abdomen. A painfully large moan comes out. I take the recording to the door, and it opens.

I enter another lab with twenty-foot ceilings. It's a clean and organized workspace with a lounge. In a common area with a kitchen, there's a TV screen on the wall. A young man with wavy brown hair sits on a couch watching the ISC rocket carry the Super Satellite up into the sky.

At the sound of the door, he spins around, anxious. But his big green eyes brighten after he sees past the blonde hair and snow gear. He jumps to his feet, wonder in his eyes.

"*Mila?* Is it really you?" For two seconds, we stare at each other. He's older now, his jaw even more defined. His shoulders wider. The frequency undulating from him is calm, despite what he must have been through. But then I remember: he is the son of a crime boss. "You're not the person I expected to walk through that door." His familiar accent fluctuates like music in the room, flooding me with memories of the Pratt, which hold both darkness and light.

"I got your message," I say, shrugging.

"It's good to see you," he says, "but if you're here I assume that means we're in big trouble?"

"Why does everyone assume that when I am present?" I grimace. "But unfortunately, you're right. Your father is here too. There's a war about to go down between your dad and Palermo. We've also got to stop a massive blackout and the sabotage of the ISC satellite."

He sighs. "Yes, I know. The weapon is already in the sky." He strides toward me, kissing both cheeks then he wraps me into a tight embrace. "Thank you for coming, anyway."

My dad races into the room, panting. Kai sent him. My dad's eyebrows rise at seeing me in the arms of a different guy this time. He has impeccable timing. "Hello," he says, slowly.

I slip from Rafael's embrace and wave him over. "Dad, this is Rafael, Cesare's son."

My father gives Rafael the usual *Jason Rivers stare down.* "So, this is your boyfriend from the Pratt?"

"He wasn't my boyfriend," I groan, remembering my earlier embarrassment at Noble's house.

"What?" Rafael says. "We had *something*...right? Well, until you met Kai."

I roll my eyes but seeing that I gave up a chance at escaping the Pratt to save Rafael from drowning on the container ship, I have to admit there was *something* between us. "Yeah, it was...friendship."

Rafael beams at me until he notices my dad, then he straightens. "And totally innocent. After I left China, we never saw each other again. Until today." He reaches out his hand. "*Salve. Rafael Di Susa.* I am not what you must think I am." Rafael pours out his charming accent for my father.

My dad stretches out a hand. "Call me Jason. I've become acquainted with your father. Better grab your jacket."

"Ah, father and daughter working together," he says, a gleam of mischief in his eyes, as he slips into winter clothing and boots. "Family business isn't always easy, eh?"

"I've learned that recently." My dad gives me a funny glance. I shrug and mouth, "Sorry."

"Let's hurry. Your family business and father won't wait too long." One by one we step over the guards, my numbers leading us to a back exit out of the building.

"How is my papá?" Rafael asks, zipping up his coat.

"Your old man has still got it," my dad says. "Let's go."

We pace down long, narrow halls designed like a maze to keep intruders out. But with the map in my head, I could take these twists and turns blindfolded.

Rafael speaks with my dad as we make our way. "Your daughter saved my life, a couple of times actually," Rafael says. "That's why I messaged her. Palermo is *pazzo*—crazy. Terra Liberata runs deep, everywhere. But Mila took down King. If anyone can stop Palermo, Mila can."

My dad keeps up a brisk pace with a smirk on his face. "Believe me," he says. "*Mila* surprises me on a regular basis with *who* she is and *what* she can accomplish."

Rafael moves closer to me, his voice low. "*Asher Ming* is working with Palermo. Have you seen him? Is he here too?"

He knows about Kai. "Yeah," I say, avoiding his eyes. "He's here."

"I'd assume so, if *you're* here," Rafael says. I give him a tight smile.

We make it to the back exit. Pulling open the door, the howling icy wind numbs my face and creeps into my extremities, but the bitter cold also clears my mind.

My numbers calculate a roughly 1,090-foot stretch to the north side of the Scale Tech campus. About three football fields away. In the snowy maze of buildings, it should take us fifteen minutes.

The three of us tuck ourselves along the side of the building, hurrying in single file along a cleared path. In this area, there are very few guards around—they must be congregating on the north side. My dad takes the lead to break the cold wind. I take the chance to talk with Rafael.

"Raf," I say, through my facemask, "when we arrive, I'll need to get to where Palermo is holding the scientist. We're going to stop the blackout."

He shakes his head. "It won't be easy. Palermo is prepared. Nobody can trace his connection to the satellites, except those few who he's either threatened or bribed to stay quiet."

I exhale in hard clouds of breath. "Tell me what you know."

With eyes forward and voice low, he says, "Terra Liberata is steeped in so many industries. Take your pick—energy, medicine, communications. But after my father refused to sell Palermo his Scale Tech shares, Palermo found me in town with both an offer and a threat. To help my girlfriend," Rafael repeats.

"You have a girlfriend?" I ask. I'm not surprised—Rafael's dimples could charm any girl.

His shoulders shrug to his ears. "*Spero.* I hope so. If she's still waiting for me after this *casino*—this mess," he says, a hopeful look on his face. A frown soon replaces it. "My girlfriend has a rare illness. Palermo claimed he could cure her in exchange for my loyalty. I was tempted, but eventually refused him. That's when his deal changed—my life in exchange for Scale Tech."

"But Palermo owns other communication companies," I say.

"Not like this one," he explains. "Terra Liberata needs

Scale Tech to control satellite communications. With the Super Satellite, they'll use it to hack any satellite or destroy their competition. Once Palermo is in control of Scale Tech, the ISC will end. Palermo always has a backup plan, and he always makes sure there are repercussions for those who betray him. *Mila*, he will destroy anyone who crosses him." We walk a minute in silence.

Repercussions. The word reverberates through me like a siren. I don't like it. Cesare also used the same word. They know what Palermo is capable of. I turn to my father beside me and grab his gloved hand. "Keep your mask on at all times. Don't let anyone see you, ok?" My dad nods. The lab comes into view.

We crouch down, taking in the scene. Multiple vehicles are parked outside the building. All are clean without a buildup of snow or ice, and slightly steaming, indicating Palermo and his men must have just arrived.

Rafael leans in. "Kai is crazy to infiltrate Terra Liberata. Are you ok with that?"

My face goes rigid. I suck in a deep breath. The answer is complicated. *Do I like him in danger?* No. *Do I believe he can succeed?* Yes. *Is he here because I forced his hand?* Most likely. But all I say is, "Actually, we broke up. It's a long story."

"*Non ci credo*," he says in disbelief. "When I saw you together in Shanghai, I had never seen such chemistry between two people before. *Sì*, I was slightly jealous, but I was never going to win." He shakes his hands at me. "*Mila, perché*? He's one of the best guys I know."

I narrow my eyes at him. "You met him for a few weeks." But the look in his eyes unfolds a different story. "That's not true, is it?"

He shakes his head. "After my papá and I went to Croatia with the Ghost Markers program, it was very stressful. PGF was in charge of our case. It was Kai who checked on us. He did more than he had to. He became a friend."

I swallow. All those times I thought he was bored with me, Kai's trips were actually about searching out Red's history and helping Rafael. He knew those things would make me happy. He was thinking long term, while I was worried about the day to day.

"I didn't know," I say, my stomach in a knot.

We arrive at the north side of the campus. A web of frequencies comes from the Solar Power Lab that is attached to the Master Satellite Control Center. Noble's frequency slips onto my radar, furthering my unease.

"Kai wanted to tell you," Rafael whispers, "but Ghost Markers is completely confidential." Rafael draws a finger to his lips. We slide up to a back door of the lab, suspiciously unguarded. I try my hand at the numerical keypad and crack the code in seconds. A torrent of frequencies moves inside the building. We sneak inside, my dad taking up the rear, uncannily silent.

The Solar Power Lab is a large clean room that contains twenty-two rows of 6x6 blue solar cells and equipment for assembling metal rigs and frameworks. Full-body zippable cleanroom bunny suits hang at stations in the back corner. We sneak inside, hiding behind the rows of solar panels.

Palermo is not here, but five of his men line one side of the facility. Among them are men I recognize from the banquet and the chase last night. They look wide-eyed and angry at the spectacle staring them down from across the inner courtyard.

Twenty-one of Cesare's men stand in ranks like a chain link fence, facing off against Palermo's thugs. Most of them are older, like Cesare, although there are a few young, strong men among them, perhaps their sons.

Then two dozen men enter from the other side of the Lab. *"È uscito di prigione."* Whispers and murmurs in Italian fill the room as they spot Cesare. "*Allora, le voci che giravano erano vere. È tornato." The rumors are true. He's returned.*

These men believe Cesare betrayed them. Their bodies harden, preparing for a fight. Unless Cesare has an old mafia trick up his sleeve, another bloodbath is about to erupt.

CHAPTER 64

∞

The tension in the room boils, but no one makes a move. Soon I understand why. They're waiting for Cesare to speak, giving him a chance to defend himself. It must be a pact within *la famiglia*.

Kai is not standing with Palermo's men, but his frequency is close by. Noble's is too. The two of them so close together is confusing. I need to get to Noble and this seems like a good time, but I can't leave yet. I hang back in the shadows with Rafael and my father, calculating the situation and looking for Kai.

I also text Harrison: *Over 50 mafiosi about to brawl. Send backup.*

Cesare steps forward, his chest puffed, and head held high. "È vero," he says, his voice echoing through the lab in Italian. "I've returned to put an end to this division. Some say I abandoned this family, my role. But I never broke my oath. The Susa-Ricci legacy was about blood, honor and loyalty." He clears his throat, a strong frequency surging from him. "Terra Liberata's power has grown far beyond Palermo. It goes against our family's oath. Civilians were always off-limits as targets. Palermo's plans will devastate billions. It's not our family's way." He stops, peering around the room at them.

Cesare walks among them, a terrifying confidence radiating from him. "My grandfather gave me this legacy because he believed in *my* leadership," he growls. "For years, I did not believe in it until I understood that true leaders make their own legacy—by standing for what they believe in. Now I'll fight for that." He stands taller, rallying them. "You once believed in me as your *Capo*. I'm asking you to do it again."

A low murmur moves over the crowd. Rafael is zinging with energy beside me.

A shiver runs over me as if Cesare is also speaking to me. His words are potent and strangely familiar. Clearly, a change has taken place in him. And his speech...it carries a truth and teachings I recognize. There's a ring to it that I've heard before.

My skin tingles with heat as Kai sneaks up next to me, moving in front of me like a shield, but his finger is to his lips. "Shh."

Cesare's voice is a roar now. "I am the heir of Terra Liberata's legacy. The rightful boss. I'm calling you back to loyalty, blood and honor. Who will answer?" He tears off his jacket and pulls up his sleeve, revealing a crest tattooed on his arm. "Join me and you will be part of a new legacy." He kisses the tattoo, then raises his fist in the air.

Rafael leans over. "Thank you, Mila." Then he removes his jacket, the same tattoo on his forearm. He storms past me and stands by his father's side, kissing the crest tattoo and pumping his fist in the air.

Two men, who used to be loyal to Cesare, break ranks from Palermo's men and join Cesare. He dips his head to them.

"Capo." They respect him even after all these years. Even after his betrayal, they are giving him a second chance.

"*Insieme siamo più forte!* We're stronger together!" Cesare yells out to the men. "Stand with me against Palermo!"

Five more trickle to his side. But it's not nearly enough,

with an unknown number of guards around.

My father doesn't understand the speech Cesare is delivering in Italian like I do, but he can already sense how this night will go down. From the glint in his eye, he won't shrink from it. He leans over to Kai. "So, are we jumping back in?"

Kai's brow tightens. "Mr. Rivers, I can't be part of this fight, or I'll blow my cover. Palermo will be waiting for Asher Ming. He's almost here," he says. "And, Jason, round two will get very ugly."

My father touches his nose, then the fresh bruise on his cheek. "There aren't enough men joining Cesare. And after that speech, I have to stand with him. Our success depends on it, right?" Then he looks at me. "What are my odds?"

I assess the situation, but the odds aren't clear yet—it all depends on Cesare and Palermo's men. Some haven't chosen a side yet. Before I respond, my dad holds up his hand.

"Don't tell me. Keeps it real. Wish me luck, sweetheart." Then he looks at Kai. "Keep her safe."

Kai dips his head. "Yes, sir."

My stomach tightens as I watch my father strut out to stand beside Cesare. How many times will this trip render me speechless? The numbers are unfolding before my eyes. The energy in the room turns dark and the crossroads is almost before me.

I turn to Kai. "I have to find Noble now."

Negative equations explode as men on both sides contemplate their next move, a gathering of power. It's easy to feel in their breath, their heartbeats, the fluctuation in their frequencies. I'm worried for my father. An all-out brawl is inevitable, which means it's time for us to leave.

Kai turns to me, a gleam of pain in his eyes. "Let's go find your man."

CHAPTER 65

∞

Our masks are pulled over our faces as we exit the Solar Power Lab, and loop around the backside to reach the Master Satellite Control Center. The tension of the mafia war behind us is so enormous that the odds of a guard recognizing Kai right now are slim. Still, more than 55% of my brain is calculating ways to keep him safe. The rest is worried about Noble.

Outside, the arctic winter sun has already started to set and under the clouds, the day is gray once more. My suit's power is at 90% and working perfectly, constantly adjusting to my body temperature's needs. If the weather is affecting Kai, I couldn't say, because he's extremely focused on our surroundings, constantly surveying for potential threats. We have an hour until the blackout is supposed to happen. And 26 minutes to find Noble and get Kai back to Palermo's side as Asher Ming. The Super Satellite is already in the sky, and unless we disable the blackout weapon, too many people will suffer.

At the entrance, Kai pulls down his mask and steps briskly up to the door. He taps in his access code, his shoulders tense. His rapid stride is all business—we're on a job, together, but a world apart.

We step into the Master Satellite Control Center lobby. Models of rockets and satellites hang from the ceiling. Scale

Tech's emblem is on the outer wall, the outline of the country of Finland surrounded by stars and radiant sunbeams.

Following Noble's frequency and the map in my head, I lead us down a white tiled hall with doors along both sides.

Kai's focus remains on the mission. "Even if Noble can prevent the blackout, Palermo is famous for his backup plans."

"There's a way to stop it," I say, believing Noble didn't come here to cause a blackout. "Noble and I foresee these things. We never do anything without a backup plan either. He'll know how to hack into the satellite to change its programming."

"Even if his father's life is on the line?" he asks.

An image of Noble watching Qadar about to "die" in Tunisia comes to mind. He couldn't think clearly. But this is different. He's known about this for months.

"He's like me, Kai, he will have thought through everything. I'm sure of it." I purse my lips. "He just needs help."

My gift picks up on another man moving quickly toward us just out of view around the corner. "Guard."

We dash behind a door.

"Allow me," Kai says, fists tightening.

I hold him back. "No," I say. "Not even one face can see you helping us. I have one taser left." Kai's about to protest but it's too late. I launch the drone. A man with a long ponytail convulses to the ground, but his eyes open on Kai for a split second too long before he passes out.

When the man stills, Kai cocks his head. "It's not a guard. He's one of Palermo's men. He doesn't know me." Kai drags him into an open room with a huge hydraulic table, then bars the door. But my calculations recalibrate with a different prediction.

"You might be wrong," I say with a hint of dread. "I think he recognized you."

Kai grits his teeth. "Nothing we can do about it now."

At the end of the hall, there is a double door leading to

the main room in the Control Center. Noble's frequency is pounding behind it.

A burst of numbers flashes for a nanosecond in my mind, splitting into a numerical crossroad before me into paths of darkness and light. I blink and it's gone. My breath catches, and I look at Kai. A tight expression is in his eyes.

"Here we are," Kai says, his voice low, a tinge of remorse. "This is where they control the satellites and where Noble is supposed to execute the final blackout."

I don't tell Kai that I can sense Noble behind the door, or that the wired bombs are producing the same amount of electrical charge as the Infinity Dome.

My heart is a blizzard of feelings. Just like the snow, it's beautiful one moment and filling me with wonder, then painfully killing me the next. Kai's and Noble's frequencies pulse at me in different ways. But right now, we have very little time and only one focus. I shrug off my feelings and swing the door open.

My heart stops. Noble is hunched over a desk. The numbers around him are dark clouds, a massive storm. Every email, chat, and memory of him is amplified.

"Hi, Digits," Noble says, without turning around. "Kai." He breathes in deep, then pushes away from the desk and stands to face us.

When he sees my face, his eyes fill with wild emotion and remorse, and he rushes over to me. I can sense Kai jolt though he remains still.

"Why did you come?" he asks sadly, the frequency in his voice tearing holes into my chest.

I can't answer. His eyes are so heavy, like they hold all the emotional weight he's ever carried, plus the fate of the world. He doesn't have to say it. Something is wrong—something neither of us calculated. But my moment of silence gives room for Kai to speak.

"She's here," Kai says, stalking forward, "because you ruined a perfectly good plan."

Noble studies Kai with an astute awareness. Both of their frequencies spike.

"I had my reasons," Noble says, calmly.

Kai cocks his head. "Because of your reasons, she almost died last night." His voice pulses with energy.

Noble's body goes stiff, but he doesn't move or back away from Kai. Noble can read him as I can. Kai is powerful, but he's clearly in control, and there's no way he'd ever hurt him. He's just upset.

"Jo wasn't supposed to follow me," Noble says. "I didn't expect her to blow up the Infinity Dome to get inside Scale Tech."

Kai laughs, a slight shake of the head. More disdain than his usual self. "Obviously, you don't know Jo very well."

Noble steps closer to Kai, a challenge in his eyes. "It didn't feel like that when her lips were on mine yesterday."

The energy of an active volcano erupts. Heat burns me to the ground.

This is the last thing we need right now, but Noble makes it worse by stepping closer to me, like I've chosen him. Did I, by coming here? Kai's words ring in my head. *You came here for him. Stick with that. You may be the only ones who can understand each other.* My eyes shoot to Kai who refuses to look at me.

To my disappointment, Kai steps back, removing the tension. "What can I say? You're meant for each other." His voice is lined with daggers. "But right now, we have bigger problems. Palermo just arrived. I have to join him. All of our fathers are involved in this mess. And the whole world is waiting to see what happens tonight. Jo claims you have a different way to stop this. So, do you?"

My eyes drill into Noble's with all the belief I've had in him since we were kids. He's the boy who looks for infinity in stars, the calm in the chaos, a thumbprint in the trees. Of course he has a plan.

Noble releases a deep breath. "I did," he clenches his jaw. "But it's a bit more complicated now."

Noble walks over to the computer. "I completed the weapon, but I built a breaker into the satellite—a failsafe that can be triggered to cancel the attack. I was never going to allow a major blackout to happen." He looks back at his father. "But Palermo had his own backup too. He modified the weapon to be activatable via a remote trigger, which bypasses the system's built-in breaker. So, in order to prevent Palermo from activating the weapon, we have to brick the remote trigger. Until that remote is disabled, Palermo will be able to execute the attack even if the breaker is triggered." Noble's mind is spinning with probabilities. "My father and I are working on a solution, but we need to find the remote trigger and we've hacked everything—it's not on Palermo and it's nowhere on this compound."

"Then I'll make Palermo tell me where it is." Kai bites down.

My numbers blur in and out. Calculations scream in two directions. Whatever happens, Kai's cover can't be blown. The whole mission and the future depend on it. I don't know how I know, but I do. It's my numbers lining up with my gut.

"No," I say, reaching out to Kai. I try not to flinch when he moves away so I can't touch him. "Don't say anything to Palermo. Just buy us time," I say. "Make sure Cesare's men win this mafia war. We'll figure this out." Somehow. Even if this room is rigged.

Kai looks at me, shaking his head. Our eyes meet and my stomach flips at the spike in frequency. I see the doubt in his face, whether he should trust me with this or not. He tears his gaze away first and checks his watch. "We don't have long." He heads to the door.

I look at Noble and mouth, "One second." Then I follow Kai, wishing I could erase the last few minutes, which certainly made his feelings of betrayal worse.

"I'm sorry," I say when we're far enough away.

"Nothing to apologize for, Jo," he says, his tone resigned. "Let's just focus on averting this crisis."

"Listen, my numbers predict if you're exposed, the whole operation will fail." The long-haired man tied up in the hydraulics room comes to mind. "You won't be able to take down Terra Liberata if you reveal yourself."

Kai doesn't say anything, but his body tightens. He used to trust my gift, but now he's debating what I've said. He also doesn't like leaving me here without protection.

"Don't open this door until I get back." His eyes are dead-serious. Agent Ramos is right. He isn't prioritizing Palermo or Terra Liberata. He's thinking about me. He'll sacrifice this mission for me if he has to. If that happens, Terra Liberata could succeed. And if Kai is caught, he'll die.

"Only if you promise not to reveal yourself under any circumstances." I hold his gaze.

"That's the thing about me, Jo. I don't make promises I can't keep." He looks to Noble then me—two people who broke our promises to him. My heart shatters as the door clicks shut behind him.

As his frequency moves away from the room, my gift buzzes with adrenaline. A crescendo of numbers shoots from me, then blurs for 3, 4, 5, seconds. I shiver, stronger this time. That eruption Noble talked about...the crossroads. Whatever is coming, it's soon.

I turn back to Noble, who exhales heavily. "Nice timing, huh?" Noble says, motioning to his father, the spitting image of an older Noble, slouching behind him in the chair. "First, I meet your dad, and now you meet mine. Josephine, this is Dr. James Adams, my father."

CHAPTER 66

∞

If I could do it over, I'd choose you.

The words of Noble's father, a man I once despised, act like a filter in my head. I'm glad they do, because otherwise, I don't know what I would have done, or what I would have said when finally facing him. For one, we wouldn't be in this situation if it wasn't for him. But more poignantly, what he did to his son still pounds in my memory. The Phoenix in me wants to stand in defense of my childhood friend.

Beside Dr. Adams, Noble's face is that of a boy who is struggling. Just like Kai can't focus because of me, Noble can't focus because of his father. Even though his father mistreated him, there's something else sparking inside Noble too. That stupid, ridiculous, stubborn thing called love, that can't be beaten down by any amount of darkness, is getting back up again, standing its ground, and shining through it all.

Dr. Adams rises to his feet. He's nearly Tank's height and build. But years that don't belong to him are in the lines of his face, a shadow eclipsing what he could have been. Regret pours off him like a sad song drowned out by the rain.

He forces a weak smile. "I'm sorry we have to meet like this. I know who you are and how important you have been to my son."

My son. That title is earned, like Qadar earned it. A deep emotion races through me. I want to be angry at this man, but I fight it, because I know what regret and change feels like. How desperately we can wish for a second chance. Even on this trip, I'm surrounded by men who proved they could change. Cesare. Chan. My father. If Red were here, he'd call me a hypocrite. There isn't a soul in this world who doesn't need a second chance sometime. Wasn't I just wishing I could take back what I did to Kai? Choose not to give him SWAY? For him to trust me again? My heart rages.

Noble is waiting for me to say something, like we can't start fixing anything until we face this problem. And his face says it all. Noble wants to give his father a second chance and he needs my help to do it. That's when I break.

I stretch out my hand to him. "Hi, Dr. Adams," I say. "I know who you are. I'm sorry about what's happened to you and your wife." His hand wraps around mine. It's warm but trembling.

"When Noble designed this new way to harness energy as a kid," he says, softly, "I had no idea it could be a weapon. He and I worked on it together before he...left. I was angry. And I believed in my son's genius. It was clearly a breakthrough in aerospace technology....so I sold it. Not understanding the consequences." He shakes his head in disgust at himself, then moves closer to Noble. "I may be a terrible father, but I'm not a murderer or terrorist. I'll do whatever it takes to fix my mistake. *Anything.*" He looks at Noble. The weight in his eyes could carry into the next lifetime. My heart sinks at the love and pain coursing from him. The feeling is all too familiar.

I take a deep breath. "We're going to stop the blackout weapon, Dr. Adams. I believe in Noble too." He nods at me, then returns to watching Noble in the same way my father watched me after I returned from China—studying all the ways Noble has changed.

I move closer to Noble, pulling him off to the side. "Why didn't you tell me sooner?" His beautiful face crumbles into a million tiny equations.

"I'm sorry," he says, releasing a deep sigh. "I never wanted you to be involved in this mess." Noble's body leans on mine like he can't carry the weight of it. "Palermo threatened to kill my dad and put my mom in a coma unless I completed the weapon and caused the blackout. I calculated it a hundred times. It wasn't a hundred percent, but the odds were good—if my father was here. I devised three countermeasures, even a way to help Rafael." He takes a breath. "Remember the glitch?"

I nod.

"It's a very stealthy copycat command program I designed to undermine the radio satellite arrays during launch. It's a worm that runs in the background of the command code that will give me complete control of the spacecraft, so I can hack the satellite unnoticed. But the scope of Palermo's network is larger than I calculated, and his tens of dozens of hackers and scientists countered me by using something unhackable."

Terra Liberata's reach sends shivers through me, but I redirect my thoughts to right here and now.

I grab Noble's hand. "I don't blame you," I say. "And I understand. I'm here to help you now, so let's figure out how to stop this blackout from happening."

Noble pulls me to the desk, bringing up a current scan that's been working in the background. "With the remote trigger, Palermo has total control over the weapon. It could be anywhere, and we don't have much time to find it."

My brain starts processing, digging through my own internal files and drawing up possibilities. "Okay, but if we can locate the trigger and disable it, you can ensure the blackout won't happen?"

"Yes. But here's our next problem. The main reason you weren't supposed to be here." He pulls up the Super Satellite monitor. He swallows hard.

"Go on," I say, even if my numbers already know what he's going to say.

"All satellites have A/B and sometimes A/B/C systems with automatic cutover. If system A doesn't respond correctly, the satellite shifts to system B or C. Palermo's team programmed it so that if anything is altered in the Super Satellite, it changes over to the next backup system. I'll have to hack them all and upload a code, which will take time, and it can only be done from this room. But Palermo has a fourth backup plan..." Noble looks at his dad again. "If the satellite deviates from the weaponized programming, this building is rigged to explode. So, we either let the blackout happen or everyone in this building dies. See, Digits? That's why I left you."

My blood runs cold. Noble came here knowing he might die, to save his father.

"No," I say, numbers and calculations pulsing through my head. I dig into everything I know. I didn't survive people like King and Madame without learning how to take down someone like Palermo. Where would Palermo hide the remote trigger? How can we stop this blackout without any casualties? "There's got to be another way. No one is going to be left behind. Can't we reroute control of the satellite to another system in a different building?"

"I've done the math, Jo. There's not enough time," Noble says, his dad hovering close behind him. "There are only a handful of people who would be able to hack the satellite as fast as I can and upload the code for the breaker. I won't let it be you."

I shake my head. "Noble, stop. There's always another way."

Calculations bleed out of me. I need to think through this

problem logically, but the lines are blurred. Each equation is tied to billions of lives and the people I care most about in the world. I need to sit down.

Every number I recorded in Helsinki recalibrates. Like missing pieces of a puzzle, one by one, they slide into place. The dimensions of Senate Square. The unique position of the Celebration Rocket stage, which was directly above the restricted underground tunnels that Kai and Palermo's men had access to. The banquet's lightshow...

The Super Satellite is counting down to one specific moment to cause the massive blackout. Then it hits me: Palermo loves a good show. That will be his downfall.

My head snaps up. Finally, my numbers come to a solution with poor odds, but they beat what we have now.

"I know a way to solve this," I say, my head clearer and sharper than ever. "You said Palermo was causing the blackouts with a nanosatellite before, right? Can you access that satellite?"

"Yes. It'll take some time, but I can gain control of it," Noble says, his eyes glued to mine. "What are you thinking?"

My mind flashes through memories that feel as fresh as yesterday. Madame. The economic crisis. The coup. Namibia. The Infinity Dome. My eyes dart to the boy beside me who has devoted his life to finding calm in the chaos. I start tapping my leg. Since China, I've dedicated my life to solving problems, to stopping trouble.

But now it's our time to cause some.

I give Noble a hard look. "If we can't stop Palermo's blackout, then we'll cause one of our own."

CHAPTER 67

∞

Noble's father nearly chokes when he hears my idea, regarding me like I'm unhinged. But I couldn't care less. I'm dead serious and Noble knows it.

Noble reads my numbers like a book. "You know where the remote trigger is, don't you?" he says.

"Yes," I say, meeting his eyes. "It's in the Celebration Rocket."

It's perfectly clear in my mind now. The location of the Celebration Rocket stage in Senate Square was strategically placed. I was under it when Kai led me through the tunnels. Which means, Palermo's men had access to it from under the city. It's the perfect play for Palermo. The Celebration Rocket is on a countdown to when the Super Satellite reaches orbit. When the rocket explodes, the remote trigger will detonate and Palermo's blackout will be initiated, then the rocket will disintegrate, destroying all evidence of the remote. It'll be Palermo's final show, and a genius way to cover his tracks.

But not if we can help it.

I grab the chair closest to Noble. "Palermo won't expect a blackout he didn't cause. It'll ruin his show, but it will also delay his whole plan, giving us time to disable the trigger and upload your code into the Super Satellite. There's also a 40% chance that the energy pulse from the nanosatellite will be powerful enough to temporarily disable any electrical trigger in the explosives. Which will give us more time."

Noble's calculations unmistakably affirm the new plan. His dad also steps up, warming to the vision.

"This could work. But the ISC won't be able to help us," he says, his mind locking on to all his NSA knowledge. "Do we have anyone in Helsinki who could get there fast enough, with the knowledge of how to disable it?"

"Actually, I do." The situation is not funny, but I smile. "The Finns and PSS."

"The Finns?" Noble asks, confused.

"Noble, this is exactly why you need to get out more," I say. "The Helsinki University STEM team helped build the Celebration Rocket with Dr. Salonen. You'd like them." I explain the rest of my plan of having them disable it.

Noble is still running through possible scenarios. "So we cause a controlled blackout to give the team time to locate the remote trigger..." He's scratching his head. He sees something I don't.

"What is it?" I ask.

"One possible hitch. The tech in the nanosatellite is faulty, which is why Palermo is using the Super Satellite instead. If we use the nanosatellite, we have to be careful," Noble says. "What scale of blackout are you talking about?"

I rattle my head from side to side, my calculations examining and discarding potential problems. "Just all of Finland."

"All of Finland?" Dr. Adams says, panicked. "It's winter!"

Noble looks at me. "He's right. It's going to cause widespread panic. And there's a chance I won't have much control over the faulty nanosatellite. What if I can't turn the power back on? Or if we don't time it right? It could potentially destroy Finland's power grid. And then we'll be the bad guys."

Noble doesn't like my idea, which makes sense. He may be a genius, and tough in his own way—he's learned to survive anywhere in the world. But inside he's made to discover fractals in tails of seahorses and coral, and harness light in the stars—not take down evil syndicates.

"A blackout is going to happen either way," I say, strongly. "But with this plan, we have a chance to stop Palermo." Even now, I can envision my plan working, but Noble's right. There's no guarantee of success. We need to process the variables—people, grids, homes, how long it would take to be safe. We don't know how much time we'll need. An hour? 24 hours? A week?

Noble's calculations are faster than mine. "I think I got it. Give me 60 seconds."

While he processes, I contact the PSS team. "Harrison? I need you to get everyone online right now." In four minutes, a sober team listens as I explain the situation and what they have to do. They waste no time at all.

"We'll contact the Finnish team immediately," Harrison says. "I'll be in touch." The line drops.

When I began this trip, I never imagined I'd be hacking state-of-the-art satellites, causing blackouts and witnessing mafia duels. But I'm here doing just that, with my dad, ex-boyfriend and Noble.

A buzz from K2 tells me that Palermo is on the move. I swipe through monitor feeds until Palermo fills the frame outside of the lab just north of this one. Kai is at his side. Palermo's men are also with them, which means they're not with Cesare. Dr. Salonen is there too. He's clearly not here of his own free will. A thug pushes Dr. Salonen from behind to get him to move faster. They are headed toward Cesare in the Solar Power Lab and soon, they'll be coming to this control room.

I swipe through the different location feeds on my watch until Cesare and his mafia gang are in view. Cesare's men are preparing to fight and forming a barrier to the entrance into the Master Satellite Control Center. They're protecting us.

I turn back to Noble, who is flying into action at his keyboard.

"They're buying us time," I tell him.

"Alright," he says, his jaw tight. "But just in case it doesn't work, we need to prepare for the worst."

"You're right," I say sharply, another idea forming. At best, this will be a national emergency. "We need to announce it. Either way, this is going to get messy, so we warn the nation." But that's not my only reason. It's time someone sent Palermo and his elite mafia a message. "We need to show Terra Liberata they're not the only ones who can play this game." My voice has turned hard like when I used to live in the Pratt.

"What? Threatening Terra Liberata is even more dangerous, Jo," Noble says as if his numbers are on auto-pilot.

"Maybe," I say, my jaw set. "But they'll know exactly what it means."

Noble stares at me. Fractals seem to pour from his eyes, but behind them he's drawing conclusions. He gives me a tight smile. "Kai was right. There's a lot I don't know about you." But then he leans in close and confident, our numbers pounding side by side. "But I can still read your numbers. There's another piece in your plan, so what is it?"

That bright blur happens again. Equations bullet out of me, and the frequencies increase all around me. Whatever it's trying to tell me, I push away for the moment, because we don't have much time. I snap my head up.

"We need a whistleblower," I say, drawing up K2. "I know just who to call."

"Who?" Noble asks, his numbers ready for action.

The hard lines on her face come into my mind. "Someone who is after the story of a lifetime."

CHAPTER 68

∞

International prize-winning journalist Ms. Carry Mines has no problem getting the story out—it's all over the news. Once we leaked enough evidence, the DIA sent a brief statement confirming it.

Within 15 minutes, news agencies all over the world pick up the story.

Breaking news: *Terrorists target power grids; Massive blackout expected in Finland—the nation prepares. ISC delays Celebration Rocket launch.*

Finnish authorities call a national emergency, grounding all planes and rerouting flights bound for Finland. People are ordered to stay indoors and prepare.

Ms. Mines was wary of the anonymous tip until the DIA confirmed it. The department issued a statement that the plot had been discovered by an undercover operation and was being contained as we speak. The final line of Ms. Mines's article read: *"Finland has their best team working on stopping this crisis."*

A half-smile, half-frown tugs on my face. The "best team", as she unknowingly calls us, are a bunch of kids, secret agents, and *mafiosi.* Now it's T-minus 20 minutes to Palermo's blackout if we can't stop it. Let's hope her words prove true.

K2 announces a call from PSS. Harrison is on the line. "The STEM team is with us and agreed to help, but Jo, there are a ton of guards in the square. Now that there's a national emergency, they won't let us near the Celebration Rocket. How do we gain access to it?"

"You're going to go *under* it," I say, the platform clear in my memory. I rattle off directions to access the tunnels below Helsinki University, including a series of longitude and latitude coordinates—60.169716 and 24.95— before Harrison interrupts me.

"Just stop," he says. "I'll have Felicia find blueprints of the tunnels. Then you send us the exact location. News flash, we don't think in coordinates."

"Right." Felicia sends a map to K2 and I highlight the location. "It's restricted, so you'll need PSS tech to break in."

"On it," Harrison says. "Leaving now. We'll call you for Noble's help with the remote trigger when we arrive."

"We don't have much time," I remind them. "And you'd better bring a flashlight. You'll be in the dark for the next several hours. Palermo's men are most likely guarding it, so bring Tank and Miles."

"This is so cool. Our own Mission Impossible, counting down to deadly odds," Harrison says in a voice-over type narration. "Should we all wear black?" Pens cuts the call before anyone can answer him, but I imagine Pens shoving him for goofing off.

Noble is at his desk, hacking codes to access the weapon in the nanosatellite. "I'm in," he says. "But the coding has been tampered with by Palermo's scientists. We can still use it to cause the blackout. I just hope we can turn it off."

"It's dark outside already," Dr. Adams remarks. "My colleagues and I wired this room so it wouldn't be affected by a blackout, but everywhere else on the Scale Tech campus will be completely dark. What about Cesare and the fight?"

I look at Dr. James as more calculations stream through me. "There's enough light outside."

Noble looks over his shoulder. "How can you act so normal about all this? Even in Tunisia, breaking into the Successor's compound was like second nature for you. You were so calm even with bombs in your fingertips."

"Was I?" I don't remember. In the moment, all I was thinking about was saving Kai and taking down the Successor.

"Yeah, you were," he says, distractedly, but there's a hint of understanding in his voice.

"How much time is left?" I ask

Noble looks at me. "We could cause the blackout now, but I need a few extra minutes before we hit go to ensure I can turn the weapon off. I'm uploading a kill-switch, in case I can't shut it down. If I don't, I can't be certain we'll get the power back on."

"Ok." I turn back to the monitors. Suddenly, the frequencies around me explode and spread to everything in the room, distracting me. It's like my brain is processing at the speed of light. Numbers, waves, patterns are bending around me, boiling up.

"What is going on?" I mumble to myself. Some part of me recognizes that the crossroads is happening, my gift is coming to a boiling point. *Please not now.* But my gift was never a thing I could turn on or off. I've only ever learned to follow where my gift takes me.

K2 buzzes. An update from PSS: *We're in the tunnels. Made it under the stage's platform. Miles and Tank took down Palermo's men. Give us five minutes to find the trigger.*

I text back, then turn to the security feed on K2 to watch Cesare on the screen as he struts up to Palermo. I quickly locate the audio and turn up the volume.

"I've come for what belongs to me," Cesare says. "Scale

Tech is mine. If you don't stop this blackout, we'll stop you."

I can't be sure, but it looks as if Cesare is still trying to buy us time.

"Trying to ruin my party?" Palermo laughs at the news. "Cousin, you've got things confused. Exposing the blackouts can't hurt me. Nor can it ruin my plans. I have far more men than those in our family business. What I've started can't be stopped."

"Then let's settle this," Cesare says. "Here and now."

This fight is going to wipe out all of them. Possibly even my father, who is standing among the ranks with Cesare's men. Not to mention Rafael. I can't let this happen. It's going to be even bloodier than before.

Kai is in the worst position. He's taking too many risks. When the battle begins, he won't be able to hurt the people he cares about. He will protect my father, maybe even Cesare and Rafael—and be exposed as a spy in the process.

Then K2 alerts me to movement on another security monitor. I pull it up in the miniature window. The man with the ponytail, who saw Kai helping me, is awake. I watch him make his way out of the room where we left him through a window. He's stumbling around the building, heading in Palermo's direction. My heart skips. He'll expose Kai.

My numbers are playing out a terrible scenario in my head. If Kai is exposed, the fallout will be far worse than today's blackout.

"Hurry up!" I shout to Noble. "Execute the blackout! Now!"

Kai is standing beside Palermo, while the thug who saw his face stumbles into the parking lot. Four more minutes until he reaches the door to the Solar Power Lab's warehouse...until he reaches Palermo.

"Noble!" I shout, spinning to face him. Milliseconds tick faster, and with every second, mortal danger is coming too close. To my dad...Rafael...Kai. The long-haired man will ruin everything. "The blackout. Now, Noble!"

"I can't...there are still too many unknowns. Give me six minutes. The kill switch is still loading. It's not worth the risk if we can't end the blackout. There's no telling what will happen."

"Kai doesn't have six minutes!" Factors are multiplying exponentially in my head. This is the only option.

Two minutes. Dr. Adams hasn't left Noble's side. He's anxiously trying to help. It's obvious he'll do anything for Noble in this moment. "Your kill switches always work, son."

The phantom frequency is pulsing inside me. Harder and stronger and pulling something from deep within me. My eyes are glued to the monitor. Kai is readying for a fight. Negative equations assault me. Our chances of success are plummeting.

That bright frequency I experienced in the frozen meadow, when hypothermia almost stole my life, floods the room with rays of light.

The long-haired man who will reveal Kai as a fraud is ten feet from the door.

Explosions go off in my brain. I stand up from my seat, sweating in my snowsuit.

I understand now why Noble couldn't say no to Palermo's schemes when his dad's life was threatened. The same feeling is raging in me now. I would do anything to protect Kai.

K2 receives an update from PSS: *We have the Celebration Rocket. Override extraction in process.*

Everything will fail if we don't do this now.

"Noble, do it!" My shout is feral.

Frequencies fly out of me, opening a floodgate of exploding light. I can't rein this in. Calculations rip through me like a flash flood and I'm swept away. I steady myself against the wall. *What is happening?*

Even as I'm overwhelmed by calculations, I'm already running to the door. On the monitors, the energy of two groups of men is released and pandemonium breaks out in the room. I race down the halls.

My skin tingles. A surge of energy zips into the room. Then everything snaps to BLACK...

But I'm not in the dark anymore.

CHAPTER 69

∞

The blackouts *were* a sign.

Frequencies race at the speed of light. Numbers pass me like a train at high speed, so fast I can't count them. My gift is erupting—just like Noble said it would.

The crossroads led me to this place. To this moment in time. My numbers knew before I did that I'd find my answers here.

My eyes are wide open as a hundred threads of energy spill out. The halls are dark, but my world is growing brighter—my gift is coming to a pinnacle, a zenith, the birth of a new lens. Endless particles, rays, and frequencies spark to life, pulsing like rainbows in the night. One after another appears in brilliant color, piercing the darkness. I don't just see their measurements anymore. I see *them.* In this moment—darkness is as light to me.

Instead of fighting the eruption, I step into it. As if my eyes were always meant to see this. My body breathes numbers as I weave through the hallway back to the warehouse. The frequencies ripple past me, swelling with aurora-like waves, each one a different wavelength, its own pattern.

I reach the warehouse where the mobster brawl is destroying the lab. When I enter, the scene is not what I expect. Every single person—on both sides of the fight—is glowing. The heat radiating from inside them, the light burning in their eyes—it's infrared light waves I'm seeing, and yet, it's more than that. It's power. It's life. It's proof that even if we are knit together in darkness within our mother's wombs, our very design is knit together with light. The darkness can never take it away. Light is racing through our veins.

I see now what burns inside of me. In this moment, it's clear how wrong it is that *humans* fight each other. It's obvious the only enemy we have is the powerless darkness, with no frequency and no way to stand against the light.

My eyes can see numerical equations stretch out of me and reach into the terrifying and beautiful things lost in the dark. A flood of frequencies crashes over me. I hear it all. Voices singing and screaming. Weapons destroying and saving. Nations rising and falling. Stars forming and dying. The darkness cowering. Sun breaking over a new day. My vow to right the wrongs in this world.

The light is so fast that everything slows down around me. The man with the ponytail slams open the door, revealing a moonlit sky. A white glow floods into the room, reflected from the snow. It's just enough to rekindle the momentum and the fighting rages on.

Shadows leap forward and fight shadows. Bodies collide in outlines of light.

The man by the door who came to expose Kai is taking in the scene. He expected the brawl, just not the blackout. He's gauging his next steps and figuring out which side is his and which is Palermo's. It buys me time. Just as he locates Palermo, who is guarded by nine men, my gift jumps into action. It choreographs a dance between swinging fists and legs; sweat and blood; equations and frequencies of light.

Like a ghost in the dark, I target the man as he runs into the fight, but I run quicker, more silently, and with one swift motion I swing a tranq-earring into his neck before he can reach Palermo. He slips quietly down to the ground, asleep once more.

I turn back to the fight. Palermo's men now storm outside as expected. Cesare commands everyone to charge them. But I don't move.

The phantom frequency is here in the room. It's faster than light but even now, it bends to whatever my gift has opened. I can see it clearly now. It's bouncing between me and another person—someone fighting effortlessly.

Then I know without a doubt...every path has led me here. To *Kai.*

The phantom frequency travels back and forth between us like a lifeline. It's a beautiful symphony looping like infinity, entwining us like two birds in one flight.

I watch him—*us*—in awe. Our frequency spikes. Even though he can't see it, he feels it as he fights, and as a man goes down, he shifts, aware of my presence in the room. His whole being responds to it. He turns my way. Faces me even though the room is shadowed.

As I move closer to him, the phantom frequency is not all I see. His voice, his heartbeat, every piece of him—instead of just one frequency between us, there are hundreds, and every one of them is the calm to my storm. Where I was blind before, now everything is clear. I lost my gift *with Kai* in China. In Tunisia, it came back in the helicopter *with Kai.* The first eruption of my gift happened in the Banquet Hall *with Kai*, and even now, he shares this eruption with me.

Lightning is never what I wanted. Kai's frequencies are the rising sun, a dawn unfolding into day, burning hour by hour, growing more intense the higher it gets. It's faithful to rise every day, every year despite the clouds, the wind or the rain...despite the night. It always shows up. It's never ending.

Kai is my calculation in the chaos.

I love him.

Every option without him is failure. Like Cesare said in his speech, we're stronger together...*brighter* together.

The eruption crests to its full height and I understand now why my numbers followed a path leading into darkness. Red was right. Light is dangerous to follow. It drives us into dark corners, because seen or unseen, it can't be stopped. Not at night. Not at the bottom of the ocean. Not in us. And when we follow it, we send the darkness running.

I'm at the crossroads. I know which way to go. This time, nothing can stop me.

CHAPTER 70

∞

Outside, the moon and the northern lights are bright enough to reflect off the snow. In trails of green and white light, the battle for loyalty and legacy gains even more momentum. Cesare has one focus—taking back what is his.

I size up the scene in less than ten seconds: The adrenaline racing through the men's bodies has completely possessed them. Punches are thrown despite the freezing temperatures. Bodies drop to the white earth in an eerie Arctic silence. Now that chaos has taken over, even Dr. Salonen has joined the fight against Palermo.

Off to the left, Kai fights two of Cesare's men. Rafael throws fists like a scrappy boy in a schoolyard fight and my dad, who's still holding his own, has Cesare's back.

Palermo is still surrounded like a king. "Finish them!" he orders his men, and heads to the parking lot.

Cesare notices and barks orders to his men. "Do not let Palermo reach his van!" His men fly off in ferocious pursuit, but Palermo's men charge the oncoming fleet. They ram into each other like linemen in a football game. Snow flies.

Kai races to defend Palermo from the flanking group of Cesare's loyals. It appears heroic but it leaves Palermo unguarded—a matador in front of a charging bull.

Cesare plows through the remaining mafiosi and squares off with Palermo. The moon's brilliance beams on Cesare as he trains his eyes on Palermo, whose face is distorted in shadows. Cesare stalks forward.

Palermo is icy calm as the thugs fight around them. "I'm going to win, Cousin," Palermo says, a wicked laugh huffing a cloud of breath. He tightens his fists. "You'll never defeat Terra Liberata."

"Right now, I'm not here to defeat Terra Liberata," Cesare says, wiping blood from his face. "I'm here to defeat you." And he charges.

The mobsters collide like warriors charging onto a medieval battleground. Both men are fierce. Blow after blow connects with flesh and bone. Wet thuds and grunts of pain fill the frigid air but the fight is strangely silent of screams.

Puffs of hot breath fill the air as both men give everything they've got to this battle royal. Palermo is taller, looking down on Cesare. But Cesare is a mass of blood, energy and sweat. The force of each hit carries a narrative of pride, history and pain.

Cesare catches Palermo in a choke hold, about to take him down but Palermo breaks free with an elbow to Cesare's gut and a spinning backhand to Cesare's head. Cesare stumbles to a knee, his bare hand stretching out to catch himself but instead sinking in the snow. Palermo sneers and snags his chance while Cesare is down. Palermo approaches and rains down 2, 3, 4, fists to Cesare's face—until the last swing. Cesare drops his chin to his chest. There's a sick crunch and howl of pain as Palermo's hand connects with the hardest part of Cesare's skull.

Cesare pops up to his feet with an unexpected strength. He lunges through the air with a powerful drive. Cesare's left shoulder pops as it drills into Palermo's diaphragm bending him in half. The men crash to the ground in an explosion of snow.

Palermo wheezes, trying to catch his breath. He rolls over, scrambling to his feet. Cesare moans and grabs his shoulder, but adrenaline is pumping, and the pain doesn't slow him down. Palermo can't breathe yet but moves slowly toward his van.

"*Codardo*! Coward!" Cesare's roar silences the night. Palermo stops and turns to face his pursuer—a moment too late.

Cesare has already wound up from the hips, and with one blow, Palermo is sent flying off his feet, landing on his back in the snow.

Cesare is over him in a flash. He bends down and grabs Palermo's jacket collar and lifts his face towards his own. His words are as commanding as the weather. "*C'è un solo capo.* There's only one boss." Cesare draws back his fist for another blow—and Palermo goes limp.

∞

I race back to Noble, commanding K2 to get PSS on the line. In less than 50 seconds, Noble is talking to Minttu and Felicia who are removing the remote trigger from the rocket.

Dr. Adams has jumped into action, his NSA training on full speed.

"Dad," Noble says calmly. "Stay on the line with them while I get the power back on."

Noble's father takes over, talking steadily. "That's right, next let's disable it completely." Dr. Adams talks them through next steps on the phone. "One last step to go… You've got it."

I come behind him, still breathless. "Thank you."

Noble looks over his shoulder. "Now to activate the kill switch in the nanosatellite and get the lights back on in this country." Noble sets to work, a determined look on his face.

I join Dr. Adams who makes eye contact with me, nodding. "*They did it.*" He's trembling with both joy and disbelief.

PSS texts stream through K2, celebrating their win but Noble's face darkens. He looks up, the dull glow of the screen monitor casting a blue shadow around him.

"What?" I ask, reading his numbers.

"The kill switch in the nanosatellite is loading," Noble says, a straight line on his lips. "It's taking some time, but the power will come back on, and our blackout here will end." Noble catches my eyes.

"Then why are you upset?" I ask. His father comes up behind Noble, listening.

Noble rubs his hands together. "Because Palermo's fourth backup has already begun," he says grimly.

"What does that mean?" I ask.

"I can now upload my code for the breaker into the Super Satellite's systems," he says, shaking his head. "But the only way to trigger the breaker is from this room, which means this building is going to blow."

CHAPTER 71

∞

The lights flicker back on, but the moment is darker than death.

If we don't act, thousands of people will suffer or die as a result of Palermo's extended blackout. They won't be able to get the power back on for months. Thoughts rage in my head of mothers trying to keep their small children warm at night, the elderly trapped in freezing homes. Food shortages, society shutting down, the chaos it will cause. And if we do act...

Noble stands and pushes me and his father toward the door. "Get out, both of you. Tell everyone to get away from this building. I have six minutes to stop Palermo's blackout," he says, numbers pound through him like a hammer. "I have to do this." He looks down into my eyes, his hand to my cheek. "I'm sorry."

"No," I shake my head, horrified. "There has to be another way. Just like we realized the trigger was hidden in the rocket. I'll get everyone outside, then we can figure this out."

Noble flies to the desk and starts hacking the Super Satellite. The energy from the bombs crisscrossing the walls jumps exponentially. The countdown speeds up with a terrifying tick.

Dr. Adams stands behind Noble, refusing to budge. He knows as I do that Noble must upload the breaker codes into each satellite system for this to work.

I alert Cesare and my father of the bombs, warning them to get everyone as far away from the Master Satellite Control Center as possible. I ask about Kai, but no one has seen him. I don't feel his frequency either. Thankfully, he's not in the building.

I turn back to Noble, who is now screaming at his dad. "Dad, get out! I have five minutes to finish this, and even then, I don't know if it will be enough time." His voice is set, his face resigned.

"No!" My voice rips through the air. I fly up to him. "There's another way."

"I've done the math, Jo. There's no other way." Noble stands. "I can do this, but please, you all have to get out. No one else knows my design well enough to hack these systems and enter the passcodes fast enough."

His father touches him lovingly on the arm and Noble's frequency explodes into a thousand threads. "You're forgetting one person." Dr. Adams stares at his son, his hand on the back of Noble's neck. "I will do it." Then, the NSA man Noble used to talk about takes over. He rips his son from the chair.

"What are you doing, Dad?" Noble shouts.

"Something I should have done since the day you were born, Noble." The energy of his voice thunders in the room. "I should have loved you and sacrificed for you every day. I can't take back the past, but I can do this. *Now you get out.*" His face is marble, deadly serious. He's already got Noble by the arm. And the determination in his eyes is forceful enough that even I am backing up.

Noble's face contorts with pain when he understands the sacrifice his father means. "No. Dad!"

My head is spinning with calculations, but his father is right. There's no other way. If we all stay, we'll all die. But I can't leave without Noble. I'm begging every number to recalibrate and give us another solution.

"Son," he says, "because of me more people could die. I don't have a lot of time to make up for what I've done. But that's not what I care about most." His voice shakes the room with a powerful frequency. "I won't let *you* die. I love you, son. I'm so proud of you. Tell your mom I love her too." Then he physically drags his son to the door. Noble is pounding on his chest. Dr. Adams shoots me a look so fierce I instinctually follow. Once we are outside, he slams the door, locking it behind him.

Noble pounds on the door, his screams ripping into my heart.

Three minutes left. It will take almost that much time for us to reach the outer doors.

My heart is breaking for him. There is nothing I can say to fix this. But right now, we have to run.

"We have to go now!" I shout, even though my own words sound like those of a traitor. Noble doesn't budge. I grab his sweater. Then I yank Noble by the arm. I might be trying to save his life, but it feels like I'm shooting him in the heart. "Please, Noble, let's go!"

Noble wrenches his arm away from me, then beats on the door for his father, like he just found something precious and can't lose it again. "Dad, please!" he screams. "You can't do this!"

"Noble, look at me!" I scream. "I won't leave you. So if you stay, I stay." He looks up at me with wild eyes. But at the sight of me and the sound of my words, he snaps out of it. He grabs my hand, and we race out into the freezing air.

Outside of the Master Satellite Control Center, we run into Cesare's men who are dragging Palermo's thugs into a nearby lab.

"Dad!" I shout, eyes frantically searching for my father and Kai. I spot Kai who is crouched at the corner of a nearby building, when to my horror, Noble releases my hand and runs back into the Control Center.

"NO!" I shout. I sprint forward but am stopped by Rafael and my dad. "Let go of me! Noble's going back for his dad! The building is going to blow! We have to stop him! Please!" I'm screaming. But I can't break free of them. They're too strong.

Kai looks at me, then dashes after Noble.

The countdown ticks in my mind, 10—9—8… Never have I hated numbers as much as this moment. When I get to the end of it…2—1—the darkness explodes into orange fire and scalding heat.

I can't see all the variables, but what I do see are numbers predicting I could lose them both.

CHAPTER 72

∞

MASTER SATELLITE CONTROL CENTER
SCALE TECH ARCTIC LABS

I'm on my back in the snow, but I am not cold. What is left of the lab is burning. It's a bonfire in the Arctic. A source of light. The energy and heat waves are so immense, it's difficult to distinguish the different frequencies. After five minutes, there's still no sign of either of them. What if I've lost them?

Vehicles in the distance approach from different directions. Helicopter rotors pump in the sky several miles away. Agent Ramos is coming. Too late. Another group is arriving too. My stomach clenches at the frequencies I feel.

The power surges back on, and with it, K2 bombards me with messages from PSS regarding the news.

Links are dropped to K2. Finnish broadcasters and a major US news outlet declare breaking news:

"The power in Finland is back on."

"US government DIA and Finnish International Security have stopped the terrorist blackout attacks on the power grids."

My father, still shaken from the explosion, helps me sit up. "Thank God. Are you okay?"

I don't take my eyes off the building. "Yes, I just need to know if Kai and Noble are...they were in there." My head aches, and the arctic air stings my cheeks again.

"I'll find out." My father runs over to a group of Cesare's men stumbling out of another building.

A figure emerges from the smoke. Rafael points and shouts to me, "Mila!"

I jump to my feet, almost losing my balance. Even through the haze of smoke Kai's frame is hard to miss. He stumbles forward, carrying a limp body. The body slumped over Kai's strong shoulders doesn't budge, but I'd know that frequency anywhere, no matter how faint and strained. It's Noble. I gasp with relief and run toward him.

Kai sets him down in front of me with a groan. I kneel in the snow, which is dirtied and speckled with blood. Noble is burned and bleeding. A large gash on his forehead is pouring blood. I try to cover it with my jacket.

My eyes flit between Kai and Noble, ignoring the conflicting frequencies. Kai risked his life to save him. But before I can thank him and ask if he's okay, Kai's instructing my father to find a first aid kit.

"Noble?" I touch his face. My numbers scan him. My eyes dart to Kai. "Will he be okay?"

"Yes. He's just knocked out. I stopped him before he could get too close to the detonation. His dad...didn't make it." Kai closes his eyes at whatever he saw back there, shaking his head as if to ward off a bad dream.

"No..." my voice is a breath in the cold. Hot tears sting my eyes, the cold temperature starkly contrasting the heat. The loss of his father. The path they were crossing back to second chances, back to trust, back to love...is now gone forever. Life is too short, too unpredictable. There are too many threats, which is why we can't back down. I touch Noble's face, tears slipping down my cheeks leaving freezing trails behind them.

Noble's freckled nose is covered with black ash and tiny burns. I check on the gash on his forehead. It's still bleeding badly.

"I'm sorry," Kai says. "I couldn't save them both."

My eyes close. The pain is a river in both directions.

I turn to Kai. His numbers tell me he's already planning his next move. He's still undercover. I don't want to lose my chance to speak with him. "Thank you," I say. "You risked your life to save him."

"For you," he says, his frequency a disaster of messy strands. "I want you to be happy." He looks away. "Noble needs medical attention. I don't know what's happened to him internally, and I don't have the tools to gauge that right now. But I can fix this."

Kai searches his pockets and takes out a small tube. He puts ointment on his thumb, then squeezes Noble's gash together with his other hand, and presses the thick paste on his forehead. It seals the wound in less than ten seconds.

I gasp. "What did you put on him?" I ask, my numbers calculating the probabilities of what I just saw. Then I remember the medicine he put on my cheekbone.

He doesn't answer me. He just stares, plans brewing behind his eyes. I flash back to the sauna where he breathed his life back into me. I need to tell him. "Kai, I—"

Movement yanks away his attention. Too many people are coming our way.

I frown. "Agent Ramos. He's almost here. Thirteen minutes more."

"I've got to go before any of Palermo's men see me." Kai's face falls. "And if I'm not gone by the time Agent Ramos gets here, I've failed. There is so much more at stake than you know."

"I'll have my team wipe the scanners and clean up the mess. Nothing will be traced to you. We'll alter evidence if we need to." I rattle this off, but it's not what I want to say. I just sit there like a fool, wishing my eyes could tell him everything. But that's not how life works.

"Get my dad back to China, okay?" Kai's look lingers on me a moment longer before he dashes in the direction of the building where they're holding Palermo.

My father comes and lays out a stretcher, ignoring his own scrapes and bruises. "The men found this." He sweeps down and starts wrapping up Noble, lifting him onto the stretcher.

My hand taps my knee. "Where are you taking him? I'm coming too." I blurt.

"Inside Lab 3. Until Agent Ramos gets here."

Noble is settled on the stretcher. One of Cesare's men helps my dad whisk him away, while Rafael guards the lab where Palermo's men are locked up. The long-haired man that saw Kai is with them. Agent Ramos will take care of him.

Most of Cesare's men have already fled the scene before the police arrive. Looks like I'll be helping negotiate more deals for immunity. Lots of testifying to come.

I sit numbly in the snow until they are out of sight. I close my eyes, trying to tap into Kai's frequency, when a negative frequency spikes instead.

Palermo is on the move, heading toward a back parking lot. I struggle to my feet, about to alert Cesare, but I snap my mouth shut, falling silent as I pick up on the frequency of the person with him.

CHAPTER 73

∞

Kai feels me walk up behind him.

He's carrying Palermo's unconscious body to an SUV up ahead. "You might be the only one who can understand this."

"What did you do to him?" I ask. When Cesare locked him up, he wasn't unconscious. It occurs to me now that his state is unnatural.

"Gave him something that will knock him out for hours." Kai secures Palermo in the SUV and shuts the door. Then he turns to me, his face masked by shadows. "I need you to trust me. Palermo will never believe me unless I get him out of here. If I want to live and finish this assignment, I have to take Palermo with me." His jaw clenches. "I'm so close. I can't stop. Terra Liberata doesn't end with Palermo Ricci. And there are other people I need to help."

He ushers me back to the emergency exit door of the nearby lab that is cracked open. We stand there as the heat rushes out.

It'll be a circus explaining to Ms. T and the DIA why I let Palermo go, but Kai's whole operation will be ruined if I don't, and worse—Kai's life and the lives of countless others will be too. Probabilities click into place. Tonight, there's no other way. If his cover's blown, all will be lost.

I nod. "I trust you, always," I say, my voice low and shaky.

He flinches at my words, like it's a whip to his heart.

"Then take this." Kai holds out what looks like a coin. "There's a hacker working for Terra Liberata under the alias, "Nameless". PGF can't hack this. Find out what's on it and get the info to Bai. I intercepted it from a messenger in Helsinki. It was meant for Palermo's eyes only. Crucial information he requested."

"I'll get it done." When I take the coin device, our fingers touch. His frequency spirals into mine. It's unfair, knowing what my touch does to him. But even if he can't see mine, it's happening to me too—and he knows it. But his numbers haven't changed. His mind is set. He's leaving.

"Stay safe," Kai says, softly. "Let my father know I'm okay. Keep an eye on him for me." He starts to walk away.

This time I won't let him leave until he knows how I truly feel. "Kai, wait," I gasp. I pull on his hand, and he doesn't remove it. "I was wrong. I'm sorry."

"Don't be sorry for choosing happiness." The sound of his voice radiates with the frequency of a thousand suns. His light races around me as if we hold each other together. But he still thinks I've chosen Noble.

Our magnetic pull is too strong, and before he turns away, I push into him, my hands on his chest. He doesn't move, but his breath hitches, eyebrows tighten.

"No, Kai. You don't understand. You're the one I want." We stare at each other, the auroras filling the sky now, waving in brilliant colors.

I place my hand on his jacket over where I had seen the infinity tattoo, and I hold it there. His heartbeat speeds up. For a moment, we are lost in each other's eyes.

"You always said if I told you we can beat the odds, you'd never leave my side. I've done the math. We can beat them." I grab his jacket, pulling him closer. I know what he needs to hear, and I don't have SWAY or anything between us this time. "I see you more clearly than I ever have. You found me by the laavu because of the light. In the tunnels too. It wasn't my tech you saw—it was our *frequency.* It was us. Do you understand what I'm saying?"

He shakes his head. "Maybe that's the difference between us, Jo. I never needed frequencies or the odds to know how I felt about you." He pulls my hand from his side and steps away. His mind is solid rock, just like Agent Ramos said he'd have to be. Bai called him a November Romeo. Maybe he was right. But I still haven't told him what I believe he needs to hear.

"You asked me what I told you in the safe house that was so important." My chest is pounding. The words are in my throat, rising to my mouth, when finally, they rush out. "I told you that I loved you."

He swallows. His body zings with power like in the Banquet Hall, but his focus is unbreakable. "You told me you loved me knowing I wouldn't remember, only to leave me? Does that even count?"

"It did to me," I whisper, stepping closer to him. "That was why I let you go. I'm sorry. I didn't want to stop you from fulfilling what you needed to do. But then, everything led me back to you. Kai, I love you. Wherever you go, wherever you are, I need you to know that. You're the one. Every path leads to you."

I reach for his face, and he lets me. I tilt my chin up towards him as he stares down at me. Our numbers are intensifying, and light is beaming. The equation that I now know is our connection is raging like a forest fire. It's hotter, brighter, and more electrifying than anything I have ever felt before with him since for once I don't hold back what I truly feel. Ever since that first day in the pool house and the connection we shared, he's made me feel safe, loved. He always came for me. He always showed up. Because love shows up.

Our eyes are locked in tandem. For me there is only one way to go. To him. He feels it too, and for a moment I imagine his hands pulling me close to him. His breath catches, then his whole body tightens.

Every muscle in him screams to pull away from me, but he doesn't budge. "You made your choice three months ago. I did too. Now I've got a job to finish. People are counting on me. I'm sorry, Jo, but it's too late." His words slay me. But he still doesn't move. Our faces nearly touch. His eyes fall on my lips. He looks at them as if they're sharp knives, but the way he leans forward—it's like he wants to plunge himself into them even though it would cost him his life. Then with calloused fingers he touches them, his heartbeat frantic. "Your lips... your beautiful lips...shouldn't remind me of betrayal." A wall rises between us. A wall I created with my choices. "Goodbye, Josephine." His words are barely a whisper and as he moves away, a cold vacuum fills the space between us.

His footsteps are black clouds, storming to the door, dark and silent.

"I'll wait."

My words stop him mid-stride.

The words escape from a place inside me with no defenses, a vulnerable place that is raw and birthed in love. This time, I'm the soldier laying my weapons down at his feet.

Cesare, my dad, Chan's second chances stream through my head like an anthem. I understand now how he felt in the safe house in Tunisia when he said those words to me...when you find a treasure worth waiting for, you do anything to get it. And he's worth it.

Kai turns, his profile to me. A knot forms in his clenched jaw, the frequency of his heartbeat irregular. There's a 97% chance he's going to speak—until three frequencies flood the back alley.

"Stay back," Kai warns me. "Out of sight."

Light footsteps—certainly not a man's—run down the alley. A girl's voice yells softly outside. "Asher! Where are you? We're here!"

The girl's voice matches the frequency in the underground

tunnels in Helsinki. Her voice is sincere, sweet, and it makes me nauseous. Especially the way Kai's frequency responds to it. He trusts this girl.

The Finnish police are speeding onto the property. Agent Ramos is just around the corner. Another car pulls up in the back alley.

I fall back into the shadows as Kai takes one last glance at the emergency door where I hide.

"Asher!" the girl cries again. "Where are you?"

"Rayne!" Kai yells as he runs to meet the girl, who's bundled up in a white snowsuit, similar to mine. "I'm over here!"

The girl sees Kai and races to him, plowing into his arms like he's her refuge. He returns her hug, protectively.

"I thought you were dead or caught," she says, full of worry. "I didn't know what I'd do." She checks him over to see if he is okay. My numbers go berserk, my temperature boiling.

This time I get a good look at her. She's beautiful, slightly older than me, her mind sharp. My numbers zip over her, memorizing her features, imperfections and all. It's clear they know each other well enough to rely on each other, but she calls him Asher, which means she is with Palermo in his new undercover world. Are lines starting to blur for him?

My whole body cools to ice like when my suit failed. Kai and the girl get into the SUV together and drive away.

The boy who found me in the real world and continued what Red started, who fought so I could sleep at night. Kai, the one I love, flees to an uncertain fate in the arms of another girl.

I touch my cheekbone, remembering the medicine he put on it, the way he stopped the gash on Noble's forehead. I gasp as it dawns on me with a shiver.

Kai called the girl *Rayne.*

CHAPTER 74

∞

I watch the helicopter lift Noble into the sky and out of sight. They're taking him to a hospital back in Helsinki where he will be in police custody. The scene with his father replays in my head, and each time, I'm gutted. My only consolation is that Noble is unconscious, sparing him from those thoughts for the moment. I just need to be there when he wakes up.

A plane is waiting for us in Rovaniemi to take us back to Helsinki. We drive back through the woods. The ride is as silent as the Arctic night. My dad is in front with Agent Ramos. Cesare and Rafael are in the middle row. They're all discussing Palermo's escape with Kai and next steps. I'm sitting alone on the backbench, staring out the window. Stars litter the sky, and the auroras shine over us like a flashlight.

My gift has evened out. The radiant glow is gone, and only a steady balance of frequencies and numbers remain, just like Noble said it would. There's a peace to it, even if in this moment I feel none.

We hop onto a plane back to Helsinki. Cesare comes back to sit with me. He's bruised, and only now is his energy winding down as the plane takes off.

He studies me. "It's okay to let people go," he says. "Some

are meant to come in for a while. Others are meant to stay forever." He puts a hand on my shoulder. "You know, the way you looked at Rafael in the Pratt was a type of love—important for the time. You grew because of it, but the season changed. It's the same way you look at Noble, but not how you look at Kai."

I flush with heat. "I didn't think you were paying any attention in the Pratt."

"Ehh, we try not to be too obvious," he says, dramatically shrugging his shoulders. "We parents are far from perfect and make mistakes every day, but we love our kids. Thankfully second chances come around, huh?"

He pats me gently on the back then returns to sit with Rafael.

When we touch down at the Helsinki Airport, there's a crowd waiting outside our gate. Chan is there with Tank and Miles. There's another frequency glinting from among the group that makes my insides groan. This is a mess I can't avoid twice.

Ms. Mines and a camera crew wait as our plane disembarks. This time she's studying each face like a hawk. When she latches onto mine, her smile is victorious, if not a bit smug.

"Josephine Rivers," she says, shaking her head. "Fancy meeting you here in Helsinki. Turns out, this is a story of a lifetime. Your little team is involved, aren't they? Where's Ms. Taylor?"

My calculations spin, but my mind is too exhausted to speak. PSS will be exposed. Ms. T will be ruined. What will happen to Noble? To Kai? I exhale hard. The probability of Ms. Mines finding out had been high to start with. I glance over my shoulder at the three dads trailing behind me, who are just as wrecked as I am.

But then Chan shoulders his way in front of me, his voice as stern as his face. "How could you think a teenager could be involved in such a heinous criminal attack?" Chan says, his presence quite intimidating.

The reporters take a step back and my father fills the gap. "I guess you weren't told the real story. My colleagues and I were asked to go undercover at the ISC Banquet, from there we—"

"Wasted no time in stopping—" Cesare adds, stepping up to the plate.

Agent Ramos comes up too, flashing a badge. "This is an on-going investigation. No further comments, except that we owe a huge debt to these men, and we're thankful no harm came to their children. Thank you."

Reporters are now snapping pictures of the three men instead, eating up the story. Just like that, PSS and I are saved. Chan and my father wrap their arms around me, escorting me away, Cesare and Rafael by our side. We really are stronger together. My eyes brim at the thought.

Ms. Mines ruffles off her embarrassment, shooting a coy glance my way as we pass her. She got what she wanted: a story. But not all stories are told the way they really happened.

CHAPTER 75

∞

SENATE SQUARE, HELSINKI

It's evening the next day. Reporters swarm the international police who are protecting three men on a stage set up in Senate Square. Chan Huang Long, Jason Rivers, and Cesare Di Susa.

After Ms. Mines went viral with the story, the ISC invited the heroes of the day in order to personally thank and honor them at their ceremony.

By now everyone has seen the headlines:

Businessmen Rivers, Chan and ex-Mafia Di Susa uncover a terrorist attack on the ISC and Europe.

Scale Tech held hostage by blackout terrorists.

NASA TIPPER stops terrorist attack. Now in custody.

To celebrate the successful launch of the Super Satellite and an end to the blackouts, the ISC will launch a new "Celebration Rocket" in Helsinki, which will burst into fireworks as a symbol of victory. The event is drawing an even larger international crowd and thousands have poured into the city.

Senate Square glows under a bright moon and a fresh dusting of snow. The cathedral looks magnificent, aged with history, a witness throughout centuries.

The PSS team and I hang back on the university stairs, listening to the din of the crowd and waiting for the ceremony to begin. Eddie looks over at me with a dawn of understanding on his face. Ever since I told him about Kai and my phantom frequency in the warehouse, he's been puzzling over it.

"What?" I ask.

He shakes his head. "I can't believe I missed it," he says, like it was right under his nose the whole time. "Two particles connected through time and space, proven to move faster than light between each other, and they can be on two sides of the planet and still feel each other. Quantum entanglement. Cool, huh?" He claps me on the back.

I smile and nod. Eddie could have told me it meant that Kai and I were cursed forever, and it wouldn't have made the slightest difference. "Thanks, Eddie."

Huge speakers start broadcasting the ISC representative's voice through the crowd, announcing the names of the three men on stage.

The three dads took the credit despite the repercussions it could bring. Chan and my dad wanted to protect me, of course, and their alliance with Cesare will make everyone think that Palermo's downfall was caused by outside forces, not anyone within his organization. This way, no one will suspect Kai was involved. My father also wanted to protect PSS and Ms. T, who was very happy to see him alive, and all her prodigies. Cesare had his own reasons for owning the spotlight. He was eager to declare his leadership and victory.

Before the dads have their moment, the ISC representative asks everyone in the audience to join in a moment of silence to honor the sacrifice of Dr. James Adams, the scientist who was held captive and willingly gave up his life to stop the attack and prevent a months-long blackout. Everyone in the audience feels the emotion of his heroic death, but those of us who know the whole story feel it most keenly.

Then a DIA spokesman takes the mic. "We knew we needed capable people on the inside to stop the terrorists. Thankfully, these brave men stepped up to the plate, and we're standing here now because of them."

Ms. Meri Elo, an ISC representative, also on stage, steps forward. "We want to honor these men for their courage." The men are each gifted with a golden satellite statue the size of my palm.

"Thank you," the three men reply and bow their heads slightly as the crowd applauds them.

Ms. Mines, also on stage as the honored reporter who uncovered the story, directs a question their way. "Businessmen with no training going undercover with such ruthless men. What compelled you to take such a dangerous risk?"

Chan and my father look at each other and smile. "Our children."

Chan clears his throat and takes the mic. "We believe in what the ISC and what Scale Tech have accomplished, and yes, we are businessmen," Chan replies, "but before business, we are first fathers. Our children inspire us to make the world a safer place."

They pass the mic to my father. He leans in, a thoughtful smile on his lips. "The ISC's theme this year is making a way for the younger generation, and by taking this risk, we not only prevented a crisis, we made a way for our kids. Being a father can be a dangerous job. But it's worth every moment."

Cheers and applause crash through the crowd.

"Nice cover story." Pens and Eddie are poking me in the back. Harrison and Felicia are laughing. I'm stifling a laugh, too, but below it, a fierce pride and gratitude for these men rumbles deep inside me—they've lost loved ones, spouses, money, children, and yet they won't back down.

Ms. Taylor stands in back with us, sighing with satisfaction. She should be up on that stage too for her role in this, but that's not her goal.

But it might be—if she knew about Rayne Carter.

Even now, Rayne's face and the way she touched Kai burns a dark hole into my memory and my stomach twists in a way I've never experienced before. I don't like it.

The reason Ms. Mines is the thorn in Ms. T's side is because of Rayne's actions. What story would Ms. Mines write if she knew the former PSS girl was not dead after all? More importantly, how will Ms. T react to the news? How will it affect PSS?

All those questions, I'll save for another day.

Right now, I sink into the night, ignoring the frequencies buzzing around me, the noise, and plant myself in the moment.

There have always been wars and crises, but in dark times, there have always been those who stood up for what was right and good. Those who saw an opportunity in the danger. Red spoke of the thousands of heroes whose names will never be known. They charge the night, like Red, unafraid of the darkness, because they know what runs in their veins.

I just wish I was sharing this moment with Kai...and maybe I am. The boomerang in the square is subtle, the air heats up. I don't have proof that he's here watching somewhere. This time, I don't need it.

I feel him, and that's enough.

CHAPTER 76

∞

HELSINKI HOSPITAL
POLICE CUSTODY WARD

The boy of fractals and lightning is awake and alive. I've waited all morning to see him. Now that I'm allowed to go in, my stomach buzzes with nerves.

All night, my heart ached as I mentally prepared for this moment. Snowflakes and coral invaded my dreams. So did Noble's screams for his father. Then I woke up to memories of Tunisia that threatened to steal me away. To me, Noble is one of the most precious souls alive. I don't want to let him go. Even though I know I have to, it still hurts. Especially now.

A police officer pushes open the hospital room door, and I slip in.

"Good morning, Mandel," I say, my voice soft as I enter. Noble is sitting on the edge of a hospital bed in regular clothes.

"Hi, Digits." His voice sneaks in and mingles with my frequency. There is a beautiful type of love in it, but it's different now.

Cameras are mounted on the white walls around us. The police have him in a private room within the Helsinki Hospital.

Even if the arrest is more of a formality, two guards sit in the hall. Agent Ramos told me they're striking some kind of deal with him.

As I move closer, I notice his eyes are bloodshot, his nose red, and scratches mix with his freckles. There is no sign of the gash. Grief hidden in his sad smile tells me there's a lot on his mind. My heart breaks.

Noble leads me to a small table near the window where the light cuts into the room and bends around us. For the first time since Tunisia, we're in a room together with no immediate threat breathing down our necks. Our numbers don't stop examining each other, but they're not pursuing each other like before. They've settled into something new and calm.

He hands me a cup of tea, and I smell dried blueberries in the fruity steam. "We really need to develop some healthier patterns for meeting up." He softly touches my cheek.

A small laugh escapes me. "Normal is never going to happen for us, Noble. It's best we stop trying." I pause, my throat tight as I notice his numbers. Just like in the Arctic, his mind is elsewhere. I count all the tiny burns on the bridge of his nose. "I'm so sorry about your dad. He loved you."

Noble can barely speak. "Yeah." He sniffs, his jaw clenching. "Thank you for vouching for me. Ms. Taylor even wrote a statement for me." His eyes crash into mine. "Qadar is on his way here. With my mom."

I reach for his hand. "Are you ready to see her?"

He nods slowly. "Yeah. It's time." I squeeze his hand. "She needs me now, and...I need her too." He fights a lump in his throat.

"So I guess that means you won't be taking PSS's offer?" I ask, a small part of me hoping. "The team would be over the moon if you did."

He shakes his head in an absolute no. "Impossible."

"Why?"

"If you're there, I wouldn't get any work done." He smirks, then scratches his forehead. We're avoiding what we don't want to say. "To be honest with you, PSS is not exactly what I want to be doing either. I accepted NASA's offer to be part of the new development team for my designs. Who knows? Maybe one day, I'll even get to go up to the stars."

Not even gravity can hold down my joy. For so long Noble hasn't been free. My eyes brim. "You're going to get your dream. To study the light in new ways, to live among the stars. You're going to change the world, Noble. I'm so proud of you."

"Thanks, but..." He gives me that shy look where he wrinkles his nose. "It was that or prison." He brushes hair from his cheek, and hands me court papers. "Consequences of my actions. I did break into nearly every satellite in the sky. And some I did just for fun. Thankfully, fifty-two agencies have testified that I didn't misuse any information, but basically worked for them for free. But I didn't do it the right way. Without honor, things go wrong. Now I've been given a second chance, and I want to finish what my dad started. He knew my designs were worth realizing. He just didn't do it the right way either." He tears up thinking about his dad. "So now it's my turn to make things right. First with my mom. We're going to live together in Tunisia."

For two minutes, we sit in silence watching the numbers cascade between us. I wonder if he can see my heart yo-yo-ing between deep pain and joy. As we stare at each other, a sad and beautiful revelation hits us—we're not exactly two rivers flowing in opposite directions, but it's clear we have our own paths to reach the sea.

"It'll be good," I finally say, when I can talk again. "How long is the deal with NASA?"

"It's a five-year contract, but I think I'll like it. Once I get used to reporting to an authority." He smirks. "I could always outsmart them, but I don't think I will this time."

"It's good for you," I say, "to finally be part of a team."

He looks out the window at a barren tree in the courtyard, his numbers surely tracing every branch. "You remember the kids in Tunisia?" he asks.

"Of course," I say. "How could I forget them?"

"I need to do this for them. For my mom, too. For so long I hid because I *was* afraid. Not anymore. After these five years, I could do anything. I could build up Tunisia's Space Program... help Dr. Salonen...the ISC. Maybe even *Cesare*." He laughs. "The possibilities are endless."

"You're going to light up the sky, Noble." I stare at him, an ache in my heart. "I'll be sure to visit."

He looks down, his frequency skipping. "So is that a 'no' to my offer?" He brushes my hand with his fingers, exhaling deeply.

Run away with me.

There's a sad smile on his lips because even if I say nothing, the numbers are clear to both of us.

He squeezes my hand. "I see."

"A part of me wishes I could," I say. The child in me yearns for it. A once well-loved dream tears a piece out of my heart—to run away with Noble and never look back. But that thirteen-year-old girl didn't know what her future held. "When we were younger, you meant everything to me, Mandel. If you hadn't been there when I was growing up, I don't know what I would've done. But we're not kids anymore..."

We lock eyes and equations rock between us. Now that we've stopped trying to figure each other out, our numbers interact with each other like life-long friends. It's comforting. I know he'll always hold a special place in my heart.

He squeezes my hand. "I don't like it but you're right, Digits," he says quietly. "We're not kids anymore, which maybe I didn't even realize until yesterday. You kept me afloat for years. But after my parents...*my dad*—" he grits his teeth, "—contacted me, I finally understood that I needed to heal in ways I'd put off. I also need to make choices for my family now. I wouldn't even be here without you, so thank you for finding me and believing in me."

He snags me into a hug, and I hold him so tightly I think I won't ever be able to let go. His voice, his skin, his cardamom scent settles into my memory, in a place I'll keep safe. His lightning has struck me hard, forever leaving an impact on my life.

He clears his throat. "I'm sorry for messing things up with Kai," he says, pulling back and tucking a strand of my blonde hair behind my ears. "You know numbers. They don't always add up. After I realized how much you both cared for each other, it was too late. He's a good guy. If you're not with me, I want you to be with him. He *did* save my life. But if things don't work out..." He smiles shyly, then turns serious. "I'm sure your calculations caught this, but Terra Liberata won't be easy for him from here on out. They'll be rooting out moles."

I nod, soberly.

K2 buzzes at me. "I've got to get to the airport." I take one last long look at him, numbers zipping over his features that will forever be ingrained in my mind. "I'm always going to love you, Mandel. I won't ever forget you."

His frequency spikes. "You're acting like this is goodbye or something," he says. "I don't believe in goodbyes. Not with you."

"What are you saying? You know something I don't?" I search his face for some kind of numerical clue, but he just smiles.

"Don't I always?" he says. "You know what the odds are. I just may see you sooner than you think." He stands and walks me to the door.

I sniffle, as he wraps me into another hug. Our embrace is

full of emotion and energy—as if everything we ever wanted to give to each other as children is wrapped up in it.

My heart is a strange mix of hopeful and sad. Noble gave his parents a second chance. We had a second chance. Now I'm wondering if Kai will ever give me a second chance.

We take one last look at each other. "See you later, Mandel."

"See you later, Digits."

Just like winter comes to an end and spring buds on trees, the boy of fractals, lightning, and snowflakes is once again in my past.

My night is over. My morning is dawning. There's a new path stretched out in front of me full of obstacles. It won't be easy, but at least it's bathed in light.

CHAPTER 77

∞

HELSINKI INTERNATIONAL AIRPORT
VANTAA, FINLAND

Goodbyes are hard.

Walking on smooth parquet floors past large windows in one of the cleanest and quietest airports I've seen, Rafael and Cesare, Chan, and my father and I come to a crossroads—three separate gates at the airport: one to Italy, one to China, and one to America. We'll all leave on different airplanes, back to our lives, not really knowing when we'll see each other again. Not even numbers can make this world smaller.

I approach Rafael first.

"Mila," he leans in, kissing my cheeks. Then he pulls back, his green eyes more hopeful than I've ever seen them. We stare at each other. What do you say after meeting like this? It was fun to see you again? I'm glad you didn't die in the bloodbath?

Rafael smiles. "Thank you. For everything. It's a new season. I feel it. But I never want you to be more than a phone call away, *va bene*? Next time answer your phone the first time." He winks.

"*Va bene. Ho capito.*" I squeeze his hand.

"Your Italian is getting so good," he says. "Next time come to Italy, okay?"

I think about Palermo and wonder where Kai is. "Maybe." Then I recognize the look of anticipation on his face and laugh. "Is your girlfriend waiting for you on the other side?" I touch my cheekbone where Kai used that salve to heal it and remember Palermo's offer to cure his girlfriend. My mind fills with new calculations.

Rafael cracks a smile. "She is," he says. "Miracle number two."

"Then I'll keep it short," I say. "We'll see each other again. *Arriverderci.*"

"*Mi raccomando*," he says. "If you ever need anything, I'm here." He kisses my cheeks once more and walks over to his father.

Cesare has been hanging back, waiting to say his goodbye. His face is bandaged, and he probably still has a concussion—but he refused to stay in the hospital.

"I like seeing him happy," he says, as Rafael goes over to talk to my dad and Chan. "Thank God, his girlfriend is still waiting for him. After China, I thought he'd never get over you." He huffs a laugh.

"I'm happy for him, too," I say. "And for you." The man in front of me looks completely different from four days ago, and radically different since I met him in China.

"*Mila.* The girl with a thousand secrets. I'd reckon my son gave you an appropriate name." He laughs. "Thank you for believing me. You, Kai, your father. Sometimes the process of becoming who we're meant to be takes a while. And those who give us a second chance help us get there."

"You turned out okay. I thought I was helping you because of your son. But now I see Rafael got a lot of the qualities I admire in him from you." I pause, thinking about all the ways he's helped Agent Ramos already. "So what are you going to do with your new *boss* status?"

He pulls on his belt. "I'm going to put those men to honest work. I'll show them who we are and what we can really accomplish. If my grandfather's legacy taught me anything, it's that a little determination pays off. Who knows, maybe I'll get Scale Tech to fund Noble's designs. I do own quite a few shares in that company." He furrows his brow. "I better learn more about it. Whatever it is, it's time to give back."

It reminds me of his call to Palermo's men in the warehouse. "That was some speech you gave back at Scale Tech. You believe those words, don't you?"

"*Eh*," he grunts. His eyes drift to a distant memory. "Seeds that were planted long ago finally sprouted. I almost didn't believe they were still inside me."

"Where did all that talk in your speech come from?" I ask him, searching his face.

He shrugs it off like it's no big deal. "You wouldn't believe me if I told you."

"Try me." I already have my own ideas.

He takes a deep breath, his shoulders relaxing. The moment he speaks fire courses through me.

"One day in the Pratt when King was busy, an old man spoke to me. Said something I'll never forget. '*You have the heart of a leader. So why have you become a slave?*' Then he looked at me and said, '*Son, pure gold doesn't fear the fire.*'"

CHAPTER 78

∞

My last and hardest goodbye is with Chan.

Two private guards wait to escort him to his plane and will accompany him all the way back home. PSS and Agent Ramos promised him extra security, for Kai's sake, until they know Chan is safe from Palermo and Terra Liberata. But even now, threats linger in the air, an undercurrent of something I don't like.

I approach him, every line in his face a map of where he's been and who he is. A father, a businessman, a friend. A protector. My heart lurches. Truly, what makes a man great is the love that is inside of him. I miss him already.

"Dad, can you give us a minute?" I ask. He nods and wanders over to the coffee stand with Tank and Miles.

"Little Phoenix." He rests his hand on my shoulder.

"Thank you for everything, Chan." My eyes fill with tears. "We couldn't have done this without you."

He tips his head and snorts a laugh. "Whenever you need me to make a lot of money and take all of your credit, I'm here for it." He smirks.

I don't remember him ever being this funny. Dr. Ling has certainly brightened up his life. And I love it.

"Well, I hope you don't mind. The bodyguards will watch you for the next few months. Cesare warned me there may be repercussions for all of us."

"If there are repercussions, I trust you will solve those too. I'm not afraid." He gets serious. "We make a good team, *Little Phoenix*. We always have. One day, maybe Kai will return and see that too."

I pull him further off to the side. The bodyguards form a barrier for us from the crowd. "I need you to know something. Kai was here in Helsinki. And in the Arctic. His assignment is with Palermo and Terra Liberata." My voice is low, my numbers revealing no one is listening.

He nods. There is no surprise on his face. "I know."

"You did?" I gasp. "How?"

"A father always feels his son." Chan hums. "I also knew that everyone was trying very hard to cover something up. I'm smart enough to know when to stay on track. How else have I become successful?"

I smile. Chan's right. He easily picked up on things back in China, whether he said anything or not.

I bite my lip. "There's more. Kai didn't leave me for the undercover job because he wanted it. He was actually going to turn it down. I forced his hand. I broke off our relationship so that he could take the job without the guilt of leaving me behind. I thought I was doing the right thing for him. I was wrong."

"Ehh," he sighs, bobbing his head. "It makes sense why he was so upset when he left. He was brokenhearted."

"I am in love with Kai," I say, my face flooding with heat as I admit this to Chan. This time I don't care. "I don't want to lose him. Right now, he, um, doesn't trust me very much. I don't know if I can win him back." I don't add that he's in even more danger because of me.

He tips his head. "Chan men don't get over our girls so

easily. He's more like me than you know." He pauses. "Thank you for telling me."

"You're not upset?" I ask.

He shakes his head. "Moli used to say—and I am sure Red copied her—*Even the darkest storm can't stop the sun from rising.* What is there will shine again," he says. "You of all people know mistakes can be redeemed."

"Then, with your permission," I ask. "I'd like to win him back."

He looks at me suspiciously. "What will you do?"

"Not sure yet," I say, even though an idea is already brewing in my head. No one will like it, but it's all I've got. It's time I start making decisions with Kai.

"I'd ask you to promise me not to do anything rash, but it'd be like asking you not to breathe." He laughs. "I wouldn't mind if you brought him home. In one piece." Then, as if Red were speaking through him, he smiles with deep understanding in his eyes. "You have my blessing."

CHAPTER 79

∞

RIVERS RESIDENCE
WEST SEATTLE, WASHINGTON

Two weeks after Finland...

"Rayne Carter is alive."

Marigold and my father, who are sitting on the couch in front of me, go silent. We were having a pleasant time discussing Red's journal—I've been memorizing every lesson, every word, along with Kai's book of poems, even if it wrecks me—when I drop the news.

For two weeks, I've debated how to tell her, but I also needed to confirm it. After my research, there's no mistake. Every number and shred of evidence confirms it. Not only is she alive, she's with Kai and working for Palermo.

I turn away from the window where a set of gray waves rolls up on our sandy stretch of beach, and focus on Marigold, whose dark eyes are now wide. "I saw her in Finland."

I explain everything from the tunnels to Kai driving away with her to the hyper-fast acting medicine that Kai used on Noble and me. Blood drains from Marigold's face and her frequency fractures into multiple oscillations crashing in the room. Yet, she remains the usual strong woman I know. Only this time I see her squeeze my father's arm until her hand goes white.

A motherly flicker of pain and love burns behind her eyes—a theme of my last few weeks. When I finish, Marigold bites back her emotion. She offers no solution, no ideas. She needs to process. I do too.

There are so many complex pieces wrapped into Rayne—Kai, Palermo, PSS, and the fact that Marigold once viewed her as a daughter, perhaps not unlike the way she's looked at my sisters and me lately. A part of me wonders if that will change now.

Marigold scoots over and gives me a tight hug. I almost choke up. I wasn't expecting her to share her feelings with me. I only started calling her *Marigold* outside the PSS office seven days ago. Still, her arms are a comfort.

"Thank you, Josephine," she says, her voice low and quiet. Then she stands, grabbing her thick gray overcoat. "I'm going to take a walk on the beach for a few minutes. Be back soon." She excuses herself and slips out the back porch sliding door.

My dad waits a minute until she's out of view then turns to me. "You know, honey," my dad says. "It won't kill you to tell us these things earlier."

I chew on the inside of my lip as I take the mug of tea back into my hands. He's right, but there was much more than Rayne Carter spinning in my head. Since watching Kai drive away with her, my mind hasn't stopped calculating.

A fire flickers in the hearth. I stare at it, the smell of pine and pitch bringing back memories of the sauna in the Arctic.

My father picks up on the fact that I don't want to talk about Rayne anymore. He shifts his legs and pours me more tea. "So, what happened with Kai and Noble?" he asks eagerly. He's waited patiently for me to broach the subject, but I could tell it was hard for him. "I figured you'd tell me by now... I'm dying over here."

"Sorry, Dad," I say, patting his knee. "You were right. I needed to find someone who was going my direction, someone I can face anything with, and I did." I pause, thinking about Kai's frequency wrapped up in mine in the warehouse. I feel him, like that whale under the boat. No matter where I go, I'll never escape him. "Kai's the one—"

"Yes! I knew it!" He pumps and swings his elbow into his side, then regains his composure. "Sorry. I just got excited. I really like Noble, but I missed Kai...Um, go on. So, you guys are getting back together?"

"Not exactly." I set my cup down. "He's really upset about what I did."

My father wrinkles his brow. "About you breaking up with him?"

"Not that part." I bite my lip, a sour look sliding onto my face. "I also drugged him."

"What?" he shrieks. "Jo!"

I shrug. "It seemed like a good idea at the time. Long story." I shake my head. "He doesn't trust me anymore. So, it's over." I don't mention the plans rumbling in the back of my mind to change that.

Dad is wide-eyed like he clearly agrees with Kai on the whole "drugging" him matter, but then he pulls my hands to his. "No, honey. I know when two people have deep feelings for one another. They don't call me the love doctor for nothing. He'll come around. You'll get back together one day."

One day. Not a specific enough number for me.

I smile at him anyway. "Thanks, Dad, I know you're just being hopeful, but it might take more than that. Whatever comes next is going to be a challenge. I feel it."

K2 alerts me of a call from China. I jump up, snapping my purse to dig out my phone. My weekly chat with Chan is back on.

"Sorry, Dad. I need to take this. He doesn't have a lot of time today." I answer the phone. "*Zao.* Morning. You're up early." I stop abruptly. "Oh, hi, Dr. Ling." Her voice is lined with panic. "Slow down. What's going on?"

My smile fades. Blood starts racing through my veins. I harden my voice to stop it from trembling. "Where is he?" I close my eyes. I'd wondered when this would happen. *Repercussions.*

I listen to every word Dr. Ling says, going rigid, resisting the urge to board the first flight to China.

"I'll figure this out," I say, my voice low and even. "I promise."

After I agree to call her later, I drop the phone into my lap. A thousand equations pound in my brain.

My dad is waiting on the edge of his seat. "What happened?"

"Chan," I say, walking to the window. I look west over the water, my calculations rising like a tidal wave. "He's in a coma."

CHAPTER 80

∞

SEATTLE, WASHINGTON
PSS HEADQUARTERS
UNIVERSITY OF WASHINGTON

Two weeks later…

The safest path isn't always the right one.

The motorcycle engine between my legs redlines at a frequency of 8000 RPMs. The road angles at 45-degrees, and the wind pounds against my chest threatening to pull me off the handlebars like a kite in a storm, but all I feel are the new possibilities stirring in my gut.

The sun grows in intensity at the full light of day. Frequencies buzz all around me. Numbers spill over the street. As I calculate the speed and the direction before me—the plan I've been devising solidifies and a path is carved out. It terrifies me. But I won't back down. I'll face whatever challenges lie ahead. For Chan. Kai. *Rayne.* For the ones who come after me.

Eddie helped make my Ducati nearly silent. I've always appreciated stealth but the quiet also gives room for my thoughts, and right now my stupid motorcycle is sentimentally torturing me. Kai is in every curve of the road, the purr of the engine, the sense of freedom. When I'm riding, I feel closer to him.

An urgent alert on K2 informs me that the team is already assembled and waiting for me. Ms. T called an emergency meeting this morning. Eddie and Felicia finally hacked the *coin* from Kai.

"It's crucial you get here quick," Eddie said earlier when he called me. "We also have other important news we need to share with you."

"I have news, too," I replied. It's finally time to tell them what's ahead for me.

As I pull into the university, the campus unfolds like a mathematical graph in a computer game in which every obstacle I dodge becomes a point in my favor, but evading threats isn't how I'll win the next game. It's keeping my eye on the finish line until I cross it.

Terra Liberata made this personal. I already sent them one message through the blackout. I'm about to send them another. They're not the only ones who can play this game—and the end is closer than they think.

Problem is, it breaks every protocol that Ms. T has given us. On one hand, there is one PSS protocol I've changed my mind about—the whole bodyguard thing. I do want one. A very specific bodyguard. And I'm going to get him. Which means there's something I need to do even if I don't want to do it:

I need to quit PSS.

∞

Com-Hall is quiet as I enter.

I take a seat, exchanging glances with everyone in the room. There's a trust between us that's rare in this world. I think of the many lines we've crossed over. We've faced life and death together and won. They're *my team*. Which is why it will be so hard to leave them.

But it's time to stop making decisions for myself, and begin making them for Kai and me, which starts by securing the antidote for Chan. If Kai knows about his father, he may never forgive me, but I have to try to get the cure. Chan's words call to me even now—*if there are repercussions, I trust you will resolve them.*

Then, regardless of whether Kai gives me a second chance or not, I'll bring him home, along with *Rayne Carter*—no matter how I feel about her.

Finally, Ms. T walks in with my dad, trailed by Agent Ramos. *Oh no. Why is he here?* If Ramos is here about another job, he'll be sorely disappointed.

"Thank you all for coming." Ms. T sits at the wooden table, hands folded. "I guess we have a few announcements."

Eddie smiles awkwardly at me, followed by the rest of the team who give me overtly obvious looks. They all clearly know something I don't.

I kick back in my chair. "By all means, please share your news first."

Ms. T, who is a bundle of nerves, and Agent Ramos, who is cool and calm, both nod at Pens, who straightens her red hair as if we were at a press conference.

"It's official," she announces. "PSS has been cleared for duty."

"For what?" I ask.

Agent Ramos hands me a legal document from the government and clears his throat. "The Special Cases Unit has officially been re-activated."

The room goes silent as everyone waits for my response. My numbers rapid fire in thirty different directions—Ms. T said she'd only activate the department if *I* would lead it. Apparently, that wasn't true. Still, how am I going to tell her I'm leaving now?

"Well?" Harrison says with a huge grin on his face. "Aren't you excited?"

I give them a tense grin and push the words past the lump in my throat. "I would be if...I hadn't come here today to quit."

The team's heads twist back and forth, their eyes bouncing from one another. Their numbers tell me they aren't surprised—I've been set up.

"Care to explain, Jo?" Ms. T is prepared for this conversation. So is my father, who wasn't supposed to find out like this.

Fine. I play along and pull out a stack of files from my backpack, throwing down a file with the face of the ex-PSS girl staring up from the cover. I grimace. Even her pretty face irritates me. By now, they've all heard the story about Kai and Rayne, and of course the news about Chan's coma.

I cross my legs, my expression tight. "There are things I need to attend to."

Agent Ramos picks up my files. "Impressive." He opens his briefcase, and pulls out the small coin device, now split open revealing a tiny chip. "But you haven't seen my files yet. Or what's on the coin, and I'm betting you'll want to."

He pulls up pages of information on a screen for all of us to see.

"Kai intercepted this tiny chip, made for Terra Liberata, through a hacker, with the alias, *Nameless*," he says. Agent Ramos gives me a patient smile and throws a brown envelope down on the desk next to my file. "Yesterday morning, after weeks of Felicia looking for *Nameless*, we located the hacker, who is now in our custody."

"So what? You want me to talk with the hacker?" I ask.

"Not exactly," Ms. Taylor says, inhaling a deep breath. "Jo, we know you well enough by now to read the signs. We understand why you're restless. I was a bit wary when the team and Agent Ramos came to me with this idea, but I'm willing to break a few rules for you."

"What do you mean?" I say.

Agent Ramos folds his hands on the desk. "We just might have a way for you to get what you want and stay in PSS, if you're willing to hear it."

He shows me what's on the coin and what I see sets my numbers on fire.

For the first time since I met Agent Ramos, and after all the assignments he's proposed that I've turned down, I finally pause.

I sit back, folding my hands in my lap. "Go on. I'm listening."

EPILOGUE

∞

AZERBAIJAN PENITENTIARY
BAKU, AZERBAIJAN

Two months later...

There's nothing left to count but time.

That's true for this card game, or any card game played in this joint. I don't even have to count cards because everyone is so predictable. I'm playing against children in my sleep—except they're older, sweaty, scheming men and women with a lot of time on their hands.

I slap a card down in front of the young Azerbaijani man. "Rakin." I smirk. "I won again. Pay up." The man scratches his chest with a growl, his angry lips tighten, and he stares me down. I stare back until he cracks and begins to laugh.

"You're incredible," he says, grabbing his belly. "Ok, teach me another so I can beat Yusif tonight."

I lean over and snatch the cards from his hands, giving him a hard look. "Not until you call your kids."

He rubs his week-long whiskers, and grunts. "You haven't changed much. I'll be back. Keep my seat warm."

After Rakin scurries down the hall, a guard in faded army fatigues enters the co-ed work area of the prison where certain prisoners from the men and women's block assist prison guards. It's break time.

The guard gives me a smoke-stained grin. It's so wide I know exactly what it means. *Visitors.* Finally. I've already spent 48 days in this correctional facility sleeping with a concrete pillow and eating greasy rice. I'm ready to be done.

As the guard beckons me to follow him, I grin back. I'm still adjusting to my short black hair and the constant pain in my jaw. Pens and Eddie created new tech that is undetectable but hidden in my teeth. It's not super convenient or comfortable.

We trail through a windowless hallway leading to the women's block of cells. I'm placed in a holding cubicle and told to wait.

A minute later, two armed guards charge through the front door, a white male and a Central Asian woman, sweeping the cells until they find me. The light-skinned woman opens my cubicle and grabs me by the arm, yanking me forward.

"Where are you taking me?" I snap, calculating and memorizing their movements. Their frequencies drift around me, until suddenly my body flushes with warmth. I block everything out until and focus on one thing. *He's close.* I feel it.

"To the boss."

I shove the knowledge away and clear my throat. "I don't have a boss."

"You've worked for him before. Palermo Ricci. Ring a bell?" She drags me out of the women's section. "You owe him."

I huff. "I gave him what he asked for—twice, in fact. It's not my fault it was intercepted."

"Which is why he is breaking you out. He's giving you one more chance," the woman says. "You should be grateful."

A sack is thrown over my head and I gag at the sharp smell

of mold. It's never been washed—the odds don't even need to be calculated. But I couldn't care less, because my heart is beating harder the closer I get to him.

We cross to the other side of the penitentiary, going outside where the air is warm. The map in my head takes over. We're near the outer gates of the prison now and heading into the restricted south block. I'm hustled into a room and the bag is ripped off my head. I gasp for air, but it's not much better without the bag. The room is filled with cigarette smoke and the pungent scent of liquor, making me choke. Five prison guards sit around a scratched-up table staring at me. I don't recognize any of their faces. And *he's* not in the room.

Once again, I'm told to wait. I don't argue. A minute later, a vehicle drives up outside.

Remember, you're impersonating Nameless. Everything I read about her comes back to me now: she played with people's minds, used game theory, puzzles, and was obsessed with John Nash, the mathematics genius.

Finally, the air pulses and tingles. I steel myself for this moment. The warmth entering the room threatens to rob me of my breath, but I set my jaw instead. Then, three seconds later, he walks in.

Kai's shoulders are back, his body slightly bulkier than he was the last time I saw him. He takes one look at me and stops. Our frequencies flip on brighter than a stadium at night. But just like in Helsinki, his eyes give nothing away. No one would have a clue we know each other—unless they could see the frequencies locking us together.

It takes everything in me to stop the forty-two muscles in my cheeks that want to break out smiling. To subdue the five hundred and eighty-eight butterflies flapping their wings at a million miles per hour inside my stomach—even if in the background I count six deadly weapons and thirteen possible threats.

The woman snaps at Kai. "Bind her, Asher."

"Who is she?" he says, gruffly. "This can't be the hacker we're looking for."

"Surprised it's a girl?" the woman says, dark eyes glaring at me. "I'm sure she won't bite. Palermo wants answers from her. If she doesn't cooperate, then she'll sleep with the others."

At the woman's threat, Kai's jaw locks tight and the numbers around him threaten to obliterate everything in the room—but he walks over to me as instructed. Kai's eyes connect with mine, burning like a fire. He's upset, to be sure, but there's more to it. I can't interpret what he's thinking. That I put myself in danger again? That I'm interrupting his mission again? That his goodbye was final?

Right now, it doesn't matter. I may be in the worst possible place, with bad odds and even worse food, but if I'm with him, I'm right where I want to be.

Kai binds my wrists and leads me 400 meters past the outer gates of the penitentiary to a black van. Three frequencies are inside it, none of them Palermo. I didn't expect him to retrieve me personally. The door slides open.

A voice, sleek and eloquent, comes from inside the vehicle. "Ahhh, the famous hacker we've heard so much about. *Nameless.*"

A woman with jet black eyes meets mine. "The girl who gets the job done. At last, you have a face. So, now that we broke you out, are you going to tell us your real name?"

My lips curl into a sly grin as I picture the new marks on my skin in black ink hidden below my clothes. Things really do come full circle.

"I don't have a name," I say, cracking my neck. "I have a *number.*"

ACTIVATED DISCUSSION QUESTIONS

1. Jo's dad explains to her how the Continental Divide helped him decide between two women he cared for. What was the idea behind that? How did it help Jo decide between Kai and Noble? Do you agree or disagree with her decision, and why?
2. Noble and Jo are both thinking about light throughout the book. What aspects of light are each of them learning about? How does this affect the paths they end up choosing at the end of the book?
3. Several characters in *Activated* have had significant "second chances" in life. Name some of them. What were their second chances, and how did they use them? Would you have given them a second chance if it were up to you?
4. Two of the names Jo went by in *Calculated* show up again in *Activated*: Mila and Phoenix. What do these names mean? (Hint: "mila" is a number in Italian, and a phoenix is a mythical creature.) How do they reflect Jo's personality and her past experiences?
5. Noble's inspiration for technological innovations often comes from the natural world (snowflakes, coral, auroras, stars, bioluminescence). Many PSS designs come from asking the question, what if? What if night vision could be incorporated into contact lenses instead of massive goggles? What if we could harness the untapped power in auroras? What do you see in the world that makes you ask, what if?

ACKNOWLEDGMENTS

Activated was the hardest book for me to write, in the shortest amount of time, and there's a whole crew of people to thank for how well it turned out.

Thank you to my publisher Rachel Del Grosso, Jake Bray, Kristin Yahner and the entire Wise Wolf Books crew for all of your hard work behind the scenes; for giving me the time I needed to make this book what it is; and for once again believing in another *Calculated* book enough to bring it into the world.

Thank you to my agent, Amy Jameson. You are my toughest critic and mightiest coach, who will do anything to make sure that my books and I get exactly what we need to be successful. If writing books were an Olympic sport, then you would have taken me to the gold.

To the producers of the Calculated film franchise, John Lee Jr., Jay Brents, Steven Wollwerth—your belief in Jo Rivers completely changed my world. This series might not even be here if it weren't for you. Special thanks also to Marco Shepherd and Tay Centineo for all of your expertise, enthusiasm, and support.

Thank you to my amazing critique partners, faithful beta

readers, and editors. Ellen McGinty, Chelsea Bobulski, Tamara Girardi, Candace Kade, Rebecca Alexandru, Becky Dean, Rebecca Woo-Krauss, Hilary Magnuson, Sarah Zhang, Katie Wong, Michelle Tsang, Jenni Claar, Katylin Wonnell, Erin Humphrey, and Ira McBee. The ladies in Kidlitnet, too! Words cannot do justice to the amount of wisdom, feedback and support you all give me. Thank you for loving me and my books.

Thank you to Meri Takkinen, my dear friend and advisor on Finnish language and culture. Your time, insight, and thoughtfulness made this book authentically shine. Special thanks also to Jessica Tamminen.

HUGE thank you to all of my engineer, optic, satellite, rocket, hacker, and technical advisors: Justin Gardner, Arthur and Kathleen Freeman, Paul Freeman, Craig Pannell and Glenn Fleishman. Your minds and passions are incredible!

Special thanks to friends who encouraged me while I was writing: My Saturday Ladies, Lionnesses, and China Friends—you constantly pour life and energy into my dreams like they are your own. I'm so grateful for you. Chris Lumry, Amanda Wengerd, Annie Su, Wayne Lo, and Kirsten Mount, your timely words refocused and encouraged me. My Street Team, especially, Megan Walvoord, Hannah Honegger, Valerie Notess, Marielle Henning, and Dakota Foster for checking in & loving on this series. Deb Limb, huge thanks for the countless times you offered your cabin for me to write my books. That was a huge blessing, but your friendship, prayers, and support are the true gift.

Thank you to all the readers who pre-ordered and sent messages sharing your deep love and insights with me over this series. I'm overjoyed at your love for my characters. This book is for you!

To my radically supportive siblings and in-laws—Terry and Diane McBee, Isaac Schmid, Olivia Ramos, and Leanne Schmid. Thank you for always cheering me on!

Thank you to my parents, Richard and Hellen Schmid. There is a reason this book is dedicated to you. The way you love, trust, and befriend your kids is worth gold. Thanks, Dad, for passing on your love of books, writing, and challenges. Thanks, Mom, for passing on your love of our Finnish roots, language, culture, and international adventure.

Thanks to my three wonderful kiddos. You challenge me more than the books and you keep me real. I can't wait to read your stories one day.

Thanks to Ira McBee, my husband—a thousand books could be dedicated to you and it just wouldn't be enough. The way you give and keep on giving is incredible. You are the wind beneath my—oh wait, you'd kill me if I used a cliché metaphor! I love you.

Thanks always to Jesus—you light up my darkness.

ABOUT THE AUTHOR

Nova McBee is a hopeless nomad and culture nerd who has lived and worked in Europe, the Middle East and Asia. She speaks multiple languages, including Mandarin, and lived in China for more than a decade writing books and teaching English and Creative Writing to teens and adults. She thrives on complex plots, adventure, making cross-cultural connections and coffee. She currently resides in the beautiful Pacific Northwest with her husband and three children.